Arthur and the Sovereignty of Britain

Caitlín Matthews is a writer, singer and harpist. She is the author of *Mabon and the Mysteries of Britain* (Arkana, 1987), *The Elements of Celtic Tradition* and *The Elements of the Goddess*. She co-wrote with John Matthews the two volumes of *The Western Way* (Arkana, 1985 and 1986) and *The Arthurian Tarot*, and has also edited three collections. She is currently preparing *Sophia, Goddess of Wisdom*.

CAITLÍN MATTHEWS

ARTHUR AND
THE SOVEREIGNTY
OF BRITAIN

King and Goddess in the Mabinogion

Illustrated by Chesca Potter

ARKANA

For my dear John: until the finding and founding of the Court of Joy, my true companion.

'But right good stories he knows, such as that none could ever be aweary of hearkening to his words.'

The Elucidation

ARKANA

Published by the Penguin Group
27 Wrights Lane, London w8 5tz, England
Viking Penguin Inc., 40 West 23rd Street, New York, New York 10010, USA
Penguin Books Australia Ltd, Ringwood, Victoria, Australia
Penguin Books Canada Ltd, 2801 John Street, Markham, Ontario, Canada l3r 1b4
Penguin Books (NZ) Ltd, 182–190 Wairau Road, Auckland 10, New Zealand

Penguin Books Ltd, Registered Offices: Harmondsworth, Middlesex, England

First published by Arkana 1989

Made and printed in Great Britain by
Richard Clay Ltd, Bungay, Suffolk

Filmset in 10 on 12pt Baskerville

CONTENTS

PREFACE

He was dubious of much that these poets asserted though they were indeed most skilled artists and remembrancers and conservators of the things of the Island, yet he suspected that they tended to be weavers also of the fabulous and were men overjealous of their status, and secretive touching their *traditio*, but then, after all, their *disciplina* was other than his and this he knew for certain that whatever else they were, they were men who loved the things of the Island, and so did he.

DAVID JONES
The Sleeping Lord

The collection of texts known as the *Mabinogion*, which Lady Charlotte Guest first published in English in 1849,[23] has perhaps suffered most because of its name. 'The Mabi- what?' is the response of those unfamiliar with the riches that the title obscures, passing over what appear to be difficult Welsh names and inexplicably remote traditional stories, which appear to have lost their motivation or purpose. However, the *Mabinogion* is a veritable treasury well worth exploration.

It has long been valued by Arthurian scholars, who have quarried its stories for early references to King Arthur. It has never been out of Welsh oral tradition and is a prime source of British mythology and folklore; it is likewise an important link, for esotericists, with the British Mysteries. For though these stories were first transcribed in the twelfth century, they arise out of a lively oral tradition and bear remarkable traces of earlier beliefs and stories.

The *Mabinogion* falls into five distinct categories, which may be summarized as follows:

1 The Four Branches (*Pedeir Keinc y Mabinogi*): the stories of *Pwyll, Prince of Dyfed, Branwen, Daughter of Llyr, Manawyddan, Son of Llyr*, and *Math, Son of Mathonwy*, which form the *Mabinogion* proper and which are drawn from the earliest mythological levels.

2 The pseudo-histories of *Lludd and Llefelys* and *The Dream of Macsen Wledig*, which concern traditions about King Lud and the emperor Magnus Clemens Maximus.

3 The stories relating to the Dark Age Arthur: *The Dream of Rhonabwy* and *Culhwch and Olwen*.

4 The romances that depict the more medieval end of the Arthurian tradition, which are paralleled by the stories told by the French story-teller Chrétien de Troyes: *Owain* or *The Lady of the Fountain, Gereint and Enid* and *Peredur*.

5 *The Story of Taliesin* (*Hanes Taliesin*), which is not properly part of the *Mabinogion* but which Lady Charlotte Guest included in her collection.

In *Mabon and the Mysteries of Britain*[111] I have already dealt with the stories appearing in sections 1 and 5 described above, as well as commenting on *Culhwch and Olwen* from section 3. In this volume I intend to comment fully on the remaining stories, following the same general layout as before. Although *Arthur and the Sovereignty of Britain* can be read as complete in itself, there will necessarily be references back to *Mabon* where points of comparison or matters for discussion turn up.

Like the texts that comprise the Bible, the stories of the *Mabinogion* are all derived from different ages and story-tellers. However, the more I study them, the more certain I am about their interconnected nature. I have been less concerned with the literary merits of the *Mabinogion* and the historicity of its sources than with revealing the mythological subtext that links the proto-Celtic Arthur with the medieval king. Such a synthesis is a dangerous undertaking, academically speaking, since it assumes a unity in a mass of variables: a fact I am not unaware of but have chosen to play down in order that the stories as they stand in this book can be appreciated by those unable or unwilling to explore the sources and parallel texts for themselves.

Our contemporary world has little concept of, or common language with which to express, the Celtic Otherworld as a living or appreciable dimension of experience.* In attempting a study of the complex mythological subtext of British tradition where the Otherworld is the main theatre of events, I have frequently chosen to use the word 'Inner' in the particular sense of 'relating to the inner or spiritual dimension' of the human psyche. For this reason the word is capitalized throughout when this specialist meaning is intended.

In *Mabon* I traced the cult of the Goddess Modron's son through the earliest stories of the *Mabinogion*. In *Arthur* my intention is to reveal the Goddess herself in her specific guise of Sovereignty. The Goddess of the Land and her many representatives seem to me to stand at the very centre of Arthurian legend. Indeed every story within this book is concerned with political sovereignty – who rules the land most effectively – or with the prime figure of the land, the Celtic Goddess of Sovereignty herself and her relationship to the king.

The known and unknown story-tellers of the Matter of Britain unconsciously inherited what the early poet–seers and sibyls knew: themes of wasteland and wounded king, cauldrons that give life, sacrificial kings whose heads are borne in mystical dishes, wronged maidens and misguided knights all lie at the heart of the matter. The empowerment of the king by Sovereignty has become the Grail quest, while the surrounding lore has fallen into a morass of courtly love and chivalric adventure.

My intention in this book is to discover the relationship of this undying king to Sovereignty, Goddess of the Land, through the medium of the related texts of the *Mabinogion*. I wish to show that the mystical marriage of Arthur Pendragon to Sovereignty animates the core of the Matter of Britain by the admixture of this world with the Otherworld. That which is related to the undying inner, spiritual realms has its own life. Buried within the narratives, stories and pseudo-histories of the *Mabinogion* lie the

---

* See C. & J. Matthews, *The Western Way*, Arkana 1985.

clues to this relationship. By reference to these stories and their Celtic and early European parallels I hope to show how the gifts of the Goddess of Sovereignty and the behaviour of her kings and champions are a recurring theme of the Mysteries of Britain.

In presenting the theme of Sovereignty in the context of the *Mabinogion* and of other Celto-Arthurian texts, I nowise wish to imply that the theory presented in this book was consciously handled by any of the story-tellers, of both oral and literary tradition, of the Middle Ages. The concept of Sovereignty by that time had lost the strength and resonance it had had in the Celtic tradition; the Goddess of the Land and all her works dwelt only within a lesser set of symbolic stories and in countless fays and Otherworldly characters; she appeared in the person of Morgan le Fay, who, as sister to Arthur, reclaimed many of the earlier images, and she featured in stories which traced the hunting of Sovereignty's beasts and in tales about the finding of the Goddess's treasures, the Hallows.

It is perhaps necessary here to define my terms and parameters. When I speak of the Divine Feminine – the Goddess of the Land, or Sovereignty – I am discussing a spiritual principle, not the status or role of women. I find it personally inappropriate to define mythological or spiritual realities by means of feminist politics. It follows, then, that when I deal with the representatives of Sovereignty, who often appear as real women – like Luned in *The Lady of the Fountain* or Enid in *Gereint and Enid* – I do not discuss them as women beleaguered in a world of impossible men, but as activators and initiators of Otherworldly power.

The *Mabinogion* does not contain stories of everyday folk and their soap-opera scenarios; to pretend otherwise is to totally misunderstand the nature of these texts. Likewise the inner realities awaiting discovery in these stories cannot be served up as evidence of modern psychological inadequacy, whereby characters from a historical or literary tradition become models for contemporary psychoanalysis. The nature of Sovereignty's empowerment is an Otherworldly one, which does not need modern political parallels to prop it up. It is doubtless possible that readers *will* find mystical reasons for the current state of Britain, or jumping-off points for feminist or psychological discussion, but these are studies which I leave to those best qualified to undertake them.

In uncovering these stories we are like tourists to a culture that is foreign to us; we have to behave like visiting anthropologists and allow the people in these stories to behave in their own way without imposing our modern values upon their actions. It follows that the more we visit these stories and meet their inhabitants, the sooner we will understand them both.

My prime aim has been to instil in readers of these stories an awareness of the Celtic Goddess of Sovereignty, for I believe that a deeper study of these and other texts will reveal a totally unguessed-at wealth of material, which, when it is assimilated, will revolutionize the ways we look at the Divine Feminine today. Sovereignty in her three or four aspects presents a challenge to those whose study of the Goddess is bogged down in third-hand research which has been meaninglessly repeated, garbled and disempowered for too long.

In specializing in the relationship of Sovereignty to the *Mabinogion* and to other Celto-Arthurian texts, I have necessarily passed over many aspects and universal implications of the wider field of studies of the Goddess. I hope that these will be pursued by other researchers and that those readers who still impatiently await my own study of the Goddess will bear with me for a little longer. Two books are now forthcoming on this subject: *The Elements of the Goddess* (Element Books, 1989) and *Sophia, Goddess of Wisdom* (Unwin & Hyman, 1990).

I am well aware that the kind of mythological archaeology I am engaged in is fraught with danger since the investigator frequently brings his or her own personality to bear upon the study, with disastrous results, descending to a cranky fundamentalism, illuminating his or her findings with an intermittent flashlight of intelligence, or else allowing guesswork, facile comparison and banal rationalization to lead the way. I hope I have not been guilty of such myself. It follows that anything I have written here invites more explanation and bears a deeper meaning than I have had room for in this study. Other definitions are as valid as my own, and there are doubtless many aspects of the *Mabinogion* which remain unrevealed to me.

As a mere mythographer my role is to guide the puzzled reader through these complex tales with some degree of clarity, to supply parallel sources for study and comparison, and, most importantly, to instil a love of Britain's native traditions into her people and sympathetic admirers. In the tide of time our understanding is crucial to their survival. For it is our guardianship and handling of these traditions that will influence their transmission to people not yet born.

Caitlín Matthews
1 February 1988
La Fhéile Bríde

HOW TO USE THIS BOOK

I am well aware that in *Arthur and the Sovereignty of Britain*, as in *Mabon and the Mysteries of Britain*,[111] more than one interpretation can be placed upon a story. It has been my endeavour to let the stories speak for themselves wherever possible. My task has been to reveal the hidden layers that underlie each story and to juxtapose parallel texts from the proto-Celtic and post-Celtic periods from which general tradition these medieval stories derive.

That being the case, I have followed the same schema as in *Mabon*. Chapters Two to Seven include short synopses of the stories discussed. These synopses should not be substituted for a complete reading of the text, and for this you will need your own copy of the *Mabinogion*. Each synopsis is followed by a discussion of the main themes inherent in each story and an exposition of parallel texts and possible sources, for further understanding. This should direct the reader towards other sources to rediscover for him or herself. A full bibliography appears at the back of the book; the authors' names (or book titles, if there is no author) are arranged alphabetically and then numbered, and all numerical references within the text correspond to this numerated sequence of books. For more specific mention of topics already discussed in *Mabon and the Mysteries of Britain*, I have given the short title and page number for the reader's easier usage, e.g. (*Mabon*, p. 164).

In the case of Chapters Five to Seven the synopses are considerably shorter than each tale merits; but so extensive are these romances that space has necessitated that I restrict the retelling and concentrate on the commentaries. Even so, each of these romances merits a book on its own, and there have been many features I have been unable to discuss due to lack of space.

Throughout the book I have adopted the simple expedient of capitalizing the word 'Sovereignty' when discussing the Goddess of the Land; when 'sovereignty' appears in lower case, I am referring to the political rulership of the land.

It should be noted that different editions of the *Mabinogion* do not always agree as to detail and that the romances in particular reveal many such variants. I have chosen to work from Jeffrey Gantz's translation,[22] as this edition is most widely available at the time of writing.

Readers who wish to have an overview of the major themes outlined in this study are directed to the appendix, *The Wheel of the Year: King and Goddess*, p. 312.

A GUIDE TO WELSH PRONUNCIATION

The following is only a rough guide for the non-Welsh-speaker who wishes to speak the names in these stories with some degree of authenticity. Welsh, though it looks full of impossible clumps of consonants, is pronounced as it is written, unlike its less logical neighbour Saesneg (English).

The vowels, both long and short, are roughly equivalent to Italian sung vowels, with the exceptions of:

u: **i**ll, or French **tu**, e.g. Pered'**ur** = Peredir
w: l**oo**k, e.g. Ca'd**w**r = Cadoor
y: p**i**n, e.g. Rhyd = Hr**i**d (in monosyllabic words and final syllables)
y: b**u**t, e.g. Cynon = K**u**non (in first syllables and in the definite article **y**)

Dipthongs are logically pronounced:

wy: e.g. Rhonab'**wy** = Hronabooee (as in French **oui**)
aw: **ou**t, e.g. Ef'r**aw**g = Evroug
oe: b**oi**l, e.g. c**oe**d = coid
ai and ei: w**i**ne, e.g. Ow**ai**n and Ger**ei**nt = Owyn and Gerynt

Consonants are as in English with the following exceptions:

c: **c**ake, e.g. **C**ai = Ky
ch: as in Scottish lo**ch**, e.g. Gwal'**ch**mai = Gwalchmy
dd: **th**ere, e.g. Llu**dd** = Hlith
f: **v**et, e.g. Gwenhwy'**f**ar = Gwenhooeevar
ff: **f**at, e.g. **Ff**lur = Fler
g: is always hard as in **G**lewlw'yd = Gleooloo'eed
ll: **hl** (raise blade of tongue to roof of mouth behind tooth-ridge and aspirate 'huh' – this roughly approximates the sound), e.g. **Ll**efel'ys = Hlevelis
rh: **hr**, e.g. **Rh**y'awdd = Hri'owth
r: is briefly trilled
th: **th**in, e.g. Ar**th**ur = Arthir

The stress falls on the penultimate syllable of a multi-syllabic word, e.g. Rhon**ab**'wy. In a two-syllable word the stress falls on the first syllable, e.g. **Ge**'reint.

ACKNOWLEDGEMENTS

Due acknowledgement must be made to the myriad scholars whose translations have made so many texts available to me for study and comparison; without their endeavours, this book would never have been started.

My special love goes to John Matthews, who has put up with my invasion of his pitch with great good humour. It is ironic that while I write on his chosen subject – the Arthurian world – he is pasturing in my field of research, ancient Ireland. However, I'd like to thank him for bringing to my attention texts I'd never heard of and pointing out connections that I might well have missed.

My thanks to Emrys, who put up with his mother's furious typing on a daily basis, with great forbearance, in return for the odd meal, story and song between chapters. Also to Sandra Mandrey, who, in the closing stages of the writing of the book, became my son's foster-mother in the true tradition of St Brigit.

To Professor Gearóid Ó Crualaoich of the Department of Irish History, University College, Cork, for his helpful advice on the appearance of dragons in Irish literature, as well as to his colleague, Professor Padraig Ó Riain, for possible relations between Nennius and the *Echtra Airt*, grateful thanks.

To Wolfe van Brussel for listening, and to Mildred Leake Day for her enthusiastic support; I need friends like you!

Special thanks to Karl Müllner for his help in translating the story that appears on pp. 242–3; his expert German combined with my shaky early Irish and vestigial Latin reveal a truly fascinating component of the Sovereignty mythos.

To Bob Stewart many thanks for enabling me to expound the material of Chapter Two at his *Life of Merlin* course in March 1987 at Hawkwood College, Stroud.

To Kathleen Herbert, a true faery-godmother, who has helped me in matters Saxon as well as encouraging me in matters Arthurian.

To Chesca Potter and Stuart Littlejohn for their illustrative genius.

Lastly to Eileen Campbell, my editor, heartfelt thanks for giving me the opportunity to finish my study of the *Mabinogion*. *Mabon* and *Arthur* are my children perhaps, but she was certainly their midwife.

For permission to reproduce copyright material grateful acknowledgement is made to Agenda Editions for extracts from *The Roman Quarry* and *Kensington Mass* by David Jones and to Faber and Faber Ltd for extracts from *The Anathemata* and *The Sleeping Lord* by David Jones.

CHAPTER ONE

ARTHUR AND THE MATTER OF BRITAIN

> If his forehead is radiant like the smooth hill in the lateral light, it is corrugated like the defence of the hill, because of his care for the land and for the men of the land.
>
> DAVID JONES
> *The Roman Quarry*

> And Sovereignty said to Niall: 'And as you saw me ugly at first but at last beautiful, even so is royal rule. The land cannot be won without battles, but in the end everyone finds that sovereignty is both beautiful and glorious.'
>
> Echtra Mac Echach Muigmedoin [my trans.]

I THE FAME OF ARTHUR – UNDYING KING

Every year many hundreds of books are published about King Arthur. These range from the very scholarly down to the umpteenth retelling for children. Only one thing keeps this industry going – a perennial love of the Matter of Britain, as the Arthurian legends are known. Together with these books there is the evidence of recent archaeology, which is attempting to give us a broader and more detailed picture of Dark Age Britain and the world in which Arthur might have lived.

The one thing that Arthurian studies do not have – and

perhaps do not entirely need – is hard, factual evidence for the existence or otherwise of Arthur. Certain broad conclusions can be drawn, to be sure, about the nature of Britain in the Dark Ages, if we go on archaeological evidence. But the literary evidence is less helpful. Just as no one has found King Arthur's sword, Excalibur, or his tombstone (despite notable attempts to forge such evidence), so no one has yet found an autographed set of Arthurian battle orders or a chronicle which mentions Arthur in any detail.

This is not a book debunking Arthur, but neither is it one that traces the evidence for his existence. In the face of the lack of evidence, the muddled literary sources and the wish-fulfilments and self-deceptions of scholarly fundamentalists who need to 'prove' Arthur as biblical scholars need to 'prove' Christ, I merely wish to state that 'proof' does not matter to me. Arthur, like Christ, has more than one kind of existence, and it is this multiple, mythological, subtextual existence that seems to me the most telling.

Arthur lives in the imaginations and group soul of the people. He is the focus and burning-glass for many aspirations, combining the heroic endeavours of the pagan world with the spiritual chivalry of Christian Europe. Arthur's grave, as *Stanzas on the Graves* tells us, is an unthinkable sepulchre; he has not died, he dwells in Avalon, he will come again. These legends have currency among the very simple and the very wise because of the Arthurian world's immediacy in human terms and because its stories operate on many levels.

The Matter of Britain is a very subtle blend of stories, history, traditions and beliefs; its followers are likewise various – literary critics, medievalists and folklorists mingle with those who like the stories for their own sake. There are others for whom Arthur has become a cult figure. He is hero and god:[120] a figure worthy to operate within the confines of a war-game or role-playing scenario,[147] a tool suitable for psychologists to apply to patients' unconscious functions and an inspiration to mythographers and esotericists.[47,86]

This Arthurian mystique had been copiously studied and extrapolated. Despite the protestations of rationalists, it will not go away. Reverence for Arthur has at various times assumed a semi-mystical fervour, which scholars have found distasteful, for it surpasses the respect properly due to a national hero and teeters on the verge of the downright heretical. How has this come about?

Most Arthurian enthusiasts have been nurtured on Malory or Tennyson: a cultural upbringing informed by the *Boy's Own* version of the chivalric age, featuring highly coloured characters who stride about uttering 'medieval-speak'. It is endemic to British society that myths, legends and King Arthur are considered the correct historical fare for children, so unless they are taught otherwise from the start, most people grow up with an over-romanticized image of history.

At the other extreme one may encounter numerous scholars who, with notable shining exceptions, seem concerned with unravelling the very last commas of Arthurian medieval romances and relating their findings to a very narrow range of criteria indeed. These scholars are normally only interested in Arthur as grist to the medieval literary mill, which became extremely busy after the engulfing of the oral by the literary transmission of stories.

But the medieval literary corpus of stories relating to Arthur is only one stratum in the excavation in question. If we seek deeper, the literary evidence is definitely thinner, but it reveals a quite different picture of Arthur. One such source is the *Mabinogion*, which, though first written down between 1100 and 1250 was the product of a rich oral tradition and preserved features of Arthur's career that might baffle someone familiar with the great king only through late medieval sources.

For a start Arthur is not a noble king based on the Norman or Plantagenet model; he is a war-lord, surrounded by his 'war-band', not above a little cattle-raiding or pig-reiving, according to the Triads.[38] In texts like Geoffrey of Monmouth's *History of the Kings of Britain*,[10] Arthur performs his own deeds rather than sending out one of his knights to perform them on his behalf. However, we are continually struck by the way in which Arthur seems to move effortlessly between the earthly realms and the Otherworld, for he seems at home in both.

And perhaps here we are at the root of the mystery, for Arthur blends skilfully into a mythological hinterland, which is only even now being comprehended. His power to excite reverence or mystical fervour is due in no small part to his connection with and relationship to deeply-rooted mythological archetypes which arise from the land of Britain. It is perhaps no wonder that the unnamed novice about whom St Ailred of Rievaulx wrote in 1141 found that 'he had frequently been moved to tears by fables which were invented and dissembled concerning an unknown Arthur', but that it was 'almost a miracle if he could extract a tear at a pious reading or discourse',[92] for the consciousness of the time more easily swarmed with native and familiar archetypes than with those propounded by St Ailred and his fellow clerics.

In the same way in which saints stepped into the shoes of native deities, so the medieval King Arthur replaced the earlier, proto-Celtic Arthur, who was in turn a resonance of a mythic archetype of ancestral memory. Mythic identities, like suits of clothes, are changed or appropriated easily. In *Mabon and the Mysteries of Britain*[111] I attempted to show how one mythic pattern percolated through British tradition to take in figures as diverse as Arthur, Bran the Blessed and Mabon. In this volume my intentions are to show another kind of mythic pattern, that of Sovereignty, the Goddess of the Land, for it is through her that Arthur earns much of the supernatural reverence with which he is surrounded. His association with her and her representatives will be detailed in Chapter Ten.

Arthur's reputation seems, from medieval accounts, to be solely based on his Round Table knights and their exploits and on his notable birth and passing into Avalon. In fact Arthur's is a submerged reputation based on deeds and exploits of which traces can be discovered in extant early literary sources. In these episodes, such as the 'Preiddeu Annwn' or 'The Spoils of Annwn' (*Mabon*, p. 107–8),[111] in which he goes in his ship, *Prydwen*, to reive the inner empowering symbols known as the Hallows, we see him in his mythic guise, fulfilling an ancient, redemptive action which will rebalance the land of Britain. As such, Arthur is the 'earliest' Grail-winner, establishing a pattern that is followed by Perceval, Bors and Galahad in the later texts.

While these exploits have been expunged from literary sources for the most part, Arthur's begetting, birth and passing remain as clear indications of his once mythic stature. His life follows the criteria laid down by Celtic story-tellers, who told tales about the separate incidents in the hero's life: his mysterious conception and birth, his fosterage and obscure childhood, his timely recognition and empowerment, his Otherworldly journey, his confinement or illness and his mysterious death.[112,137] These features continue to be emphasized even in medieval sources.

The story of the conception of Arthur shows an interesting parallel to the usual mythic conception of a hero, which is of one earthly and one Otherworldly parent. According to Geoffrey of Monmouth,[10] Arthur is conceived in Igraine by the expedient of Merlin's transformation of Uther into the semblance of Gorlois, Igraine's husband. Although Uther is an earthly father, the fact that he appears in the shape of someone else makes him more than human at that point. (A similar set of criteria applies to the conception of Galahad: see p. 74.)

Arthur is not raised by his natural parents but is fostered, in the traditional Celtic way, by Sir Ector, according to Malory.[25] Layamon, on the other hand, tells of Arthur's fostering by the Lady Argante, Queen of the Faery.[43] He is recognized as Uther's son and the rightful king by his act of pulling the sword from the stone.[10] He journeys to Annwn in order to win the Hallows, which will heal the land and empower him.[111] His enfeeblement and disempowerment are the result of his separation from Gwenhwyfar (Guinevere), and he is borne to Avalon to be healed of his wounds, but does not die.[11]

Such a mythic framework can be constructed using the most available of medieval texts. What becomes clear is that Arthur is more than mortal, though how much more so may be debated. William Blake, whose own mythic instinct was sure and uncanny, was in no doubt:

The giant Albion, was Patriarch of the Atlantic; he is the Atlas of the Greeks, one of those the Greeks called titans. The stories of Arthur are the acts of Albion, applied to a Prince of the fifth century, who conquered Europe, and held the Empire of the

world in the dark age, which the Romans never again recovered . . . And all the fables of Arthur and his round table;
of the warlike naked Britons; of Merlin; of Arthur's conquest of
the whole world; of his death, or sleep, and promise to return
again . . . All these things are written in Eden.[53]

Whether in Eden or the Otherworld the fame of Arthur is
undying, rooted more deeply than we can know in the mythic
beginnings of our race. Dark Age battle-leader or medieval king,
mortal or demi-god, Arthur is, primarily, Guardian of Britain.
And the acts of Arthur are indeed those of Albion and thus of
Britain, for Albion is one of its ancient names. This story and its
place in our mythic history became the core of Europe's first
literature; it was a story that became embellished beyond belief
and was served up to kings and noblewomen, pored over fer-
vently by clerics in secret and recited openly by trouvères and
troubadours alike. This story was the Matter of Britain.

II THE MATTER OF BRITAIN

King Arthur and the Knights of the Round Table offered considerable scope for the medieval story-teller. Indeed, one might say
that the Matter of Britain was the first soap opera: no matter how
many times it was boiled up, there was always a new variation to
be found. That these variations may have been borrowed from
other, non-Arthurian sources has been one of the major concerns
of Arthurian scholarship, which compares text with text to arrive
at some kind of authoritative conclusion. Such findings usually
discount the oral tradition, but that is where we must make our beginning.

The extent of Arthur's fame before the writings of Chrétien de
Troyes in the second half of the twelfth century can only be
guessed at. Certainly at this time Arthur and his court inhabited
the oral rather than the literary tradition, and were probably
best known among the British (who were in the process of
becoming the Welsh, being called *wealas*, 'foreigner', by their
Saxon neighbours) and the Bretons, who were expatriate Britons

6

living in north-west France. Traces of the colonization of Brittany can be found in the story of Macsen Wledig (see p. 63). If it had not been for the Bretons, it is unlikely that Arthur and the Matter of Britain would have had such a literary impact on Europe, for their story-tellers drew directly on the shared British and Breton oral tradition and were responsible for the transmission of many stories into French literary tradition.

In the course of time, literary tradition cross-fertilized oral tradition throughout Europe. It is one such cross-fertilization that has given us the Arthurian romances of the *Mabinogion*, which will be discussed in detail in Chapters Five to Seven. *The Lady of the Fountain*, *Gereint and Enid* and *Peredur* are all paralleled in Chrétien de Troyes's *Yvain*, *Erec and Enid* and *Perceval*. In a book of this size it is impossible either to fully explore the nature of the parallels or to provide the full critical apparatus needed for such a study, although references will certainly be given here, if only briefly. Readers whose interest leads them into this vast field may consult the bibliography, where details of critical works are given. Those who are sufficiently interested might do well to read Chrétien's stories[7] and draw their own conclusions.

I am well aware that this field is strewn with scholarly reputations, the owners of which have chauvinistically supported their national legends and literary traditions. The fact remains that there is insufficient evidence to state categorically either that Chrétien's stories pre-date those of the *Mabinogion* or vice versa. I personally hold that both were derived from a then existent and now defunct oral tradition, and that the texts we read today show traces of cross-fertilization. We have no knowledge of how numerous or how widespread were the story-tellers, *conteurs* and trouvères throughout Europe; their influence on literary tradition is all that we can be sure of. Links between Wales and Brittany are certain. The existence of even one Breton or British story-teller-turned-*conteur* at the court of Marie de France would account for a great deal of the familiar content of Chrétien's work. Certainly Marie, great-granddaughter of the 'first' trouvère, William IX of Aquitaine, would have drawn to her court story-tellers of all kinds and traditions. If Chrétien's writings did precede the *Mabinogion* or if he drew from a common source, he undoubtedly worked from a first-hand source rather than from a chain of oral tradition because the similarities between the texts are too close. Chrétien's text is polished and courtly; it rationalizes the Otherworldly happenings. The *Mabinogion* has less polish and more concern for showing Otherworldly events having their impact on the earthly realm.

A long oral tradition informed the Matter of Britain. Both British and Irish story-tellers drew on a common fund, particularly of characters:

> which were once shared among *all* Celtic peoples and moved about freely among them, to be appropriated [not only] to different heroes as local and national interests dictated – to King Conchobar mac Nessa, Cu Chulainn, and Finn mac Cumhaill and the heroes who surrounded them in Ireland – but [also] to Arthur and to his attendant warriors in Britain.[56]

These common Celtic and proto-Celtic themes (those adopted from existing native beliefs) were inherited by the expositors of oral tradition, who:

> gave to the story-tellers in Celtic countries the immense repository of imaginative, colourful, and even fantastic story-themes on which their high reputation was based, and which proved to have such a rare attraction for foreign audiences. (ibid.)

We should not be surprised to find that the Matter of Britain was whole-heartedly adopted in Europe and that the majority of Arthurian romances are to be found written in French. Norman French was the language of the greatest political unit in France, Brittany and Britain in the twelfth century. Story-tellers needed patronage from the well-to-do, and to wealthy courts they undoubtedly went. And while poets and story-tellers still exercised their ancient function in benighted parts of Wales and Brittany, their role became increasingly anachronistic as Europe began to open up. Movements of clerics, appointments of bishops and the establishment of monasteries throughout Europe under the regime of St Benedict brought learning to the wealthy as well as providing the skill for the transcription of oral stories and their transmission in written form. As the professional errant story-teller became an established part of French courts, the Matter of Britain began to take shape.

In his commentary on Geoffrey of Monmouth's 'Prophecies of Merlin',[10] a twelfth-century cleric, Alain of Insulis, wrote:

> What place is there within the bounds of the empire of Christendom to which the winged praise of Arthur the Briton has not extended? Who is there, I ask, who does not speak of Arthur the Briton, since he is but little less known to the peoples of Asia than to the Bretons, as we are informed by our palmers who return from the countries of the East. The Eastern peoples speak of him as do the Western, though separated by the breadth of the whole Earth.[92]

Arthur became, in short, the hero of medieval Europe. This view was at odds with that held by native Britons, for whom Arthur became an emblem of national resurgence: the king who would come again to rescue his people from the yoke of foreign oppression. Even among the Bretons this myth was a living tradition in the twelfth century:

> Go to the realm of Armorica, which is lesser Britain, and preach about the market places and villages that Arthur the Briton is dead as other men are dead, and facts themselves will show you how true is Merlin's prophecy, which says that the ending of Arthur shall be doubtful. Hardly will you escape unscathed, without being whelmed by curses or crushed by the stones of your hearers . . .(ibid.)

Arthur lived on in a land that had been colonized over seven centuries earlier by expatriate Britons, who settled in Brittany after fleeing from the social and political upheavals of fourth and fifth century Britain.

However instrumental Arthur may have been as a piece of propaganda during the centuries of Saxon and Norman incursion, Britons had no doubt about one thing. As one early manuscript (*Llyfr Gwyn Rhydderch*) chauvinistically states about Britain's sovereignty:

9

> no one has a right to this island except only the nation of the
> Cymry, the remnant of the Britons, who came here in former
> days from Troy.[51]

Whatever else this statement implies, the fact is clear that Britons
looked back further than Arthur for their inspiration. Troy
loomed large: though how greatly it figured before the writings
of Geoffrey of Monmouth is not entirely clear.

According to Geoffrey, Brutus, the great-grandson of Aeneas,
came to Britain and established his lineage there. On what basis
is this pseudo-history (others would call it a fable) founded?
Virgil's *Aeneid* has seldom been out of the hands of readers since
its composition in the first century BC; it tells of the founding of
Rome and was therefore a tool of Roman expansionism. The
fact that it has often been the first book from which latimers, or
translators, con their Latin, and its intrinsic qualities as a story
and its poetic composition have much to recommend it; both of
these facts have ensured its continued popularity. The *Aeneid* and
the *History of the Kings of Britain*[10] are virtually contiguous; as a
sequel to the *Aeneid*, Geoffrey's chronicle vaunts the Roman and
Trojan antecedents of Britain's kings. But was this the only source
for the idea that Britons were descended from the remnant of
Troy's survivors?

Taliesin, the semi-mythical seer–poet reveals himself to be a
prophet of the Britons by means of his poetic omniscience:

> Oh! what misery
> Through extreme of woe,
> prophecy will show
> On Troia's race!
>
> A coiling serpent
> Proud and merciless
> On her golden wings,
> From Germany.
>
> She will overrun
> England and Scotland
> From Lychlyn sea-shore
> To the Severn.

Then will the Brython
Be as prisoners,
By strangers swayed
From Saxony.

Their Lord they will praise,
Their speech they will keep,
Their land they will lose
Except wild Walia.

Till some change shall come,
After long penance,
When equally rife
The two crimes come.

Britons then shall have
Their land and their crown
And the stranger swarm
Shall disappear.

All the angel's words,
As to peace and war
Will be fulfilled
To Britain's race.[23]

He speaks here, of course, of the incursion of the Saxons. But his first few words align him with the 'remnant of Troy' as if he were that legendary race's prophet (see *Mabon*, p. 122).[111] *Hanes Taliesin* may not be accurately dated to before Geoffrey of Monmouth's time; certainly this passage seems to be connected to the tradition concerning Merlin's release of the two dragons, which is documented in *History of the Kings of Britain*.[10] It is part of a mythos that is looking to its ancestral roots, whether real or imaginary. Furthermore, we should not overlook the preponderance of genealogies that arose during the centuries of Saxon and Norman rule, wherein British poets and clerics recited or transcribed their patron's illustrious line, invariably linking it into a Roman, Arthurian or saintly lineage. Inventing ancestors is not a new game, but how much is genuine remembrance?

It has been suggested that Geoffrey's *History* is Britain's version of the Irish *Book of Invasions*.[51] In this book, the *Lebor Gabala Erenn*,[8] the history of Ireland's many invasions is told; it was compiled over a vast period of time, incorporating many ancient traditions and linking them to Biblical ancestors. In this book we hear of the descent of the Irish from the peoples of Greece, Egypt and Spain – the route by which the invading tribes that settled in Ireland were supposed to have travelled. Such claims have been dismissed as akin to Geoffrey's fabrications – false and misleading. But there is now reason to suppose that this tradition was not so far wrong.

The origins of the myths of a race are hard to trace but are usually tenacious of their tradition; errors of detail are common; general report is usually near the truth. If the Irish could trace their ancestry back to Greece, it is equally possible for the British to have a tradition that spoke of Trojan forebears. It is known that Geoffrey borrowed from Nennius' *British History*,[28] but Nennius himself drew upon all kinds of manuscripts and traditions which are no longer available to us. Geoffrey further said he was indebted to Walter, Archdeacon of Oxford for the loan of 'a very ancient book written in the British language', of which his *History* was a translation. Of such books – since vanished – scholars are very properly suspicious. We will never know, but it is likely that this lost book might indeed have been the 'British Book of Invasions', couched in the same language and based upon the Irish model.

Whatever the truth of the matter, a new myth supplanted the Trojan one: that of Arthur, who repelled the incursion of the Saxons and who, after a necessary period during which Britain would suffer untold wrongs under the Saxon yoke, would come again to restore Britain to her former greatness. Such national myths, we must remind ourselves, cannot be fundamentally employed in our own era since:

> Our Ancestors obtain'd the Kingdom thus,
> And left the ill-got Recompense to us;
> The very Lands we all along enjoy'd,
> They ravish'd from the People they destroy'd . . .

as Daniel Defoe wrote in his satire *Jure Divino*, in which he further reminds nationalist sympathizers that we are all 'Blended with Britains [sic], who before were here'.[101] Myths of racial purity and dominance have no currency in this century; they have proved bankrupt – as are all spiritual mysteries employed in the service of Mammon. Sovereignty has her own methods of assessing worthy champions for her empowerment: they may be rich or poor, noble or of common stock, British or of another race – but they will be right for Britain if *she* chooses them. Only her champions are entitled to know the name of the land, the mother of us ...

The name of the game, the subtextual energy of the Matter of Britain, is about sovereignty: who holds the land and by what mystical right? It is only those kings and invaders who draw their empowering emblems and mystique from the deep, mythical framework of the land who are successful. For us to appreciate how Arthur and the related champions of Britain in the *Mabinogion*, discussed in this book, truly function, we need to investigate the role of kingship and its relationship to the land.

III THE CALLING OF THE KINGS

The *Mabinogion* is a primary document in the Matter of Britain. It draws on the earliest mythic archetypes of both pseudo-history and the cross-fertilization of stories from the British oral tradition with French romances. Each one of the stories discussed in this book shows a hero or champion who is battling for sovereignty of one kind or another. Lludd has to overcome three dreadful scourges, which ravage his country (Chapter Two); Macsen seeks a dream-woman and succeeds in becoming the ruler of Britain (Chapter Three); Rhonabwy is despondent about the state of his native Wales, but his dream reveals a combat for another kind of sovereignty between Arthur and Owain (Chapter Four); Owain becomes the king of an Otherworldly realm (Chapter Five); Gereint's story reveals a complex relationship between several characters who strive for sovereignty on many levels (Chapter Six); while in Peredur's adventures the empowering symbols of Sovereignty are sought and found (Chapter Seven). How each of these characters achieves his aim will be revealed in successive chapters, but in some way or other they are all archetypal kings.

Each of these characters may justifiably be called a king or champion because each is accountable to Sovereignty, the God-dess of the Land. But we must not take the medieval notion of kingship as our model here; Arthur, his knights and champions, as well as the other mythical kings, are drawn from a totally different frame of reference. In order to understand the nature and complexity of Sovereignty's relationship with the king, we must examine the basis of Celtic kingship.

The rites of kingship retain a magical and mystical significance even in our own times. The distillation of ages of tribal ritual still raises an atavistic shudder in some of us as we watch the British coronation ceremony today. It is difficult to express in words just what causes such a primitive reaction within us, but it is clearly con-nected with the way in which the monarch is presented as the repre-sentative of the tribe to the Otherworldly guardians of the land.

More deeply moving is the way in which the king was married to the land. Irish texts speak of the *banais rigi*, or the 'wedding of the kingship'.[70] This ritual understanding obtained in many parts of the world, but was particularly upheld within the Celtic nations. It is possible that:

> In the elder days, when the succession passed through the female line, the Sovereignty [sic] resided in the person of the queen, who, as high priestess, was also the reincarnation of the Great Earth Mother and chose from among her warriors a man to mate with, lead her warband, and after the cycle of seven years, become the king-sacrifice and die to ensure fertility for the soil and prosperity for the tribe.[158]

We will see, in the succeeding chapters, just how this ancient understanding lies hidden within the stories of the *Mabinogion* as well as in the Arthurian legends. Matrilinear considerations are still visible in, for instance, Mordred's attempts to win Arthur's throne. While Mordred is Arthur's son, he is also Arthur's *sister's* son: a role variously filled by Anna, Morgan or Morgause, depending on the traditions one wishes to draw upon (see Chapter Ten). We will also see the way that the insult to Gwenhwyfar – which occurs in *Owain, Gereint and Enid* and *Peredur* – dishonours the land, for Gwenhwyfar is Arthur's Sovereignty in the flesh. For this reason the role of 'Queen's Champion' is a prime honour at Arthur's court: both Gereint and Peredur take up this role. Lancelot later succeeds to this role in the French romances.

The 'wedding of the kingship' held mystical connotations. At his king-making the king would mystically conjoin with his king-dom by stepping into the sacred footprint on the inauguration stone up on to which his tribe raised him. This stone was symbolic of the land. Such a stone can be seen at Dunadd in Strathclyde, Scotland, where the Scottish kings were 'made'. Another famous stone was that of Fal at Tara in Ireland, which would cry out under a destined king. By this means the king aligned himself with his sacred ancestors and simultaneously established a con-tract with the ground beneath his feet. The anvil into which the sword of kingship is thrust in the later traditions of Arthur is merely an extension of the royal king-making stone: only the rightful king may draw it out. It is a supreme example of the kingly marriage with the land. In John Boorman's film *Excalibur* (Orion, 1981) the imagery of sword and cup is superimposed in such a way that the answer to the Grail question 'Whom does the Grail serve?' becomes 'The land and the king are one.' We will see in Chapters Seven and Nine how the Grail is but one of the Hallows guarded by Sovereignty and wielded by the rightful king or champion.

Late survivals of the 'wedding of the kingship' were recorded in the twelfth century, the time when the major Arthurian and Grail texts were transcribed. Giraldus Cambrensis recorded one such in his *Irish Itinerary*, where he described the inauguration of an Ultonian king (a king of Ulster):

> When the whole people of that land has been gathered together in one place, a white mare is brought forward into the middle of the assembly. He who is to be inaugurated . . . embraces the animal before all, professing himself to be a beast also. The mare is then killed immediately, cut up in pieces, and boiled in water. A bath is prepared for the man afterwards in the same water. He sits in the bath surrounded by all his people and all . . . eat of the meat of the mare which is brought to them. He quaffs and drinks of the broth in which he is bathed [by] . . . dipping his mouth into it.[60]

Here Sovereignty is represented by the white mare, which, as we saw in Chapter 2 of *Mabon*,[111] may be equated with the archetypal Goddess represented by both Rhiannon and Epona. The Indian parallel to this ritual, the *asvamedha* ritual in which a queen symbolically mates with a (dead) stallion, has a close cultural overlay with the rite that aroused Giraldus' clerical distaste.[130]

But not all survivals employed sacred bestiality. In 1170 Eleanor of Aquitaine decided to inaugurate her son, Richard – the future Lionheart – as Duke of Aquitaine. She arranged a symbolic marriage between him and St Valéry, the legendary martyr and patroness of the district, who had doubtless assumed the attributes of a local goddess of Sovereignty. The saint's ring was placed on Richard's finger 'in solemn token of his indissoluble union with the provinces and vassals of Aquitaine'.[100]

Kingship and marriage are very similar contracts. While there is harmony and mutual respect between the partners, both marriage and reign are likewise harmonious; when love is withheld or abused, then the contract is severed. Throughout the Grail legends it is this relationship between land and king that is crucial to the story, for the land and its bounty are interwoven with the destiny of the rightful king.

The duties of a king were strictly entailed: if his rule was just then his land and people were fertile and content, as this ancient Irish text relates:

> So long as he preserves justice, good will not be lacking to him, and his reign will not fail ... By the Prince's justice, every right prevails and every vessel is full during his reign ... By the Prince's justice, fair weather comes in each fitting season, winter fine and frosty, spring dry and windy, summer warm, with showers of rain, autumn with heavy dews, and fruitful. For it is the prince's falsehood that brings perverse weather upon wicked peoples and dries up the fruit of the earth.[146]

This statement will doubtless remind readers of Lerner and Loewe's musical *Camelot*, in which Arthur praises the climate of his land where the seasons conveniently match ideal weather conditions!

There are plenty of examples in Celtic literature of an unfruitful land caused by a wrongful or unjust king, as we will see in Chapter Two, where Vortigern's reign is discussed. Although Lludd himself is a good king, his kingdom suffers under three plagues which wreak devastation, and he must find a solution. Sometimes the perturbation is much deeper, an enduring evil left over from a past age, which no king has yet rectified or appeased: such is Lludd's problem, and Manawyddan's, too, in the third branch of the *Mabinogi* (*Mabon*, p. 63).[111] Sometimes the forces of the land are out of alignment because the king's wife is an unworthy representative of Sovereignty, such as Conn's Otherworld woman, Becuma (see p. 46): their marriage is no true union, and the land reflects this imbalance by failing in milk and grain.

The king's union with the land, with Sovereignty, is a very special one. There is an exchange of energies and powers: the king swears to uphold his land and people and to be true to them, while Sovereignty gives him Otherworldly gifts enabling him to keep his oath. At base the Celtic concept of Sovereignty is related to the Middle Eastern concept of Wisdom, known as Sophia, who consorts with kings as the creative and wisdom-bestowing mystic woman, either as an angelic presence or in the person of an earthly woman. Solomon and Sheba are the prime couple of this paradigm. In British symbolism, Arthur and one of Sovereignty's representatives – not necessarily Gwenhwyfar – are understood to take these roles.

Arthur's relationship with Sovereignty is an extraordinary one, for not only does he himself relate to Otherworldly and earthly women who represent some aspect of the Goddess, but also his role extends to select knights of his court, who can be seen as his champions, relating similarly to the figures of Sovereignty. These knights are usually those closely related, by blood, to Arthur: his nephews and cousins, for example, Gwalchmai (Gawain), Gereint, Culhwch, Goreu and Owain.

This custom may be more clearly understood if we look once more at Celtic kingship customs. Primogeniture was not introduced until the time of the Norman kings. Celtic kingship was elective, the successor being drawn from suitable candidates within one royal clan claiming a common ancestor. The king chose and appointed his successor, or *tanaiste* (literally 'second'), during his own lifetime. The choice was with the approval of the clan's elders and assured the succession in the event of the king's sudden death. Such an appointment was made at a great gathering of the people known as a *feis*, or assembly, so that the whole clan knew who the *tanaiste* was. It is perhaps significant that Gereint, Culhwch, Goreu, Owain and others are publicly honoured by Arthur during such an assembly. Arthur is also seen to leave his court for the express purpose of finding his appointed champions Owain, Gereint and Peredur.

Part of the king's contract with Sovereignty was outlined by the number of *geasa* laid upon him by men of wisdom at the beginning of his reign. A *geas* is a prohibition or obligation binding one on pain of the loss of honour. A king might not lose honour, since it not only diminished his authority but also mystically harmed the land. In an Irish story concerning Arthur, *The Story of the Crop-Eared Dog* (*Echtra an Mhadra Mhaoil*), Arthur says:

> Good people . . . *there are many geasa upon me*, and one of them is to convene the chase of the Dangerous Forest at the end of every seventh year. If the chase should prove favourable for me the first day, to leave the forest; if not, to stay the second day, and the third concerning the hunt. And I shall not break my *geasa* . . . *for he is a person without prosperity who breaks his geasa* [my italics].[138]

This chase is emblematic of Arthur's seven-year-agreement with Sovereignty, which has to be ratified in order for his reign to continue. As we will see in Chapter Six, the chase for the White Hart is part of this tradition and is one of the rare occasions when Arthur himself engages in the action of the story.

One of Arthur's famous *geasa* was never to eat until a wonder had appeared before him; the best-known tale about the proving of this *geas* is *Sir Gawain and the Green Knight*.[31] We are already familiar with a similar *geas*: that upon Pwyll to climb to the top of the Mound of Arberth whereupon he might see a wonder or be wounded (*Mabon*, p. 22).[111]

The two-edged nature of *geasa* hinges upon the capacity for selflessness of the man concerned: as long as he lives a redemptive life, given over to the service of his people, he is king in truth; but there usually comes a moment when he must decide between his *geas* and his contract with Sovereignty, and his own interests. This usually takes the form of a life/death decision, such as when Cu Chulainn is invited to eat a roasted dog by the Morrighan in the *Tain bó Cualigne*: his *geasa* include an obligation to accept food when it is offered to him and a prohibition against eating dog's flesh, since it is his totemic beast. He eats and accepts the consequences, but his contract as Ulster's champion is at an end.[88]

But at all times the king is bound to uphold the law, which is most binding upon him:

> The king must have patience, self-government without haughtiness, speak truth and keep promises; honour the nobles, respect the poets, adore God; keep the Law exactly without mercy. Boundless in charity, care for the sick and orphans; lift up good men and suppress evil ones; give freedom for the just, restriction for the guilty. At Samhain (November 1st, Hallowmas) he must light the lamps and welcome the guests with clapping. He must appear splendid as the sun in the Mead Hall.[158]

So goes an instruction of Cormac mac Airt, known as the Irish King Solomon, famed for his laws and noble institutions of learning; but this might well be a description of Arthur in his great hall, the most resplendent of kings in that supposedly Dark Age. And Arthur shines yet in the hearts and imaginations of many as the upholder of the Light against the Dark, but there are few to mark the nature of his union with the land, and that is the underlying purpose of this book; for, as mentioned in Chapter One of *Mabon*, this will enable us to call forth the Pendragon and to name the land, correctly identifying the aspect of Sovereignty appropriate to our time.

IV THE GODDESS OF THE LAND

The Goddess of Sovereignty has long been acknowledged by scholars to be an intrinsic part of the Celtic world; she is viewed by them as a literary type or an ancient survival of pre-Christian times. As we examine the evidence for this, we may be astounded to find that, far from being a cultural cliché or an abstraction, the power of the living Goddess is paramount. She appears in many guises: as an Otherworldly maiden whose beauty dazzles; as a bountiful queen, bestowing the gifts of the land upon her people; as Dark Woman of Knowledge, *Cailleach* or Loathly Lady she appals with her ugliness, but not for long. The dark aspect of the Goddess is but the last waning crescent, which will turn to new moon in the twinkling of an eye to reveal her as Princess of Beauty, Youth and Gladness.

Each of our stories shows how she interacts with the protagonists of a tale: she may appear to heroes and kings, urging them on to find her gifts or to champion her cause; she may assume the shape of a mortal woman, using her as an exemplar of the Goddess; or she may use many earthly women in one story so that each of her aspects is manifested. And here we must beware that we do not impute goddessly status to mortal women. Though the gifts of the Goddess are manifested at every level of existence, we must neither confuse these levels with each other nor impose modern psychological or feminist values on these medieval stories.

The Divine Feminine may have been officially expunged from Christian worship, or lodged in a niche reserved for the Blessed Virgin, but the Goddess and her works did not vanish from the consciousness of a people who had revered her at stream and in grove from the dawn of time. The Goddess haunted the medieval imagination, as a glance at any text will testify. While Europe may have been nominally Christian, believers evidently approached the new expression of deity with images drawn from their own native mythic traditions.

While the official political apparatus of medieval society may have been harsh to women in its laws and social judgements, we can still perceive a great gentleness and reverence between men and women of all kinds. The barbarism and cruelty which some have perceived as the mainspring of medieval times was no worse than that which has typified this century. Feudal society was not far advanced beyond that of the tribe, for whom all life was sacred, plant, beast and humankind. However, those who would equate the gentle, peaceful time of the prehistoric tribe with a 'matriarchal' society need to think carefully about their definitions and take off their rose-coloured spectacles before they vaunt the Goddess as the gentle earth-mother, and women as her automatic peacemakers. The Goddess wore many faces and her rites were not exclusively female. If I take space to stress this point here, it is only to remind certain readers that, in the divine economy, as in the human, there is a measure of balance in all things: women *and* men, muses *and* daemons, goddesses *and* gods.

Times change but stories endure. The Goddess passes into the shape of Sovereignty, and into many other guises, which I have not discussed in this book. She passes also into the guise of the land itself personified.

Primarily the Goddess of Sovereignty is the *genius loci*, the spirit of the earth beneath us, who in many different countries assumes a localized appearance and a set of symbols appropriate to her cult. The first localized cults of the Blessed Virgin were built upon this understanding, giving us 'Our Lady of' this or that place. Every country has its own Sovereignty, who is emblematic of that country's political identity. Britain's prime symbol once appeared on the common penny as Britannia: a personification first portrayed on Roman coins of the conquest period, showing Britain arrayed with the spear, shield and mural crown of Minerva. This symbolic representation, once in everyone's pocket, now appears only on the fifty-pence piece.

Yet examples of Sovereignty in British tradition are hard to find. In my discussion of the Sovereignty themes in the *Mabinogion*, the reader will notice that I have frequently resorted to Irish texts to explicate the text in question. There is a good reason for this. Although British – what we would now call Welsh – tradition embodied and preserved a good deal of evidence for Sovereignty, this occurred mainly in the oral tradition only and has been subsequently lost. The Irish tradition, whose poets and story-tellers merged almost imperceptibly with that other professional class, the Christian clerics, preserved both an oral and a written tradition, which, for reasons of geographical isolation and other cultural features, have come down to us in a nearly complete body of lore. The loss of a parallel Welsh tradition is partially made up for by the preservation and transmission of British stories in Breton and French traditions where they emerged to form the Matter of Britain. 'Whatever the reason may have been,' says the respected scholar Rachel Bromwich, 'there can be no doubt of the great value for comparative purposes of early Irish literature.'[56]

Glenys Goetinck has rightly pointed out that 'for many scholars "Celtic origin" and "Irish origin" have become synonymous. Welsh tradition has been regarded as . . . a channel through which Irish legends filtered to the continental romancers.'[74] The *Mabinogion* does preserve a truly British tradition which though it is paralleled frequently in Irish tradition, does not necessarily draw directly upon it. We must posit a common heritage, remembering that the 'cultural norm' was dictated by a professional class of poets and story-tellers, highly trained in transmitting 'classified information' by way of their arts. Their stories would have provided a common store of tradition in imagery and song, which would have been as potent, if not more so, than the media culture that is common in our own time on both sides of the Atlantic.

I believe that once the reader has assimilated the evidence both within the *Mabinogion* stories discussed in this volume and in *Mabon*[111], as well as in the parallel and comparative stories in the commentaries, he or she will hold the keys to a new understanding of the Goddess. It will be seen that expressions of the Divine Feminine did not suddenly cease in early Romano-British culture but, in the post-Celtic period, developed in a totally new way, spreading organically by means of the oral tradition into the deep levels of national consciousness. Although many may feel that this process diminished the Goddess's power, I believe that the reverse is true. When a deity steps down from a shrine and is seemingly exiled from its cult, two things may happen. That deity either gradually fades from memory or becomes newly enshrined in the hearts of the people: this is what happened to Sovereignty, whose function as the bestower of wisdom and power was enhanced by the skill of story-tellers beyond the scope of a local cult.

That a few localized aspects of the great Earth Mother of primitive belief should have melded together and survived to form one of the major figures not only of Celtic and Arthurian tradition but also of the redemptive Grail legends is astounding, but this is what happened. The foundation mysteries of the Goddess underlie the Matter of Britain, as does the Succession of the Pendragons with all its ancient resonances of earlier beliefs. The process of this unfolding comprises the matter of this book.

The most clearly defined portrayal of Sovereignty is found in early Irish literary tradition, where she is called Eriu – Ireland herself. A late fourteenth-century poem by Gofraigh Fionn Ó'Dálaigh addressed to his future patron, Tadhg Mainistreach, Lord of Desmond, shows us Eire as the Goddess of Sovereignty awaiting her true husband:

> Patience awhile, O Eire!
> Soon shalt thou get a true spouse.
> He is not yet a grown man,
> O Eire, thou home of comfort.
>
> O smooth plain of Usneach,
> fair Temhair of Da Thi,
> I know him who shall wed thee,
> a hero child whom thou shalt love.[102]

The Goddess of the Land who awaited a worthy consort was a well-established theme by the time of this poem, but the Irish had achieved a high degree of skill in portraying Sovereignty as the consort of kings, as we find in the following story, *Echtra Mac Echach Muigmedoin* (*The Adventures of Eochaid Muigmedon's Sons*). It concerns primarily Niall of the Nine Hostages, who was a historical High King of Ireland from AD 379–405. I give the fullest synopsis of this story since it establishes a primary source for Sovereignty's relationship with the king.

King Eochaid Muigmedon had four sons by his wife, Queen Mong-find. He had also a concubine called Cairenn Casdubh, a captive from Alba. She gave birth to Eochaid's son, Niall, beside a well, and was forced into slavery by Mongfind and had to abandon her child. He was found by a wandering poet, Torna Eces, who fostered him until the boy was nine and had long golden hair. Eochaid recognized his son formally at court, and Niall's first deed was to clothe his mother in the royal purple, bringing her toil to an end.

When the time came for Eochaid to appoint his *tanaiste*, he sent all five boys to the smith, Sithchenn, who was also a druid and prophet. He tested the boys to see which should become king by setting fire to his smithy and standing by to see what the boys would do. The four eldest boys rushed into the flaming smithy and brought out a chariot that was being repaired, a vat of wine, some weapons and a bunch of kindling, but Niall brought out the anvil, the tongs, bellows and hammers – all the tools of the smith's craft – so that Sithchenn's choice fell upon him.

Mongfind was dissatisfied by this outcome and demanded another test. The boys were then armed as men and sent off hunting to see how they would fare. They killed a boar and set up a fire but they were soon very thirsty. In turn each of the four eldest boys went in search of water but each one encountered the same hideous hag, who guarded a well from which she allowed none to drink save the one who kissed her. In turn all fled. Lastly, Niall himself came and saw her:

> every joint and limb of her, from the top of her head to the earth, was black as coal. Like the tail of a wild horse was the gray bristly mane that came through the upper part of her head-crown. The green branch of an oak in bearing would be severed by the sickle of green teeth that lay in her head and reached to her ears. She had a middle fibrous, spotted with pustules, diseased, and shins distorted and awry. Her ankles were thick, her shoulderblades were broad, her knees were big, and her nails were green. [70]

Niall agreed not only to kiss her but lie with her as well. When he kissed her he found that:

> there was not in the world a damsel whose gait or appearance was more lovable than hers! ... Plump and queenly forearms she had; fingers long and lengthy: calves straight and beautifully coloured. Two blunt shoes of white bronze between her little, soft-white feet and the ground. A costly full-purple mantle she wore, with a brooch of bright silver in the clothing of the mantle. Shining pearl teeth she had, an eye large [and] queenly, and lips red as rowanberries. (ibid.)

Amazed, Niall asked who she was. And was told, 'Lordship is mine; O King of Tara, I am Sovereignty.' She commended him for his perseverence in the face of her ugliness and gave him to drink of the well, bidding him not to give his brothers any until they acknowledged him as his father's *tanaiste*. And so Niall became High King, reigning long and prosperously, he and his line after him. [58]

In this, one of many king-making stories in which Sovereignty appears, we note that she is primarily a transformative goddess, changing from hag to maiden, renewed by Niall's acceptance of all that kingship entails. It is this very element of transformation from hag to maiden that helps us track the parallel developments of Sovereignty within British and Arthurian tradition. Niall's success is dependent upon many factors, not least of which is his early boyhood deed of freeing his mother from slavery. (There are many elements in this story that are strongly reminiscent of Rhiannon and Pryderi. Even the poet, Torna Eces, 'Thunder Knowledge', who fosters Niall, is strikingly similar to Teyrnon Twrf Liant, 'Lord of the Raging Sea'. The hag's horse-like hair may also indicate a parallel with Rhiannon (see *Mabon*, Chapters 2 and 4).[111]

By freeing his mother from servitude, Niall has already set in motion the transformative chain of events that will make him king. His action of seizing the anvil is also significant, especially if we parallel the sword-in-the-stone motif, which similarly establishes Arthur's kingship in a competitive test. Perhaps the part of this story that is most indicative of Sovereignty's empowerment is her guardianship of the well. Invariably Sovereignty gives to drink of her cup to the rightful kingly candidate or champion. In this, as we will later see, she is the prototype of the Grail Maiden. More importantly she is the guardian of the Hallows, the Otherworldly empowering elements that underlie the kingly regalia of the king-making ceremony. The Hallows – often formalized into the spear, the sword, the cup and the cauldron, though appearing in many variations – may not be handled by any save the rightful king or most worthy champion. In the test or quest by which they are found, Sovereignty often assumes her guise of hag, although she is by no means restricted to that role.

The transformative Goddess of Sovereignty is a unique feature in Irish and British tradition, rarely encountered elsewhere in such a profusion of expressions, except perhaps in Indian or Tibetan tradition, where aspectual qualities of deity are prominently stressed. This same method of understanding deities and inner archetypes was once commonplace in the proto-Celtic era, but is no longer so in an age when Deity, whether male or female

Aspect	Maiden	Mother/ Foster-mother	Hag/Cailleach
Aspect of royal rule	Princess	Queen	Queen Mother
Appearance	Beautiful maiden	Royal woman	Ugly hag or the Black Maiden
Symbolic colour	White (sometimes red)	Red (sometimes white)	Black
Function	She invites	She empowers	She guides and warns
Empowering drink	The red drink of lordship	The milk of fostering	The dark drink of forgetfulness
Title in the Grail legends	Grail Maiden/ -bearer	Queen of the Hallows	Grail messenger
Other titles	Sovereignty, Flower Bride	Sovereignty	Loathly Lady, Dark Woman of Knowledge

Figure 1.1: *The Shape of Sovereignty*

in expression, has virtually become a featureless two-dimensional concept or a concept totally absent from the consciousness of many people.

In order to help the reader conceptualize the features of Sovereignty in a very generalized sense, Figure 1.1 gives a simple formula, which lists the names, aspects, functions and characteristics of Sovereignty that I have employed in this book. This schema is by no means the last word and should be employed only as a rough guide. Sovereignty is too subtle and transformatory a goddess to be pinned down and decoded in this fashion.

There is nothing immovable about this schema: as we will see, Sovereignty chooses her own methods of making herself known. She may use more than three aspects in which to reveal herself, as she indeed does in *Peredur* (see Chapter Seven). There is a case for her appearing in four aspects, especially if one considers the evidence of the Arthurian legends, where the admonitory Black Maiden, who shares all the features of the *Cailleach* except age, is a transitional figure between the hag and maiden aspects. She

presents an aspect of the Goddess identifiable to anyone familiar
with Celtic mythology: that of the woman warrior who often acts
as bodyguard or resourceful companion to the champion, as
Luned does for Owain (see Chapter Five).

The symbolic colours above are derived from a number of
textual sources, which comprise a familiar set of details corresponding to the aspects outlined above. The woman who possesses all
these colours in her appearance – white of skin, red of cheek and
lip, black of hair – is the ideal woman over whom the champion
languishes; she may appear in dream or, as in Peredur's case, the
champion may see these colours in vivid juxtaposition and en-
vision a dream-woman. This ideal woman is none other than
Sovereignty, who combines all these colours and their symbolic
qualities within her own person.

The warrior-woman aspect of the Black Maiden may be said to
combine black and white as her colours; these are frequently
represented by the chessboard of combat, another emblem of the
land or of Sovereignty herself. The Black Maiden, as a fourth
aspect of Sovereignty, fulfils the role of tutor in some of the
stories, as Luned does for Owain (see Chapter Five). Or she is the
satirist–challenger, which is how the Black Maiden appears to
Peredur (see Chapter Seven). This role can be traced throughout
Celtic literature, from the women warriors who teach heroes
battle skills, like Scathach, to the appearance of the Morrighan as
a satirist – both of whom figure largely in the story of Cu
Chulainn.[88] The Black Maiden battles hard to bring her protégé
to self-knowledge and responsible action; in many ways she is an
active champion of Sovereignty and corresponds to the male
figure I have identified as the Provoker of Strife, an archetype
fulfilled by Iddawg, Efnissien and Cai in the stories of *The Dream
of Rhonabwy*, *Branwen, Daughter of Llyr* and the romances. These
men are irritating troublemakers in whom we can perceive the
role of Sovereignty's guardian (see Chapter Eight).

Sovereignty is not a passive archetype, nor some kind of negative cypher whose sole purpose is to empower kings and heroes. As
a goddess and in her human representatives she exists in her own
right and actively chooses to promote, obstruct or dismiss her
chosen candidates. She and her candidates continually modify

and develop their relationships. As the essential quality of the land personified, Sovereignty has the right to change her mind and frequently does so. Arthur himself is not exempt from her strictures.

Arthur's brilliant early career is mostly overshadowed in later texts by his own seemingly passive stance: a king who does not hazard his person but who sends out his knights instead. As we shall see in Chapter Ten, his inability to retain Gwenhwyfar (Guinevere) is a symptom of the kingly relationship with Sovereignty. His enmity with Morgan is similarly significant. The demise of the Round Table Fellowship is nothing less than the reordering of the land in Britain under a new regime, according to Sovereignty's decision. It is not for nothing that medieval story-tellers frequently include a set-piece dream in which Arthur meets the Goddess as Fortuna, upon whose wheel he has been both elevated and abased.[3,25] But of these subtle relationships between Arthur and Sovereignty we will speak more in Chapter Ten.

The point at which the historical and mythic concepts of Arthur meet and merge is perhaps best seen and understood in the undying king's defence of Britain. Arthur's timely welding together of the scattered kingdoms of Britain to form a palladium against barbarian invaders thrust him into mythic prominence. But he was only one of many such defenders dating back before Bran the Blessed, whose head was buried at the White Mount in London to prevent invasion – a talismanic burial, which, say the triads, Arthur abhorred, since he wished to fulfil this role alone, and he supervised the lamentable disinterment of the head of Bran.[38] Vortimer, the erstwhile King of Britain, Vortigern's son, similarly asked for his body to be dismembered and buried at the ports to defend Britain from Saxon invasion (ibid., Triad 37).

Even earlier than Vortimer was Constantius Chlorus, the imperial commander of Gaul, who, in the late third century AD, routed the usurping Allectus, murderer of the British emperor Carausius whose seamanship had effectively defended Britain from foreign invasion. Constantius Chlorus was subsequently active in restoring Britain and in strengthening its borders. His defeat of Allectus was marked by the striking of a golden medallion; on the reverse of his portrait appears a kneeling woman, the spirit of London herself, welcoming his appearance with the legend: *Redditor lucis aeternae* – 'Restorer of the Eternal Light'. This tradition seems to have been borrowed from coinage of Carausius, whose coins call him *Restitutor Britanniae* – 'Restorer of Britain', and hail him *Expectate veni* – 'Come, awaited one.'[49]

If Arthur ever found time to strike such coins himself, none has survived, yet these titles might well be used to refer to him, since he deserved them as much as, if not more than, Constantius or Carausius for his defence of Britain's sovereignty. Historical tradition affords Arthur the title *Dux Britanniarum*, the old Roman military title given to those who defended the northern frontiers, and Nennius attests to many battles that Arthur fought in Britain's defence, notably the eighth battle, which:

> was in Guinnion fort, and in it Arthur carried the image of the holy Mary, the everlasting Virgin, on his shield.[28]

Geoffrey of Monmouth, calling on this tradition, gives his own version of this incident, placing it at the Battle of Badon:

> And across his shoulders, a circular shield called Pridwen, on which there was painted a likeness of the Blessed Mary, Mother of God, which forced him to be thinking perpetually of her.[10]

British tradition was not slow to afford Arthur the status of a Christian king and emperor, whose defence of his realm was but an extension of his defence of Christendom. The two passages above have been disputed in that Nennius' text implies that Arthur carried the Virgin's image on his shoulder rather than his shield, due to a confusion between two old Welsh terms, *ysgwyd* (shield) and *ysgwydd* (shoulder).* However, if we consider Geoffrey's singular slip in confusing *Pridwen*, Arthur's ship, famed from long British usage, with his shield, we find an interesting implication.

The meaning of the word *Prydwen*, Arthur's ship, may unlock for us the true relationship of Arthur to the land of Britain in a more mystical sense. *Prid*, *pridd* or *pryd* may mean, variously, 'dear', 'earth' or 'beauty'. The suffix, *wen*, from *gwen* or *gwyn*,

---

* See J. Lindsay, *Arthur and his Times*, Frederick Muller, 1958.

means 'white' or 'blessed', so that *Prydwen* might signify the White or Blessed Earth'. Prydein is, of course, one of the names of Britain. Perhaps beneath the writings of Nennius and Geoffrey we may discern Arthur's true championship of the Lady of Britain, the indwelling Goddess and Sovereignty of the Land, on whose defence Arthur's thoughts were perpetually set.

According to ancient tradition it was in the ship *Prydwen* that Arthur sailed to gain the empowering Hallows of Sovereignty, reiving them from the Underworld of Annwn: a feat which, says the poet Taliesin, caused him to wear a 'mournful mien', since out of three shipfuls of men only seven returned from that place. It is precisely because of his care for and his defence of the Blessed Earth of Britain and its *genius loci*, Sovereignty, that Arthur is remembered: a duty which marks him out from other men and incorporates him into Britain's landscape, as the poet David Jones wrote:

> if his forehead is radiant like the smooth hill in the lateral light, it is corrugated like the defence of the hill, because of his care for the land and for the men of the land.[84]

CHAPTER TWO

LLUDD AND LLEFELYS

> Britons then shall have
> Their land and their crown,
> And the stranger swarm
> Shall disappear.
> *Hanes Taliesin*

Do not allow your sword hilt – a misfortune would be had –
yonder to one of the Coraniaid; to destroy the poison as Lludd
once did, you supply the holy water on behalf of our nation.

> Lewys Mon to his patron
> (medieval Welsh poem)

I THE TESTING OF LLUDD

In the first story of this discussion we find all the necessary
ingredients for our study: kingship, Britain's sovereignty and
Otherworldly manifestations of disorder and challenge. All of
these factors feature in the testing of Lludd in his new role as king.
The story is short and simple and relates the adventures of Lludd,
King of Britain and his attempts to rid his kingdom of three
plagues, which threaten his sovereignty. In *Hanes Taliesin*[23] the
story is alluded to as 'The Contention of Lludd and Llefelys',
which may well have been an earlier title; if this is so, it is an

intriguing one since it suggests a development untouched in our narrative. Lludd and his brother, although Kings of Britain and France respectively, do not really contend in this story. However, a further facet is added to this lost tradition in the work of the twelfth-century bard Llewelyn Fardd, who alludes to our story thus: 'I am an eloquent lad who is known in the court, like the contention of Lludd and Llefelys.'[38]

As will become clear from the discussion on pp. 48–50, the function of the Wise and Innocent Youth is paramount in both our story and the parallel and source texts that accompany it. This is the role of the young Merlin, for example, who, as Emrys, confounds Vortigern's magicians (see section II). Perhaps, in some lost original of our story, Llefelys acted in a similar way in a supportive vindication of his brother's kingship. It is in such a mode that Taliesin helps his young patron, Elphin, at the court of King Maelgwn (see *Mabon*, pp. 114–16).[111] A possible folkstory variant for the contention of the two brothers is investigated on p. 50.

The incident of the dragons (who *do* contend in this story) we find paralleled in Geoffrey of Monmouth's *History of the Kings of Britain*.[10] Britain's sovereignty is here represented by the red dragon – still the national emblem of Wales. It is likewise the device or totemic beast of the greatest line of kings, the Pendragons, and is, ultimately, the beast of Sovereignty herself. In the evolution of the Arthurian legends we continue to accumulate traditions relating to the dragon. At the latter end of the corpus we find in John Boorman's film *Excalibur* that not only is Merlin the arch dragon-priest, attached in a prophetic and magical role to King Arthur, but also that the land of Britain itself is understood to be the dragon. When the King is wounded (by the adultery of Guinevere with Lancelot), Merlin is de-activated on the magical levels and the land is rent: the powers of the dragon are no longer safely syphoned through the roles of king and priest but are loose to wreak havoc in the kingdom. Wasteland, unnatural rites and weak kingship result.

We must view the dragons in this story in a similar light. The emblematic beast of Britain – the red dragon – does battle with the foreign dragon. Both Taliesin in the *Mabinogion*[23] and Merlin in his prophecies[150] speak at length about this combat and its consequences for the people of Britain. The overcoming of the red dragon by the white will ensue, say Merlin and Taliesin, followed by a return of Britain's primacy before the ending of the world. The historical, allegorical and mythological meanings of the prophecies of Merlin are dealt with exhaustively in R. J. Stewart's book *The Prophetic Vision of Merlin*.[150]

Lludd and Llefelys

* (1) Beli the Great had three sons, Lludd, Caswallawn and Nynnyaw as well as a fourth, Llefelys. Lludd reigned after his father, rebuilding London as his chief fortress. Llefelys married the King of France's only daughter, becoming king of that country in his turn.

(2) Three plagues fell upon Britain: (3) the arrival of the Corannyeid, who overheard anything that was uttered in the kingdom, so they could not be overthrown; (4) a scream was heard every May Eve which robbed men of their strength, made women miscarry and children to become mad, while animals and soil alike became barren; (5) the king's court was mysteriously robbed of its provisions. (6) Seeking his brother's advice, Lludd set off for France very secretly. Llefelys met him in mid-ocean with his own fleet. To avoid the Corannyeid overhearing, Llefelys counselled that they speak only through a bronze horn. But whatever was said was misunderstood by the other. Llefelys had the horn washed out with wine, which removed this contrary set of spirits. He then advised his brother on how to deal with each of the plagues.

Lludd returned and implemented his brother's advice. (7) He summoned all his people together with the Corannyeid, mashed up the insects, which Llefelys had given him, with water and threw the water over the assembly. It destroyed the Corannyeid but left the British unharmed. (8) He then measured the length and breadth of the island to discover its centre, which was found to be Oxford. There a pit was dug and a vat of mead was placed in it with a silk sheet over it. Two dragons came fighting. When they were tired they sank down on to the sheet in the form of piglets, drank up the mead and fell asleep. They were immediately bundled into the sheet and locked in a stone chest and buried in the most secure part of the kingdom:

* See following commentary (p. 34) for notes.

Snowdon. This ended the screaming. (9) Last, Lludd himself prepared to stay up all night and catch whoever stole his court's provisions. He had a tub of cold water ready to immerse himself in if he felt sleepy. He saw a heavily armoured man enter with a basket into which he put all the food. They struggled and Lludd overcame his adversary, making him grant restitution and serve him for ever afterwards. So were the three plagues overcome and peace restored to Britain.

Commentary

1. Tradition credits Beli with many descendants. He is none other than Beli Mawr (the Great), ancestor of the Welsh princes. Geoffrey of Monmouth calls him Bellinus. Tradition also credits Beli with marrying Anna, the cousin of the Blessed Virgin Mary, while in the triads he is called the father of Arianrhod. Lludd is none other than King Lud, who, in the *History of the Kings of Britain*,[10] renamed Trinovantum as Caer Lud. In our story Lludd is indeed named as the refounder of London, as it afterwards became. Ludgate, near modern Fleet Street, still bears his name. Statues of him and his brothers appear in the porch of the church of St Dunstan-in-the-West in Fleet Street.

Caswallawn appears in *Branwen, Daughter of Llyr* as the oppressor and usurper of Britain, one responsible for the Enchantment of Britain (see note 2 below). Nynnyaw, or Ninian/Nennius, plays no part in our story, although Geoffrey credits him with a hand-to-hand combat with Julius Caesar in his *History*.[10] The many muddled genealogies that stem from Beli Mawr speak of a Nwyfre who is father of Lliaws, who is married to Beli's daughter, Arianrhod. As this would make Lliaws the son-in-law, do we have here a possible explanation for Llefelys, who nowhere else appears as a son of Beli? Nynnyaw and Nwyfre are sufficiently similar to cause this confusion, while Lliaws and Llefelys sound very similar when pronounced (see *Mabon*, p. 74).[111] Llefelys in our story, however, is credited with gaining a very favourable match with the (unnamed) daughter of the King of France. He seems to have taken on the role of Wise Youth in this story (see note 6).

2. The Enchantments of Britain are a perennial theme in oral

and early literary tradition. Two specific instances spring to mind in the context of this story: the enchantment that falls upon Dyfed in *Manawyddan* (see *Mabon*, p. 57)[111] and the wasteland of the Grail legends. In the first of these a mist covers Dyfed and takes away all living things. It is caused by the Otherworldly workings of Llwyd ap Cil Coed, the enemy of Pwyll's family. In the Grail corpus, the wasteland may be caused by one of several things, the chief of which is the wounding of the king and this is closely associated with the rules under which Sovereignty as Goddess of the Land operates – a blemished or wounded king cannot rule and his failure to abdicate is reflected in the fertility of the land. However, in the *Didot Perceval*[32] it is the fault of Perceval sitting unworthily on the Perilous Seat; likewise a mist descends and a great scream is heard.

Triad 36 speaks of the Three Oppressions that came upon Britain. The Welsh word used to describe these is *gormes*, or *gormesiad* for the plural, which gives the sense of 'plague' or 'foreign oppression' (see note 3). The Enchantments in this story are thus concerned with the sovereignty of Britain. It is not clear how Lludd's reign should have merited these plagues since his rule is a fair one, with no hint of a rupture in the king's traditional relationship with the land; but, as we will see, these plagues are mainly of Otherworldly origin, arising from deep within the land to challenge or test Lludd's kingship.

If we look into the Triads and into parallel Arthurian tradition, we will find that similar problems pursue Arthur's career as king. He is described in Triad 26 as pursuing and seeking to destroy an Otherworldly pregnant sow called Henwen. It is prophesied that 'the Island of Britain would be the worse for the womb-burden'.[38] At first the sow gave forth wheat, bees and barley, but her next offspring were not so beneficial to the Island. She bore three contentious beasts: a wolf-cub, an eagle and a kitten, the last of which grew up to become the fearsome Palug Cat, eventually killed by Cai.[105] We see further to these devastations that Arthur provokes trouble by uncovering the head of Bran the Blessed: this is called one of 'Three Unfortunate Disclosures' in Triad 37. The burial of Bran's head was initially described as one of 'Three Fortunate Concealments', since its interment was for the protection of Britain from invasion. Arthur's hubris in wanting no other but himself to defend Britain causes considerable trouble.

The Three Fortunate Concealments and Three Unfortunate Disclosures are very relevant to our understanding of Britain's sovereignty. They are:

A the head of Bran, buried to protect Britain from invasion, which Arthur dug up out of hubris;
B the bones of Gwrthefyr the Blessed (Vortimer), which protected Britain from Saxon oppression: these were disinterred by Gwrtheyrn the Thin (Vortigern) out of love for Ronnwen, (Renwein, Rowena) Hengist's daughter;
C the dragons that Lludd buried at Dinas Emrys; it was Vortigern's fault they were uncovered since he tried to build his tower over their resting place.

These three concealments are clearly intended for the safety of Britain, and in each case it is a king who disinters or uncovers them. We will learn more of Vortigern in note 8 and section II.

We are perhaps unused to conceiving of Arthur as an irresponsible king. It is possible that Triad 20 can elucidate a lost tradition concerning Arthur's action. In this he is called one of 'Three Red Ravagers of the Island of Britain', or is appended to the triad thus:

But there was one who was a Red Ravager greater than all three: Arthur was his name. For a year neither grass nor plants used to spring up where one of the three would walk; but where Arthur went, not for seven years.

This is an indictment indeed, and one which clearly follows the tradition that it is Arthur's rupture with Sovereignty which causes the wasteland.

The acts of the king are never discrete ones: they have far-reaching repercussions throughout the life of the land and its people. The story of Lludd is too vestigial to establish the causes of his three plagues, but we may be sure that they are closely related to the nature of his early reign and that, like Arthur, it lies within his strength to put things right again.

3. The Corannyeid seem to stem, etymologically, from the Breton faeryfolk, the Korrigans. These beings were said to be descendants of the female druids, whose spells maliciously interfered with the lives of ordinary people; they robbed families of children, substituting changelings and worked much petty magic. According to Breton folk tradition they dance and sing and are not able to stop their singing unless someone passes by and asks a favour. If the client is successful, he receives a gift; otherwise he is afflicted by their enchantment.[109]

Like the Welsh Tylwyth Teg (the Fair Family), as the faerykind were called, the Corannyeid seem to be omniscient, hearing everything that is uttered; this is partially why all faery peoples are spoken of in terms of great reverence or careful respect, lest they blight the lives of mortals in any way. Of course this omniscient hearing is also a power that Math ap Mathonwy has in the Fourth Branch story (*Mabon*, pp. 72–6).[111]

Triad 36 tells that the first of the Three Oppressions upon Britain comprised:

> the people of the Coraniaid, who came here in the time of Caswallawn son of Beli; and not one of them went back. And they came from Arabia.[38]

This information conflicts with our story, in which it is Lludd who has to deal with them. However, there may be a half-forgotten reason for this, since Caswallawn is frequently mentioned in regard to the enchantments of Britain. In *Branwen, Daughter of Llyr* he actually causes destruction himself, by usurping Bran's role as king during his absence in Ireland (see *Mabon*, pp. 38–40).[111] However, Caswallawn is known also, traditionally, as a rival with Julius Caesar for the hand of a British princess, Fflur. This lost story is most intriguing and we have reference to it only in the triads. Since Caswallawn is obviously associated with the struggle against the Romans, it has been suggested that although Triad 36 speaks of the Coraniaid, perhaps the term should properly be 'Cesaryeit', the Romans or followers of Caesar.

4. The scream that sounds over Britain every May Eve has precedents in British tradition. This magical time, when the

barriers between the worlds are down, is when Rhiannon loses her child, Pryderi, in *Pwyll, Prince of Dyfed*; likewise it is when a giant claw tries to carry off the foals of Teyrnon in the same story (see *Mabon*, pp. 21–23).[111] Taliesin also manifests himself at this magical time.

When Culhwch is striving to gain entrance to the hall of Arthur in *Culhwch and Olwen*, he threatens to let out a shout that will be audible throughout the kingdom of Britain and will blight pregnant women with miscarriages and render virgins barren. The effect of the dragon's shout in this story is as devastating as the Dolorous Blow, which causes the wasteland in the Grail legends. It is significant that it is only the British dragon that screams, not the foreign dragon.

The shriek is closely related to other manifestations of Britain's wronged Sovereignty. In *Owain*, the Lady of the Fountain gives a lamentable shriek when her champion is killed by Owain; it is said to sound three times, like a triple *ochone*, or a keen. A similar shriek is set up by Enid in *Gereint and Enid* when her husband is carried in upon his shield as though dead; it is only her shriek when Earl Limwris attempts to rape her that revives the wounded Gereint and makes him spring to her defence. In these examples the Goddess of the Land's representatives utter the cry that the land itself often makes in other Celtic contexts.

The wail of the *beanisidi* (banshee), often heard at the death of certain individuals, is that of a tutelary spirit of a place or family and is thus related to the cry uttered by Sovereignty's representatives. More telling, perhaps, is the stone that cries out under the true king in Irish sovereignty stories: the Lia Fail or Stone of Fal. This stone is related to the Arthurian tradition of the Perilous Seat: the seat at the Round Table that is reserved for the destined Grail-winner, whom, we will see, shares in the king's sovereign duty to the land in a special sense. This stone seat, emblematic of the land, cries out terribly when the wrong or unworthy knight sits upon it, as indeed Perceval does.[32]

In some senses the shriek of the dragon is the voice of the land itself crying out under oppression. We have yet to see just how the Goddess of Sovereignty uses the dragon as one of her many guises (see Chapter Nine).

A discussion of the most obvious parallels to this episode, notably the story of Vortigern's tower, follows in the next section.

5. The blighting of Britain is matched, in a microcosm, by the theft of the provisions from the King's courts. The loss of a year's supply of provisions sufficient to feed the King and his retainers represents a considerable loss for Lludd. This is almost the only episode in British tradition to show the bounty of the Grail or cauldron working in reverse (see note 9).

6. In the following section, where we compare parallel texts, we see that the role of the Wise and Innocent Youth is a paramount feature of this story. In *Lludd and Llefelys* there is no exact parallel, save that Llefelys is described as 'handsome and wise'. This text is at variance, since it says specifically that Llefelys did not know why his brother was coming, yet he took out his fleet to meet him; however, when they embrace, Llefelys says he knows why Lludd has come. It would appear that Llefelys has the ability of ancient poet-kind, that of *dichetul dichennaib* (see *Mabon*, p. 124)[111] or spontaneous knowledge, which arises from psychometrically touching his brother.

The Corannyeid or their agents seem to infiltrate the horn through which Lludd and Llefelys discuss the three plagues in surely the earliest episode of 'bugging' in British history! Llefelys is discerning enough to know the solution and swills out the horn with wine. This is the first time that alcoholic measures are taken in this story; the dragons are similarly disposed of later by being made drunk. Here, perhaps, we have the remnant of the two brothers' contention, since the horn causes them to misunderstand each other. We will see that this misinterpretation, caused here by the Corannyeid, is reflected throughout the Sovereignty tradition. In the *Dream of Rhonabwy* we find Iddawg, the Churn of Britain – so called for his propensity to stir up strife – in much the same role; it is he who bears the offer of a truce from Arthur to Medrawt (Mordred), but delivers it in such a way as to provoke the Battle of Camlann. This character is identifiable within the Sovereignty tradition as the Provoker of Strife: a role that Efnissien in *Branwen, Daughter of Llyr* also fulfils (see Chapter Eight).

7. The Corannyeid bear a close similarity to the Saxons of

Nennius' account[28], in which Hengist calls a similar meeting, pretending to make peace, at which all the British are slain. In *Lludd and Llefelys* it is the Corannyeid who are overcome. They represent the danger of the archetypal enemy of Britain's sovereignty, which is the threat of a former race of overthrown people. Their Otherworldly prescience and malevolence remind us strongly of the Fomorians and Fir Bolgs who similarly afflict the Tuatha de Danaan in the Irish mythological cycle.[8]

The measures that Lludd takes to overcome the Corannyeid may have been influenced by two existent traditions, one from the Bible, the other from the *Vita Merlini*. Just as the land of Britain and its people are purged of the Corannyeid, so too does Moses purge the Israelites by grinding down the idolized golden calf into powder, scattering it on the water and making the people drink it (Exodus 32:20). In the *Vita Merlini* Merlin is purged of his madness by drinking from the waters of a new fountain which springs up. At this point in the text Taliesin speaks at length about the curative properties of different springs.[11] In both cases the healing waters are harsh and purgative: a symbol of Sovereignty's power manifesting itself through the land. In Celtic heroic tradition, Sovereignty's champion is invarably wounded deeply; his healing is effected by a *Cailleach*, who alternately plunges him into a cauldron of poison and a cauldron of cure – the first one to toughen him up, the second to heal him (see p. 177).

8. Llefelys advises Lludd to find the centre of Britain and there to prepare the pit ready for the dragons. This is found to be Oxford, which seems an odd sort of centre if we are considering the modern map of the British Isles. Lludd's kingdom extends from the Welsh coast to East Anglia, west to east, while for Oxford to be at the centre, it can extend no further than from the south coast up to as far as the Humber. However, sacred centres of countries are not necessarily always centrally positioned, except in the roughest sense. As Alwyn and Brinley Rees have shown in their *Celtic Heritage*[137] the sacred *omphaloi* of Ireland are all to be found in Meath, where the functions of kingship, learning and sovereignty are all mystically present, making up a series of *temenoi*

(sacred enclosures), in which the other four provinces are essentially represented. A similar set of characteristics is apparent in modern Britain, where the governmental centre is London while its scholastic centre is still Oxford.

Triad 37 speaks of Lludd's action in burying the dragons as one of the Three Fortunate Concealments. It is likewise mentioned as one of the Three Unfortunate Disclosures that Vortigern uncovered them. This triad is specifically concerned with the mystical protections by which Britain's sovereignty is safeguarded; the other two concealments are the Head of Bran, which, as we saw in *Mabon*, (p. 47)[111] was uncovered by Arthur, who could not endure the thought of anyone other than himself as Britain's protector, and the bones of Gwerthefyr the Blessed (Vortimer), who was Vortigern's son.

Vortimer stood against his father and fought off the Saxons. He was, according to Geoffrey of Monmouth,[10] made king by popular demand while Vortigern was deposed, proving himself a champion of Sovereignty in a special way by fighting four battles against the Saxons and, at his death, requesting to be buried on the Saxon shore so that 'Wherever else they may hold a British port or may have settled, they will never again live in this land.'[28] Both Nennius and Geoffrey state that this request was ignored, and his remains were interred, according to the respective chronicles, either at London or Lincoln. Triad 37 ignores both accounts and specifically says that Vortimer's remains were buried at the chief seaports of Britain.[38] Further discussion about Vortigern's role and the dragons follows in the next section.

The fact that the dragons become pigs may seem curious at first, but, as we noted in *Mabon*,[111] they are chthonic creatures, that is, associated closely with the Underworld whence they are supposed to derive, according to *Math, Son of Mathonwy* (see *Mabon*, pp. 73–5, 77).[111] During his madness Merlin addresses his remarks to a pig in the forest of Celyddon:

> Little pig, be not sleepy,
> Terrible tidings come this way . . .
> A distant prophet has predicted
> That kings of foreign blood-ties –

> Gaels and Romans, treacherous Britons,
> Will bring ferment to this land. [my trans.]

In this obscure poem, 'Yr Oianau' ('The Greetings'),[152] the pig seems to represent the dormant spirit of Britain. It would seem that there is a distinct sequence in which the beasts that are emblematic of Britain become dragons when the land is active and pigs when the land is passive.

9. The stealer of the provisions is described as a mighty magician and as a giant, but he remains unnamed in the story. There are two similar incidents in related traditions in which we can find traces of this last plague. In *Pwyll, Prince of Dyfed* Rhiannon gives Pwyll a bag into which a beggar can put food, but it will never be filled until a gentleman or nobleman puts both feet inside and tells the bag it has had enough. By this ruse her former suitor, Gwawl, is trapped. Rhiannon's bag is clearly an Otherworldly receptacle whose appetite is as capacious as a giant's. Since the Otherworldly dimension is infinitely expandable, it can take any shape. The other tradition that this last plague calls to mind is the hamper of Gwyddno Garanhir, Elphin's father in *Hanes Taliesin*. This hamper is one of the Thirteen Treasures of Britain, said to be guarded by Merlin in his retirement on Bardsey Island. Its main property is that food for one man can be put into it and food for a hundred can be taken out afterwards.

As we saw in *Mabon*,[111] the rightful king or Pendragon needs the empowerment of the Thirteen Treasures or other sacred objects of Sovereignty's regalia in order to be a true king. Arthur goes to Annwn in his ship *Prydwen* in order to win these objects, including the cauldron, the prototype of the Grail. In *Lludd and Llefelys*, Lludd, although in every respect a brave and generous king, has yet to win his kingship from the empowering Other-worldly forces of the Goddess Sovereignty. It would seem probable that the unnamed giant is indeed Gwyddno, with whom he has to wrestle. That an Otherworldly agent is at work we need have no doubt, since the provisions always disappear at night and all watchmen are overcome with deep sleep. Lludd cannot depute any champion to act for him in this enterprise, but keeps watch himself and stays awake by splashing himself with water.

42

The overcoming of the three plagues or *gormesiad* is likewise a feature of *Peredur*, in which the hero defeats the nine witches of Gloucester, three serpents and the Black Oppressor as well as the devastating unicorn, whose horn dries up the waters. And indeed, as we have noted, the resonances between this story and the underlying features of the Grail legends are very strong. When the king is in harmony with his kingdom, then the land flourishes; when he is out of union with Sovereignty, the result is wasteland, disorder and dissension. But the one who overcomes these *gormesiad* is the king's nearest companion, his champion or his poet–seer, whose courageous deeds or prophetic insight enable him to uphold his sovereign's rights in the land by putting right the imbalances within the kingdom. Such a one is the Grail-winner, Peredur, or the youthful prophet, Merlin, or the youth who stands in the place of Sovereignty's son.

II SOVEREIGNTY'S SON

Reading *Lludd and Llefelys* we cannot but be struck by the obvious parallels between it and Nennius' account of Vortigern's tower.[28] This latter incident is better known in the version by Geoffrey of Monmouth,[10] but there are closer parallels to be drawn from Nennius' earlier account.

In Nennius we read of Vortigern's disastrous career, in which he is made king by default, sustaining his sovereignty by the expedient of inviting the alien Saxons to act as his federal troops – this despite the universal disapproval of his people. He compounds this enormity by marrying the daughter of Hengist, the Saxon chief, who is called Renwein, or Rowena, by Geoffrey. As if this were not enough, Vortigern shows himself lost to reason by marrying his own daughter as well. By her he has a son called Faustus.

It follows that St Germanus comes to Britain in order to call a synod of the British clergy, with whom he intends to denounce Vortigern and his unchristian deeds. Knowing this, Vortigern instructs his daughter to place her son in Germanus' lap and accuse the saint of fathering the child. Germanus says, 'I will be your father and will not send you away until a razor, scissors and comb are given to me and you are permitted to give them to your father after the flesh.' The boy turns to Vortigern, who is both his father and his grandfather, and bids him cut his son's hair for him. Vortigern is thus outfaced by his own son, shamed before the synod who accuse him, rightfully, of incest, and from whom he flees.

Thereafter he goes to Snowdon and there tries to build a stronghold, but the tower keeps falling down. His druids advise that he find a boy without a father whose blood may be sprinkled on the foundations. His men discover a boy playing at ball who is miscalled 'fatherless' by his rival playmates. The mother is questioned and denies ever having lain with a man. The boy is then brought to the tower and there questions the druids about the foundations of the edifice. They cannot tell what lies there. The boy reveals that there is a lake under the foundations and that two vessels are buried there. The druids cannot guess what is contained therein. A cloth lies in between them and in it are two dragons, says the boy, one white and the other red. The cloth is the kingdom, the red dragon that of Britain and the white one that of the Saxons. The lake is the world, he further reveals. He tells Vortigern to find another stronghold, since he himself will remain in the present one. He then reveals that he is Ambrosius, or Emrys, the Overlord.[28]

This account is followed closely by Geoffrey's, with a few variations, notably the additions, in Nennius, from the *Life of St Germanus of Auxterre*,[28] who did indeed visit Britain; this has been historically attested. In the *Life of St Germanus* Vortigern shows himself to be a model 'bad king': he commits every action alien to the coronation oath of a British king by actively inviting enemies over the threshold and putting them in positions of trust; he commits incest and reverts to ancestral paganism and human sacrifice. But there are three youths who stand between him and the rightful kingship.

As we have already stated, he is deposed by his people in favour of his son Vortimer whose heroic deeds against the Saxons earn him eternal popularity but an early death, so that Vortigern resumes the throne once more. Vortimer, though called Blessed, is unable to stem the successive waves of invaders with his own sacred burial, which is supposed to act as a palladium against further sea-borne forays. However, he acts as an admirable champion of Sovereignty.

Set against this stalwart son who redeems his father's deeds is the son born of incest, Faustus, who, due to the patronage of St Germanus, becomes a saint. Vortigern is unable to use this sinfully begotten child for his own ends: in fact, Faustus causes Vortigern's downfall. Vortigern has, in effect, no rightful sovereignty at all. He is a usurper who has to be bolstered up by his country's natural enemy. Even his last stronghold will not remain erect due to some undisclosed trouble.

It is at this point that we meet the young Merlin, in this story called Ambrosius or Emrys, who, in Nennius' account, is the rightful ruler. Merlin Emrys and Ambrosius Aurelianus were frequently conflated among chroniclers who were often reliant on oral tradition alone for their compilations. In the legendary history of Britain it is indeed Ambrosius Aurelianus who succeeds Vortigern as king, but in this version we may assume we are seeing a manifestation of the Pendragon's own priest and prophet in the shape of Merlin Emrys.

Emrys is able to state exactly what is wrong, not only with Vortigern's tower, but also about his reign. For the Snowdonia stronghold is a microcosm of the state of Britain itself. Emrys, as we learn from subsequent traditions about Merlin, is begotten of a daemon or spirit of the air upon his mother, who, like the Virgin, 'knows not man'. He is an innocent youth, yet full of wisdom. He is Sovereignty's own son, her vindication, and so is never endangered by Vortigern's evil designs. He is destined to reveal the state of Britain and send its unlawful king packing, and he banishes Vortigern with these words:

'Go forth from this fortress, for you cannot build it, and travel over many provinces, to find a safe fortress, and I will stay here.' ... So the king gave him the fortress, with all the kingdoms of the western part of Britain, and he went himself with his wizards to the northern parts ... and there he built a city, that is called by his name, Caer Gwrtheyrn.[28]

Vortigern relinquishes the sovereignty into the hands of

Sovereignty's own son until 'the king shall come again', or a rightful Pendragon is inaugurated. Thus Vortigern is thwarted by three young men: his own sons, Vortimer and Faustus, and Emrys.

There is a parallel or possibly a source text from which both this story and that of *Lludd and Llefelys* stem. It comes from the repertoire of the professional Irish poet and was certainly circulating in Ireland before the tenth century, where it was one of the 350 stories that had to be learned by the qualified poet. It is the *Echtra Airt*, or *The Adventures of Art*.

> Conn, King of Ireland took to wife Becuma, an Otherworldly woman who had been banished from the Land of Promise by the Tuatha de Danaan for committing adultery with Manannan's son. She was really in love with Conn's son, Art, but preferred to be queen. During their reign neither corn nor milk could be found in Ireland, and Conn called his druids to find the cause of this affliction. They told him that it was because of Becuma that Ireland was barren of food, but that if the son of a sinless couple could be found and slain at Tara, where his blood might be mixed into the soil, then the famine might be averted. Conn travelled to the Otherworld, where he was hosted by Rigru Roisclethan and her husband, Daire Degamra. Seated in a crystal chair was a youth, Segda Saerlabraid. He befriended Conn and, when he heard about Conn's errand, begged to be allowed to go to Tara with him. For Conn lied, saying that he needed a youth such as Segda in order that he might be bathed in the waters of Ireland and so heal the land. His parents were dismayed and revealed that, among their kind, people never mated unless it was to conceive a child and he was the only fruit of their union. However, Segda and Conn returned to Ireland, after Conn had promised many sureties for Segda's safety.
>
> The druids insisted that their advice be implemented: that Segda should be killed and his blood mingled 'with the blighted earth and the withered trees, so that its mast, fruit, fish and produce' might be increased. Seeing the men of Ireland ready to kill him, Segda asked to be put to death willingly. Just then a lowing cow, followed by a woman, came on the scene; she demanded to know what was happening. She asked the druids to tell her what was in the two bags hanging from the cow's sides, but they couldn't tell. 'A single cow has come here to save an innocent youth,' she said. 'Let the cow be killed and her blood mixed with the soil of Ireland and on the doors of Tara.' When the cow had been killed, the two bags were examined:

inside were two birds – one with one leg, the other with twelve. They rose above the host and fought each other; the one-legged bird being victorious. The druids were still unable to interpret the meaning of this, and the woman said, 'You [the men of Ireland] are the bird with twelve legs and the little boy is the bird with one, since it is he who is in the right. Let those druids of yours be taken away and hanged.' Then she told Conn to put Becuma away, else Ireland would lack a third of its produce. In a further incident, Art causes the downfall of Becuma by his Otherworldly adventures in which he brings back a suitable bride, Delbhchaem, with whom he ousts Becuma and succeeds to his father's throne.[4]

This tale is in the forefront of the Irish king-cycle and tells of Art, who actually reigned in the third century. The parallels between this and both *Lludd and Llefelys* and the story of Vortigern's tower are remarkable. Instead of foreign invaders, Ireland is afflicted with barrenness because of Becuma's unsuitability as a bride (or as a representative of Sovereignty). Like Vortigern, Conn has a suitably kingly son. Conn's visit to the Otherworld to find the sinless youth must obviously be likened to the search for Emrys. Here, however, the boy's mother is significantly called Rigru, 'the Queenly One', while her son, Segda, is called Saerlabraid, 'Noble Speech'. We have here a portrait of Sovereignty and her son. In the subsequent episode at Tara, when Segda is about to be killed, he is saved by the woman and the cow: she is none other than Rigru herself, come to save her child and reveal where the true Sovereignty of Ireland lies. She refutes the druids, as Emrys does in Nennius' account of Vortigern's tower.

That we are dealing with a parallel text or a text from a common source is evident from the use of birds rather than dragons in the text. There is no word for dragon or serpent in early Irish, except when borrowed from British or Latin tradition. The Gaelic concept of 'monster' is that of a water-serpent (*nathair*), though Scots Gaelic tradition supplies us with *nathair sgiathach* or 'winged serpent'. The twelve-legged bird here stands not for foreign oppression so much as injustice or lies – a totally false premise on which to establish kingship. The one-legged bird stands for the truth or justice of Sovereignty, whose champion is her own son, Segda.

Historical Character	Reigned	Text	Date of Transcription
Lud	1st century BC	*Mabinogion*	14th century AD
Art mac Conn	c. AD 220	*Echtra Airt*	13th century, but in oral poetic repertoire pre-10th century
Vortigern	AD 425–455	Nennius[28]	c. AD 828–9
Vortigern	AD 425–455	Geoffrey[10]	c. AD 1136

Figure 2.1 *Common Sources of the Two Dragons of Sovereignty*

The Sovereignty motif is, as we have stated, most strongly represented within Irish tradition, where the nature of sacral kingship is ever stressed. The task of dating the three stories is a difficult one. If we examine Figure 2.1, we will see how the evidence falls.

It will be seen that the earliest historical character, Lud, appears in the latest transcription of these three traditions, while the latest historical character, Vortigern, appears in the earliest transcriptions. The common themes of the stories are set forth in Figure 2.2 for easy reference. The stories' protagonists lived within five centuries of each other and each had a place in oral tradition; that each of them should share a common Sovereignty story such as the uncovering of the dragons and the refutation of supposedly wise men by, or on behalf of, a boy or youth is remarkable. We can conclude only that a common source, which is now lost to us but which understood the symbolic language of Sovereignty, was responsible for all three stories. That each protagonist should pass so quickly into oral tradition and become associated, by inference, with the struggle for sovereignty and for kingship is indeed fortunate for our argument. The workings of oral tradition and the Mysteries of Britain are seldom so clearly revealed as in this story.

The Wise and Innocent Youth, who is Sovereignty's son, is Mabon as well as Merlin Emrys and Segda, a role perhaps shared by Llefelys. Mabon's profound influence underlying the texts of the *Mabinogion* has already been noted in *Mabon and the*

Texts	Beasts	Imprisoned Within	Centre	Wise Youth	Parentage	Invaders/ Representative of False Sovereignty	Wasteland/ Plagues Caused by	True Representatives of Sovereignty
Lludd and Llefelys	dragons	stone chest	Oxford	Llefelys	earthly	Corannyeid	dragon's shout	Lludd
Nennius' account of Vortigern's tower, and Geoffrey of Monmouth	dragons	two vessels	Snowdon	Emrys	daemon/ woman	Saxons/ Vortigern	Vortigern marries own daughter and invites Saxons to Britain	Ambrosius and the Pendragons
Echtra Airt	birds	two bags	Tara	Segda	Otherworldly parents	Becuma's tainted powers	Conn marries Becuma	Art and Delbhchaem

Figure 2.2: *Table of Comparisons of* Lludd and Llefelys *with Parallel Texts*

Mysteries of Britain;[111] in this set of related stories the innocence of Mabon is revealed as a manifestation of Sovereignty herself. He is shown to be the forerunner of the Pendragon or rightful king in these stories; one who clears the ground in advance by revealing corruption and the causes of the land's disorder.

III THE CONTENTION OF THE TWO BROTHERS

As we have seen from these parallel stories there seems little basis for *Lludd and Llefelys* ever featuring a contention, as the earlier title suggests. However, there is a story from Welsh tradition that may embody a fragmentary and half-understood piece of the original. It is significant in that it speaks of two brothers, obviously of Beli Mawr's lineage, who argue about the sovereignty of their land. Even more interesting, from the point of view of this book, is that Arthur himself emerges as rightful Pendragon of Britain.

The story is retold by John Rhys, who did much field research in nineteenth-century Wales, drawing on oral folk-memory and traditions then prevalent.

> There were two brothers who were kings, called Nyniaw and Pebiaw. One moonlit night Nyniaw said to his brother, 'See what an extensive field I possess.'
>
> 'Where is it?' asked Pebiaw.
>
> 'There,' said his brother, 'the whole firmament.'
>
> 'Well, as to that,' said Pebiaw, 'see how many sheep and cattle I have grazing in your field.'
>
> 'Where are they?' asked Nyniaw.
>
> 'There, the great host of stars, each of golden brightness, with the moon to shepherd them.'
>
> 'Well, they shall not graze on my field,' replied Nyniaw. And the two kings fought, embroiling both kingdoms and their subjects in terrible war so that they were nearly exterminated.
>
> Rhitta Gawr, King of Wales attacked them because they were obviously both mad. He conquered them and shaved off their beards. But when the other twenty-eight kings of Prydain heard of this treacherous assault, they raised up armies and stood before Rhitta to avenge Nyniaw and Pebiaw. Rhitta conquered every one of them

and shaved off their beards, making himself a gigantic cloak into which the beards were decoratively worked.[139]

This story is continued in Geoffrey of Monmouth. Arthur never fought a stronger man than Retho (Rhitta), the Giant of Mount Arvaius. Rhitta once sent to Arthur to send him his beard so that he might fix it above those of the other British kings whom he had overcome, or else to come and fight him in single combat. Arthur slew Rhitta, taking not only his beard but the cloak of beards as well.[10]

Now, it might well be asked, what has this story got to do with *Lludd and Llefelys*? At first sight, nothing much. But if we look at the name of Nyniaw, or Ninian, we realize that this is none other than the brother of Lludd, according to both the *Mabinogion* and to Geoffrey of Monmouth (where he is called Nennius).[10] As we have already stated, the name Llefelys does not appear anywhere as the brother of Lludd or son of Beli except in the *Mabinogion* (see p. 34). Who, then, is Pebiaw? We must remember that we are dealing with folk-tradition, not the pseudo-respectable chronicles of literary tradition. Pebiaw is obviously an onomatopoeic doublet for Nyniaw, like Jack and Jill of the nursery rhyme, or like some of the uncouth characters who appear in *Culhwch and Olwen*: Lluched, Nefed and Eissiwed (Oh, Cry and Shriek).

We might overlook the story altogether if Rhitta Gawr didn't appear in it. His reappearance in a separate context in Geoffrey's *History*[10] makes this folk-incident significant to the sovereignty of Britain. The contention of Pebiaw and Nyniaw is in itself as inconsequential as the sayings of the Men of Gotham in folk tradition, but there are certain elements which, even in folk-story, retain a familiarity from mainstream tradition.

First of all there is the motif of shaving off the beards. Rhitta's object in shaving off the vanquished kings' beards is symbolically clear: he robs them at one stroke of their manhood and their sovereignty. We have already encountered this shaving motif in Nennius' account of Vortigern's incestuously conceived son and St Germanus – admittedly only a parallel story to *Lludd and Llefelys*, but still close enough to our original story. Further we recall the many similar shaving incidents in *Culhwch and Olwen*, which revolve around the vanquishing of a giant (see *Mabon*, Chapter 6). The original story, if any can be found in this tangle of similarities, is in such muddy water that we cannot guess at the original transcription.

Secondly we find from Rhys's field research that Nyniaw and Pebiaw were changed into oxen for their sins and that they fell into a lake in Cardiganshire.[139] They are locally called *Uchain Pannog* (Pannog's Oxen). Two contending brothers here become beasts – not dragons or pigs, as in our story, to be sure, but an interesting transmogrification nevertheless. A similar story is told of Twrch Twryth in *Culhwch and Olwen*.

Thirdly there is the contest for the sovereignty of Britain, which appears in all versions of the story. Rhitta takes the place of Vortigern or the foreign invaders, undermining the manhood and sovereignty of the kings of Britain by taking their beards. The contention of Nyniaw and Pebiaw is the result of their hubris: their kingship is only of an earthly nature and does not extend to the heavens. Perhaps in the earliest story their punishment was indeed to be turned into the oxen that each claimed to own – the oxen or stars in the field of the firmament. Perhaps concealed under all this detritus there is the identity of one of the treasures of Annwn, which Arthur goes to seek in the 'Preiddeu Annwn' (see *Mabon*, p. 107–8):[111]

> They know not whose the brindled, harnessed ox
> With seven score notches on his collar.

Thus reads one of the most mysterious poems in Welsh tradition. This ox may be one of the hidden treasures of Annwn or one of Sovereignty's secret symbols. Any more than this is sheer conjecture. I leave it to the reader's intuitive reading of the texts.

The contention of Nyniaw and Pebiaw is clearly a mythic parable tumbled into folklore, and its use for comparison with Lludd and Llefelys may be slight, but we see that an act of hubris underlies this story, as we do in the career of Arthur, whose descent to Annwn to fetch the cauldron and the other Hallows, or whose disinterment of Bran's head, are deeds for which he pays the full price.

All we can conclude is that Arthur, as rightful Pendragon,

overcomes Rhitta the Giant. Nor does the story rest there; it was considered to be of sufficient importance for Malory to incorporate into *Le Morte d'Arthur*,[25] in which Rhitta appears as Ryons, King of Ireland, who demands the submission and beard of Arthur. It will be remembered that it is to Ireland that Arthur directs his quest for the cauldron, one among the many treasures of Annwn, which he goes to seek in the *Culhwch and Olwen* story.

There may be a further mystery locked in this tradition of Rhitta, since an early genealogical tradition states that Eigr, Arthur's mother Igraine in later stories, was first married to a certain Rhica of Cornwall (see Figure 10.2, p. 264). Eigr, as we shall see, is of prime importance in British tradition as a representative of Sovereignty in the line of the 'Daughters of Branwen' – those women who bear the royal blood of Britain (see p. 267). Since this Rhica appears nowhere else, no certain identification of him with Rhitta can be made. But since Arthur was the son of Eigr's second husband, Uther, it is perhaps not unlikely that Arthur should seek to overcome the man who once held the kingdom of Britain because he had been married to Eigr, the sovereignty-bestowing woman who produced the short-lived Succession of the Pendragons.

In both the folk-story and the story of Vortigern's tower, a contention precedes the coming of the Pendragons. In *Lludd and Llefelys*, Lludd is established safely in his kingship, having solved the mystery of the three plagues with the help of his brother. We would indeed be fortunate if the knotted threads of this story were less tangled; as it is we must be content to leave the knots alone and merely appreciate the impressionistic colours of these stories.

The reign of Lludd or Lud tells the story of Britain's sovereignty before the coming of the Romans: a lost era of legend. But the Roman occupation, rather than erasing past glories, has contributed to legends concerning Britain's kings. It is in such a context that we turn to Macsen Wledig: the Emperor of the West.

CHAPTER THREE

THE DREAM OF MACSEN WLEDIG

> . . . our own Elen of the Army-paths . . .
> She for whom the Imperator
> could not sleep
> nor ride out with his comites and duces
> . . . nor could he
> find solace of his most loved falcon
> nor from any venery
> which formerly
> had been some respite from
> the tedium of affairs of state.
>
> DAVID JONES
> *The Kensington Mass*

I BRITAIN IN ROMAN RIG

The history of Britain is tenacious of its traditions. While it has been properly proud of its native achievements, it has not been slow to turn its defeats into greater victories and capitalize on disaster. This has been nowhere more apparent than in the aftermath of the Roman occupation. The desperate struggle to repel invasion, which typified the early centuries of the first millennium, was modified into either an acceptance of Roman rule or a localized resistance, which soon emulated Roman tactics, customs and standards.

By the time *The Dream of Macsen Wledig* was transcribed in the Middle Ages, Wales – the remnant of Britain still faithful to her deepest traditions – had already undergone the further indignity of Norman oppression. These new invaders were but pigmies in comparison with the Romans, who gave Britain a new understanding of her sovereignty. The notion of many petty kingdoms being welded together under one dispensation became fact: an idea on which the legends of Arthur are firmly based. Threat of invasion no doubt helped, but it was from the Roman model that Britain learned to combine its forces effectively. Rome lent authority and cohesion to the embattled kingdoms of Wales long after her armies had left these shores, up until the Normans imposed their government upon the Welsh princes.

We have only to look at the genealogies to learn what pride Britain took in her Roman connections: past glories of imperial ties are reflected in many family lines. But the prime story of Rome's wedding with Britain is best told in *The Dream of Macsen Wledig*, where Britain's sovereignty is overcome in a mystical manner, which enhances defeat and vaunts national pride.

The eponymous hero of this tale, Macsen, is none other than Magnus Clemens Maximus, a Spaniard who had served in the Roman army in Britain and who was proclaimed Emperor of the West by the disaffected troops of the previous Emperor. In this story he marries Elen, daughter of Eudaf, a Welsh nobleman: but this is only the evidence of legend. That he did, indeed, marry a British wife of a noble line is very possible, but history does not name her. In fact, history has little to do with this story, except in a rather circuitous way.

What has come down to us, via legend and oral tradition, is often more discursive than the fragmentary chronicles of the times that have survived, but the identities of both Macsen and Elen have been inextricably mixed up with other personages of similar names or functions. It is as though the Tudor period survived only through oral tradition and scraps of known history, and that tradition credited Philip of Spain with marrying Mary, Queen of Scots. Imagine the further confusion resulting from these figures being conflated with, say, Philip Howard, Earl of Arundel and with Mary Tudor. All four were roughly

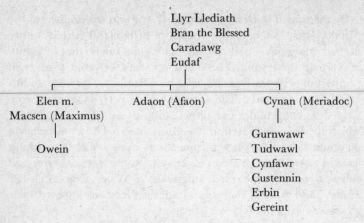

Figure 3.1: *Mythological Descent of Gereint from Llyr*

contemporaneous, all were Catholic; Philip of Spain and Mary, Queen of Scots were both associated with invasion attempts; both Mary, Queen of Scots and Philip Howard were imprisoned and put under threat of execution, although only Mary was beheaded; both Philip of Spain and Mary Tudor were zealous monarchs who impressed their faith upon their countries with considerable force; although both were considered martyrs of the Catholic faith, only Philip Howard and not Mary, Queen of Scots achieved canonization. Such would be the difficulties for any future researcher of such an unprovable past.

Similarly Macsen or Maximus was confused with the emperor Maxentius as well as with the Roman senator Maximianus, while Elen was invariably conflated with St Helena, mother of Constantine the Great. In order to minimize confusion I append two genealogies showing the place of Elen and Macsen in the mythological descent of one of the *Mabinogion* later heroes, Gereint, and the historical descent and relationships of St Helena (Figures 3.1 and 3.2)

Historians are unsure whether St Helena was a British princess or a barmaid from Bithynia in Turkey, but Britons would be unwilling to relinquish their imperial or saintly connections with her. She lives on in British tradition in the shape of the Elen in our

Cole of Colchester   Maxentius
            | |
Helena m. Constantius Chlorus   _   Maximian
            | |
    Constantine the Great   m.   Fausta

Figure 3.2: *Helena's Imperial Connections*

story, Elen of the Legions, maker of roads, defender of fortresses, representative of Sovereignty herself; while Magnus Maximus' disastrous career has been glorified into an idealized campaign in which Britain supports his attempt on the Imperial city of Rome.

The Dream of Macsen Wledig

(1) Macsen Wledig was Emperor of Rome. (2) One day out hunting he grew weary and lay down to rest under a canopy which his men raised, made of a shield atop their spears. He dreamed he saw the highest mountain in the world and then, travelling through the most beautiful country he had seen, he came to a port where he set out to sea until he came to the most (3) lovely island. He crossed it and came to a castle. (4) Entering it, he saw two youths playing chess and behind them a man carving chessmen. (5) Nearby sat a beautiful maiden in a golden chair who permitted him to embrace her. (6) Just then, the shield-canopy collapsed, waking Macsen. So smitten with love was he that he was unable to settle to his duties and only wanted to sleep. Wise men counselled that he send out messengers to find the woman of his dreams. After a year there was still no sign of her. (7) Macsen was advised to go back to the scene of his dreaming-sleep and there he was able to dispatch messengers in the correct direction. They came to Arfon in Wales and recognized their master's dream-castle. Entering it, they immediately hailed the maiden as (8) Empress of Rome. (9) She refused to come with them, saying that if Macsen loved her so much he should come himself. The messengers returned, guiding Macsen to Britain where he (10) conquered the Island of the Mighty, taking it from Beli, son of Manogan. He came to Arfon and found the castle, where he saw Cynan and Afaon playing chess, while their father, Eudaf, carved chesspieces. He claimed Elen for his Empress. (11) As her morning gift, Elen claimed the Island of Britain for her father, Eudaf, the three offshore islands for her own and three strongholds to be made for her in Britain, at Caer Seint

[Segontium], Caerlleon [Caerleon on Usk] and Caerfyrddin [Caermarthen]. (12) Elen was responsible for building the roads which connected these strongholds.

However, in Macsen's absence an ancient custom of Rome had been invoked: an emperor might not stay outside his land for more than seven years – the period of Macsen's sojourn in Britain. (13) Another emperor had been created. Macsen returned to Rome, conquering France and Burgundy on the way. But he was unable to raise the siege which he had set at Rome's gates. (14) It was not until Cynan and Afaon, with their troops from Britain, came to Macsen's aid that they were able to take Rome. (15) The Britons stormed Rome during the noon-time break for dinner, and though Macsen feared that they would hold it for themselves, the British relinquished the city to him. (16) Macsen awarded his brothers-in-law leadership of the war-troop that had successfully besieged Rome so that they might conquer lands of their own. Afaon eventually returned to Britain, while Cynan settled in Brittany where he and his troops married with the Breton women, but cut out their tongues that the British speech might not be corrupted.

Commentary

1. This is not strictly accurate. The career of Magnus Maximus can be summarized briefly as follows: he served with Theodosius in Britain, possibly holding the title of *Dux Britanniarum* (Duke of Britain – originally the title of the military Roman governor based at York), and was proclaimed Emperor of the West by his troops. (At this point there were joint emperors governing the eastern and western halves of the sprawling Roman Empire – a task beyond a single man.) The true Emperor of the West, Gratian, engaged Maximus in battle when the latter landed in Europe, but was defeated. Maximus took control of Gaul and Spain as well as northern Italy, where he was strengthened by British troops. Representations were sent to Theodosius, his old comrade-in-arms who had now become Emperor of the East, that Maximus should be recognized as Emperor of the West. Maximus occupied Rome in AD 388 but was defeated a few months later when Theodosius' troops cornered him in Aquileia. He was beheaded and his son Victor was subsequently killed. Theodosius

provided for Maximus' daughters. Of Maximus' unnamed wife we know only that she was very attentive to St Martin of Tours, who dined with Maximus but who was unimpressed by his jumped-up pretensions of imperial glory. The ninth-century inscribed stone called the Pillar of Eliseg in Valle Crucis, Wales, attests to Vortigern's Marriage to 'Severa, the daughter of Maximus the King who slew the King of the Romans'.[145]

The similarity in the names of generals and emperors of this period has not helped transmission of Maximus' history; Nennius, who knew of the tradition regarding the meeting of Maximus with St Martin, nevertheless ascribes Maximus' career to Maximianus, who took the British troops to Britanny (see notes 14 and 16). Geoffrey of Monmouth likewise calls him Maximianus and makes him a Roman senator and nephew to King Coel (Cole).[10]

2. Macsen's dream has all the quality of an Irish *aisling* – a mystic vision dream or dream in which a representative of Sovereignty appears to the hero. This genre of story is of great antiquity in Celtic tradition; it has descended via the Grail romances in which Sovereignty is depicted by both beautiful Grail Maiden and Loathly Lady, as well as via medieval romances and native folk-stories. Scholars have suggested that the *cyfarwydd* (story-teller) of this story was well acquainted with the Irish genre.[95] Some parallel examples follow in sections II and III of this chapter.

In effect Macsen's dream takes him across the western expanse of the Roman Empire wherein the land is laid out as on a map. He crosses the Alps and comes to Britain. At the embarkation point Macsen significantly boards his ship by means of an ivory bridge: an allusion to the Emperor's title *Pontifex Maximus*, which was bestowed in token of the Emperor's sacral kingship, which literally 'built a bridge' between this world and that of the gods. (Interestingly Gratian, the emperor assassinated by the historical Maximus, was the first to refuse this pagan title in AD 373; the title is currently held by the Pope.)

3. Macsen sees the land of Britain for the first time in his dream and arrives at the city of Caer Seint (modern Caernarvon). As Segontium – its Roman appellation – it was strongly garrisoned

from the time of Agricola (AD 80) to about AD 380, the time of Maximus' withdrawal from Britain with the better part of Britain's troops. It is also the place where Bran the Blessed was staying when he received Branwen's starling (see *Mabon*, p. 42).[111]

4. The unfolding dream reveals a wealth of symbolism proper to Sovereignty. Macsen sees Elen's two brothers playing *gwyddbwyll*, a form of chess in which the kingpiece is defended by a small company of men against the opponent who has a larger number of opposing and more mobile men; the object is for the kingpiece to reach the edge of the board. Eudaf, Elen's father, is carving new pieces for the board. As we will see from *The Dream of Rhonabwy* and *Peredur*, the *gwyddbwyll* board or chessboard is one of the prime symbols of the land and is usually possessed by a representative of Sovereignty. The pieces upon the board symbolize Britain's men and their opponents, a usurping or invading force. Although Eudaf is making new chess-pieces, he is attired as a nobleman and sits in an ivory chair on which two eagles are carved – symbolic of both Roman imperialism and of the British eagle of Eryri (Snowdon). Eudaf appears also in Chrétien's *Perceval*.[7,92]

5. Elen's beauty is compared with that of the sun: she is radiant and queenly – a fitting representative of Sovereignty. It is notable that she is first seen seated, or established in her kingdom. In section II we will discuss the parallels between this episode and the Irish Sovereignty narratives. Macsen sits beside her; the *cyfarwydd* remarks that the chair was as comfortable for two as it had been for one – an allusion to Macsen's forthcoming marriage with Elen and the alliance between Rome and Britain.

6. Just as in the days of modest cinema when love-scenes were curtailed just prior to the happy couple getting into bed or establishing more intimate contact, so here is Macsen rudely awoken by his makeshift canopy toppling down on him. He is enchanted by love for a woman he has never met – as Culhwch is by his love for Olwen (see *Mabon*, p. 93).[111]

7. He is unable to find his dream-woman until he returns to the

place of his dream, where he is able correctly to determine the path of his dream-flight over Europe.

8. The British princess is hailed Empress of Rome. This story turns upon the fact that the land is represented by the person of Elen. Her inner potency as guardian of the land of Britain is recognized and she is entitled Empress of all the known world under Roman occupation. There is also a subtextual connection between pagan Goddess and Christian virgin, as David Jones observed in his *Roman Quarry*:[84]

> We'll mix their Bride-lights with the lights of Syriac God-bearers, and gusty flames they coax within the wattle hedge shall call to carried flame lit from Demeter's torch – til, in the woof of time there'll be but one queen of the candles, and by whatever name they call her she'll be in Roman rig.

9. Elen's reply is not that of a conquered land, submissive and meek. She makes it clear that if she is worth Macsen's impassioned love, then she is worth his personal attendance.

10. Here the story slips back in time. Beli was the father of Lludd in our previous story, four centuries prior to Maximus' time. The *cyfarwydd* has telescoped the whole Roman occupation from Julius Caesar's first attempts upon Britain in 55 BC up until nearly the time of Rome's retreat from Britain in AD 407.

11. The custom of the 'morning gift' – a gratuity, usually involving an endowment of land or valuables, which was given by a husband 'in return' for the gift of his new wife's virginity – was a custom common to both the Welsh and the Saxons.[19] This enabled the wife to retain part of her dowry which, in the event of divorce or separation, was not liable to distraint. It was also helpful to the widow, as she retained lands and properties of her own. Both the laws of Hywel Dda (c. AD 950) and the Irish Brehon laws, operative until the sixteenth century, allowed a woman sole rights to her clothing and produce. The morning gift was called the *cowyll*, and, in the case of a king's daughter, was always given in land – the extent was dependent on the status of the husband. Considering Macsen's status as Emperor of Rome,

Elen does very well and is enabled to retain the whole of Britain on her father's behalf, as well as the three chief Cities of the Legions for herself.

12. In Welsh legend Elen is known as Elen Lluddog, or Elen of the Hosts. She is also remembered by the network of Roman roads which connected Segontium with the rest of Wales and England, parts of which are still extant. They are locally known as *Sarn Elen* or Elen's Road. In actuality the improvements to roads were probably undertaken by Constantine and by Constantius Chlorus, the husband of St Helena, but in some way their work has been attributed to, or put under the aegis of, Elen. The persistence of this legend suggests that Elen or St Helena has been subsumed into a native cult of some now vanished tutelary goddess of the ways.

13. Our story here puts the usurper, Maximus, in the position of being usurped. As stated above, Maximus killed Gratian and ousted his successor-apparent, Valentinian, Gratian's half-brother. Maximus did indeed rule Gaul and Spain in the brief period before his downfall; his occupancy of Rome is also undisputed.

14. There is a persistent tradition and some archaeological evidence to support the statement that Maximus was partially responsible for emptying Britain of its troops. While the major withdrawal of Rome from Britain is officially dated AD 410, successive commanders, each with his own axe to grind, had been drawing on the strength of British levies for some time. Maximus was but one of these. Triad 35 speaks of 'The Three Levies that departed from this Island, and not one of them came back'.[38] One of those mentioned is 'the army that went with Elen of the Hosts and Maxen Wledig to Llychlyn; and they never returned'. The three armies are known as 'The Three Silver Hosts of the Island of Britain'. The understanding running beneath this triad is that the levies are the currency of the island, poured out of Britain's purse, leaving it beggared. This was not far from the truth, for the next seventy to eighty years were dark times for Britain's defence of her sovereignty. The Llychlyn or

Lochlin of the triad usually means Scandinavia, although it was often more generally applied to mean any foreign country; however, the likelihood is that Llydaw (Armorica) is intended (see note 16).

15. Since this is a British tale, it is the British troops who save the day for Macsen. Totally ignoring the courtesies of warfare they attack the city during the two emperors' lunch-break. The implication of this story is that although Britain had become subject to Rome, she could easily have imposed her sovereignty upon Rome – if she had wanted to. Macsen's brothers-in-law are true to their sister's husband, however.

16. During the troubled latter years of Rome's occupation of Britain, there had already been a steady trickle of emigrants leaving these shores for Brittany. The 'official' founder of these colonists was known as Conan Meriadoc, who, as we see from our story, is none other than Cynan, Elen's brother. Afaon or Adaon stays in Britain while Cynan carves out lands of his own.

The episode of cutting out the Breton women's tongues is an onomastic story derived from the Welsh for Armorica, *Llydaw* (lled-taw = half silent). Nennius puts it graphically thus:

> For the Armorican British, who are overseas, went forth there with the tyrant Maximus on his campaign, and, since they were unwilling to return, they destroyed the western parts of Gaul to the ground and did not leave alive those who piss against the wall ... They are the Armorican British, and they never came back, even to the present day. That is why Britain has been occupied by foreigners and the citizens driven out ...[28]

Clearly, Maximus' withdrawal with Britain's prime troops rankled deeply. Although their presence in Britain might well not have counted for much, Britons could not help wondering what might have been. Interestingly, Cynan and Cadwalladyr, a seventh-century king of Gwynedd, appear in the *Armes Prydein*, or *Prophecies of Britain*, (c. AD 930) as two promised deliverers who will liberate Wales from the Saxon yoke. Since Arthur's own ancestors derive from the Breton colonies, it will be seen that

Brittany's role as liberator loomed prominently in the British imagination.

II GODDESS OF THE DREAM-PATHS

The figure of Elen within this story is a primal example of the Goddess of Sovereignty. This is a role she shares with many other female characters within the *Mabinogion* as well as with others from parallel Celtic literature and oral tradition. Elen is primarily a representative of the land of Britain itself, marriage to whom confers regal status. But there is a level of the story which operates in a more mystical sense than just as a bald parable of Roman occupation.

Elen, like the many famous Elaines of later Arthurian romance, is a special princess. She is one of the 'Daughters of Branwen',[48] those representatives of Britain's sovereignty, who carry in their veins the blood of the Grail family. The Daughters of Branwen will be dealt with in more detail in Chapter Eight, but we may say here that the term is based on a lost triadic tradition which is mentioned in *Branwen, Daughter of Llyr*, where Branwen is called one of Three Ancestresses or Three Matriarchs of the Island of Britain. This term seems incongruous, since Branwen has only one child, Gwern, and he is killed: she, therefore, has no descendants. However, if we take this title to mean one of the Three Sovereignty-bestowing Women – women who represent the Sovereignty of Britain in their own person – we might indeed begin to comprehend. The Daughters of Branwen are those women whose royal blood engenders sovereigns, though the women themselves are rarely queens in their own right.

Elen belongs to the archetype most frequently appearing in Irish *aisling* (vision) tradition as the dream-woman, the faery-mistress who leads the hero to the Otherworld, the queenly woman who pours the cup for the rightful king. In *Mabon* we encountered many figures of Sovereignty who were goddesses in their own right; in this volume, we meet earthly women who embody Sovereignty in their queenly or heroic lives.

What, then, is the purpose of the dream within the Sovereignty tradition? We note that, significantly, it is always a man who has the dream, and that he always dreams or has a vision of an Otherworldly woman. Here we see in operation the basic esoteric law of polarity, whereby the energies of male and female are paired and endlessly reflected down all levels of existence from the divine to the human. I have dealt with the subject further in *The Western Way*.

Just as men and women mate on the physical plane, so do women dream of men and men of women on the psychic plane. By this means, sexual fantasy enables non-incarnate spirits or daemons to become incarnate; or, on a more mundane level, spiritual attributes are imparted to the bodies of children or to creative works. This esoteric law of polarity is expounded in *Vita Merlini*[11] and also in C. S. Lewis's writings about Merlin, who was himself the son of a mortal woman and a daemon.[89]

Dreams about women whom they desire above all else impel heroes to go on quests, each to discover his own strengths and shortcomings, to encounter spiritual challenges and to gain the woman he loves best. This is primarily Peredur's preoccupation, as we shall see in Chapter Seven. For in Celtic-derived stories there is no sense of duality in searching for a great spiritual good in the shape of a beautiful woman, as all the earliest Grail stories show. Sin and shame are for the later Grail stories, when medieval morality has branded the tradition with its fierce stamp.

Dreams of Sovereignty or her representatives are necessarily dreams of kingship and spiritual empowerment: dreams that have the power to disenchant the wasteland or the barren soul. So while men dream of the women they love best, their fantasy images, this will always be directed in one of two ways: they will project the fantasy image upon every woman they meet – as happens to Peredur at the outset of his quest – or upon that one woman or special symbol that represents her king-making or spiritually liberating power – Elen, the Grail, etc.

Let us examine a few of these dreams, bearing them in mind as we read through the rest of the *Mabinogion*. So numerous are the possible examples from Celtic tradition, that we shall confine ourselves to an examination of only a few. The first is the *Aislinge Oenguso*, the *Dream of Oengus*, which is found in Irish tradition. Oengus was the son of Dagda and Boann. One night he dreamt about the most beautiful maiden, who vanished just as he was about to embrace her. The dream recurred every night for a year until Oengus became ill from frustration. Doctors were called to attend him, and one divined that the cause was a woman. Bodh, King of the Sidhe of Munster, undertook to find her. She was discovered among 150 other maidens near a lake; they turned into swans every other year. The maiden was called Caer Ibormeith. Oengus shared her swan-form, mating with her in this shape, and eventually brought her back to his home Brugh na Boyne.[8]

Now, this story relates the history of two Otherworldly beings, as Oengus or Angus mac Og was one of the Tuatha de Danaan, and Caer was the daughter of King of the Sidhe in Connacht, but the theme of consuming love engendered by means of a dream is quite clear. Caer appears to Oengus in order to be freed from her swan-shape, drawing him to her by means of a dream. This theme, the quest of disenchantment, appears in related stories as we shall see, and is crucial to an understanding of Sovereignty's shape-changing ability. But while the *aisling* or dream-vision became an integral part of the later Irish tradition in which the poet dreams of a beautiful woman, the representative of Ireland who draws to her a champion or poet who can voice her sorrows through his verse, it is almost absent from British tradition. Elen in our story does not appear as a sorrowful or distressed woman: she is always beautiful, poised and competent. She appears, in fact, like 'some fair daughter of the Celestial Powers',[66] a queen of the Otherworld, like Caer. Indeed, in classical Irish *aisling* poetry, the woman who appears to the solitary poet in his vision is called a *speir-bhean* (literally, 'sky-woman'). This vision-woman is the true native muse, who takes the dreamer along the ancient dream-tracks to deeper knowledge than the waking consciousness can remember or grasp.

Sometimes the *speir-bhean* appears as a messenger, as in the story of Bran, who begins his wonder-voyage only after being visited by a faery-woman, who brings him the silver branch on which blooms blossom from the apple-trees of Emain Abhlach, the Irish Avalon. She sings to him of that wondrous place, and specifically tells him about the Land of Women (*Tir na mBan*).

Bran mac Febal is invited to make a voyage thither; it is an Otherworldly land which offers the pleasures of the earthly paradise and immortality. Bran makes the voyage, stays in the Land of Women but finds that return home is impossible, since he has already entered the timeless realm of the Otherworld and his mortal companions and family are long since dead.[146]

In this story Bran is given a vision of paradise and actually mates with the Queen of the Land of Women herself. Here the vision-woman is a messenger and foretaste of paradisaical bliss; she is not, as in later tradition, associated with or representative of a heavenly vessel of power such as the Grail (see Chapter Ten). But the empowerment of the hero with an Otherworldly object (usually a vessel or weapon) is a theme that we find in later Celtic and Arthurian tradition in great profusion. This search is symbolic of the quest for sovereignty – either of a king over his land, or of a hero over other strong men. As we have seen, Elen is representative of Britain's sovereignty, whom Macsen gains, whereas the Queen of the Land of Women is a form of Otherworldly Sovereignty, granting Bran power over the Blessed Isles.

Specific instances of Sovereignty appearing in a dream are rare, but there is one such appearance in *Baile in Scail* (*The Shadow's Prophecy*). Here, Conn of the Hundred Battles steps upon the stone of Fal, brought by the Tuatha de Danaan from the Otherworldly island of Falias. The stone shrieks under him, but his druids are unable to tell him anything else about it save that he will be king. Conn is then enveloped in a mist from which a horseman emerges to invite him to his house. Conn rides on and finds himself at a rath [hill-fort] where the horseman is ready seated as host. Before him sits a beautiful woman, dressed richly, and beside her a silver vat full of red ale and a golden ladle and gold cup. The host is none other than the god Lugh, and the woman is the Sovereignty of Ireland. She asks Lugh for whom the cup shall be poured. 'For Conn,' replies Lugh. Again she asks the question, and Lugh gives the name of Conn's descendant and successor as king. This is repeated until the number of Conn's successors is known. The rath and people vanish, leaving Conn with the ladle, vat and cup in his possession.[58]

Although this story shows a vision rather than a dream, we see how Sovereignty pours out a drink for Conn, who is to be the rightful king. As we shall see in Chapter Nine, this story is closely associated with the Grail legends and shows the connections between Sovereignty and that spiritual vessel of empowerment. Sovereignty appears in archetypal form for Conn, and their spiritual marriage is symbolized by his receipt of the vat of ale with its ladle and cup. He gains a land, not an earthly wife, and becomes a king: even the land itself, in the shape of the Inis Fal, cries out under his royal foot.

In these three examples we see how the dream or vision reveals the faces of Sovereignty and the ways in which she is won. First of all, the dream presents an ideal vision: a beautiful land or woman. Following the dream is the quest for the place or woman, or the answer to the vision. In this way the Otherworld affects the earthly realm, presenting visions of unattainable beauty and longing; the earthly realm responds by searching until that longing is assuaged by finding. The interconnection of the worlds is finely wrought in Celto-Arthurian tradition. For every land has its inner or archetypal Sovereignty as Goddess of the Land, who is represented by an earthly woman or women destined to become queen of that land. The vision-woman who appears in the dream of heroes is then a sending or premonition, forging links of fantasy between the Goddess and the woman who is in the mind of the dreamer. He will be satisfied by no woman other than the one who is most like his fantasy.

Elen's description is very close to that of Sovereignty in *Baile in Scail:* both she and Sovereignty are seated in a chair, clad in the glory of the sun. In Irish tradition there is a definite link between the inner, archetypal Sovereignty and Lugh, who is the culmination of all heroes and kings. (Lugh himself, like the earlier Manannan, appears as a vision-man to women, and fathers many heroes by them.) Elen is dressed in red-gold with rubies and pearls adorning her; she is in every respect Britain's answer to the classical Irish Sovereignty figure. In our story Elen reaches out, on behalf of Britain, to Macsen, sending her image along the dream-paths to awaken a virtuous and worthy champion for Britain, and a strong, handsome husband for herself. Nevertheless there remains a certain aloofness in her character, as though she were not acting on her own behalf: perhaps discernible here are the remnants of an earlier story about her, in which she embodies British Sovereignty in a more explicit way.

If that is so, then we have no British originals to draw upon, only successors to the figure that Elen embodies. Looking at these we may find some interesting 'descendants' of Britain's Sovereignty. In so doing we will anticipate many of the themes that will recur throughout this book, but the very complexity of Sovereignty demands that we unfold many of her themes and aspects along the way in order to gain a full overview of the *Mabinogion*'s treasury of stories.

III THE FAIR UNKNOWN AND THE LOATHLY LADY

We mentioned earlier the Irish *aisling* tradition. This poetic genre had its main flowering in the seventeenth and eighteenth centuries and was an expression of Ireland's oppression under the invader's yoke. The *speir-bhean* appeared to the poet who could make an appeal, on her behalf, to the exiled heroes of Ireland to come and save her from marriage to an unworthy husband. She appeared as the 'Brightest of the Bright . . . the Crystal of all crystals', who was to be married to a ragged churl.[66] She appeared, in fact, as a form of Ireland's Sovereignty who needed to be rescued from oppression and restored to her full loveliness again. By the late nineteenth century W. B. Yeats was writing of the old hag, Cathleen ni Houlihan, the ragged representation of Ireland's Sovereignty, whose youth had been squandered and whose land laid waste by a foreign power.

A similar pattern can be traced in British tradition. The early Irish models of Sovereignty were modified by British folk-traditions and further incorporated into Arthurian tradition throughout the Middle Ages. But within both Irish and British developments of her archetype, Sovereignty demonstrates her age-old facility for shape-changing. Like the land that she represents, which undergoes seasonal changes, Sovereignty changes from winter hag into spring maiden.

The oldest tales of Sovereignty reveal the pattern of an ancient test. One such story is *The Sons of Daire*, in which the four sons of King Daire pursue a magical fawn along the river Shannon.

After slaying it they enter a hut, where a fearsome hag sits by the fire. She demands that one of the brothers lie with her that night or she will transform them all into monstrous shape. One of the brothers, Lughaidh Laidhe, who actually slew the fawn, volunteers. As they lie down he observes that the hag has been replaced by a beautiful maiden. She informs him that she is Sovereignty of Alba and Eire and that he will have a son who will become a great king and likewise cohabit with her.[58]

The true hideousness of the hag is fully stressed in this text:

> High she was as any mast,
> Larger than a sleeping booth her ear,
> Blacker her face than any visage,
> Heavy on each heart was the hag . . .
>
> She was one continuous belly.
> Without ribs, without separation,
> A rugged, hilly, thick, black head
> Was upon her like a furzy mountain.[70]

We recognize the hag aspect of Sovereignty as a representation of the land awaiting a worthy king. This is but one of many texts in which Sovereignty changes from hag to maiden in Irish tradition; the theme will be further discussed in Chapter Six. In British tradition the hag recurs as the Loathly Lady, linking the ancient archetype of a sovereignty-bestowing goddess with the medieval Grail-bearer (see Chapter Seven).[115] While Sovereignty's ability to shapeshift from hag to maiden in a twinkling was a totally voluntary function in earliest traditions, later story-tellers failed to understand the subtleties of this transformation and rationalized it by making Sovereignty's ugliness the effect of a magical enchantment.

In these later stories, where Sovereignty appears as a Loathly Lady, either she is truly an ugly old hag, or she is enchanted into a monstrous shape, such as a dragon, worm or serpent. The means of disenchantment in both cases remained true to the original stories: a kiss was sufficient. In medieval romance, where the latter story soon abounded, this kiss was known as the *fier baiser* or daring kiss. In this kind of story, Sovereignty was represented by two women: the maiden messenger who summoned the hero in person to his quest, and the enchanted maiden who was in monstrous form. One story wherein these themes are in their transitionary state is *The Fair Unknown*.

The story of *The Fair Unknown* (*Le Bel Inconnu*) appears in a variety of versions during the Middle Ages. The main version was written by Renaut de Beaujeu in about 1185–90. R. S. Loomis has discovered what he considers to be connections between this story and that of Macsen Wledig.[92] While these connections are, in my opinion, slight enough, there are other connections which we will find between *The Fair Unknown* and other stories within the *Mabinogion*. For that reason it seems best to give the story here and refer to it further on in the book. The version given below is from the English metrical *Libeaus Desconus*, written about 1350.

> The hero of the story was brought up by his mother, who kept him secluded, calling him only Beau-Fis (Handsome Son). He accoutred himself in a dead knight's armour when he was grown up and went to Arthur's court at Glastonbury. Because the boy could not name himself, Arthur called him Libeaus Desconus (the Fair Unknown). He was knighted and taught arms by Gawain. A maiden called Elene rode into Arthur's hall demanding help to rescue her mistress who was imprisoned in the castle of Sinadoun. Libeaus Desconus claimed the adventure and Arthur granted it to him, to Elene's disgust, since she expected an experienced knight to ride with her. After many adventures, they came to Sinadoun where Libeaus Desconus learned from the steward that the lady of the castle had been imprisoned by two clerks: Mabon and Yrain, his brother. They were magicians and kept the lady in durance until she granted Mabon her hand in marriage. Libeaus Desconus entered the castle and found there only minstrels and beautiful furnishings. As he proceeded, the music ceased and the castle shook as with thunder. He fought Mabon and Yrain, overcoming them, but their bodies vanished. Dismayed, he prayed to the Virgin and saw a worm with the face of a woman emerge from a wall. Libeaus was transfixed with terror as the worm twined about him and kissed him. As she did so, the wings and tail fell from her and she appeared as a naked woman. She said that she had been enchanted by Mabon and Yrain, and that she would marry him, bestowing him her possessions. The lady was dressed, crowned and married him.[30]

In the earlier *Le Bel Inconnu* the lady tells the hero his name after he has kissed her: he is the son of Gawain by a water-fay and he is called Guinglain.

We are immediately struck by certain points in this story. The Fair Unknown, like Peredur, is a 'son of his mother', raised in ignorance of arms. There is little doubt that *Libeaus Desconus* furnished Malory with the material for shaping Gareth, or Beau-Mains, whose story this one much resembles.[25] The maiden messenger, Elene, is impatient with her mistress's champion, but in all other respects behaves in much the same manner as Lunet in *Owain*, as we shall see; both women represent the Black Maiden aspect of Sovereignty. Loomis has made much of the fact that the name Elene is combined in this story with a visit to a castle in Snowdon (Sinadoun) and has pointed out that these points tally with *The Dream of Macsen Wledig*: both have a woman called Elen and both are set in Snowdonia. That both tales share these aspects may not be entirely accidental, but the links between them cannot with certainty be identified from literary sources. If we look under the story at the symbolic shapes that emerge, then we may come to another conclusion.

The enchanted lady is held prisoner by Mabon and Yrain, brother enchanters. As we have already seen in *Mabon* (p. 157),[111] Mabon is a figure who was inherited by medieval story-tellers and was used in a way very different from his original function; instead of being Mabon the prisoner, he became Mabon the *im*prisoner. He also took on the function of cowardly enchanter, due to story-tellers misunderstanding the Celtic symbolism surrounding his mythos. That Mabon should be linked with a character called Yrain is interesting, since Yrain is etymologically linked with both Urien and Owain. As we have already seen, (*Mabon*, p. 161)[111] Mabon is the son of Modron, but then so is Owain, according to another story, by Urien of Rheged. The author of *Libeaus Desconus* knew the tradition that made them brothers. This may further explain why in Chrétien's version of *Gereint, Erec and Enid* the red knight in the enchanted garden is called Mabonograin: a possible linking of the names Mabon and Owain to create one character who is both prisoner and champion of the Otherworld garden (see Chapter Six).

The woman disenchanted by Libeaus Desconus is in the form of a wyvern according to *Le Bel Inconnu*, although the English version calls her a worm. This is consistent within British folk-

tradition, where many ladies are so enchanted by jealous step-
mothers (see Chapter Five). This kind of enchantment must be
seen as an alternative to the Loathly Lady's enchantment in British
tradition. According to this story-line, the Loathly Lady – who
appears in Chaucer's *Wife of Bath's Tale* as well as in Arthurian
tradition as Dame Ragnell – is bespelled into ugliness by Morgan
le Fay, or a stepmother.[78] In both stories she is able to give the
answer to a question upon which the life of the hero depends:
'What is it women most desire?' She will only vouchsafe this life-
saving answer if the hero agrees to marry her. The answer reveals
that the Loathly Lady is indeed a direct descendant of Celtic
Sovereignty: 'Women desire to have sovereignty,' or, more pro-
saically, 'Women desire to have their own way.' (See p. 273.)

Here the kiss demanded by Sovereignty has become a marriage;
and the ritual question has emerged from a tangle of traditions
merging. Instead of Sovereignty representing the land and all
that royal rule entails, she has descended, still in her shapeshifting form, as an enchanted woman who represents all women.
It is a fascinating diminution of the original theme, but still
instructive. The most famous disenchanter of the Loathly Lady is
Sir Gawain whose son (by a faery) rescues the enchanted lady of
the castle of Sinadoun. About him and the role of the champion
of Sovereignty we will have more to say later.

But what of Elen and her part in this schema? There is perhaps
a way in which Elen of Caer Seint, the Lady of Sinadoun and an
Elaine of another Arthurian story are connected in an intimate
way to the themes of both Sovereignty and the Grail quest, in the
light of the dream/vision we have discussed.

The connection lies at the far end of the Arthurian tradition,
the work of Malory, who derived the most part of *Le Morte
d'Arthur*[25] from the *Vulgate Cycle*, itself a compendium of traditions
about the Matter of Britain. The *Vulgate Cycle* represents, in a
vast canonical form running to five volumes, the entire Matter of
Britain from the coming of Joseph of Arimathea with the Grail to
the death of Arthur. Within it are found many stories reworked
from ancient sources as well as a boiling-down of many early
medieval Arthurian romances. The Lady of Sovereignty has been
transmuted in this collection from Goddess of the Land to

Grail-bearer in a way that we can distinguish quite clearly. The episode of Malory's in which this understanding is most clearly demonstrated lies within Book Eleven of *Le Morte d'Arthur*, in which a hermit comes to Arthur's Round Table and explains that the Siege (seat) Perilous (which, like the Lia Fail, cries out under the rightful possessor of that seat – at least in the *Didot Perceval* text[32]) shall be occupied by one who will be conceived that year and who shall win the Holy Grail. After this incident:

> Lancelot rode out until he came to the tower of Corbin. The people there all acclaimed him as the best of knights and begged him to release a maiden from the enchantment of being in a boiling tub of water. She had been bespelled by Morgan le Fay and the Queen of Northgalis. Lancelot took the naked woman by the hand and drew her out, since only the best knight was so able. The people of Corbin further begged Lancelot to deliver them from a serpent that was in a nearby tomb. On the lid of the tomb was a prophecy concerning the conception of Galahad ('the which lion shall pass all other knights'). Lancelot then dispatched the serpent whereupon King Pelles approached and asked his name, explaining that he himself was cousin to Joseph of Arimathea.
>
> Lancelot then went with him to Pelles' castle where, as they sat at table, there entered a maiden bearing the Grail. Lancelot asked what this meant, and was told that it was 'the richest thing that any man hath living'. Then Pelles began to devise how Lancelot might be got to sleep with his daughter Elaine, for by them only might the Grail-winner be conceived. With the help of Dame Brisen, who knew of Lancelot's unfailing love for only Guinevere, Pelles commanded Elaine to go to the Castle of Case and ready herself. Brisen caused Elaine to take Guinevere's outer appearance and sent a ring to Lancelot to arrange an assignation with his mistress and queen. And so Lancelot slept with Elaine thinking that she was Guinevere. On that night, Galahad was conceived.

Under this late Arthurian story, itself the culmination of many story-tellings, we can perceive a significant subtext, which illuminates Sovereignty's association with the themes of disenchantment and vision-woman. Malory is silent upon the identities of either the enchanted maiden or the Grail Maiden in this extract, but the likelihood is that both are presumed to be Elaine. The land of Corbin, consistent with the enchanting of the land of Sovereignty, is a wasteland awaiting the best knight in the world in order to be released. The maiden under enchantment, representing the land of Corbin, has been associated here with the 'maiden transformed into a serpent' theme that we spoke of above; although Malory makes these separate incidents, they follow upon each other too significantly not to be connected. It is possible that Lancelot, in some lost oral tradition, disenchanted the maiden who had been transformed into a serpent and who dwelt among the tombs awaiting release, by means of the *fier baiser*.

Lancelot appears here as the best knight in the world: a theme we shall find again and again in the literature of Sovereignty, for only the best or most worthy hero can champion Sovereignty. He arrives at Corbin for one destiny only, to him unknown – to engender Galahad, who will surpass his father and become the Grail-winner. When the Grail Maiden enters, and she may be identical to Elaine who is Pelles the Grail guardian's daughter, Lancelot asks the significance of this and is given a significant answer: 'the richest thing that any man hath living'. Does Pelles refer to the Grail or to its bearer? Is he being purposely evasive? A similar confusion occurs in von Eschenbach *Parzival*,[40] where Feirfitz, the particoloured pagan half-brother of Parzival, is brought into the presence of the Grail. Because he is a pagan, he can only see the Grail-bearer, not the vessel itself. And in order to win the beautiful maiden, he becomes a Christian.[39] This is consistent with the pattern of a more ancient sovereignty, as we have already noted: that the vision-woman is both incentive and prize, whereas the later stories show the vision-woman becoming merely a messenger or adjunct of the spiritual vessel or Grail.

What of Elaine herself? Her role in Malory's story seems outrageously passive, condoning her father's dream of spiritual destiny by means of a cheap deception. However, we need to read this episode with the mirror of Sovereignty in our hands, for a deep and archetypal pattern is worked out here. With the agreement of Pelles and the connivance of Brisen, Elaine becomes a simulacrum of Guinevere, for the sole reason that Lancelot will respond sexually to no other woman but Arthur's queen. Elaine becomes then a kind of succuba, a dream-woman or embodied fantasy. While Lancelot responds physically to his supposed

Guinevere, Elaine evokes the psychic image of the Grail-winner that her father has foretold will be born of the Grail guardian's daughter and the best knight in the world. An ancient pattern is reworked to great effect: instead of the Loathly Lady being transformed into a beautiful woman by the kiss of a hero, Elaine is the means of disenchanting the wasteland by becoming the mother of Galahad, the Grail-winner, by means of Lancelot's singular passion for Guinevere.

Elaine is thus an authentic sovereignty-bestowing woman. She is a Daughter of Branwen, a vessel of the blood of the Grail family. She is literally a Grail-bearer, carrying both cup and child. Similarly we saw that Rhiannon (see *Mabon*, p. 70)[111] is the bearer of Gwair (which means both hay and the mystery name of Pryderi, her son).

So we see the cross-tracked and sometimes tangled line of Sovereignty's influence. Elen, the queenly representative of Britain's blood and Sovereignty, becomes the wife of Macsen Wledig by means of a dream. She exercises her ancient role as Goddess of the dream-paths, probably inherited from an even more remote figure who is lost in British tradition. The Elene of *Libeaus Desconus* may derive in part from our Elen, but more important to us is the linkage between the themes of the enchanted maiden and the Loathly Lady in that story. Lastly, Malory's Elaine shows us the final pattern of Sovereignty: she still bears the sovereignty-bestowing power, but in the form of the Grail; she accepts only the best hero as her mate; she brings peace and plenty to the land by engendering the hero who will represent her, the one who will find the Grail and heal the wasteland, bringing an end to all enchantments; she assumes a dream-form in order to evoke her destined mate's *eros*, but transmutes that *eros* to *agape*, selfish into selfless love, for the healing of the world.

So is Sovereignty transformed from a king-making goddess to a Grail-bearing maiden. In order to bear her transformations in mind more clearly, the reader is referred to Figure 3.3.

Source	Transformed From	Transformed To	Means of Transformation	Sovereignty's Gift
Ancient Irish Sovereignty Stories	hag	Goddess of Sovereignty	kiss/cohabitation	kingship of Ireland to champion and descendants
Loathly Lady (Dame Ragnell/ Wife of Bath) Traditions	enchanted hag	beautiful maiden	marriage/kiss/ allowing maiden/hag to decide the 'right' answer	answer that saves the life of/ disenchants the hero/king
British Folk Tradition (Kemp Owyne/ Libeaus Desconus)	serpent/ monster	beautiful maiden	kiss	her lands by marriage to the hero
Arthurian Grail Stories	hideous damsel/ messenger	Grail Maiden/ Grail-bearer	Grail question successfully answered	spiritual kingship
	(enchanted wasteland also becomes transformed to fertile land)			

Figure 3.3: *Patterns of Sovereignty's Transformation*

CHAPTER FOUR

THE DREAM OF RHONABWY

The sage has invented a battlefield, in the midst of which the king takes up his station. To left and right of him the army is dispersed, the foot-soldiers occupying the rank in front. At the king's side stands his sagacious counsellor advising him on the strategy to be carried out during the battle.

FIRDAUSI
Shahnama

And then he saw around him so many birds that all the air about him was full of them and they were blacker than anything he had ever seen.

Didot Perceval

I THREE NIGHTS IN AVALON

The Dream of Rhonabwy is one of the most mysterious tales in the *Mabinogion*. It is nearest in nature to *Culhwch and Olwen*. In it Arthur is still the King of the Heroic Age with a mere patina of medieval overlay; his men are the same warriors as those listed in *Culhwch and Olwen*, and are not yet medieval knights. Many ancient and curious remnants are littered about this story, and perhaps some of them would still have been intelligible to a medieval Welshman, though they are certainly not so to us. As with many of the earlier stories of the *Mabinogion*, it is the traditions to which the story alludes that explain it, and these have been left out of the narrative. Fortunately it is possible to reconstruct from existing parallel sources some of the cultural underpinning necessary to our understanding.

The central question that the reader needs to ask is: 'Are Owain's ravens real birds or are they a troop of men called ravens?' The story leaves us in no doubt that real ravens fight Arthur's squires:

> clapping their wings in the wind . . . they seized some by the heads and others by the eyes, and others by the arms and carried them up into the air.[22]

These are not figurative ravens, but real scavengers of the battle-field: the kind of carrion birds once commonly seen after any bloody fray. Although the action of the story takes place within a dream, we need not be dismissive of the dream's contents for that reason. Indeed, hidden within the story and its dream symbolism lies the identity of one of the chief exemplars of Sovereignty, in the person of Owain's mother (see p. 96).

The location of the story in twelfth-century Wales – the world in which Rhonabwy has the unfortunate task of hunting down one of his own countrymen – is offset by the location of the dream in which he meets Arthur and his mighty host. From an all-too-real world of Wales in disarray, Rhonabwy awakes to a dream of the Otherworld, where the strength and glory of Britain is an ever-living reality. Since the Celtic conception of the Otherworld was not one of gloom and decay but of a paradisaical present in which it is possible to fulfil all the normal actions of one's earthly life, Arthur and his men engage Osla Big-Knife in a rematch of the Battle of Badon. Once the reader understands the time-scale of the dream to be that of a living Otherworld 'reality', the story becomes a lot clearer. Although men are wounded and even die in the combat of the Ravens, they, like the pieces on the *gwyddbwyll* board, will be set up on the field of battle another day.

Central to the dream is the *gwyddbwyll* game that Owain plays against Arthur. As we shall see, this game is a combat for sovereignty, but not in the usual sense, since it takes place within the Otherworld and, like the Battle of Badon, is a combat whose outcome has already been decided in linear time.

Owain is Arthur's nephew, the son of Urien of Rheged. We will meet him again in *The Lady of the Fountain*, where he is the chief protagonist. He is not called Arthur's nephew in the story, although we know from parallel and later tradition that Urien married Morgan, Arthur's half-sister. Owain ap Urien Rheged was an historical character, existing a good two generations after the passing of the Dark Age Arthur c. AD 530 at Camlann. Like many other heroes of roughly the same era, he became drawn into the Arthurian corpus. Because of his unique links with both Arthur himself and with the Otherworldly queen, Modron, his mythos is of great significance to our discussion of this story.

The Battle of Camlann ended the brief independence of the British – barely 120 years had elapsed since the Romans left this island. Rhonabwy knew, as any well-brought-up youth should, the stories of that fatal battle. That he should meet its survivors in his dream and encounter those who actually died there is wonderful enough; that he should be permitted to witness the game between Arthur and Owain – itself a ritual challenge of Sovereignty's king and champion – is a great privilege. In that combat more than the fate of the game is staked.

There are many interesting parallels between *The Dream of Rhonabwy* and the early Irish story *The Destruction of Da Derga's Hostel*. As we saw in *Mabon*, the borrowing of Irish themes and motifs is very common within the *Mabinogion*; not because the British story-tellers lacked their own themes or innate skills but because Britain and Ireland shared a common tradition of stories and mysteries. No story could be so apposite to Britain as *The Dream of Rhonabwy*, which draws straight from the British Otherworld tradition and which is deeply concerned with our native Sovereignty, yet Irish themes from *Da Derga's Hostel* are still apparent.

Rhonabwy's dream is not of a common order: but then he sleeps on an ox's hide, unconsciously following an ancient druidic practice of inducing prophetic dreams by incubating within the skin of a sacred animal. The original method was to sleep in a bull's hide: perhaps it is the *cyfarwydd*'s unstated and ironic comment on the state of Wales that Rhonabwy sleeps in the skin of a castrated bull – an ox. Whatever his intention, the story-teller certainly allows Rhonabwy a full vision of Arthur and his men within the realms of Avalon.

The Dream of Rhonabwy

(1) Madawg, ruler of Powys had a brother, Iorwerth, who was displeased by his brother's position and his own obscurity. Although Madawg offered his brother the position of commander of his troops, Iorwerth preferred to go raiding in England. Three hundred men were sent to search for him, including Rhonabwy. (2) With a company of his fellows, Rhonabwy sought shelter at the house of Heilyn the Red. It was a singularly dilapidated household, and the company were offered very poor hospitality. (3) Rhonabwy went to sleep on a yellow oxhide on the floor and there he dreamed that he and his companions were crossing the plain in Montgomeryshire. (4) They were overtaken by Iddawg, who had been the cause of the conflict at Camlann. Sent by Arthur to deliver a message of truce to Medrawt, Iddawg framed the message as rudely as he could. (5) They came to where Arthur was encamped on an island in the middle of a ford. Arthur expressed sorrow for Britain that such little men now guarded it. (6) Iddawg pointed out to Rhonabwy the stone in Arthur's ring: it had the property that whoever looked on it would remember all that he saw. They watched several troops of differently accoutred men ride by, including that led by (7) Afaon, son of Taliesin, who splashed Arthur and his bishop with water. (8) Caradawg mac Llyr, Arthur's chief counsellor, expressed doubts that so many men would be contained in that space, especially as they were scheduled to fight the Battle of Badon against Osla Big-Knife by noon. They watched the coming of other troops and then noticed a commotion in the middle of the assembly. (9) This was caused by all the men wishing to see Cai's great prowess at riding. (10) Arthur was armed by Cadwr of Cornwall, (11) his mantle placed on the ground for him to sit upon, and his (12) *gwyddbwyll* placed ready for a game with Owain ap Urien. (13) They played and after a while a man came to tell Owain that Arthur's squires were harassing his ravens. Although Owain requested Arthur to call his men off, Arthur played on. Three times in all, messengers came with reports of the worsening plight of the ravens until Owain (14) finally told the messenger to raise his standard in the thick of the fighting. The combat was reversed. Messengers came to Arthur to tell of how the ravens were overcoming his squires. Although Arthur requested Owain call off his ravens,

Owain played on. (15) Three times this happened until Arthur squeezed the gold chess-pieces into dust. Owain caused his standard to be lowered. (16) Osla Big-Knife sent envoys to request a truce of six weeks for the fighting of their battle. (17) Arthur consulted his men about the suitability of the truce. (18) Twenty-four donkeys arrived burdened with gold and silver – the tribute of the islands of Greece – while the bards were singing a eulogy in praise of Arthur. The truce was agreed upon and the gold and silver awarded to the poets. Cai exhorted everyone to be in Cornwall ready to fight Osla at the end of the truce. (19) Such was the sound of their acclamation that Rhonabwy awoke, after a sleep of three days and nights. No one is able to tell this story without a book because of the many colours and various equipment and clothes mentioned.

Commentary

1. The geographical and historical setting of the story is entirely accurate. The scene takes place in central Wales – Powys – over which region Madawg ap Maredudd did indeed rule from 1138–1160. There was a good deal of unrest and political strife following his death until his grandson, Llewellyn the Great, took possession of Powys. This preamble, which tells of a renegade Cymro (Welshman), is offset by the loyalty shown by Arthur's host in the main story of *The Dream of Rhonabwy*. Indeed, as we will see, the whole story revolves around the dichotomy of medieval Wales, which looked to an ideal Arthurian kingdom but which actually lived in a far-from-ideal state, being partially governed by English kings.

2. Celtic hospitality was universally warm and lavish – according to the circumstances of the host. It was everywhere an honourable thing to feed strangers, just as it still is in parts of rural Greece today. The house of Heilyn the Red is not simply poor, but is downright inhospitable: dung and urine make the floor muddy, the food is poor and the fire smoky. This episode can be compared with the visit of King Fedlimid to the house of Gulide the Satirist. In this early Irish story Gulide sends his daughters – Fly, Smasher and Scream – out to his guests to give an account of the hospitality to be expected: the old food was eaten, the new food

hadn't arrived, the women were pregnant, the cows were dry, mice swarmed about the floors and the benches were rotten.[137] The house of Heilyn represents the state of Wales, impoverished by its overlords, willing enough to offer hospitality, but too poor to provide the best.

3. Offered a choice of beds Rhonabwy chooses the yellow ox's hide and wraps himself up in it for the night. Little does he know that this action triggers his dream. In druidic usage such a sleep in an ox's hide brought prophetic and precognitive dreams. In *The Destruction of Da Derga's Hostel*[8] a bull-feast (*tarbh-feis*) is prepared on the death of King Eterscel in order to determine who will be the next king. A druid kills a bull, eats a broth of its flesh and a spell of truth is chanted over him. By such a method the new king, Conaire, is recognized. This is not the only similarity between these two texts, as we shall see. The setting of a story within a dream is not a common Welsh tradition, although it is often utilized by Irish story-tellers.

4. Just as Rhonabwy's real-life errand is to search for a renegade Cymro, so now he meets with another in his dream. Iddawg, the Churn of Britain, was the chief cause of the last battle fought between Arthur and his son/nephew, Medrawt (Mordred). He, along with six others, escaped the slaughter of Camlann, according to tradition, and he says that he completed his penance for this act after seven years at the Grey Stone in Scotland. Rhonabwy has certainly gone back in time and no mistake. The survivors of Camlann are variously given as follows:

> Here are the names of the men who escaped from the battle of Camlann: Sandde Angel's form because of his beauty [sic], Morfran son of Tegid because of his ugliness, St Cynfelyn from the speed of his horse. St Cedwyn from the world's blessing, St Pedrog from the strength of his spear, Derfel the Strong from his strength, Geneid the Tall from his speed. The year of Christ when the battle of Camlann took place was 542.[38]

There is an obvious parallel with the seven who returned from Ireland with Bran (see *Mabon*, p. 46)[111] and with Arthur from Annwn (ibid., p. 107). See also note 8.

5. The scene of Arthur's encampment shows the king surrounded by his counsellors and retainers. When he sees Rhonabwy and his companions, he laments that Britain should be governed by such little men as these. It is now obvious that Rhonabwy is indeed in the Otherworld by the power of his dreaming. He meets the archetypal warriors and guardians of Britain's former greatness, and doubtless feels about this encounter as a young man about to go to the Crusades was reported, by Giraldus Cambrensis, to have felt:

> What man of spirit can hesitate for a moment to undertake this journey when, among the many hazards involved, none could be more unfortunate, none could cause greater distress, than the prospect of coming back alive? [12]

– though, doubtless, Rhonabwy's distress was more from failure to measure up to the ideal warrior.

6. As all dreamers know, dreams fade rapidly once one is awake. Iddawg shows how Rhonabwy may recall all that he sees by dint of looking at Arthur's ring. Despite a list of Arthur's goods, weapons and possessions, this is the solitary mention of his ring (see notes 10 and 11). However, C. S. Lewis made this ring the object of a mystery question which Merlin sets Ransom, the successor to the long line of Pendragons:

> 'Where is the ring of Arthur the King? . . .'
> 'The ring of the King . . . is on Arthur's finger where he sits in the House of Kings in the cup-shaped land of Abhalljin [i.e. Avalon] . . . For Arthur did not die; but our Lord took him to be in the body till the end of time . . . with Enoch and Moses and Melchisedec the King.' [89]

This novel, *That Hideous Strength*, shows the continuity of the tradition begun here.

7. The striking of Afaon's horse by Elphin is significant also. Elphin is here described as Arthur's sword-bearer. He is the same Elphin who rescued Taliesin from the weir and was in turn rescued by Taliesin from imprisonment by Maelgwn (see *Mabon*, p. 116).[111] This episode in *The Story of Taliesin* is traditionally

supposed to correspond with the freeing of the youth Gwair (a type of Mabon) from imprisonment in Annwn. In the Succession of the Pendragons, the Pendragon always frees his successor from Otherworldly detainment, as Arthur frees Gwair in the 'Preiddeu Annwn'. The identification of Elphin as a type of Mabon is established in our story, where Elphin stands before Arthur as his sword-bearer. We will also remember that Taliesin bade Elphin's jockey strike all Maelgwn's horses as he overtook them in the race. Here Afaon, the son of Taliesin, splashes Arthur with water and his horse is struck by Elphin. Iddawg's comment on this action is strange: he praises Afaon as the wisest and most accomplished youth in the kingdom, while Elphin is called a perverse and over-anxious boy.

Triads 7 and 25 describe Afaon as one of three 'Bull-chieftains' and 'Battle-Leaders' of Britain. He is further described as having avenged his death from his grave – an allusion to a lost tradition. Elphin is always known as 'the unfortunate'. That he should be described as over-anxious is strangely familiar; Pryderi, another type of Mabon, is similarly called 'anxiety'. This mysterious passage shows that the *cyfarwydd* was familiar with related traditions of these characters.

8. The Battle of Camlann, at which most of those mentioned in this story perished, was fought about A D 530. The Battle of Badon – Arthur's greatest victory – was fought about A D 495. Badon is generally identified as Caer Baddon or Bath. Osla Big-Knife, who also appears in *Culhwch and Olwen* as the bearer of a large knife, which spanned all rivers so as to enable Arthur and his host to cross water, is not so easy to identify. This mention of him in *Culhwch and Olwen* establishes a distinguished tradition of the Sword-bridge in Arthurian legend, but although he appears here as Arthur's ally, he is, in fact, anything but in historical terms. 'Only one English king is directly stated to have fought at Baddon and his name was Oesc of Kent,'[123] which is sufficiently like Osla to be acceptable. But it is more likely that Octha, the kinsman of Hengist whom Vortigern allowed to settle in the lands north of the Wall is intended; this area, agreed to be Dumfries, takes its name from the Frisians who settled there.

Caradawg mac Llyr is also called Caradawg Freichfras or Strong Arm. Triads 1 and 18 speak of him as the Chief Elder of Britain and one of three Battle-Horsemen. In Welsh and Breton tradition he was incorporated into the noble genealogies. In Arthurian literary tradition he was translated into French as Karadues or Carados Briefbras; the French story-tellers did not understand Welsh and many stories abounded concerning his 'shortened arms'.

9. Cai's reputation as one of Arthur's chief warriors gradually declined over the years. Here, as in *Culhwch and Olwen*, Cai is still one of the 'Battle-Diademed Men' (Triad 21) of the Island of Britain. With Bedwyr he performs great feats of supernatural strength and cunning. It is only later that he becomes the discourteous Kay, as we can see in the later romances of *Peredur* and *Gereint and Enid*. His prowess at riding causes the host to look as though it is 'turning inside out'. It rather looks as though the *cyfarwydd* is using a poetical allusion common at the time of this story's transcription. The Battle of Camlann became a byword for futility, furious combat and tumult.[38] The word *cadgamlan*, derived from Camlann, was coined to express 'a confused mob or rabble', such as is caused by Cai's prodigious riding here.

10. The arming of Arthur is unique among stories concerning his exploits. As stated elsewhere it is rare that Arthur performs any feats on his own behalf in the later legends. *The Dream of Rhonabwy*, apart from supplying a further list of Arthur's host (see note 17), goes into great detail concerning his possessions. The sword that Elphin bears is brought to Arthur by Cadwr of Cornwall, who holds Arthur's personal domain in trust for his king. The sword has two golden serpents on the hilt: when it is unsheathed, flames of fire issue from the mouths of these serpents, dazzling the faces of his foes.

11. Arthur's mantle, Gwenn (white), is placed on the ground. It has two properties: nothing that is not white can be placed on it, and anyone wrapped in it becomes invisible. This mantle is listed as the Thirteenth Treasure of Britain (see *Mabon*, p. 52).[111] The mantle of invisibility is likewise used by Caswallawn in *Branwen*,

Daughter of Llyr, although he uses it to usurp Bran's throne and cause death to Britain's faithful troops. It is clearly one of Sovereignty's empowering Hallows, like the *gwyddbwyll* board (see note 12). The fact that it allows things only of the same colour as itself to be placed on it seems puzzling at first, but white is the prime colour whose purity belongs to the worthy – kings, heroes, maidens and queens. The implication is that it cannot be used for evil purposes.

12. This is the second appearance of the *gwyddbwyll* board in this book. Wherever serious matters of sovereignty are debated, there we will find this gaming board. The exact method of playing *gwyddbwyll* is uncertain, but it is likely to be similar to other games of the period, like the Irish *brandubh* or *fidhchell*, which had two sets of men: the kingpiece and his companions, and the opposing men. There is an extant Irish poem from the works of Tadhg Dall O hUiginn which speaks of the *brandubh* board as a microcosm of Ireland itself. The centre square represents Tara (the sacred centre of Ireland), while the surrounding four squares to north, south, east and west are the royal seats of Ulster, Munster, Leinster and Connacht respectively.[13] There is an unwritten tradition, which can be surmised from the folk-traditions and oral culture of the Celtic (and other) nations, that the king often wins his kingdom (or retains it) by winning a board-game between himself and an Otherworldly king. This is significant in respect of our story, as we shall see.

13. The mysterious game begins, and with it an equally mysterious series of messengers appears. Those who come to Owain do not greet Arthur first, as courtesy demands that they should. To Owain's repeated request that Arthur call off his squires from Owain's ravens, the king merely says, 'Your move,' in the manner of one who has the game sewn up. The nature of this game and the significance of Owain and the Ravens will be discussed below.

14. It is only when the raven-standard is raised that Owain's side gains the upper hand. This action is talismanic, and Owain seems to allow it only as a last resort. If we look at parallel Celtic tradition,

we will see just why. There is a firm tradition that battle-standards were somehow empowered *in their own right* to wreak vengeance and slaughter.[116] The Fairy Flag of Dunvegan, in the keeping of the MacLeods, was given to the ancestors of the MacLeod clan to be used only in great need. It traditionally stopped a cattle-plague, extinguished a fire and aided the clan in battle: but it is removed from its chest only *in greatest need*.[121] It is regarded as an Other-worldly gift which empowers mortals. Of course, the standard, as with any heraldic device, is but a manifestation of a tribe's totem. Owain's particular right to use this device is discussed below.

15. Arthur ends the conflict by crushing the chess-pieces. The game of *gwyddbwyll* has been operational on two levels: as a board game and as an actual combat. At the same time Owain orders the lowering of the raven-standard and there is peace between both kinsmen.

16. The truce by arrangement may seem farcical to modern understanding, to which the chivalry of war is a thing of the past, yet such truces were frequent and acceptable in the Middle Ages, when hostilities would break off, by agreement, in honour of a major feast of the Church. The duplicity of the Briton's lunchtime assault on Rome in *The Dream of Macsen Wledig* is a rare event in historical terms. The Battle of Badon to be fought here is by way of a repeat match: since neither side exists in linear time but only in the ever-living 'reality' of the Otherworld, they can refight old battles with impunity.

17. The extent and power of Arthur's reign is due entirely to his ability to combine with fellow kings and leaders of Britain. This story, like *Culhwch and Olwen*, gives us a full list of his allies and chief officers. These lists represent the earliest literary examples of Arthur's court, an earlier and far more authentic numeration than that of the later Round Table knights. Although the casual reader who wishes to read the story and not get delayed by these lists is tempted to pass them over as full of difficult Welsh names, it is worth looking closely at them, for they reveal a good deal about the way in which Arthur was understood.[120]

Many characters from other parts of the *Mabinogion* appear in
this story. Edern ap Nudd (who is called the King of Denmark
here!) we will meet again in *The Lady of the Fountain*. Apart from
Arthur's usual warriors, Gwalchmai (Gawain), Bedwyr (Bedevere) and Cai (Kay), there are Trystan and Morfran (the son
of Ceridwen and Tegid), and Gwrhyr and Menw, who both
helped to find Mabon in *Culhwch and Olwen*. Peredur, who we will
meet later on, is mentioned in the same breath as Goreu and
Mabon: a significant juxtaposition. The tradition that Arthur
had children other than Mordred is not generally known: but
Llacheu is mentioned here as Arthur's son. In later Arthurian
romance he becomes Loholt and is said to have been killed by
Cai (see also p. 297). Present also are some anachronistic kings,
including William of France (Gwilym) and Howel of Brittany.
The story-teller is at pains to show the extent of Arthur's power.
Ironically Gildas ap Caw is included: the same Gildas the Priest
whose chronicle *The Ruin of Britain* was written in the period of
the historical Dark Age Arthur, which singularly fails to mention
him.[13] The silence of Gildas on the subject of Arthur has been
variously interpreted as either a complete lack of such a king at
that time or the purposeful ignoring of a tribal enemy. (Gildas's
father, Caw, a Pict of the northern Clyde, was probably subdued
by Arthur).[123]

18. So vast is Arthur's power and influence that even the islands
of Greece send him tribute. This is in contrast to the numerous
mentions in oral tradition of Britain having to send tribute to
Rome: this is a memory of the ignominious period after Julius
Caesar's attempted invasion of Britain, when many minor kings
kept their titles and lands only by dint of paying such tribute.
The lands of the extreme east, Greece included, are often cited by
story-tellers in lieu of the Otherworld, as we will see in Chapter
Seven.

The praise-song that the bards sing to Arthur is so obscure that
only Cadyryeith understood it, says the text. As he is called 'Fair
Speech', we must conclude that he is himself skilled in poetic
conventions. This obscurity on the part of professional poets was
often remarked upon in the Middle Ages and later, attesting to a

lore and tradition which had its own allusive symbolism, the full implications of which only another poet could comprehend.

19. The death of the oral tradition and the new fashionable literary tradition is alluded to here: so complex and various are the colours and armaments that no one is able to tell the story without a book. Such a statement does a disservice to the actual memory of story-tellers of both Ireland and Wales, whose professional repertoire (in Ireland at least) included some 350 stories, many of which were not only longer than this one but also exceedingly more complex in their descriptions. But with the onset of literacy in the noble and clerical classes – especially the latter, who would have been professional poets or story-tellers in a non-Christian society – the skill of memorizing was forgotten.

Just as Macsen was awakened at the climax of his dream, so Rhonabwy awakes after his prodigious sleep because of the acclamation of Arthur's host.

II MODRON, QUEEN OF RAVENS

Owain's Ravens have been universally understood to mean his troops in this story, in much the same way that Achilles' men are called Myrmidons (ants). However there is, I believe, a deeper significance to *The Dream of Rhonabwy*; in order to discover its inner meaning we will need to look at some parallel texts relating to Owain and his family.

Why Owain should be associated with ravens is to do with the secret of his birth. This has already been mentioned in *Mabon*, p. 161,[111] but a brief summary of his conception follows.

There was a ford at Llanferres where people dared not go due to the sounds of dogs howling and barking. Urien of Rheged came to the ford and there met a woman who was washing. He lay with her and she told him that she was the daughter of the King of Annwn, fated to wait there until she conceived a son by a Christian. Her name was Modron. Returning at the end of the year, Urien found that she had had two children by him: Owain and Morfudd. These twins were also mentioned in Triad 70 as one of three 'Fair Womb Burdens': 'Owain Son of Urien, and Morfudd his sister, who were carried together in the womb of Modron ferch [daughter of] Afallach'.[38]

This late sixteenth-century oral story, combined with the triad, gives us an extraordinary key with which to open the door of a great mystery. Owain is of joint Otherworldly and mortal parentage, just as Pryderi is in *Pwyll, Prince of Dyfed*. Moreover he is the son of Modron. As I have already discussed, Modron is a title, not a personal name. It means 'Mother', and is applicable to many women who represent the Goddess as mother of the Mabon, or Son. The identity of the woman whom Urien meets is not difficult to discover. Later tradition speaks of Arthur's sister, Morgan, being married to Urien and of her being the mother of Owain. What clinches the identification is Morgan's own parentage: in the *Gesta Regnum Britanniae* (c. 1235), her father is given as Rex Avallonis – King of Avalon.

The tradition of Morgan in Arthurian tradition is a strangely tangled one. She appears as Arthur's sister (or half-sister) only in later texts. She first appears in Geoffrey of Monmouth[10] as Morgen, chief of nine sister prophetesses and healers. Chrétien de Troyes makes her Arthur's sister in *Erec and Enid*.[7] Later tradition makes of her an evil enchantress at odds with Arthur; her enmity is at the root of all later versions of the Round Table's decline (see Chapter Ten).

If we look at Morgan in the earlier traditions, we will find her likeness to the Irish Morrighan: the triple-aspected goddess who appears as the Dark Woman of Knowledge, as the Washer at the Ford and as the Battle-crow or raven. What is surprising is that the name 'Morgan' is never used as a female name in Welsh tradition, although it is common enough as a male name (see p. 143). Geoffrey of Monmouth called her Morgen. We cannot look to Welsh tradition to furnish a prototype of Morgan from any genealogy or chronicle earlier than Geoffrey. In so far as she can be identified with the name Modron, she is present in earlier tradition only as Owain's mother and the daughter of the King of Avalon or Annwn. So where did Morgan originate?

Geoffrey of Monmouth may have been a Breton born in Wales: if this was so, then we need look no further for our evidence.

Morgan le Fay is a character in her own right in Breton tradition, where she appears as Queen of the Otherworld, as a giver of gifts and haunter of wells and springs. Whether she stems from the same tradition that Pomponius Mela spoke of – the Nine Korrigans, or prophetic sisters, who lived on a holy island off the coast of Brittany – or from some other source, this tradition is remarkably close to Geoffrey's account of Morgen in the *Vita Merlini*.[11]

The lineage of Morgan in oral tradition has been too badly tangled for complete certainty of reconstruction; however, it is remarkably consistent. It is as though a common tradition concerning a prototype Morgan existed and has been parcelled out among the Celtic nations. It is only by assembling the evidence from each country that a complete Morgan can be found.

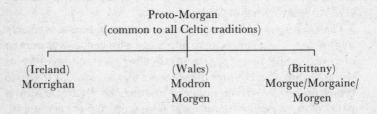

Figure 4.1: *Morgan in Celtic Tradition*

If we look at the characteristics of each of these seemingly separate women, we will see a 'family' likeness to one archetype: that of the Consort/Healer of the Dead Hero or Pendragon.

MORRIGHAN appears as a Battle-crow or raven, scavenging the battlefield. She also appears as the Washer at the Ford, to warn warriors of their impending death; the clothes that she launders are the bloody garments of a man she meets at the ford. She is at enmity with a chosen hero (in particular Cu Chulainn) whom she first loves and then, on being refused, hates, hounding him to his early death.

MODRON appears as the Washer at the Ford in order to conceive a child by a Christian man. She is the daughter of the Underworld

King, and people fear to frequent the ford because they imagine they will meet the Washer in her aspect of death-bringer. Modron bears a son/Mabon who will be her champion in battle. Likewise, by right of his maternal descent, Owain bears the raven upon his standard.

MORGEN/MORGUE/MORGAINE appears as an Otherworldly priestess, whose island or *temenos* is a place of healing and learning. She is the royal virgin of Avalon, who heals Arthur's wounds with her own skill; she keeps him with her as her consort after the Battle of Camlann.

The proto-Morgan, the great Celtic goddess who can appear as the Battle-raven or the hag washing the clothes of those destined to be slain, is also the Dark Woman of Knowledge, whose healing skills restore the wounded king and who is destined to bring forth a new Mabon to replace him in the outer worlds. The composite of these three women creates the later Morgan le Fay of Arthurian tradition. Meanwhile we are able to see that the daughter of Afallach, or Modron/Morgan, is fully at liberty to bequeath the aid of her raven-totem to her son/Mabon, Owain. If this is so, what then is the real nature of Owain's *gwyddbwyll* game with Arthur and of the combat between their respective troops?

We are fortunate that a further strand of this tradition, directly relating to *The Dream of Rhonabwy*, is extant in a later twelfth-century text known as the *Didot Perceval* (also called the *Prose Perceval*).[32] This relates a unique narrative concerning the exploits of Perceval and his quest for the Grail. Written in French, and closely related to the works of Robert de Boron, it yet retains some ancient features which doubtless strayed in from contemporary British oral tradition. One episode in particular concerns us here: that of Perceval's combat at the ford with a character called Urban of the Black Pine.

> While on his quest, Perceval came to a ford near which a pavilion was pitched in a beautiful meadow. A knight came from the pavilion and challenged Perceval's crossing. They fought and Perceval overcame his opponent; he would not grant him mercy until he told his tale. The knight said he was called Urban, son of the Queen of the Black Pine. He had been a knight of King Arthur's and, while on adventure, he had followed a maiden seated upon a mule. He was

unable to overtake her. Eventually she led him to a castle and there Urban fell in love with her, promising that he would pitch his pavilion at the ford and challenge all comers. He had held the ford for the best part of a year, at the end of which time he expected to win his maiden. Perceval said that he did not wish to guard the Ford Perilous himself, and he told Urban that he need not guard the place any longer. Then a great noise sounded and a shadow overcame them both and a voice was heard to say:

'Perceval li Galois, accursed may you be by whatever we women can contrive, for you have caused us the greatest sorrow today that we could ever have . . .' Then it addressed Urban and forbade him to stay and guard the ford. 'If you stay there longer, you will lose me.'

As Urban made haste to go, hundreds of black birds filled the sky and started to attack Perceval. Urban helped him beat them off; Perceval wounded one bird so that it fell to earth where it became a woman. Amazed, Perceval asked the meaning of the transformation. Urban said that, 'the voice that you heard was she who called to me, and when she saw that I could not escape from you she changed herself and her damsels into the semblance of birds and they came here to oppress you . . . this one whom you wounded, she was the sister of my lady, but she will suffer no harm, for within the moment she is in Avalon.' Urban recognized Perceval as a worthy man and the best knight in the world, and Perceval went on his way.[32]

We will be returning to this theme in Chapter Seven, but it is evident that much of the mystery of *The Dream of Rhonabwy* is solved by this passage. The Ford Perilous is the boundary of the Otherworld where the maiden rules as queen. Like Pwyll in pursuit of Rhiannon, Urban was not able to catch up with his maiden. He is set to guard the borders of the Otherworld after the fashion of a knightly *Rex Nemorensis* (see p. 116). Perceval, because of his successful challenge, should by rights become the champion of the maiden, although he abrogates this duty in the text. He is cursed by the disembodied voice of the maiden and then physically attacked by her in her shape of a black bird, and though he is able to bring down one of the birds, it is not killed but becomes a woman and is spirited to Avalon to be healed.

The maiden is evidently a shadow of Modron/Morgan: she appears in raven shape and has the power to heal her sister in Avalon. It has been authoritatively established that Urban is based on Urien. In modern Breton folk-tradition the Forest of Brocéliande is Morgan's domain. Overlooking the Fountain of Barenton in the forest, is the famous Pine of Barenton, on which Otherworldly birds sing. In the *Didot Perceval* Urban is the son of the Queen of the Black Pine. Taken together with the encounter at a ford, we have the complete key to *The Dream of Rhonabwy*.

Owain is the champion of his mother's kin, the people of Avalon, who have the ability to shapeshift into ravens. As the grandson of Rex Avallonis he champions the Otherworld in a game against Arthur, who, since his defeat at Camlann, is a newcomer to Avalon. Why should he do this?

The long enmity between Morgan and Arthur is persistent throughout later tradition, though its real reason is misunderstood. In early tradition Morgan – as we shall continue to call this representative of the Great Mother, Modron – stood for Britain's Sovereignty, and it is because of Sovereignty and his union with her that the Pendragon is able to reign. Arthur's career and his relationship to Sovereignty's aspects are clearly shown in the schema below.

INITIATING MOTHER/RETIRING ASPECT OF
SOVEREIGNTY: Igerna/Igraine, Arthur's mother
FLOWER BRIDE/EARTHLY ASPECT OF SOVEREIGNTY:
Gwenhwyfar, Arthur's wife
OTHERWORLDLY CONSORT/INNER SOVEREIGNTY:
Morgan, Arthur's healer and receiver

These aspects of Sovereignty will be discussed in greater detail in Chapter Ten.

Sovereignty does not allow her earthly consort – her Pendragon – to reign beyond his rightful time. If we recall the pattern of the Succession of the Pendragons, we will see this:

MABON – the Wondrous Youth, the Pendragon's champion and *tanaiste* (successor)
PENDRAGON – the king who, with Sovereignty's empowerment holds the land
PEN ANNWN – the Withdrawn Pendragon who becomes King of the Underworld

In *The Dream of Rhonabwy* Arthur is the Withdrawn Pendragon; Owain, born to Modron and therefore a Mabon in his own right, stands ready to challenge his uncle, Arthur, for the Pendragon-ship. A close look at any of the late Arthurian romances will show that, as in earlier tradition, Morgan acts as Sovereignty, con-tinually presenting her champions at court where they try to oust Arthur or overcome him by combat or magical skill. In early tradition Owain becomes the son of Modron, who as a prototype of Morgan, may be seen as a sister of the Pendragon; Owain, her son, is thus Arthur's nephew and in a prime place to be his *tanaiste*. Within Celtic tradition the complex webs of familial relationships were guided by an older system of reckoning descent and succession through the female. This meant that the nephew or sister's son of a king had a greater right to the throne than the king's own son (who would have been born to a woman outside the royal blood). This situation is clearly shown in later Arthurian tradition, where the sons of Morgause by Lot – Gawain, Gaheris, Gareth and Agravain – are at odds with Arthur, aware of their prior claims to the succession. The culmination of this tradition is, of course, seen in the birth of Mordred, conceived upon Morgause by her half-brother, Arthur. Mordred is thus both his father's son and his nephew, which strengthens his claim to reign after his father. (He also attempts to reinforce this by abducting Guinevere in the later traditions – a curious turnabout to an earlier understanding of Guinevere as the Flower Bride and earthly representative of Sovereignty. See Chapters Six and Ten.)

That Owain is rightfully a Mabon we need have no doubts. The lost legends of Mabon as a character in his own right are only vestigially present in *Culhwch and Olwen*, but traditions about him filtered through into Continental developments of the Ar-thurian legend, and it is here that we find him again, in Chrétien's *Erec and Enid* as Mabonograin. Scholars argue over the etymology of this name, but it is possible that the traditions of Mabon and Owain – who are both sons of a woman bearing the title of Modron – have been combined to provide Mabonograin: Mabon and Ivain (the French name for Owain). Interestingly Mabono-grain is the nephew of Eurain (Urien) (see p. 71 and Chapter Six).

Owain is, then, the champion of Morgan; the ravens are his Otherworldly kindred and the contest is to determine the kingship.

III THE GAME OF THE GODDESS

The *gwyddbwyll* board appears many times in the *Mabinogion* and is central to the theme of Sovereignty, as we shall further discover in Chapter Seven. The board appears in the list of the Thirteen Treasures of the Island of Britain:

> The Chessboard of Gwenddolau ap Ceidio: if the pieces were set, they would play by themselves. The board was of gold and the men of silver.[38]

The identity of this Gwenddolau is not hard to find: he is the Gwenddolau who was the patron and protector of Myrddin ap Morfryn or Myrddin Wyllt – Merlin the Mad. He was the leader of one of the factions of the Battle of Arfderydd (AD 573), described in the Triads as one of the Three Futile Battles of the Island of Britain. It was brought about 'by the cause of the lark's nest'. Gwenddolau perished at this battle, causing Merlin to lapse into madness at the sight of the fray and the loss of so many of his family and friends.

Gwenddolau's reputation was high among poets, who describe him as generously open-handed. The allusion to the battle in which he met his death being caused by a lark's nest is very obscure, and though 'a lark's nest' may possibly indicate 'a trifling matter', knowing the nature of Celto-Arthurian texts, there is likely to be a more specific meaning. Gwenddolau appears in another triad concerning one of the Three Fortunate Assassinations. This triad tells of:

> Gall son of Dysgyfdawd who slew the Two Birds of Gwenddolau. And they had a yoke of gold on them. Two corpses of the Cymry they ate for their dinner, and two for their supper.[38]

Nothing more is known about these birds, but it is indeed unusual that there should be another tradition concerning the owner of a magical *gwyddbwyll* board and a pair of carrion birds, so similar to those in *The Dream of Rhonabwy*.

Owain was a fellow countryman and contemporary of Gwenddolau, for they were both men of the north, though they are clearly separate historical characters. Nikolai Tolstoy argues persuasively for the stubborn pagan adherence of Gwenddolau against his Christian enemy Rhydderch, who is described in the Black Book of Carmarthen as 'the defender of the faith'.[152] Tolstoy instances the fact that Gwenddolau was Merlin's patron and the fact that the chronicles describe Gwenddolau as causing a battle fog – a magical device often employed by druids, according to many Irish texts, to confuse their patron's enemy – as evidence of his pagan belief.

If we look at the career of Owain in the following two stories of Owain and Gereint, we find that Owain himself is a clear proponent of the old pagan ways, since he not only encounters and marries the Lady of the Fountain – a manifestation of Sovereignty – but also later on, in *Gereint and Enid*, becomes the King of the Enchanted Games – the contest that all visitors to Owain's castle must undergo. The Enchanted Games, like the game of *gwyddbwyll*, can have only one of two possible outcomes: success or failure. If successful, the candidate for the games emerges from the enclosed, paradisaical garden as the champion of Sovereignty; if he is unsuccessful, the candidate is summarily beheaded by the Red Knight who guards the garden, and his head is stuck on the surrounding palisade.

It is difficult to say whether or not the mythos of Owain has overlapped with that of Gwenddolau, but clearly there is some kind of connection. We should recall that the Thirteen Treasures of Britain are traditionally supposed to be guarded by Merlin in his Glass House on Bardsey Island, and that Merlin's patron was Gwenddolau – historically speaking.[38]

The *gwyddbwyll* board in Gwenddolau's possession is one of the prime symbols of Sovereignty herself, since it represents the land of Britain over which so many champions, invaders and defenders have fought in game after endless game. In *The Dream of Rhonabwy*, the board is in Arthur's possession, since he is King of Britain, for all that the time-scale of the story indicates that he is in the

Otherworld. But the pieces on the board, moved by the hands of Arthur and Owain, are represented by their respective troops, who 'play by themselves'.

The game that Owain and Arthur play is nothing more than the Game of the Goddess – the ultimate contest as to who shall have sovereignty over the land. This theme is echoed on every possible level of the story, since Rhonabwy's master, Madawg, seeks to overcome his brother Iorwerth in historical time; Arthur seeks to overcome Osla Big-Knife in a replay of Badon Field; and Owain seeks to overcome Arthur in a more mythological sense for the position of the Master of the Goddess's Game.

It would be indeed tempting to draw up the *gwyddbwyll* board exactly according to the story of *The Dream of Rhonabwy*, for the placement of the troops on the field seems to suggest the positioning of men upon a gaming board. Triad 59 speaks of the Battle of Camlann as being caused by one of Three Unfortunate Counsels of the Island of Britain, in which Arthur is advised to divide his troops in a threefold manner with Medrawt (Triad 59). This probably refers to the placement and command of Arthur's household troops or *teulu*, usually numbering 300 men.

In *The Dream of Rhonabwy* there are indeed three separate troops: those of Rhufawn Pebyr (who asks if Rhonabwy's company might be divided among the battle-disposition), those of March and those of Edern ap Nudd. In the very visual setting of this story we may envisage these three companies assembled on the plain before the island in the ford where Arthur sits: Rhufawn's company are in red liveries, March's in white with black colours and Edern's in darkest black, as befits the son of the Underworld.

Seated centrally in the field are Arthur and his household warriors, counsellors and servants. On either side of Arthur are Bedwini, his bishop, and Gwarthegydd ap Caw. Before him stands his champion Elphin, while his servitor Eirin, and Earl Cadwr, who arms the king, stand ready to accoutre and equip Arthur. Behind the king is Caradawg ap Llyr Marini, his chief counsellor. Arthur's horseman, Cai, rides among the host, dressed in his white and red colours.

This story makes much of colour, detail and equipment, which might be overlooked as a story-teller's convention. However, we find that these colours and details are very exact as well as visually compelling. The tents and mounts, colours and emblematic beasts of the separate messengers who come to Arthur and Owain all bear investigation.

The messengers who come to Owain and the tents from which they come are:

Selyf – from a white, red-topped tent, flying the black serpent

Gwgawn – from a yellow tent, flying the red lion

Gwres – from a spotted yellow tent, flying the golden eagle

The messengers who come to Arthur and the mounts on which they ride are:

Blathaon – on a dapple-grey horse, helmet crested by a yellow-red leopard

Rhufawn – on a white horse, helmet crested by a yellow-red lion

Hefeidd – on a black horse, helmet crested by a griffin with a stone of power in its head

We note that except for Gwres, who bears a severed head on his spear, Owain's messengers are on foot and carry only swords, while Arthur's messengers are all mounted with swords and spears. Arthur's men bear beasts of royalty upon their helms. Gwgawn, Owain's second messenger, comes from a tent flying what will become Owain's emblem in *Owain*; when he has overcome the Lady of the Fountain's husband, Luned arms him with a golden lion shield. The eagle is clearly an emblem of royalty, and as for the tent from which Selyf appears, there we find the colours of Sovereignty clearly arrayed: the white, the red and the black with the serpent over it as a banner. The serpent or dragon is the totemic manifestation of Sovereignty just as much as the other beasts are. We have already noted the connection between the transformatory Goddess and the dragon: we will encounter this again (see p. 240).

These two sets of messengers may represent the different moves that were possible upon the *gwyddbwyll* board: a game which no one has yet successfully reconstructed.[90,104] Owain's messengers in their tents may remind us of rooks or castles, while Arthur's messengers may seem identical with the knights of modern chess, but there can be no such identification, since the two games are culturally far removed from each other.

Arthur closes the triple contest and just manages not to lose his men only by the expedient of squeezing the golden *gwyddbwyll* pieces into dust; otherwise Owain's ravens would have beaten him completely. As the owner of the board, as King of Britain, he calls for the end of the game/battle, and the comical 'rematch' of Badon is planned with as much deliberation as that of any football manager faced with 'match called off' because of bad weather.

The Game of the Goddess is played on many levels. Sometimes she utilizes the formal framework of a *gwyddbwyll* game, as here, but more often she sets up complex quests, tests and contests into which her champions blunder without the least knowledge that they are playing her game at all. It is a case of winner takes all, with the gamble that failure means death. It is a game which Owain is well qualified to enter, and into which Gereint after him finds himself inextricably drawn.

CHAPTER FIVE

THE LADY OF THE FOUNTAIN

What will the naiads . . .
do now, poor things:
            the lady of the *ffynnon*
Es Sitt that moves the *birket*, fays *del lac*, the donnas of the
lyn, the triad-*matres*, the barley-tressed *mamau* and the
grey-eyed *nymphae* at the dry *ffynhonnau* whose *silvae*-office
is to sing:

VNVS HOMO NOBIS
        (PER AQVAM)
RESTITVIS REM.

DAVID JONES
Anathemata

I THE LION AND THE UNICORN

In *The Lady of the Fountain*, or *Owain*, as we shall call this story for
convenience, we perceive the evolution of Owain from Lord of
Ravens to Knight of the Lion. In *The Dream of Rhonabwy*, Owain
appeared as a powerful Otherworldly lord, able to call upon his
mother's people for assistance: in *Gereint and Enid* we will see how
he resumes his Otherworldly guise as King of the Enchanted
Games. In *Owain* he does not stray far from the Celtic earthly
paradise; indeed, we see how he is drawn further into its realms
by becoming the champion of the fountain and the husband of
Sovereignty's representative.

The Lady of the Fountain remains unnamed in the *Mabinogion*, although Chrétien calls her Laudine; she is merely referred to as 'the Countess'. She is, in fact, not the lady of an earthly domain at all, but the powerful mistress of an Otherworldly realm. As we shall see, the real Lady of the Fountain is Sovereignty herself. Like Diana, the goddess of the grove, the Countess needs a champion to guard her fountain; the one who overcomes that champion becomes the new champion and consort of the Countess. We shall speak more of this theme in section II.

Owain and his Countess are represented by the lion and the unicorn in a mythic sense: that same pair of beasts about whom the famous rhyme runs:

> The Lion and Unicorn were fighting for the crown.
> The Lion beat the Unicorn all about the town . . .[50]

These beasts are today the heraldic supporters of the Royal Coat of Arms; the royal lion of England and Scotland and the mystical unicorn of Scotland were adopted as the supporters of James VI's armorial bearings. (The rhyme above referred originally to the manner in which the lion and the unicorn changed sides during their heraldic associations with the crowns of England and Scotland.) These heraldic beasts have their roots in the British consciousness in a deeper sense, for they are totemic of Sovereignty and her champion. In the course of this story Owain acquires a new set of arms as a result of having slain and succeeded the Lady of the Fountain's husband: the golden lion is his new crest. The Lady of the Fountain herself is a representation of Sovereignty, and, as we shall see in both *Gereint and Enid* and *Peredur*, the Goddess is symbolized by both the white hart and the unicorn.

Throughout the course of our study of the relationship between Sovereignty and her champion we note that the Goddess is not submissive, mild and biddable: she is a powerful force, armed with subtle skills and deep wisdom. Here, in *Owain*, we find that the Lady of the Fountain is no exception to the rule. She opposes Owain until he is championed by Luned (pronounced Linnet), who acts in this story as a form of the Black Maiden. Luned is a far more sympathetic character than her mistress, whom she in some senses represents. The struggle of the lion and the unicorn is a perennial one: the lion, Sovereignty's would-be champion, fights the Goddess's proven champion, the unicorn. As we shall see, this is a story in which a number of substitutions take place and chief among them is the exchange of one champion for another.

As we read *Owain*, we are aware of certain lacunae in the text: these may be partially supplied from Chrétien's *Yvain*, which the reader is invited to read for comparison's sake. Hidden within the text also are reflective images which mirror the Otherworldly 'reality' into which Owain falls; these reflections are apparent between the characters of the story, who continually mirror or double for one another.

There are overlaps between *Owain* and *Libeaus Desconus* (see p. 70): both heroes go to champion a lady at the behest of her handmaiden messenger; both overcome a serpent and both rescue a lady from imprisonment or death. Furthermore, both maiden messengers are similarly named. We shall see further parallels between these stories and the folklore version of the Loathly Lady, in which she is enchanted into the form of a monster.

Most remarkable is the striking number of shared themes between *Owain* and the Gawain cycle of stories, in which host and oppressor are one and the same. Tying all these together is the theme of the damsel representing Sovereignty, who presents a talismanic gift to her chosen champion.

The Lady of the Fountain

(1) While Arthur held court at Caerleon upon Usk one day, Owain ap Urien, Cynon ap Clydno and Cai ap Cynyr were talking together, while Gwenhwyfar sewed by the window. There was no gatekeeper, although Glewlwyd Mighty-Grasp acted as one. Arthur felt sleepy and begged his companions to tell stories while he slept. (2) Cynon told a story against himself in which he had ridden seeking adventure. He came to a beautiful land wherein stood a shining fortress where he had been royally entertained. The company there directed his steps to an adventure. They told him to seek a certain mound (3) whereon he would see a great black man with one foot and one eye in the centre of his forehead. This Cynon did. The black forest guardian

demonstrated his sovereignty over the animals of the forest and directed Cynon to (4) a great tree beneath which was a fountain; on the stone next to it was a silver bowl. He was to fill the bowl with water and throw water on the stone. At the sound of thunder, a great shower would fall, stripping the tree of leaves, (5) but a flock of birds would alight and sing. Then a black rider would come and challenge him. All fell out as he had been told: the black rider taxed Cynon with causing the death of many beasts and men because of the shower he had caused to fall. They fought and Cynon was ignominiously overcome.

(6) Owain suggested that they ride and find the place again, but Cai cast aspersions upon him. Gwenhwyfar rebuked him. Just then Arthur awoke, and while the company went in to eat, Owain slipped away. He discovered the place and all befell him as it had to Cynon, but he overcame the black rider by wounding him severely. Giving chase, Owain followed him to a castle where the portcullis was lowered so that Owain and the front half of his horse was within the castle and the back of the horse outside. (7) A girl came and offered her friendship to him. (8) She gave him a ring which, while it was concealed within his fist, would render him invisible. She then led him to a chamber and served him. They heard a cry, followed by an outbreak of lamentation. She told Owain that the lord of the castle, whom Owain had fought, had died and was to be buried. (9) Owain watched from a window as the widow followed her husband to the church. Although she had marred her appearance with mourning, Owain fell in love with her. The girl explained that her mistress was the Countess of the Fountain, and although the lady must loathe Owain, nevertheless the girl would go on his behalf to court the Countess.

(10) The girl, Luned, pleaded with the Countess to accept a new husband. Luned reminded her that her lands could be held only by strength of arms and that they needed a defender quickly to hold the fountain. Luned would go to Arthur's court and procure a warrior forthwith. The Countess gave her reluctant permission. Pretending to go on a journey, Luned returned to her chamber and then came again to her mistress to announce the arrival of a Round Table knight. Luned arrayed Owain (11) in yellow garments bearing the device of a golden lion. The Countess was not convinced by this ruse and called together her retainers to decide what she should do: either that one of them should marry her, or that she should be married to a man from outside their realm. They decided on the latter course and,

amid splendid preparations, (12) she was married to Owain. All the retainers of the Countess swore him fealty.

Three years later Gwalchmai was walking with Arthur, who expressed great sorrow at Owain's absence. Taking a small company, Arthur went to seek Owain. They followed the route of Cynon's story and (13) Cai threw water on the stone. Many of Arthur's servants were slain in the shower. A black rider came, pitched his tent and on the morrow they jousted. First Cai was overcome and then Gwalchmai fought the black rider. The Black Knight recognized Gwalchmai and identified himself as Owain. Both men attempted to relinquish their arms into each other's custody, but neither would accept mastery of the joust. (14) Arthur then bade them give their swords to him. Owain led them back to the castle where he had been preparing a feast in honour of Arthur's foreseen coming for three years. Arthur sent messengers to beg the Countess's leave for Owain to accompany Arthur back to his court, which she reluctantly granted.

While Owain was feasting with Arthur, a woman rode into the hall and dragged the ring from his finger, taxing him with treachery. (15) As she turned to go, Owain recognized Luned and he recovered his memory of what had happened in the Land of the Fountain. Grief-stricken, he set out to wander the four corners of the earth. (16) He grew unkempt and became accustomed to the company of animals. In his wild state he came to the park of the second Countess, where she found him asleep in a weakened condition.

The Countess gave order for his tending. Her damsel anointed him and left a horse and clothing nearby, which Owain took. She then greeted him and told him about the land he was in. Since the Countess was widowed, she had only one house remaining from the depredations of a neighbouring earl. The damsel took Owain back and healed him with the Countess's ointment, despite that lady's annoyance at her handmaiden having used so much.

In three months he was well enough to overcome the earl and offer him as hostage to the Countess, in payment for having used up so much ointment. The earl returned the Countess's lands and property. Although the Countess bade him stay, Owain left to continue his wanderings. (17) He encountered a lion trapped in the cleft of a rock, unable to leave it because of a serpent which leapt up. Owain slew the serpent and found himself followed by the lion as by a greyhound. The lion brought Owain a buck to eat. While they were eating it, Owain heard a cry. (18) It was the voice of Luned. She had been imprisoned in a stone chamber because of a quarrel she had had with two of the Countess's chamberlains concerning Owain, whom they had reviled in her hearing. She had rebuked them and was even now awaiting Owain to defend her, but she had no one to search for him. Owain shared his food with her and then left her, getting directions from her to the nearest castle to shelter.

(19) Owain was served well there, but the company were the saddest he had ever seen. The earl told Owain that the reason was that his two sons had been seized by a marauder who would kill them before their father's eyes unless the earl rendered up his only daughter to him. The giant marauder approached the castle the next morning, and Owain fought him, but the lion helped his master kill the giant. Restoring his sons to the earl, Owain rode off to rescue Luned. He arrived just in time to see two men seizing her to put on a pyre. In order that the fight be fair, Owain locked the lion in Luned's prison, but it burst out and killed both Owain's assailants. They both returned to the Land of the Fountain, where he once again took the Countess to him and they lived together at Arthur's court.

(20) Owain went then to the court of the Black Oppressor, where twenty-four maidens were sadly kept. The Oppressor had killed each of their men. Owain fought him, and the Black Oppressor begged for mercy, since it was prophesied that Owain would overcome him. He would give up his evil ways, cease to be a robber and turn his court into a hostel for both weak and strong. This Owain accepted. He took the twenty-four maidens to Arthur's court, where he was welcomed. Afterwards he returned to his ancestral lands with the 300 swords of Cynferchin, his grandfather and his flight of ravens, who were victorious wherever they went.

Commentary

1. In many early Arthurian tales Arthur's court is not held at Camelot but at Caerleon upon Usk, one of the great legionary cities, as we have already seen in *The Dream of Macsen Wledig*, in which it is called by the Romans Castra Legionum. The insistence upon there being no gatekeeper for so great a court may seem strange. According to *Culhwch and Olwen* Glewlwyd Gafaelfawr is the gatekeeper only on the first of January: the rest of the year his post is filled by Huandaw, Gogigwr, Llaesgymyn and Penpingyon. In *Culhwch and Olwen* it is obvious that Glewlwyd is an ancient figure whose exploits are shared by Arthur. An ancient

Welsh poem, 'Pa Gur', preserves a dialogue between Arthur and Glewlwyd, in which Arthur is obviously the man seeking entrance and Glewlwyd is the porter at the gate, possibly at the fortress of Wrnach the Giant. He is but one of several 'gatekeepers' who appear in *Owain*.[87]

Significantly Arthur sleeps during the relating of Cynon's tale. As we have already seen in *The Dream of Macsen Wledig* and *The Dream of Rhonabwy*, in which part of the action occurs in a dream, Cynon's tale can be seen as a dream of Arthur's. Within this sleep many mysteries are revealed under the aegis of the Sleeping Lord,[84] just as in the myth of the Golden Age, where 'the things which Zeus premeditates, Kronos dreams' (see *Mabon*, p. 54).[111]

Cai fulfils his traditional role as Arthur's butler here by going to fetch Cynon food and drink to sustain him during his telling.

2. Cynon unfolds a tale of an Otherworldly journey undertaken in the supreme hope that he will meet someone who can overcome him or whom he can best in order to prove himself invincible. At the shining fortress he is served by a man dressed in yellow, who is possibly a figure inherited from an Irish story (see section III for a discussion of this theme). Cynon inadvertently insults Gwenhwyfar in his story, saying that the least beautiful of the women attendant upon him at this fortress was more beautiful than Gwenhwyfar arrayed in her best, but the queen does not make any remark, nor do his listeners spring to her defence. This is explainable only if the women in question are faery-women or fays.[58] The insulting of Gwenhwyfar is a recurrent theme in the romances, as we shall see in Chapters Six and Seven.

3. The monstrous black guardian, or Wild Herdsman, whom Cynon encounters springs whole and entire from Celtic mythology. He is a *bachlach* carrying a club, a herder of animals, and, as we shall see, is crucial to our understanding of this story. We are reminded of the figure of Cernunnos from the Gundestrup Cauldron (see *Mabon*, p. 138),[111] except the Wild Herdsman here is a one-legged and one-eyed man. Certainly he seems reminiscent of the father of Goreu in *Culhwch and Olwen*, Custennin, the mighty shepherd who never allows his flock to stray and

whose breath could blast a tree. The Wild Herdsman is an interpreter and guardian, a way-shower of great perspicacity. He shares his role with Merlin in Celto-Arthurian mythology, where Merlin becomes a lord of the forest during his madness and seclusion.[152] See section III.

4. The great tree near which the Wild Herdsman sits is the axial tree of tradition, the tree of knowledge: the *axis mundi* around which are grouped times, dimensions and objects of power within Celtic tradition. Such trees occur within many mythologies. They connect the earthly world with both Underworld and overworld and, in some cultures, have been physically represented as the shaman's ladder. The fountain under this axial tree is a direct descendant of the Celtic Fountain of Knowledge, whose waters enlighten the ignorance of the earth and fructify the gardens of the Otherworld. As we will see in section II, Chrétien and others associated this fountain with the famous Fountain of Barenton in Brittany. We recall also that Rhiannon and Pryderi vanished in a thunderstorm and mist (see *Mabon*, p. 64).[111] The appearance of thunder and rain within the Otherworld represents a reversal of normality, an enchantment which is being worked out.

5. The flock of birds that alights on the tree is of Otherworldly birds akin to both the birds of Rhiannon, which conduct souls to blissful existence in the paradisaical realms of peace, and the birds encountered by both Bran mac Febal and St Brendan in their wondrous voyages[146] which sing of the wonders of paradise.

The Black Knight is nameless in *Owain*, but Chrétien calls him Esclados. He is the champion of the Lady of the Fountain, defending her lands against all comers. At his hands Cynon learns that he is not, after all, the most *puissant* knight he once thought. It is interesting that the Black Knight taxes Cynon with the destruction of both men and beasts who have been caught in the hailstorm. As we shall see, the Wild Herdsman and the Yellow Man have much in common.

6. Cai lives up to his nature as unmannerly churl by insulting Owain's avowal to seek the place. We note that Arthur does not awake until the story is complete. Owain's successful encounter with the Black Knight leaves him in a sad predicament: caught

between two gates, with half a horse under him. It is possible that this incident at the gate is a medieval retelling of an Irish story in which Cu Roi mac Daire has a revolving fortress (see p. 126). There are notable overlaps between *Owain* and the cycle of Irish stories that gave rise to the Green Knight's challenge in Arthurian legend, as we shall see.

7. Owain is befriended by Luned. The role of Luned in *Owain* is hard to accept as she stands. She takes the role of messenger and confidante throughout and is self-effacing with regard to her personal love for Owain. We need to look again at the lady in *Libeaus Desconus* (p. 71) who comes to fetch a champion to free her mistress. That messenger is called Elen. Luned is a variant of the Welsh Eluned, itself a name similar to Elen. The similarity between both women is close enough to warrant further attention.

In later Arthurian literature Luned becomes Linnet; with her sister Lionors, or Lyones, she has more to do with the Orkney clan than with Owain. Linnet, in fact, becomes the wife of Gaheris, while Lionors marries Gareth. Linnet rides to Camelot to fetch a knight to rescue her sister besieged by the Red Knight of the Red Laundes, in much the same way as Elen comes to fetch Libeaus Desconus; like Elen, Linnet is fobbed off with a young, unnamed knight, Beaumains, which is Kay's cruel name for Gareth, who comes to court incognito. The overlaps are easy to find between the early and later stories.[25,92]

In Chrétien, before the literary existence of either of his brothers, Gareth or Gaheris, it is Gawain who loves Lunet. Chrétien makes a play on Lunet's name and on Gawain's reputation as a knight whose strength waxes as the sun comes to midday by referring to them poetically as the moon and the sun.[7]

8. The ring that Luned gives Owain is mentioned in a supplement to the Thirteen Treasures of Britain as a ring of invisibility. In this last property it is similar in function to the thirteenth treasure: the Mantle of Invisibility, which belongs to Arthur and which is also used by Caswallawn to usurp Bran's kingdom.[22] In Malory, Lyones gives Beaumains a ring which saves him from loss of blood.[25] Owain hears three cries of lamentation, the great triple

ochone (mourning-cry) at the death of the Lady of the Fountain's champion-husband.

9. Significantly Owain falls in love with the Countess while she is wretched, grieving and unkempt of appearance, being covered with self-inflicted wounds. In effect he has fallen in love with a Loathly Lady under whose veneer of unloveliness he yet discerns a beautiful woman. As we have seen from the tales concerning the hag aspect of Sovereignty, Owain's avowal of love immediately makes him worthy to replace the Lady's husband.

10. In Chrétien we learn that Lunet is known for her outspokenness;[7] she apparently was sent by Laudine, her mistress, on an errand to Arthur's court and was so rude in her behaviour that no knight would deign to speak with her, save Owain. This archetype, clearly related to the Black Maiden, became known as the *Damoiselle Maldisante*. This incident is absent from *Owain*, but Luned is certainly still very forthright in her speech. We learn, in her harangue of courtship on Owain's behalf, that only a knight of Arthur's court can defend the Fountain.

11. Owain is armed by Luned in the fashion of Celtic heroes who are destined to win the arms of their mother or lady, representing Sovereignty. He also gains a fresh livery: the golden lion. This device is foreign to Owain's native totem of the raven, and it would be interesting to know for certain whether Chrétien's *Yvain*, the Knight of the Lion, suggested it. In the context of our story it is a prophetic arming, since Owain later wins a lion as his companion.

12. This is the only mention of canonical marriage in the whole of the *Mabinogion*. Even in *Gereint and Enid*, Gereint and Enid are laid in Arthur and Gwenhwyfar's chamber and there they sleep together; while in *Peredur*, Peredur seems to form several casual liaisons of varying degrees of intimacy. Owain's marriage lasts three years without interruption.

13. This incident in which Cai purposely provokes the hero of our story and is then justly overcome in combat appears in all three romances. Similarly in all three Gwalchmai (Gawain)

appears to make peace and tactfully to approach the hero. Gwalchmai's role seems to be that of intermediary between the harsh reality of Cai's bluster and the fay, often distracted air adopted by the hero acting under Otherworldly influence. Significantly Gwalchmai intervenes in order to help the hero, whether it be Owain, Geraint or Peredur, to express himself. This usually occurs at a crucial point when the hero is defending Sovereignty in some manner, as Owain is here by acting as the Countess's champion. Owain has adopted a third set of colours; he has become the new Black Knight of the Fountain. Perhaps because they start fighting at the stroke of noon (the time of Gwalchmai's greatest strength; it diminishes after noon), neither Gwalchmai nor Owain can beat the other.

Gwalchmai is described in Triad 75 as one of Three Men of the Island of Britain who were most courteous to Guests and Strangers.[38] He is perhaps helped in this regard by the fact that Triad 91 also names him as one of Three Fearless Men of the Island of Britain.

14. Owain virtually relinquishes his championship of the Fountain into the hands of Arthur: 'Give me your swords,' says Arthur, 'then neither of you will have overcome the other.' There seems to be something of a lacuna in the text here, for the implication is that Owain is granted leave to remain with Arthur for three months, but stays for three years instead. In Chrétien, Laudine lets Owain go for a year and gives him a ring, which acts as a shield against wounds.[7] In both stories, Owain stays away longer than the time agreed.

There is here an echo of a theme common in medieval romances: the temporary absence of the hero from his faery mistress. This theme is central to many medieval stories and *lais*, including *Désiré*[134] and *Lanval*,[59] in which an earthly knight has an assignation with a faery woman at a spring. They cohabit for a while, but the hero fails to return or vouchsafes the name of his mistress to others – a thing he has sworn never to do, since it also reveals her nature.

In Chrétien, at this point in the story, Gwalchmai launches into a long speech about the inadvisability of staying so closely yoked to a woman to the detriment of manly deeds.[7] Of course this theme accords closely with the theme of Sovereignty, who has here become a faery woman. Medieval romancers failed to handle this theme according to its original lights and recast the hero as a henpecked man tied to a woman's apron-strings in many tales, including, as we will see, *Erec and Enid*, Chrétien's version of *Geraint and Enid*. We will take this up again in section II.

15. It is clear that Owain's has been an Otherworldly sojourn, since as soon as he returns with Arthur to court, he totally forgets his adventure and that its outcome resulted in his being married! It is not until Luned strips the ring from his finger that Owain remembers all that has passed. It would appear that the text has a lacuna here since the ring in question has not proved to be a ring of invisibility, although the wearer is invisible only if he hides the stone. It is likely that, as in Chrétien,[7] the Countess gave her husband a ring on their parting to act as a remembrance and magical communication between them, in much the same manner as the Beast gives Beauty a ring in the French faery story. But Owain wears the token unworthily, failing to honour the bestower of the ring until Luned takes it from his hand. Like Arthur's ring in *The Dream of Rhonabwy*, Owain's is a ring of remembrance. However, the ring of invisibility, like the Otherworldly silver branch given to Bran mac Febal,[146] may function as a token of Sovereignty's faith in her champion: while he possesses it, he is in communion with her.

16. With full memory restored to him, Owain suffers the pangs of remorse and self-reproach. The madness into which he now falls is a classical reaction to shock in Celto-Arthurian legend. Owain, like Lancelot and Merlin, who also go insane temporarily, is stripped of every normal faculty, resigning his position as knight and champion of the Fountain in order to live among wild beasts.[107,149] This period of insanity has its healing properties, however. The curative effect of living close to nature is adopted by Celto-Arthurian madmen as a form of therapy, in which they regard the wonders of creation and understand their own relationship with both plant and animal life. Owain becomes, in

effect, a wild man, familiar to the medieval mind as a wood-wose: a species of mythical being thought to haunt the great forests which still covered Europe at that time. Hair grows all over his body, like an animal.

The subsequent incident, in which Owain is discovered by a countess and her damsel, is likely to confuse the reader. Does the story-teller, who leaves both ladies unnamed, intend us to understand that the woman who finds Owain is the same as the Lady of the Fountain, and that her damsel is Luned? If we refer to Chrétien, it would appear not, for the lady who finds him is called the Lady of Noroison.[7] Whatever the common source for both *Owain* and *Yvain*, there is a point of confusion here.

Owain receives exactly the same treatment as in the former episode when he arrived at the Countess's castle: he is tended by the maiden, given arms and made well without the Countess's knowledge. The incident of the healing ointment is interesting. In Chrétien, the Lady of Noroison gets her lotion from Morgan le Fay, who, as we will see (p. 143), is perhaps also responsible for healing Gereint in a later story. The duplication of incidents attests to a lost original story, in which Owain's finding of the Fountain and his championship of the Lady is paralleled by his restoration to sanity and championship of Sovereignty in a more direct sense. At this remove it is impossible to piece together the evidence. It is likewise possible that both countesses and their maidens are intended to be the same women, only in another form. The important thing is that the women effect Owain's partial restoration to sanity.

17. Having accepted the second countess's championship and then relinquished her hand in marriage, Owain rides on to champion a lion. Scholars have written endless commentaries on how Owain's lion is derived from all kinds of medieval and classical originals, including Androcles' lion or St Jerome's.[46,127] Certainly the lion enjoyed the status of 'king of the beasts' from medieval times onwards, and the epithet 'lion' was applied to many kings and heroes both historically and in literature. Perhaps we can approach the appearance of the lion from another viewpoint.

Owain at this point is hardly reconciled to human company. He has only recently emerged from a state of semi-bestiality and is in the process of winning back self-respect, regaining the high status he once enjoyed through force of arms. Luned once armed him with the heraldic device of the lion, which he forsook to wear the black livery of the Lady of the Fountain. Within this story an extraordinary transformation is happening: Owain, having once succeeded to the place of the Black Knight, now succeeds to the role of the Wild Herdsman – the master of beasts. Only Owain fulfils the dual roles of Knight of the Fountain and Wild Herdsman in one, lifting them out of their former alignment and ennobling them with all his personal qualities. In so doing Owain has assimilated the roles of his challengers and, by means of his madness, now emerges as a new man (see Figure 5.2, p. 129).

18. The imprisonment of Luned and her fortuitous discovery by Owain is very sketchily dealt with in our story. In Chrétien, Yvain inadvertently hears, from her own lips, of Lunet's love for him. But both stories tell that, despite Lunet/Luned's impending execution, Yvain/Owain rides off to find shelter for the night. It is possible that in the proto-story Owain was totally disenchanted from his madness by the sound of Luned's voice; for so is Lanzelet released from his enchantment in Ulrich von Zatzikhoven's story.[42]

19. The next incident is drawn from a common Celtic theme, the *Ridere gan Gaire* (The Knight without Laughter), in which the impending demise or already accomplished death of a knight's offspring causes him such sorrow that he is unable to make merry.[68] This incident occurs in *Peredur* also (see p. 176). Luned's plight is thus considerably heightened during this intervening episode. In Chrétien, Yvain similarly rescues the knight's children, who are discovered to be Gawain's nephews and niece. Chrétien also tells a long story about a pair of sisters, the elder of which succeeded to their father's estates, totally disinheriting her younger sister, who went in search of a champion. This incident is paralleled by the story of the two sisters Lyones and Linnet in Malory.[25] Lyones and Linnet seem to be later identities for Laudine and Lunet in Chrétien, and for the Lady of the Fountain and Luned in *Owain*.

20. The last episode of our story is paralleled in Chrétien by Yvain's adventures at the Castle of Evil Adventure, where the King of the Isle des Puceles (Castle of Maidens), in order to save his own life, promised a tribute of maidens every year to a pair of diabolic brothers. These maidens were retained at the Castle of Evil Adventure and there were made to embroider in a kind of Otherworldly sweat-shop for the devils' profit. Yvain rescues them. This episode is reminiscent of *Libeaus Desconus*, in which Mabon and Yrain keep the Lady of Sinadoun captive. In Chrétien's *Perceval* we find a similar Castle of Maidens which Gawain visits (see p. 266).

Owain in our story defeats the Black Oppressor, whose identity, as we shall see, is not hard to discover. If we turn back to the beginning of *Owain* and read about the shining fortress where the Yellow Man plays the Hospitable Host and where maidens sit round the hero embroidering, we will experience a sense of *déjà vu*. For the Black Oppressor is none other than the Yellow Man in another guise. This duplication of characters is all part of the mirror image set up between the earthly realms and the Otherworld. It is perhaps more clearly seen in *Peredur*, but *Owain* is full of astounding reflections which are hard to ignore.

II REX NEMORENSIS

It has been pointed out by numerous scholars that *Owain* bears traces of a famous Roman myth: that of *Rex Nemorensis*, the King of the Sacred Grove. The sanctuary of Arician Diana, near Lake Nemi, was protected by a priest who remained in office only as long as he could fend off other contenders. In the sanctuary grew a tree whose branches might never be broken, save by a slave who, in order to become a worthy contender for the office of Diana's priest, had to tear off a bough.[73]

While we might conveniently call this myth by its Roman title, we must remember that this story is not confined to one culture but does indeed occur frequently within Celtic and Arthurian sources. That there may have been a marriage made between Latin and Celtic myths during medieval times is very probable. The cult of Diana, the huntress and protectress of women, spread speedily throughout Europe with the expansion of the Roman Empire; native cults of goddesses of the sacred grove were long established in all lands of Celtic occupancy. The most famous of these woods, complete with its own spring, was that of the Brocéliande in Brittany, where the Fountain of Barenton was celebrated in local tradition and medieval romance. Here Morgan, Nimue, Niniane and Diana had their meeting in one archetype.[134]

Chrétien, if he was indeed working from a British original, made his spring conform to the verbatim reports of Barenton, even making his whole story of *Yvain* cross the Channel at one point, without explanation, in order to encompass this phenomenon. The fountain or spring was well known to medieval writers; Alexander Neckam, the twelfth-century scholar, wrote:

> It is said that there is a fountain such that if water is drawn from it and thrown upon a stone which is near that fountain, a storm arises from the stone . . . much rain suddenly falls, with hail and vehement wind.[96]

The Norman chronicler Wace actually visited the spring in order to see faeries and, while ruefully disappointed in his wish, reported:

> Thither hunters are used to repair in sultry weather; and drawing up some water with their horns, they sprinkle the stone for the purpose of having rain . . .[96]

That the fountain in *Owain* or the Fountain of Barenton have little to do with the historical cult of Arician Diana is obvious, since our spring and stone *generate* rain whereas Diana was worshipped on 13 August in order to invoke her help to *avert* storms injurious to the harvest.[73] The similarities are gratuitous, though they were certainly enhanced by classically minded medieval writers. What of the Lady of the Fountain herself?

What becomes apparent from our reading of the story is that the Countess and Luned correspond to two faces of Sovereignty: the mistress of the Otherworld or inner Sovereignty, and her representative messenger or outer Sovereignty. We will see that this dual identity occurs within the Grail stories also: the Grail messenger corresponds to the dark face of Sovereignty, the wasted land, and the Grail-bearer corresponds to the beautiful face of Sovereignty, the fertile land. The Countess is not able to leave her land, except through the person of Luned, her messenger. But her land cannot be governed except by a worthy champion whom she must find in the earthly realm and bring to the Otherworld. This situation is the theme of countless Celtic and medieval tales wherein the Otherworldly woman has to draw to her realm an earthly man to play the part of her champion or consort.

We have already seen how Bran mac Febal is coaxed to visit the Land of Women (p. 66). There the Otherworldly queen sends one of her maids as a messenger, bearing with her a branch of the paradisaical tree of bliss. Her form and her song are sufficient to incite Bran to set sail. When he arrives, the queen begs him to stay with her, but Bran's men are homesick. She tries to bind him to her by magical threads, but he departs, only to find that time, which in the Land of Women passed pleasantly and easefully, has sped past and all his generation in Ireland are long dead.[146]

From the tradition exemplified above arise the many tales of men who wander into Faeryland, become the consort of the Queen of Faery and there remain with her. Thomas the Rhymer is one such, but his service is concluded after seven years, during which time he learns Otherworldly knowledge.[64] The length of time that the hero spends with the Inner Sovereignty varies greatly, and although he sometimes becomes her champion, unable to leave her until he is bested by another man who becomes her consort, this is not always the case.

The question arises: why does the Goddess of Sovereignty retain certain men in her domain? This is an important question, since it is relevant to all three romances: Owain becomes the Countess's champion; Gereint fights such a champion in the Enchanted Games; Peredur is retained in the service of many mistresses. What strange pattern is being enacted in this retention? What is its purpose?

The classical pattern of Diana and the priests of Nemi is only a partial explanation, and it cannot be totally accommodated within the Celto-Arthurian mode. We are left with the evidence of parallel texts. On the face of it there seem to arise four kinds of re-tention:

A The fostering in Faery of such characters as Lancelot and Mabon as children. Both babies are removed from earthly danger and raised in the Otherworld.

B The tuition of the hero by Otherworldly women or goddesses, as occurs in the stories of Gwion/Taliesin and Peredur.

C The retention of a champion who serves a term but is replaced by another: Mabonograin (in Chrétien's *Erec and Enid*), Lancelot and Owain.

D The retention of an earthly knight or king as the consort of the Otherworldly queen: Arthur and Bran mac Febal. This consort does not return from Faery, at least not within the same life cycle.

It will be seen that this pattern corresponds, with variations, to the Succession of the Pendragons discussed in *Mabon* (p. 164).[111] The roles that Sovereignty takes in each of the four 'imprison-ments' above are as follows:

A The Lady of the Lake and Modron function as mothers to Lancelot and Mabon respectively.

B The Dark Woman of Knowledge appears in her role as teacher to Gwion/Taliesin and Peredur as Ceridwen and the Hag of Gloucester respectively.

C & D To Mabonograin, Bran, Lancelot and Arthur and to Owain, Sovereignty appears in her beautiful aspect as Otherworldly queen and consort in the shapes of the Orchard Woman and Morgan. (Though Morgan is not successful in retaining Lancelot as her consort, she does succeed in retaining other medieval heroes including Ogier, Renoart and Alisander l'Orphelin.)[79]

Each of these partnerships demands an exchange of power, by which both earthly and Otherworldly realms are energized. The mother nourishes her fosterling or own child in order that he may become the champion of her rights, just as the Dark Woman of

Knowledge or the Loathly Lady teaches her secrets to her initiates so that her pupils may be empowered to act on her behalf. Knights and heroes who experience this kind of fostering generally prove worthy to be Sovereignty's champion or consort. Those who enter Sovereignty's service are rarely released from it. Theirs is a bargain which goes beyond personal concerns or earthly lifetimes. Her champions may be temporarily released in order to visit the earth once more – as Owain is – or they may be allowed to live their whole lives in the earthly realm as kings in the service of the Outer Sovereignty, the land itself, as Arthur does, only to be drawn back into the paradisaical realms once again at the end of his reign.

The seemingly malicious enmity with which Morgan pursues her half-brother, Arthur, in the later Arthurian stories can be properly understood in this light, as can the mysterious 'imprisonment' of Merlin by Nimue/Viviane. The partnership that both Arthur and Merlin enjoy with the Otherworldly powers is not broken by death. Their whole lives are shot through with miraculous happenings, difficult tests, the averting of dangers and the bestowal of blessings. Neither Arthur nor Merlin is born or dies in the normal way: their conceptions are planned by the Otherworldly powers, their deaths are really passings back into the paradisaical realms. Both men follow the patterns discussed in *Mabon*; Arthur follows the Succession of the Pendragons (*Mabon*, p. 164) while Merlin follows the Poet's Wheel (*Mabon*, p. 127–8).[111]

The pattern is less easily seen in Owain's career from the evidence of this story alone, but it will be seen that he fits into the Succession of the Pendragons. (See Fig. 5.1, p. 121.)

In his last role Owain becomes the master of the Enchanted Games (see p. 129) in *Gereint and Enid*, while his role as champion knight is told in *Owain*. We deduce his role as Mabon from the sixteenth-century oral story of p. 90, which speaks of his conception by Modron (as Morgan) and Urien. We note, too, that Owain follows in his father's footsteps as guardian of the Otherworldly borders of the Goddess's realm, for Urien, as we saw on p. 93, becomes a guardian of a ford, the Knight of the Black Pine, while Owain likewise guards the Fountain. Both men are defenders of

Owain's Role	Sovereignty appears as	Her role
Mabon (the Wondrous Child destined to be a champion)	Modron/Morgan (in *The Dream of Rhonabwy* and *Macgnimartha Owain*, p. 93)	mother
Pendragon (the champion knight worthy to be king)	Lady of the Fountain (in *Owain*)	consort
Pen Annwn (the withdrawn, Other-worldly King/Guardian of Knowledge)	Orchard Woman (in *Gereint and Enid*)	Otherworldly queen

Figure 5.1: *Owain and the Succession of the Pendragons*

the wells, bound in the service of the primal Goddess of Sovereignty who can change from woman to raven, from beautiful maiden into ravaged hag in a twinkling.

The man who has once dreamt of her or received her token is never again free to be his own man, living an ordinary existence. He is in service both in and out of time. He is bound to come at the call of his Otherworldly mistress, whatever shape she may assume. It is in such faith that Owain appears in a late ballad as Kemp Owyne.

In this remarkable song Owyne's lady (or sister, in some versions) Isabel is transformed into a worm or serpent by her stepmother. Isabel is doomed to remain thus until Owyne returns from overseas and gives her three kisses. He comes and she bids him kiss her, but he is warned to beware touching her, either tail or fin. She gives him three tokens in exchange for three kisses: a belt, a ring and a sword that will prevent his blood from being spilled.

> He stepped in, gave her a kiss,
> The royal brand he brought him wi';
> Her breath was sweet, her hair grew short,
> And twisted nane about the tree,
> And smilingly she came about,
> As fair a woman as fair could be.[64]

We immediately notice the likeness of this story to the original Sovereignty transformation by means of a kiss and pledge. Like Libeaus Desconus, Owyne is able to free his mistress from enchantment only by means of the *fier baiser*. Her gift of talismanic tokens brings us immediately back to *Owain*, in which Luned gives Owain a ring when he is in danger. We remember also that Owain defeats a serpent which is attacking the chained lion, and that immediately after that incident he hears Luned's voice asking for rescue. Does *Kemp Owyne* preserve a lost part of the original story in which Sovereignty's role was more clearly defined? Around the area of Bamborough (where the ballad and its legend were supposed to have been enacted) schoolgirls used to call boys who championed them against bullies 'the Childe o' Wane', remembering Owain and his role. That was in the last century: a not inconceivable time for Sovereignty's champion to be remembered, if the traditions are as persistent as we have seen.

This ballad marks the strange manner in which both Owain and Gawain are connected, for hidden within *Owain* are a series of mirror-like themes which draw upon the long-standing cycle of Gawain stories and an even more ancient tradition of pre-Celtic origin.

III THE HOSPITABLE HOST

During the course of both *Mabon* and *Arthur* we have had cause to mention the medieval romance of *Sir Gawain and the Green Knight* more than once. It certainly holds more than a few clues to our unravelling of the mystery at the heart of *Owain*. Briefly the story goes as follows.

> While Arthur was holding court at Christmas time, a gigantic Green Knight came into the hall and challenged the court to a Christmas game: the challenger was to behead the Green Knight, providing that in a twelvemonth and a day hence the Green Knight might return the blow. Arthur would have taken up the challenge himself at the dumbstruck silence in his court, but Gawain came forward and offered himself. No sooner had he beheaded the Green Knight when the

knight stood up, gathered up his head and bade Gawain meet him at the Green Chapel in a year and a day.

Gawain started out in search of the place late in the year and arrived at a castle on Christmas Eve, where the lord, Sir Bertilak, and his lady made him welcome. In attendance on the lady, and held in great honour, was an aged crone, her ugliness richly adorned with fine clothes and jewels. Gawain agreed to stay until New Year's Eve and be led to the nearby Green Chapel. In the interim he and Bertilak agreed to an exchange: Gawain would rest at home with Bertilak's beautiful wife, and Bertilak would go hunting; each man would exchange what each had won during the day.

The Lady Bertilak visited Gawain's bedchamber three times. They exchanged courtesies, pretending that Gawain was a prisoner and she his captor. Gawain offered her his knightly service and assured her that she was his sovereign lady. She kissed him on each occasion, which kiss Gawain dutifully gave to Sir Bertilak on his return in exchange for the game obtained in his hunting. (From each beast slaughtered, Bertilak offered 'the raven's fee' – the piece of gristle adhering to the breastbone, which huntsmen threw to the carrion.) On the third occasion the lady offered Gawain a ring, which he refused, but she persuaded him to accept her girdle made of green silk, which protected its wearer from death. Although Gawain rendered Bertilak the kisses, he hid the gift of the green girdle.

On the day appointed, Gawain was directed by Bertilak to the Green Chapel. He saw a mound beside a roaring stream, which had an entrance at one end and a hole in either side: this he took to be the place. The Green Knight emerged from the 'chapel' and Gawain bent down for the blow. He made two feints with the axe and just nicked Gawain's neck with the third stroke. He then revealed himself as Sir Bertilak. Gawain's whole visit had been a test of fidelity, and the third blow was because he had concealed the green girdle. Bertilak likewise revealed that the old crone's identity was 'Morgan the goddess', and that her purpose in sending Bertilak as Green Knight to the court of Arthur was to drive the knights mad and to terrify Guinevere to death. He commended Gawain as the most courageous and truest of knights and invited him to return to the castle. Gawain refused and returned to Camelot where he told the shameful account of his doings to much laughter. Gawain said he would henceforth wear the girdle to remind him of this event and keep himself humble. Arthur announced that all knights of the Round Table should likewise wear a green baldric as a special honour.[31]

There are, of course, many similarities between the two stories. The point of the challenge is that only the bravest and most worthy knight can be successful and that the Green Knight is the messenger and agent of Morgan. The two women, Lady Bertilak and Morgan, represent the two aspects of Sovereignty, with Lady Bertilak behaving in an intimate fashion with Gawain, as Luned does in her attendance upon Owain. Gawain accepts a talismanic token, though here he refuses the ring. The Green Knight's appearance at the Green Chapel is overwhelmingly reminiscent of the Wild Herdsman at the mound.

There are two 'champions' present in this story. Bertilak is working on behalf of Morgan. The text tells us he is an elderly man, implying that he is a champion of long standing in Morgan's service. This is further hinted at in Bertilak's gift of the 'raven's fee' when he is out hunting: we have already seen how Morgan/Modron's totemic beast is the raven and that this bird is a frequent symbol for the Dark Woman of Knowledge. Gawain, although he makes a courtly game of it with the lady, champions Lady Bertilak, whom we may see as an aspect of the Goddess of Sovereignty in her beautiful form.

Despite the medieval and Christian overlay of the story, *Gawain and the Green Knight* reveals hidden depths. The Sovereignty theme, which follows Gawain's whole career, is somewhat constrained into the format of enchantment and courtly honour, but it is clear enough. Instead of one figure assuming two different guises as does Bertilak, we have Lady Bertilak and Morgan appearing together as polarized aspects of Sovereignty: the dual identity is preserved only by Bertilak, her former champion. What to Gawain is a shameful incident in his life (paralleling the shame of the self-assertive Cynon in *Owain*) is made into a great honour of chivalry by Arthur, who turns the green girdle into something approaching the Order of the Garter. This last incident brings us squarely back into alignment with the original Sovereignty theme: only worthy champions can serve her or are fit to mate with her. Arthur himself has already wed Sovereignty as king, both mystically with the land and by wedding Guinevere, who acts as Sovereignty's representative in the earthly realm (which would partially explain why Morgan, as the Inner Sovereignty, is often cast in an antagonistic role against Guinevere, as in *Gawain and the Green Knight*). The Round Table knights, by extension of Arthur's mystical marriage, are all entitled to wear Sovereignty's green girdle as a badge of their king's allegiance and honour.

Gawain's own special duty in the service of the Goddess is dealt with more fully in another book,* but the poet of *Gawain and the Green Knight* has this to say about Gawain's future armorial bearing – the pentacle or endless knot which is the device he bears after the game:

> First he was found faultless in his five wits,
> Then the fellow failed not in his five fingers.
> All his faith on earth was in the five wounds
> Of Christ on the cross, as the creed doth tell.
> Where'er this Man in melée was placed
> His thoughts were upon them above other things;
> So that all his force he found in the five joys
> That the Fair Queen of Heaven had felt in her child.
> For this cause had the Knight in comely fashion
> On the inside of his shield her image depicted,
> That when he viewed it his valour never failed.[31]

After the game:

> On his shining shield shaped was that knot,
> All with red gold upon red gules
> Called the pure pentangle among the people of lore. (ibid.)

It will be seen that Gawain does not alter his allegiance in any way. He serves the Blessed Virgin and, like Arthur in the earliest texts, carries her image on his shield, which gives him courage. He merely exchanges the Christian for the pagan image of the five-fold pentacle, which is here the badge of Sovereignty herself.

We must return to Owain's role within our story. Although certain passages of *Owain* are doubtless lost, a very clear pattern emerges from the remaining text. Loomis has cited the similarities

---

* John Matthews, *Gawain: Knight of the Goddess* (Aquarian, 1990).

between *Owain* and an Irish story from the Ulster cycle, *Bricriu's Feast*.[8] It is fortunate that we have the evidence of this story, since it is the lineal forerunner of *Sir Gawain and the Green Knight*.

In *Bricriu's Feast*, the heroes of Ulster are set against each other to contend for the sovereignty of the 'Hero's Portion' – a cut of meat awarded only to the best warrior. Bricriu incites their jealousy and contention, being a satirist and a twisted man, justly avoided by most of Ulster society. [We have already mentioned his likeness to Efnissien in *Mabon*, p. 41.] So troublesome and uncontrollable do the heroes Conall, Laegaire and Cu Chulainn become that Conchobar sends them to his neighbours, Medbh and Ailell, to decide between them. Although the heroes are awarded a beautifully ornamented cup apiece, none is satisfied and their king sends them on to meet Buide mac mBan (Yellow, son of Fair). He also greets them hospitably but sends them on to Uath mac Imomain (Terror, son of Great Fear), a terrible giant. Again, none is satisfied with the verdict, and they go to Cu Roi mac Daire, whose wife, Blanaid, warmly welcomes them all.

Cu Roi's rath is magically protected: it revolves like a millstone so that no one can find the entrance every night. Each man protects the rath from a giant who comes every night to attack it. Cu Chulainn bests him and makes him promise Cu Chulainn the victory, which is agreed. However there is still dissension among the heroes when they return to Conchobar. As they argue, a great *bachlach* (club-carrying herdsman) comes into the hall and challenges the warriors to a beheading game. One warrior accepts the challenge but is dashed to discover that the *bachlach*'s head returns to his shoulders and that he will come the next night to claim the return blow. In turn the *bachlach* offers the challenge to Conall and Laegaire, who fail to meet their return appointments. Only Cu Chulainn, in the full sight of his people and king, bends his head for the return stroke. The *bachlach* proclaims Cu Chulainn the champion worthy to have sovereignty over all other warriors. Then the *bachlach* vanishes. It was Cu Roi mac Daire who in that guise had come to fulfil the promise he had given to Cu Chulainn.[8]

Again we see the immediate similarities that link *Bricriu's Feast* with *Sir Gawain and the Green Knight*, but more interesting are the parallels between *Bricriu's Feast* and *Owain*, for they are certainly present. The part of Bricriu is played by Cai in *Owain* who, similarly, tries to cause dissension between knights. The figure of Sovereignty is present in both Medbh, the Queen of Connacht, and in Blanaid, Cu Roi's wife, who, as we saw in *Mabon*, p. 49,[111] rejects Cu Roi in favour of Cu Chulainn in a later story (cf. Chapter Nine).

The heroes are hospitably entertained by a Yellow Man, just as Owain and Cynon are when they enter the Otherworldly realms for the first time. And, like the Ulster heroes, both encounter a terrible figure immediately afterwards. In the Irish story, terrible giants are reduplicated at every angle of the story, but they are similarly described as the *bachlach*, whom they all mirror. While Cu Roi's wife entertains them, Cu Roi himself returns as the giant who threatens the rath, so he is both host and aggressor, like Bertilak. (Rachel Bromwich has noted that Bertilak is derived from the Irish *bachlach*.)[38] The turning rath whose gate can never be found after sunset is possibly the origin of the portcullis incident in *Owain*. The beheading game, which in *Sir Gawain and the Green Knight* happens in the Green Chapel and in *Owain* is restricted to a combat at the Fountain, happens in full view of the court, who cannot dispute the outcome that Cu Chulainn alone has the sovereignty of warriorkind.

This text further explicates the mysterious appearance of Glewlwyd at the beginning of *Owain*, who is present in such a gratuitous way. When the *bachlach* comes into the hall he utters these words:

> Neither in Erin nor in Alba nor in Europe nor in Africa nor in Asia, including Greece, Scythia, the Isles of Gades, the Pillars of Hercules, and Bregon's Tower have I accomplished the quest on which I have come.[8]

These words are familiar to us from *Culhwch and Olwen*, in which Glewlwyd goes to ask Arthur's permission for Culhwch to enter the hall:

> I have been also in Europe, and in Africa, and in the islands of Corsica, and in Caer Brythwch, and Brythach, and Verthach; and I was present when formerly thou didst conquer Greece in the East. And I have been in Caer Oeth and Annoeth, and

Caer Nevenhyr; nine supreme sovereigns, handsome men, saw we there, but never did I behold a man of equal dignity with him who is now at the door of the portal.[23]

Another lost part of the *Mabinogion*'s riddle falls into place as we compare these words, for as Cu Roi defends Conchobar's kingship by testing the sovereignty of his warriors, so Glewlwyd defends Arthur's kingship from the incursion of unworthy men into his hall. Both Cu Roi and Glewlwyd are gatekeepers of ancient kind and have a direct bearing on the role of Owain as champion of the Fountain.

The parallels between the three stories can be found in Figure 5.3 where the reader can appreciate them at a glance. It will be seen that Owain passes through a number of encounters and assimilations of roles. He first meets the Yellow Man, who is the hospitable host who welcomes him to the borders of the Otherworldly realms of adventure. He next meets the Wild Herdsman, who shows him the way to the combat of the Fountain where, finally, he meets the Black Knight, the current champion of the Countess. Thereafter Owain succeeds to each of these roles. He himself becomes an hospitable host to Arthur and his men, even acknowledging that he has been preparing a feast for this occasion for three years. He becomes mad on leaving the realms of the Countess and befriends the wild beasts, growing hair all over his body in likeness with their condition. Like the Wild Herdsman he discovers an ability to master animals, especially the lion, traditionally believed to be the king of the beasts. He takes over the role of Black Knight as defender of the Fountain and husband of the Countess. But, before the story ends, he is instrumental in establishing the Black Oppressor as a hospitable host who will aid wayfarers, rather than attack them.

There is a pleasing circularity and reflection of images throughout the story.

Although the aspect of the beheading game is absent from *Owain*, the Enchanted Games of *Gereint and Enid* are a reflection of this theme, for, as we will see, the champion of the orchard beheads his opponents. And it is consistent that Owain, like Bertilak in *Sir Gawain and the Green Knight*, should be portrayed as

	Owain	Bricriu's Feast	Sir Gawain and the Green Knight
Purpose of Adventure	to find an adventure which only the best knight can fulfil	to gain sovereignty of one hero over all other warriors	to defend the sovereignty of Arthur's kingship; the outcome also determines the best knight
Sovereignty's Game	Enchanted Games (in *Gereint and Enid*)	beheading game	beheading game
Hospitable Host	The Yellow Man	Cu Roi and Buide mac mBan	Sir Bertilak
Talismanic Token	Ring of Invisibility/ring which guards wearer from bloodshed	cups awarded to each hero	green girdle which guards wearer from death
Guardian of Sovereignty's Realms	Wild Herdsman	Bachlach and Uath	Green Knight
Goddess of Sovereignty	Lady of the Fountain	Medbh	Morgan
Her Messenger/ Representative	Luned	Blanaid	Lady Bertilak

Figure 5.2: *The Game of Sovereignty in Celto-Arthurian Tradition*

the reluctant and ageing gamesmaster in that story. An exchange takes place between Owain and the Black Knight just as the Black Oppressor becomes the Hospitable Host. Is it possible that the Yellow Man of Owain's first encounter is, like Sir Bertilak, a host who is also an aggressor? From the evidence of our parallel stories it looks likely.

We perceive another pattern arising from this story, which is a clue to the Sovereignty tradition. Just as Sovereignty assumes two forms, so does her champion. He is both hospitable host and champion, presenting an ordinary countenance and a darker, threatening face. Owain is not exempt from this pattern of behaviour, for, though he tries to resume his former life with Arthur's court, he plunges into madness rather than maintain his guise as Black Knight, who must attack and kill all comers to the Fountain or be killed himself. By a circuitous route he is able to overcome his destiny for a short while, but in the end he must appoint a proxy champion. Owain avoids his destiny by handing over the sovereignty of the Fountain to Arthur as supreme over-lord and king, for Arthur is also Sovereignty's man. But, as we shall see in the next chapter, Owain returns to his post as King of the Enchanted Games: no longer fighting himself, but still opera-tive through his proxy champion. This is a pattern repeated throughout the Arthurian legends by Arthur himself, who ceases to ride out or hazard his own person in single combat: he appoints several knights (usually his nephews) to act on his behalf.

Below the many layers of this tradition is a pre-Celtic duality left over from a former time. In this tradition the Wild Herdsman or *bachlach* together with the Dark Woman of Knowledge in her many guises rule in the native or tribal Underworld as King and Queen of the inner realms of knowledge. We have already spoken of their role in *Mabon*, p. 144.[111] Their persistence throughout the *Mabinogion* in various roles is sufficient to point to an earlier level of tradition. They are the same couple who left the deep lake in Ireland, bearing with them the Cauldron of Rebirth. They are the primal parents of Britain's native mystery tradition, the inner guardians of knowledge and wisdom (see Chapter Eight). Within *Owain* we see them still in their developed guises as the

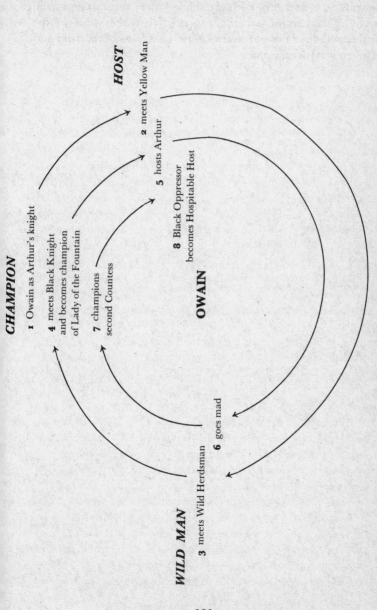

Figure 5-3: *The Figures of Champion, Host and Wild Man in Owain*

Lady of Sovereignty and her consort, who encompasses many disguises in her service. Both are shapeshifters and can appear in bright or dark forms, according to need. It is they who are the Lion and Unicorn of our inner vision: guardians of the land and its sovereignty for all time.

CHAPTER SIX

GEREINT AND ENID

MORGAN: Daughter, dear daughter oh what are you looking for?
GWENHWYVAR: An apple-tree in an orchard oh that is what I
am looking for.
MORGAN: ... What will you do when you find it, dear daughter?
GWENHWYVAR: I will call out the white stag that runs wild
beneath the branches.

JOHN ARDEN & MARGARETTA D'ARCY
The Island of the Mighty

I THE RITES OF SUMMER

The closest resemblance between Welsh and French traditions can be found in *Gereint and Enid* and Chrétien's *Erec and Enid*. *Erec and Enid* is often called 'the first Arthurian romance' because it was the first work from Chrétien's pen, but he cannot be credited with being the story's 'onlie true begetter'.

Despite the sophisticated courtliness of the story, *Gereint and Enid* reveals a number of more archaic aspects. We discover, for example, that the love of Gereint and Enid is set within a wider context of the Games of Sovereignty, wherein the White Hart, the Sparrowhawk contest and the Enchanted Games are separate tests at which the hero must succeed. Lying somewhere beneath the surface of the early part of the story are traces of the

Abduction of Gwenhwyfar – a variant of a once popular theme for spring and summer revels. Gwenhwyfar's position as the Flower Bride or Spring Maiden is consistent throughout Arthurian tradition and is often hinted at, as here.

Without an understanding of the mythic archetypes and patterns underlying *Gereint and Enid* it is impossible to form a fair judgement of the story; without them, Gereint himself is merely a bully on the make, and Enid a wilting violet. Certainly Gereint undergoes radical changes in attitude throughout the story, especially with regard to Enid, whom he eventually comes to value in a more mature light; but we cannot read this story as 'social realism' with modern psychological insight, because that is not its true context nor the story-teller's intention.

Enid goes from rags to riches in quick succession, but her transformation has less to do with her marketable value as a wife than with her role within the story as Sovereignty's representative. Although Chrétien rationalized the original story to eradicate its coarser elements, it is obvious that the adventures of Gereint or Erec take place against an Otherworldly backdrop where faery women, dwarfs and black knights exert their influence on the world of humankind.

Gereint and Enid is undoubtedly the clearest of the three romances to uncover, because Chrétien's *Erec and Enid* is virtually a counterpart to the Welsh text: what is missing in one is supplied in the other. Chrétien's boast that *Erec and Enid* – the tale that most professional story-tellers fragment and corrupt – shall be remembered as long as Christendom endures may well be warranted. It gives us pieces of the pattern surrounding Sovereignty's empowerment of men and women more clearly than many texts within the *Mabinogion*.

It is perhaps the most human story, because it deals, on all levels, with the mutual love and trust that should exist between partners, whether those partners are man and woman, king and queen, or the king and his land. The prime symbol of this love is the White Hart, which appears at the beginning of the story and which acts as the Goddess's messenger, summoning Arthur and his men to the chase. Its appearance in both Irish and Breton texts helps us locate mythic details which are common to *Erec and Enid* and *Gereint and Enid*.

Innerworld Roles and Designations: Represented By:

Mythic level	Supreme and Champion	Sovereignty	Mabonograin and Orchard Woman
Archetypal level	Summer King	and Summer Queen	Arthur and Gwenhwyfar
Mundane level	Untried Champion	and Spring Maiden	Gereint and Enid

Figure 6.1: *The Mythic Structure of* Gereint and Enid

The appearance of the Otherworldly orchard at the end of the story gives us a rare view of Sovereignty surrounded by her regalia, holding court, as it were, sitting in judgement on her champions. The Orchard Woman appears in many texts, which will be further discussed in Chapter Nine along with that mysterious incident of the Enchanted Games which Chrétien terms 'the Joy of the Court'. Owain appears again, a much more mature figure than in the former chapter, as the master of the Enchanted Games, which Gereint undergoes in a great Celtic *tour de force* that restores him to his senses, to his sovereignty over his lands and to the fair and long-suffering Enid once more.

Gereint and Enid

(1) Arthur held court at Caerleon upon Usk one Whitsun. Whenever his court assembled for a major feast, thirteen churches were set aside for their use: one each for Arthur, Gwenhwyfar, the steward Odiar the Frank, and their companions; and one each for Arthur's nine captains, especially Gwalchmai. Glewlwyd Mighty-Grasp was gatekeeper at only one festival, sharing his duties with seven others. (2) On Whit Tuesday a forester of Arthur's, Madawg from the Forest of Dean, brought news of a pure white stag that had been seen. Arthur gave orders to hunt it. (3) Gwenhwyfar begged to watch the hunt. Gwalchmai suggested that whoever was successful in cutting off the stag's head should present it to his lover. Arthur rode forth early, but Gwenhwyfar slept late. (4) With only her maid, the queen rode out alone, when they met with Gereint out riding; he agreed to accompany the queen. They met with a dwarf bearing a whip, and a richly dressed woman in the company of a mud-spattered knight of

great size. Gwenhwyfar's maid asked the dwarf who the people were, but he refused to speak with one so low-born and struck her across the face with his whip.

(5) Gereint rode to the maid's defence and was struck by the dwarf. As he was unarmed he forbore to punish the dwarf and got Gwenhwyfar's permission to ride after the knight. He rode after the party and saw them enter a castle in a walled town. (6) He found lodgings for himself in a run-down hall outside the town. The household consisted of an old man and woman dressed in ragged, once-fine clothing, and a beautiful maiden who tended to the needs of Gereint and his horse herself. After they had sent out for good food for their guest, (7) the old man told Gereint that he had once been earl of the castle in the town, but that he lost the title and lands to his nephew. Gereint asked about the preparations of armoured men he had seen in the town. (8) He was told that there was to be a game tomorrow which the young earl played: two forked sticks would be put in the ground, with a silver rod resting on them, on which a sparrowhawk would be set. Every man had to bring his lady and joust for the sparrowhawk. The knight whose dwarf insulted Gereint had won it two years running. If he won a third time he would be known as the Knight of the Sparrowhawk. The old man offered his own armour and horse for Gereint's use, but warned him that he could not enter the tournament without a lady. (9) Gereint asked if he might enter the joust in honour of the old man's daughter. He promised to love and serve her loyally if he survived. The girl's father consented. They all rose early to make the challenge to the presumptive Knight of the Sparrowhawk, and Gereint jousted with him. The old man acted as Gereint's squire, and his family cheered Gereint on. He offered Gereint the spear which he had been given when he was knighted; he was able to unhorse his opponent thus, and they fought on foot. (10) Seeing Gereint wounded and flagging, the old man urged Gereint to remember the insult to Gwenhwyfar. He was thus able to disable his opponent who begged for mercy. Gereint would only grant it if the knight made good the insult to the queen in person. (11) Gereint asked his opponent's identity; he was revealed as Edern ap Nudd.

The young earl invited Gereint to his castle, but he refused and returned with the old man who was called Ynwyl. The young earl sent his servants to furnish Ynwyl's court with food and clothing. (12) Gereint forbade the maiden to wear anything but her shift and mantle until they came to Arthur's court where Gwenhwyfar would dress her. Gereint was able to reinstate Ynwyl to his lands and titles, and with Ynwyl's daughter he rode off to Arthur's court.

(13) Meanwhile, Arthur had been hunting the White Hart. His own hound, Cafall, cornered the beast and Arthur beheaded it himself. Cadyrieth noticed that Gwenhwyfar was unaccompanied and Arthur gave order for her to be accompanied home by Gildas ap Caw and the clerics of the court. (14) There was dispute over who should have the head; Gwenhwyfar made everyone wait until Gereint came home. Edern, his lady and dwarf arrived and submitted themselves to the queen, and told the whole story of events so far. (15) Gwenhwyfar forgave him and Arthur took sureties for Edern himself, along with Caradawg ap Llyr, Gwallawg ap Llenawg, Owein ap Nudd, Gwalchmai and others. (16) He also bade Morgan Tud, his physician, attend Edern. Gwenhwyfar's watchmen warned of Gereint's approach and Gwenhwyfar thanked him for avenging her. (17) Gereint introduced her to the maiden in whose person the queen was avenged. The maiden went with Gwenhwyfar to her chamber and was there attired according to her rank. The king and queen themselves gave up their bedroom for Gereint and his maiden. (18) The queen proposed that Enid be given the Hart's head. The couple remained at court engaged in tournaments and companionship for three years.

(19) Word came from Gereint's father, Erbin, in Cornwall that Arthur should send back Gereint to defend his lands, as his father was ageing. (20) Arthur allowed Gereint to go, accompanied with a host from the court. (21) Erbin relinquished the rule of his lands into his son's hands. Cadyrieth listened to the suppliants and Gereint received the homage of the Cornishmen. Gereint's companions advised him on his best method of ruling.

(22) Gereint's reputation had spread so far that he no longer exerted himself, preferring to stay in his court with Enid. His retainers grew discontented. Erbin challenged Enid as to whether she was not the cause of Gereint's lethargy. She denied this. One morning, while they were in bed, Enid woke, lamenting her husband's lapse from deeds of greatness. Gereint awoke and, seeing her tears, assumed that she was in love with another. (23) He ordered that horses be brought for them and that Enid should wear her worst riding habit. He swore she should not return until she saw that he had not lost his strength. He left the realm in Erbin's hands and mounted his horse, telling Enid to ride out ahead. (24) Whatever she saw or heard about him, she was to remain silent until he spoke first.

Enid overheard robbers planning to attack them and warned Gereint. He rebuked her and fought off the robbers, taking their armour and horses. This happened twice more, until there were twelve horses laden with armour. They met a boy taking food to the mowers in the fields and were fed by him. He went to the town and told the Brown Earl about them. The Earl later persuaded Gereint to lodge with him. Seeing how badly Enid was treated, the Brown Earl encouraged her to love himself and forsake Gereint. Enid asked him to come and carry her off, as though she were agreeable. While Gereint slept she set his armour ready and woke him to warn him. Although angry, he readied himself, and they left their hostel, leaving eleven horses and armour as payment. The Brown Earl and eighty men followed them, and Enid, seeing the dust of their pursuit, warned Gereint, but he ignored her. Gereint defeated all eighty knights and the Brown Earl and they set off on their way.

(25) They approached a walled city set in a lovely valley which, they were told, belonged to Gwiffert Petit or Y Brenhin Bychan. Gereint was warned not to cross the bridge and go that way because the Little King allowed no knight on his lands without challenging him. Shortly, a little armoured man encountered them, challenging Gereint who overcame him. The Little King begged mercy and bade him rescue him if ever he met with trouble. Refusing the Little King's invitation to come to his court, Gereint rode on, although sorely wounded. (26) While they rested in a forest, they heard hunting horns and the approach of Arthur's court. They were spotted by a servant and Cai came to investigate. Although he recognized Cai, Cai did not recognize him and Gereint refused his name to Cai and fought him. Cai retreated and Gwalchmai came to see for himself. Although more courteous than Cai, Gwalchmai was soon fighting Gereint and recognized him.

(27) Gereint refused to see Arthur, so his pavilion was set nearer Gereint and Gereint was persuaded to see his cousin. Arthur begged Enid to leave off following her husband but she was determined to follow him still. Gwenhwyfar gave her tending while Morgan Tud saw to Gereint's wounds. They continued on their way the next day. Hearing a scream Gereint went to investigate and found a young woman lamenting her dead knight. Three giants had attacked them. While Enid tended the woman, Gereint set out to find the giants. As he killed the third, his wounds burst open. He staggered back to Enid and collapsed. Hearing her screams, Earl Limwris rode up. He buried the knight and had Gereint borne back to his hall. Although the

Earl thought Gereint dead, Enid thought otherwise. Earl Limwris offered himself as a protector and lover to Enid, but she refused him. She would neither eat nor drink until Gereint did. The Earl boxed her ears and it was her shrieks which wakened Gereint out of his coma. Appearing to rise from the dead, from the hollow of the shield in which he had been laid, Gereint started up and slew the Earl. (28) When he looked on Enid, Gereint felt two sorrows: for the loss of her looks and for the realization that she had been in the right. They rode on and were met by the Little King, who rescued the wounded Gereint and tended him.

When Gereint was better they rode on and found the domain of Earl Owain. (29) A man warned them against going there as there was a hedge of mist and enchanted games within that hedge from which no one returned. No one was permitted to lodge in the town except those who went to Owain's court. They were sent on to the court where they were received with honour: Gereint seated to one side of Owain and Enid to the other, with the Little King next to Enid and Owain's countess to Gereint's side. Owain considered Gereint and was grieved that he had ever instituted the enchanted games if a good man like Gereint was to be lost. He told Gereint to stop worrying about the prospect, since he was not obliged to go and, if Gereint would grant it, the games would be abolished. Gereint however said he was eager to go.

(30) Gereint approached the hedge. On every stake but two of the hedge was set a man's head. The Little King asked to accompany Gereint, but Owain forbade it. (31) Gereint entered the mist and emerged in a fair orchard wherein was set a red tent next to an apple-tree from which hung a horn. Inside the tent was a maiden sitting in a golden chair with a vacant seat beside her. She warned Gereint against sitting in it because its owner never permitted this. (32) A well-armoured knight challenged Gereint and they jousted. As Gereint went to behead him, he begged mercy, granting whatever Gereint should desire. He wished for nothing else but the abolition of the games, and ordered that the mist be dispersed. (33) The knight told Gereint to blow on the horn for not until he had been overcome and his successful assailant had blown the horn would the mist go. (34) The company met together and peace was established between them. Then Gereint returned with Enid to his own realms which he ruled wisely with her henceforth.

Commentary

1. We hear further about our old friend Glewlwyd, the porter or gatekeeper; the story-teller relates details which cross-reference to *Culhwch and Olwen*, in which Arthur's court is composed of wondrous warriors, each with his magical property. But we are no longer in 'Dark Age mode'. The importance of Arthur's company and their different needs are acknowledged by the provision of thirteen churches wherein they might hear mass honourably. The assembly is particularly large since it is Whitsuntide, one of the major feasts of the church's year.

2. The appearance of the White Hart is the signal for Otherworldly interpenetration of the earthly realm. We saw how Pwyll was inveigled into Annwn's domains by the hunting of a similar beast (*Mabon*, p. 23).[111] The White Hart, like the unicorn, bore a mystical significance, which wove the joint strands of pagan and Christian Europe together. The White Hart is the Otherworldly beast, representing the high powers of the gods – it is sometimes of the Wild Hunt and its lord, and is sometimes the emblematic beast of the Goddess, as we shall see. In Christian tradition the White Hart became a symbol of Christ or of the Christian soul, yearning towards the waters of salvation.[144] Its appearance here is the signal for an ancient ritual enactment by Arthur and his court: for the Hart is to be hunted after the custom of his father, Uther (see note 14).

3. In both Chrétien's *Erec and Enid* and in *Lanzelet*,[42] the awarding of the stag's head to the fairest lady is well established, though here Gwalchmai suggests it. While Gwenhwyfar sleeps late, Arthur departs with his squires, among whom is Amr or Amhar, his son. This is a rare reference to any child of Arthur's. According to Nennius, one of the wonders of Britain was a spring called Llygard Amr near which was buried 'a son of the warrior Arthur, and he killed him there and buried him'.[28] The grave is supposed to be unmeasurable because its dimensions seem to change. Of Arthur's killing of Amr there is no extant story. Also one of his squires is Goreu, who, we will remember, is Arthur's cousin and, according to the Triads, the one who released Arthur from

imprisonment (*Mabon*, p. 96).[111] Certainly the juxtaposition of these two young men is significant: perhaps their stories, lost to tradition, suggested parallels in the mind of the story-teller?

4. Here Gereint champions Gwenhwyfar, becoming both her escort and her avenger. The insult to the maid is really an insult to Gwenhwyfar herself. We have already noted that the insulting of the queen occurs in some form in each of the romances, and here she is particularly vulnerable. Gereint himself has no lady and so behaves as 'queen's knight' when Edern's dwarf strikes the queen's damsel. As we shall see, Arthur is unable to champion Gwenhwyfar both because of his absence at the hunt and because he is cast in an archetypal role.

5. It is possible that in the original sources of this story was some faint remembrance of Gwenhwyfar's abduction by Melwas, a story which appears in the *Vita Gildae*.[21] Melwas was king of the Summer Country – clearly an Otherworldly domain. Here Gwenhwyfar is insulted by Edern ap Nudd, the Eternal Son of Night – a medieval variant on the Underworld lord jealous of the Flower Bride.[95]

6. As in *The Dream of Rhonabwy*, where the hero finds himself in a ramshackle hall, so Gereint takes lodgings in a decrepit court. His first vision of Enid is hardly propitious to their love. But unlike Pryderi who found manual work repugnant to his upbringing (*Mabon*, p. 60),[111] Enid willingly stables Gereint's horse and performs tasks more suitable for a page than for a gentlewoman.

7. The dispossession of Ynwyl, Enid's father, is very like that of Custennin, Goreu's father (*Mabon*, p. 97).[111]

8. The joust of the Sparrowhawk was a very popular motif in medieval romance and can be found in many related texts, including *Libeaus Desconus*. Like the hunting of the White Hart and the Enchanted Games, the Sparrowhawk contest is one of the games that Sovereignty sets in order to establish both her champion and her representative.

9. The Sparrowhawk contest is not open to a man without a mistress to champion, so Gereint selects Enid in what seems to us

an arbitrary way. But this is Gereint's only way of legitimately attacking Gwenhwyfar's insulting knight, Edern.

10. Ynwyl spurs Gereint's flagging efforts with remembrance of the queen's insult in a theme time-honoured in Celtic literature: only by being wrought to great rage can the hero exert his fullest powers. Laegaire, Cu Chulainn's charioteer, urges his master on to perform his greatest feat – the salmon-leap – against Ferdiad in the Ulster cycle.[8] Gawain is similarly encouraged by a hermit when attempting to rescue Guinevere in the *Vulgate Cycle*.[33]

11. Gereint avenges Gwenhwyfar and sends Edern back to Caerlion for judgement. Edern ap Nudd survived into later Arthurian romance as Yder fiz Nut. On the famous Modena archivault Edern turns up as Isdernus with a certain Winlogie, whom commentators have identified as Guinevere.[87] This may indeed give us a faint connection between Gereint and the Abduction of Guinevere, which the Modena archivault supposedly illustrates.

12. This is the first time that Gereint forbids Enid the wearing of suitably noble clothing. His insistence on her wearing her old dress is not to humiliate his intended bride but to submit all his affairs to the judgement of Arthur and Gwenhwyfar, so that he may receive his bride, suitably attired by the queen, as his prize.

13. The suggestion, noted above, that Gwenhwyfar's abduction might have once played a part in this story is strengthened here. Arthur bids Gildas take the queen home. Gildas ap Caw was a historical chronicler and monk writing in the sixth century. His life, the *Vita Gildae*, written by Caradoc of Llancarfan, relates how Gildas personally reconciled Arthur with Melwas who was retaining Gwenhwyfar.[21] Although Gwenhwyfar suffers no rape in *Gereint and Enid*, she is unaccompanied by armed men and thus a prey to abduction.

14. The bestowal of the White Hart's head is, in *Erec and Enid*, a cause of turmoil, for the killer of the Hart is allowed to kiss the fairest maiden, which all good knights will defend. This is called 'the custom of Uther Pendragon' after the man who instituted it. The same custom is mentioned in *Lanzelet*,[142] where Arthur hunts

the White Stag, but, as he is about to practise 'the custom of Uther', Guinevere is abducted by King Valerin, a neighbouring vassal-king. All this is clearly significant to the strange roles adopted by both Gwenhwyfar and Arthur in *Gereint and Enid*. Arthur, when he is engaged in the hunt for the White Hart, is no longer an earthly king and husband but a sovereign lord with droit de seigneur as once practised by both European and Irish kingships. Gwenhwyfar reverts to her guise of Flower Bride: the Spring Maiden over whose possession the Bright and Dark Lords fight. Arthur, while he exercises his 'custom of Uther Pendragon', cannot champion the queen in this battle: Gereint substitutes for Arthur and fights Edern, who, in some early version, played the part of Melwas (see p. 156).

15. At the conclusion of these Otherworldly challenges to normality, Gwenhwyfar exercises her queenly rights of forgiveness and charity, at Arthur's bidding. The Celtic custom of taking sureties for the good behaviour of an offender – a kind of bail – is upheld by Arthur's court.

16. Edern's wounds are tended by a person called Morgan Tud. Lucy Paton[134] has written extensively about this healer and proposes that Morgan le Fay cannot be intended here. However, Morgan's salve heals Erec in Chrétien. Paton establishes that Morgan is a common enough male Welsh name, but is not applied to women. In Geoffrey she is called Morgen (derived from 'sea-borne': mor-gen).[10] As we shall see later on, Morgan is not absent from traditions relating to the Gereint story, and it is perhaps possible that she is remembered here.

17. Gereint's words to Gwenhwyfar: 'Here is the girl for whose sake you were avenged,' immediately help us to place Enid's role in this story. She is a substitute Gwenhwyfar, in terms of the insult: a focus to help Gereint avenge the queen. But Enid herself is far more than this. She is a representative of Sovereignty: a bride fetched from out of another world. The fact that Enid is dressed in the queen's own clothes and is honourably received points to this, as does a later episode in *Erec and Enid* (cf. p. 159).

18. The bestowal of the White Hart's head upon Enid is the queen's suggestion. In Chrétien's *Erec and Enid* it is at this point

that Arthur upholds the custom of Uther Pendragon and gives Enid a kiss: this may once have replaced a feature in the story which might have disturbed courtly listeners – the droit du seigneur or the sovereign lord's right to the first night with the bride. While there is little to suggest that this custom widely obtained in Britain, it was certainly common enough among the French. Irish legal tracts of the earliest period and certain stories still speak of the king's circuit of the land, on which he slept with the wives of notable lords. It is during one such visitation, for example, that Conchobar mac Nessa is present at the birth of Cu Chulainn.[8] It is Arthur who is destined to win the White Hart – a task which might be dangerous to an ordinary man, if we are to judge from similar romances, such as *Graelent*[26] and *Guigamor*,[134] in which the hero departs into Faery after a magical beast and is thereafter lost to humankind. The risk that Arthur takes in absorbing the Otherworldly dangers of the hunt in his own royal person is compensated by his pairing with the most beautiful maiden. In effect, he is the Hunter King so familiar from traditional spring rites in which a man takes the place of a proto-Robin Hood character and a woman the Spring Maiden, or Maid Marian. But instead of taking Enid to his own bed, Arthur bestows her upon Gereint, who, as the queen's champion, is the hero of the hour.

19. Gereint's duties now become mundane. He has won a fair bride and now goes to 'beat the boundaries' of his land, but he has many trials to undergo before he is worthy of either bride or land.

20. It is worth while comparing the list of Arthur's court that is given in *Gereint and Enid* with that appearing in both *Culhwch and Olwen* and *The Dream of Rhonabwy*. Apart from the established kings and lords whose experience will help Gereint, he takes with him many of the younger men, notably Goreu, Gwair (the prisoner of Annwn), and Peredur.

21. Gereint makes a circuit of his land in the manner of Celtic rulers, exchanging gifts and taking promises of service. Thus he establishes his sovereignty over his inherited domain, though things soon change.

22. This theme of the hero who appears to be so in the grip of a woman that he fails in manly duties is one common to both Gereint and Owain, for both stand so accused by their *meinie* (company). The medieval texts abound concerning this dichotomy between love of one's mistress and duty to one's lord, but the earlier ones reveal an older pattern: the ideal of the inner mistress or Sovereignty is projected on to an earthly woman so that the hero seems in thrall to his wife though he truly serves the Goddess herself. Enid's unfortunate remarks put her in much the same position as Psyche, who loses her husband, Cupid; like Psyche she is forced to undergo a series of trials in order to win him back (see section II).

23. Until Gereint comes to himself and is reconciled with her again, Enid must assume a ragged appearance. She becomes, in effect, a dolorous lady, akin to the Dark Woman of Knowledge or the Black Maiden, who assumes a woeful appearance but still faithfully accompanies the hero in his wasteland search, like Luned and the Grail messenger. The ensuing episodes are to show Enid that Gereint has not lost his manly strength.

24. The encounter with robbers is paralleled by Gareth's ride with Linnet in Malory.[25] Enid's enforced silence, like that of Rhiannon or of Chaucer's Faithful Griselda,[6] seems a stock medieval harassment for wilting damsels; however, Enid's silence (which she is unable to maintain because of her love of Gereint) hides her real power and self-possession. It forces Gereint into more and more ludicrous tests of his strength, which we can see as all part of the Games of Sovereignty.

25. Gwiffert Petit, the Little King, has aroused a good deal of scholarly speculation. It has been suggested that he derives from Auberon, King of Faery, or indeed from Gwiddolwyn Gorr, who appears in *Culhwch and Olwen* as the dwarf whose magic bottles kept drinks warm from the east to the furthest west.[92] Gwiffert is a friendly opponent and one who, once bested, gives hospitality to his vanquisher. There is a good deal of the *gruagach*, or friendly brownie, about him; in many Gaelic stories, the *gruagach*, himself king over his own domain, agrees to companion the hero and help him in his quest.[61]

26. In one of the most amusing episodes of the story, Gereint exchanges a very literal conversation with Cai. This is the ubiquitous 'taunting by Cai' and 'appeasement of Gwalchmai' episode that occurs in all three romances.

27. Gereint's childish behaviour is patiently balanced by Enid's insistence on following him. In Chrétien, Earl Limwris is the lord of Li Mors, or death. But Enid refuses him as she refused the Brown Earl. It is her shrieks that cause Gereint to revive in a macabre scene, which causes the castle's occupants to flee in terror.

28. Enid's love has brought Gereint back from the dead, and now he acknowledges her in a moment of sorrowful revelation. He at last deigns to protect her at the approach of his old ally, Gwiffert Petit.

29. We now reach the heart of the story, where Gereint and Enid meet with Owain, who is now master of the Enchanted Games. This is Gereint's supreme test. Later Arthurian tradition parallels this incident with the *Val sans Retour*, into which knights go but never return.[33] In *Erec and Enid* Owain becomes Evrain and his castle is called Brandigan – the Raven's Castle. We note that it is Owain who institutes the games.

30. There is no disparity between the garden or orchard as described by Chrétien and that of *Gereint and Enid*, and both tales have much to complement and illuminate each other. Common to both is the hedge of stakes with men's heads upon them. This is a common feature of Celtic folk stories: the hero invariably arrives to find one stake vacant ready for his head, as does Art mac Conn when he goes to win his bride, Delbhchaem.[4] Gereint's garden is derived from native sources, Chrétien's is closer to the Breton land of the fays; both are types of terrestrial paradise.

31. Chrétien's description of the garden is of an orchard which bears fruit summer and winter alike, though it is impossible to leave the orchard if any fruit is plucked: a consistent description of the Faery realms where mortals must not eat if they wish to return from them. In Chrétien the Enchanted Games are called

the Joy of the Court, an expression which has given a good deal of confusion, since the *Joie de Cort* can mean the Joy of the Court, horn or body, depending on slight variant spellings. There is a way in which all three can be seen as valid, and I shall be discussing this aspect in Chapter Nine, where we compare the combined evidence. The mystery of 'the Joy', as it is called, is dependent on the subtle exchange that passes between the mistress of the orchard and her champion. For the woman in the golden chair is none other than Sovereignty herself, complete with the emblems of her cult: the horn, the apple-tree and the golden seat. The vacant seat reminds us forcibly of the Siege Perilous in which Perceval sits in the *Didot Perceval* (*Mabon*, p. 65).[111]

32. Gereint's unnamed opponent is called Mabonograin in Chrétien, and is yet another guise of Mabon himself, as eternal prisoner. We note that he is a prisoner of the orchard in so far as he has sworn never to leave it undefended nor leave his lady alone.[7] So he has become what Gereint's *meinie* accused their lord of being: the thrall of a woman. We may ponder the significance of Mabonograin's appearance in collusion with Evrain or Owain in *Erec and Enid*. This is not the first time we have noted the joint appearance of these men in one story: in *Libeaus Desconus* Mabon and Yrain are brother magicians, while Mabon and Owain share a conception story (*Mabon*, p. 161).[111] Their close association is further borne out in *Gereint and Enid*, for although the Welsh story omits the champion in the orchard's name, in *Erec and Enid* he is named Mabonograin. One commentator has seen this name as a twinning of Mabon/Owain.[132] (See also Chapters Three and Four.)

If we consider Owain's career, some of this will get clearer. In the previous chapter we saw how Owain relinquishes his guardianship of the Fountain and returns to Arthur's court. Now Owain, having been a champion who beat his challengers, becomes a challenger and setter of tests himself, becoming master of the Enchanted Games. Instead of defending the orchard himself, Owain appoints a proxy champion – his doublet, Mabonograin.

33. The blowing of the horn dispels the mists of glamour and enchantment that surround the orchard, for the Games of

Sovereignty are ended. The significance of this episode will be discussed in Chapter Nine.

34. Gereint is rightful lord not only of his own lands, but also of the inner realms belonging to Sovereignty. The seal of this association is set by Enid, Gereint's wife and Sovereignty's representative.

II THE HUNTING OF THE WHITE HART

One of the central features of this story is the hunting of the White Hart. All hunts in early literature are laden with symbols of mystery and power, but none more so than *Gereint and Enid*. But what is the real significance of the White Hart? We have already noted its affiliation with Christian symbolism as an emblem of spiritual yearning. Both the White Hart and the unicorn have been applied to Christ himself as emblems of unique power: both animals were believed to be able to find medicinal herbs and were considered impossible to catch without the help of a virgin. While there are aspects of this later understanding, particularly within Chrétien, it is to an earlier set of symbols that we shall look next.

As the forester tells Arthur, 'it is pure white, and out of arrogance and pride in its lordliness it will travel with no other animal.'[22] It is clearly marked out as the proper quarry for a king. Its appearance marks the assumption, by Arthur, of a ritual role – as the Huntsman consort of Sovereignty, whose beast the White Hart is. Like the unicorn, which will lay its head unprotesting in a virgin's lap while the huntsman slays it, so the White Hart's head is awarded to the most beautiful maiden from whom Arthur is expected to exact a kiss – a token of a more explicit surrender which the Spring Maiden once rendered to the Huntsman King.

Of the three tasks that are to be achieved in this story, Arthur hunts and kills the White Hart while Gereint wins the Sparrowhawk contest and the Enchanted Games. Taken together these contests can be seen as part of a once widely observed set of ritual games, which I will term here the Games of Sovereignty.

The finding and fetching of the Hallows (*Mabon*, p. 48)[111] is the task of the king, and the winning of Games of Sovereignty is the task of the best of the king's companions and warriors. The fact that Gereint does not alone achieve the three contests but shares the rostrum with Arthur, whose prize, Enid, he gives to Gereint in marriage, is very significant, and emphasizes that Gereint is acting as a champion of Arthur and thus, by extension, of Sovereignty also.

But how may we establish the mythical occurrence of such a set of ritual games and with what warranty? Of the many Celtic stories that relate to both Sovereignty and the hunting of a wondrous beast, let us look at one of the most relevant parallel texts in Irish tradition: the *Sons of Daire*.

It is told how Daire reverently celebrated the games at the fair of Tailltiu. She was the foster-mother of the mighty god, Lugh, who had inaugurated games in her honour every year at Lughnasad, 1 August. Tailltiu had cleared the plains of trees in order to help Ireland become cultivated. Such was her labour that she died:

> Long her sorrow, long her weariness,
> In sickness was Tailltiu after heavy toil.
> To her came the men of Ireland,
> To whom she was in bondage.[146]

As earth mother and progenitor of agricultural skills she was reverenced at her games every year.

Daire had five sons, and because of a prophecy that one of them named Lughaidh would succeed to the Sovereignty of Ireland, Daire called each of them Lughaidh. Daire inquired of a druid which of his sons should be king. 'The one who succeeds in overtaking the golden doe which shall appear at this fair,' he said. Shortly a golden doe did appear and was chased by Daire's sons as far as Beann Eadair, where a magical mist descended. One of the sons overtook the doe, another killed her, and so each had their part in hunting the magical doe.

A great snow fell and they each went in turn to find a house to sleep in. One by one they encountered a hideous hag who refused each shelter unless he slept with her. Each refused her and was told he had refused the kingship and sovereignty of Ireland; she named each of the Lughaidhs by their part in the hunting, e.g. the one who had flayed the carcass was called Lughaidh Corb forever afterwards.

At last the final man came to the house, he who had overtaken the doe, and he slept with her. She named him Lughaidh Laidhe and transformed herself so that 'the light of her countenance was as the sun rising in the month of May'. And she identified herself thus:

'I say unto thee, O mild youth,
~~With me the arch-kings cohabit,~~
I am the majestic, slender damsel,
The Sovereignty of Alba and Eire.'

She promised that his son should win her and combine the skills of druid, prophet, poet and king.[129]

So we see that at the ritual games of an earth-goddess, the kingship of Ireland is decided by the outcome of a hunt. Significantly Lughaidh Laidhe overtakes the doe in order to win the Sovereignty: similarly Pwyll tries to overtake Rhiannon, whose pace is always just faster than his own (*Mabon*, p. 27).[111] As to the games of Tailltiu (Teltown in modern Irish) Maire MacNeill has collected all known traditions surrounding this festival in her colossal study *The Festival of Lughnasad*.[103] Most modern animal fairs in the British Isles are held in a season or on a date once sacred to a local deity in whose honour sacred games were held, animals bartered and marriages arranged. The fair of Teltown was most particularly associated with matchmaking, and there are legends extant concerning the abduction of a woman into a nearby faery hill to become a *beansidi* (woman of the sidi, the faery hills) as well as traditions relating a duel fought over a woman between either two giants or a giant and a hero, and of a brawl which is the outcome of the insulting of a woman. The chief protagonists in most folk traditions relating to this festival are Lugh, the mighty God of Light, Crom Dubh, literally, the Black Bent One (a harvest deity, symbolic of summer's end), and Tailltiu herself, Lugh's foster-mother, who occupied in early tradition a similar position to that now enjoyed by St Brigit as the foster-mother of Christ in native Gaelic tradition. If we also remember the *Baile in Scail* story (p. 67), in which Lugh enjoys a particularly powerful partnership with Sovereignty, with whom he prophesies lines of kings, we have a fascinating series of overlays with *Gereint and Enid*.

The festival of Lughnasad represents the mythic pattern of a God of Light and a God of Summer's End in combat for a Goddess of the Land. This pattern lies behind the archetypal roles played by Arthur in *Gereint and Enid*, where he appears as the Hunter of the White Hart; by Edern ap Nudd, who attempts to abduct or at least insult Gwenhwyfar, and who represents the darkness of winter; and by Gwenhwyfar, who is representative of the Goddess of the Land, no longer the Spring Maiden but the Summer Queen. At another level of the story these roles are enacted by Gereint, as Arthur's champion, defender of the queen and contestant in Sovereignty's games; by the Brown Earl and Earl Limwris, as well as by Mabonograin, as the representatives of the failing Otherworldly powers; and by Enid, who, as an unwed maiden, represents the Spring Maiden or Sovereignty's messenger.

If we turn to Chapter Eight we will find a list of such triplicities which interact in a similar way within the *Mabinogion*. We note that each of the levels on which *Gereint and Enid* may be understood in its Celtic context revolves around the theme of loving partnership. This is the real meaning at the heart of *Gereint and Enid*, for the White Hart betokens true love and exchange of powers, whether it be between the king and Sovereignty, the king and his queen or the hero and the heroine. There is a reciprocal love and duty between each of the protagonists which goes beyond courtly love and chivalric honour. This is the 'love strong as death' that poets speak of, love that is need and desire, sacrifice and patient acceptance. It is within this context that Enid must be understood, for her role is least easy to comprehend.

Perhaps it will be easier to come to terms with Enid's unsympathetic role if we look at the *Lay of Guigamor*, one of the Breton *lais* recorded by Marie de France,[26] for here the tradition of the White Hart and the patient lover is combined.

· Guigamor was trained as a knight at Arthur's court, where he soon excelled all others at chivalric feats; but his knightly prowess was not matched by his enthusiasm for courtly love. In fact he gave no thought to women at all, for which everyone thought him strangely incomplete. He chanced one day to go hunting when he found and wounded a white doe, which bore antlers on her head. But the arrow with which he wounded her rebounded on him and struck him in the thigh. As he lay on the ground, the doe spoke her dying words to him, saying: 'Vassal, you have done me wrong and will never avoid your destiny which is this: no medicine will heal your wound. The only way you may be healed is by a woman who will suffer such pain and sorrow as no woman in the world has endured before. *And to dolorous lady, dolorous knight.* For your part you shall do and suffer so great things for her, that not a lover beneath the sun ... but shall marvel at the tale.' So saying, she died.

Guigamor made his way to a harbour in which was anchored a miraculous ship. Lying upon a bed fashioned by workmen in King Solomon's time, he was transported, without agency of man, to the opposite shore. The king of that country, an old jealous man, had married a beautiful young maiden whom he had immured within a tower in an orchard, with her niece as attendant. Only a priest held the key, in order to administer the sacraments to her.

Walking in the garden, the two women saw the ship miraculously arrive and, seeking to give honourable burial to the knight on board, they brought him into the orchard. The queen fell in love with him and heard his tale. She offered to hide him until he was well again. During this period of healing Guigamor likewise fell in love with the queen. After a year and a half the queen had a foreboding that she would soon lose him and she asked him to give her a shirt that she might set in it a knot as their covenant to each other: that he would never love another woman except the one who undid the knot. Guigamor likewise fastened a belt about the queen, which was similarly fastened so secretly that none but he might undo it.

The king's chamberlain saw Guigamor with the queen and told his master. Hearing Guigamor's story, the king judged that he might go free but only by being put into the ship by which he had arrived, and the fates must guide it. Guigamor arrived safely home and was welcomed by his squire and taken to his castle where he refused to make merry or to take a wife save only her who could unloose the knot in his shirt. Soon all the women in Brittany heard about this and came to make the attempt but all failed.

Meanwhile, for the space of two years, the queen had been imprisoned in a grey tower, bound and joyless. She was lamenting her lost love and wishing she could either come to him or cast herself into the sea, when she found the door miraculously open. She escaped and, finding the self-same ship awaiting her, was borne across the sea to Brittany to the castle of a lord named Meriadus.

Meriadus, finding the queen within the ship, thought her to be a faery, so fair she was. He sheltered her and bade her love him, but she refused him, saying only he who could loose her belt might have her. Meriadus then exclaimed that there was a knight who would likewise yield to no other save she who could unknot his shirt. Meriadus arranged a tournament to which Guigamor came and recognized the queen. Meriadus bade her loose the knight's shirt and so she was able. Then Guigamor, seeing that it was truly his mistress, and hearing her story, begged Meriadus to release her to him. Meriadus refused him and, after a long campaign, was successfully besieged by Guigamor, who slew him and carried off the queen to his own lands.[26]

In the *Lay of Guigamor* we see the interwoven themes of the White Hart and the power of love to overcome. The destiny that the doe lays on Guigamor is in the nature of a *geas* or proscription and, as will become increasingly obvious in this study, is a feature of many stories which deal with Sovereignty and her successors in medieval literature. The *geas* is the command of the Goddess in these stories, shaping the hero's destiny, a challenge to overcome, fail or balance in some way. Guigamor's problem is his lack of love for any woman. In this he is a perfect candidate for Sovereignty's contest. Marie de France points out a very obvious classical archetype in this story, for the wounding of Guigamor by his own arrow is the moment when the possibility of love enters his heart, like one of Cupid's darts. But the wounding of the hero by his own weapons or hounds is also a feature of myths concerning the Goddess of Venery, Artemis or Diana. Here the chase for quarry becomes the quest for love.

Guigamor's queen is imprisoned in a tower within an orchard, which becomes a *temenos* where love can develop. Both she and Guigamor undergo sorrow and suffering for their love. The miraculous ship that transports them is a descendant of the faery *curragh*, or crystal boat, which bears heroes to *Tir na mBan*, the Land of Women; as a barque shaped by Solomon's craftsmen, it will appear again in the *Quest del San Graal* as the ship that carries the Grail-finders to the city of Sarras.[29] The many correspondences between this story and that of *Gereint and Enid* lead to the existence of a common source or a tradition of related stories.

Even the abduction and enforced captivity of the queen by Meriadus is paralleled by the abduction of Gwenhwyfar by Melwas that underlies *Gereint and Enid*.

Here the importance of the White Hart is fully revealed: it comes as a messenger from the Otherworld to lead the hero into a contest which goes beyond human strength and knightly prowess. It is by love, trust and enduring patience in times of sorrow that the lovers are reunited. And although Gereint and Enid are not separated physically, there is no communication between them. The White Hart leads Gereint to find Enid and marry her, but the Games of Sovereignty enable him to fully love her.

III IN THE APPLE ORCHARD

It is in the apple orchard that all is revealed in this story, although we are forced to turn to *Erec and Enid* in order to corroborate our findings. Let us focus on this episode and its antecedents.

Throughout Celtic and Arthurian literature the orchard is a paradigm for the terrestrial paradise. It is *Insula Avalonis*, according to Geoffrey of Monmouth, the Isle of Apples.[11] Gaelic tradition locates it on Arran in the Firth of Clyde as Emain Abhlach: for us a significant identification, since Mabon's own stamping ground in the Firth of Solway is not far distant, and Chrétien calls the guardian of his orchard Mabonograin.

In *Erec and Enid* the Knight who successfully sounds the horn will have greater renown than any other man living, for so will the Joy of the Court be announced. This mysterious term, as we know, is Chrétien's name for the Enchanted Games of *Gereint and Enid*. Erec approaches the lady of the orchard, only to be challenged by a Red Knight whom he overcomes, and he demands to be told why the Red Knight is in the garden. The Knight relates his story. He had once been at the court of Erec's father, King Lac. His mistress, the lady of the orchard, had asked him a favour without specifying its nature, to which he agreed. Immediately he had been knighted by Evrain (Owain), whose nephew he was, the Red Knight's mistress demanded he obey her favour, which was never to leave the place they were now in until some knight should overcome him by force of arms. And so he had been forced to defend the garden, unwillingly killing many knights because of his former promise. But now that Erec had overcome him, he was free to leave and return to his uncle's court, for which reason all at that court will be joyful. For this reason is the Joy of the Court so named. He bids Erec blow the horn to signify the coming joy, and reveals himself to be none other than Mabonograin, a knight no longer remembered in his country. The ladies of the court immediately compose and sing a Lay of Joy and acclaim Erec.

And so Erec becomes a freer of Mabon and, if we follow the convention of the *Rex Nemorensis* combat, the new guardian of the orchard – except, of course, the games are now abolished, since the enchantment is lifted.

Chrétien's Orchard Woman is very much an earthly lady, peeved at the frustration of her plan to keep Mabonograin imprisoned. This retention of the hero by an Otherworldly woman is a theme we have already encountered in *Owain* and which occurs again and again in Celto-Arthurian literature. In the romances of *Graelent*, *Désiré* and *Guigamor* all three knights are similarly held captive by a faery woman who holds power of life and death over them. Chrétien's rationalization of a faery woman is at odds with the rest of his story, but something interesting is revealed at this point; when Enid goes to comfort the lady, she finds that they are in fact cousins, just as Erec and Mabonograin discover that they were raised in the same court, almost as foster-brothers.

Erec and Enid are thus shown to be the earthly counterparts of Mabonograin and the Orchard Woman. Erec breaks out of his obsessive love of Enid that caused him to give up knightly sports, which Mabonograin was unable to do, while Enid rejects the abject obedience that the tyrannical Orchard Woman extorts from her lover in favour of her own loving obedience and watch-fulness (see Figure 6.2, p. 156).

It is interesting to note, following the last section, that Mabono-grain is laid under a *geas* and forced to accept or deny his destiny,

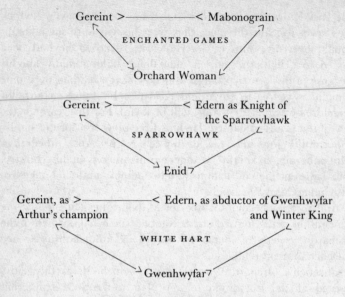

Figure 6.2: *The Ritual Games*

whereas Erec swears his love to Enid but does not fulfil it in a mature way.

If we return to *Gereint and Enid* we will find that the mysteries of the story are unravelling before us. It becomes clear that we have here a story in which three distinct levels are in operation, which, without reference to each other, render our understanding void. These levels can be seen as centring upon the three female protagonists of *Gereint and Enid*: Enid, Gwenhwyfar and the Orchard Woman (see Figure 6.2).

The Orchard Woman is the Sovereignty figure within *Gereint and Enid*, and though she has a seemingly negligible role in the action, she is none the less the prime mover of events. It is her White Hart that the court hunt and that acts as her messenger to summon Arthur and his men to Otherworldly adventures at her games. Her appearance in a type of earthly paradise at the conclusion of the story marks Gereint's restoration to his real self. For up·until that point he has been seeking to become whole. His championship of Gwenhwyfar is a courteous response to his lord's

lady; his entrance in the Sparrowhawk contest rests upon his
having his own lady, and he picks upon Enid almost arbitrarily.
The reader is half aware that, like Guigamor, he is not a man
accustomed to the love of women. His temporary infatuation
with the joys of married love is replaced by a complete reversal of
behaviour. Instead of cherishing Enid, he puts her through much
mental torment and physical danger in order to prove his manly
prowess, only succeeding in appearing foolish to his peers and
almost killing himself. It is only his brush with death that brings
him to his senses and impels him to aid Enid struggling in Earl
Limwris's arms. The final seal of his adventures is his meeting
with Sovereignty, the ultimate mistress of mistresses, whose garden
is death to any knight who cannot fight her champion. As
Gereint has never showed any modesty about what is due to him,
so here he sits in the vacant chair by Sovereignty's side. He has
learned, through the trials of combat and much unnecessary
trouble, that true love is his friend and requires a balanced
response. It is in this way that he truly earns the right to his
lands, for, as we have already noted, a man cannot use his people
unjustly nor waste his lands – as Gereint has done by ill-treating
Enid – and be worthy of his sovereignty. Only a man who can
submit to love, whatever its appearance, in sickness and in
health, can rule justly.

The Orchard Woman offers Gereint the final challenge to
submit to Sovereignty's rules: only a man just and honest, truthful
and loving may hold the land or partner Sovereignty's representative.

Gwenhwyfar's part in the story is not the mythic role of the
Orchard Woman, but that of archetypal queen. As Gereint
strives to find himself and be reconciled with Enid, so Arthur
once strove to win his wife and hold her against abduction. The
newly made king has many trials ahead of him. He must be
empowered in his kingship by the Hallows, the mystic symbols
of his reign. These he obtains by undertaking the hazardous
Underworld Foray, as in the 'Preiddeu Annwn' (*Mabon*, p. 107–
8),[111] holding them balanced in his kingdom until his reign is
concluded, when they are returned to their bearers, as Excalibur
is returned to the Lady of the Lake, or the Grail to Sarras.

The other main test for the new king is the finding of a suitable wife. This woman has to be, in mythic terms, Sovereignty's representative, the young Flower Bride or Spring Maiden, in whom all the qualities of the fruitful land are immanent. Gwenhwyfar embodies all these qualifications, and it is not surprising that every stratum of the Arthurian legend has some story in which she is abducted or propositioned by rival kings. We may view Lancelot's love and final abduction of Guinevere from the stake, in late tradition, in this very light. From this point onwards the institution of the Round Table ceases to be effective, civil war breaks out and Arthur is forced to fight the last battle of his reign and pass back into Avalon. Some versions tell of Mordred imprisoning Guinevere in the Tower of London in order to force her into marriage with him: a clear signal that the queen who was once a Flower Bride remains important to claimant kings.[87]

It is easy to forget at the beginning of the Arthurian story that Arthur, like Gereint at the beginning of this story, was a landless warrior who, even after he had been inaugurated as king, had to put down numerous revolts until he won the right to marry his bride. Gereint, by his championship of Gwenhwyfar, shows his desire to serve Sovereignty's representative in the person of his queen. The fact that Gwenhwyfar's insult is cancelled by Gereint's championship of Enid at the Sparrowhawk contest is a sign that the mantle of Flower Bride, or Spring Maiden, falls upon Enid. We remember that Gereint refuses to let Enid wear fine clothes until he brings her to the queen, who dresses her from her own wardrobe.

Enid then represents the final level of the story, the earthly woman who becomes Sovereignty's representative. We may be sure that if Gereint's choice had fallen upon some other woman, he might never have won the Sparrowhawk contest, nor would his chosen lady have been presented with the White Hart's head. But because Arthur assumes the guise of the Goddess's Huntsman, taking the Otherworldly dangers inherent in such a chase upon himself, he gives Gereint an unparalleled prize. At this point in the mythic structure, Arthur might well have chosen to take Enid for himself and repudiate Gwenhwyfar as a faded flower, perhaps increasing the length of his reign as a result of marrying the

Flower Bride aspect of Sovereignty. But such a thing does not come to pass. Enid is accorded the highest place at court next to the king and queen. Her role is Queen for the Feast, just as Gereint's is Honoured Champion of Sovereignty for his defence of the queen. Such roles have to be earned, and both Enid and Gereint have trouble in good measure. Like Guigamor and his queen: 'and to dolorous knight, dolorous lady'.[26]

If Enid's claim to be Sovereignty's representative looks negligible, let us look at the evidence. Rachel Bromwich has suggested some possible meanings for the names Erec and Enid, as these appear in Chrétien. She derives 'Erec' from the Breton *Bro Weroc*, 'the land of Guerec', and suggests that 'Enid' derives from a territorial Breton district, the once-powerful tribe of the Veneti, as *Bro Wened*. While this is ingenious, she in no way urges our acceptance of such derivations, although she, too, recognizes aspects of Sovereignty about Enid.[56]

We have already seen in Chapter Three how the legends of the transformed hag attach to Sovereignty's mythos. Might not Gereint's insistence on Enid assuming her worst dress and the deterioration of her beauty have a relevance to this hag motif? As a Tattered Lady, Enid can hardly be a Loathly Lady, though Gereint certainly treats her as such. However, we have seen how the Irish story of the *Sons of Daire* (p. 149) combines the themes of the White Hart and the transformed hag who bestows sovereignty upon the hero. Here Gereint can be said to cause his Spring Maiden to suffer an unseasonal frost, for, equipped with the loveliest wife and kingly domains, he abandons his duty, becoming a morose husband and absentee landlord.

The end of *Erec and Enid* is substantially different from that of *Gereint and Enid* in that the story concludes with the crowning of Erec and Enid. They are received by Arthur and Guinevere in a scene which echoes their former arrival and acclaim. The queen is 'so above herself with joy that you might have used her for hawking',[7] at the sight of the pair. Their joy is somewhat blunted at hearing of the death of Erec's father, King Lac. Arthur says: 'We have to go from here to Nantes in Brittany. There you shall bear the tokens of kingship, a crown on your head and a sceptre in your hand: this favour and this honour I bestow upon you.'[7]

Arthur endows Erec and Enid with many riches, including ivory thrones and a rich robe woven by four faeries, depicting four of the liberal arts: geometry, arithmetic, music and astronomy. Guinevere clothes Enid herself, while Arthur provides crowns for them both. And so they are crowned in the presence of all.

It is indeed a pity that no part of this episode is retained in *Gereint and Enid*, for, as the reader will be aware, it is of supreme importance. Erec is confirmed in his lordship as king and at Arthur's behest. It is obvious that, having made Gereint his champion in so blatant a manner, Arthur could not relinquish the kingship of Britain to his knight. Gereint's lands are in Cornwall and not Brittany, as in Chrétien, but he is none the less their true lord at the end of the story, with his own Flower Bride by his side. And in the land where the White Hart once ran, the magic mist lifts from the Otherworldly Orchard; the Orchard Woman and her champion depart, leaving only Gereint and Enid to flourish in their turn.

CHAPTER SEVEN

PEREDUR

Who caught the blood?
I, said the Fish,
In my little dish:
I caught the blood.
TRADITIONAL
The Death of Cock Robin

Of no account was he held at first, yet afterwards was his
accoutrement right noble, and so thoroughly did he search out
amidst the land ... that he found the Court ... Perceval li
Galois was he.

The Elucidation

I IN THE WASTELAND

With *Peredur* we reach the last of our commentaries on the
Mabinogion and find perhaps the most complex and pied of the
stories. *Peredur* has excited more interest and more study than any
other of the texts that comprise the *Mabinogion* because of its
Grail associations. But, as a quick reading will inform anyone,
this story is quite unlike later and more sophisticated texts which
relate the Grail quest.

Although there are many talismanic gifts in *Peredur* – rings,
cups, spears and swords – there is no classic Grail cup. The vessel

that is borne during the procession of the Hallows at Peredur's uncle's castle is described as a *dysgyl*, a wide, shallow dish, and it contains a severed and bloody head.

Everything in *Peredur* leads us to look to earlier texts for clarification, for, although the story-teller was aware of Chrétien's *Perceval*, he did not draw on it extensively. That there was a proto-story in circulation can be proved from cross-reference to other texts in which Perceval appears.[74] *Peredur* proves to be in the same tradition as the *Amadan Mor* stories about the Great Fool who accomplishes wonders, wins a wife and lands and vindicates his wronged family. There is also a distinct overlay with the *macgnimartha* (youthful exploits) stories of Celtic tradition, especially with those of Fionn mac Cumhail.

The motivation for Peredur is not a quest for the Grail but a threefold purpose: to avenge his family, to find his intended wife, and to alleviate the Enchantments (*gormesiad*) which are upon the land. This last theme is the only appearance of the 'wasteland' motif, familiar from other texts. The quest for the Grail, which we can see here to be one of the Hallows is ultimately derived from Peredur's search for lost sovereignty, to avenge his father's loss of his lands. One later romance actually calls Peredur 'Perdles-vaus', or 'He who has lost the valleys', in a French rationalization of his name. But though Peredur's quest starts as one of vengeance, like Maelduine the voyager who begins his *imram* (voyage) for a similar reason,[146] the journey proves more fruitful.

There is also a subsidiary quest interwoven in *Peredur*, the search for a name or a truer understanding of that name. Peredur is acclaimed by name by three Otherworldly people: the dwarfs, the Witches of Gloucester and the Black Maiden. Elsewhere he is entitled 'the Dumb Knight', 'the Knight with the Spear', or 'the Knight of the Mill'. In Chrétien his mother calls him nothing but 'dear son'. This is consistent with the Celtic tradition of the hero having to earn his name, for, though he may have a childhood name, it is by his deeds that he earns his adult name.

There are many inconsistencies within the text, and the reader is advised to refer to more than one translation of *Peredur*, for each varies slightly depending on which manuscripts were used. The Gwyn and Thomas Jones text is particularly helpful[24].

However, the reader is struck by the way the narrative falls over itself to get to the next incident and by the duplication and triplication of characters and events. Why does Peredur not marry the Disinherited Maiden? How can Peredur's career be reconciled with his role in the other *Perceval* texts?

The answer to the first question will emerge as we study the many female figures within this text. While Gereint encounters knights, footpads (outlaws) and other combatants, Peredur seems fated to fall in with unmarried women and a great many guises of Sovereignty. This will form the discussion of section III of this chapter.

The answer to the second question will perhaps disappoint avid Grail-seekers. Because of the nature of *Peredur* and the many cross-currents of earlier tradition that emerge from the text, I have chosen to concentrate on *Peredur* in its proto-Celtic context. A full comparison between this and the many other associated texts, including the *Didot Perceval*,[32] Chrétien's *Perceval*[7] and von Eschenbach's *Parzival*,[40] not to mention the later texts, would render this chapter book-length; I shall not attempt such a comparison here, but I shall make reference to specific points which elucidate *Peredur*. The reader is directed to the bibliography for the other texts and to Glenys Goetinck's study of *Peredur*.[74]

I have chosen a rather unusual framework for comparison, which most Grail scholars would eschew, drawing parallels between *Peredur* and its Irish cousins – oral folk-stories collected in the nineteenth century, which illuminate many of the more obscure and primitive aspects of the story. I offer no apology for this. The Grail corpus has suffered comparisons with the cult of Adonis,[73] the Orthodox liturgy,[157] Middle Eastern astrology,[40] Templar relics[67] and Cathars from Outer Space.[159] Such analogues may prove diverting to the scholar, but they are hardly helpful in illuminating what is basically a proto-Celtic story, in its British mythological context.

Peredur reveals a wealth of Otherworld characters and archetypes which are readily identifiable from a pan-Celtic understanding of native mythology. Most striking are the many female characters who throng this story. Their functions and natures are discussed at length in the third section of this chapter.

Peredur

(1) Earl Efrawg had seven sons; he and the first six were killed in wars and tournaments, leaving the last, Peredur, to be raised by his mother, who determined that her remaining son should be raised in ignorance of warfare. (2) They lived in seclusion in the forest. Peredur, however, soon showed his strength and prowess, despite ignorance of arms, as well as his amiable stupidity. (3) On seeing three knights ride by, Peredur asked what they were. His mother said they were angels. But the riders soon enlightened him and he resolved to follow them. (4) His mother, shocked, nevertheless gave him advice about courtesy in such an unworldly way that he was subsequently misled into danger and discourtesy. He was to: recite a paternoster when he saw a church, take food and drink if he had need and they were not offered, if he heard a woman cry out he was to attend immediately, if he saw a jewel to take it and offer it to another, and to pay court to beautiful women. (5) Providing himself with makeshift weapons and a mount, Peredur rode into the forest where he saw an unattended tent with a maiden inside. He snatched up food unasked, took the maiden's ring and kissed her. Meanwhile the Proud Knight of the Clearing returned, accused his lady of unchastity and swore that she should not remain in the same place for two nights together.

(6) Peredur came to Arthur's court and there witnessed a knight throw wine at Gwenhwyfar and strike her. Cai mocked Peredur and was angered when a male and female dwarf, hitherto dumb, greeted Peredur by name and acclaimed him best of knights. Cai struck both dwarfs and bade Peredur follow the knight who had insulted the queen. Peredur overcame him and tried to drag the corpse out of the armour until Owain unfastened it for him. Peredur bade Owain tell Arthur that he served him faithfully but that he would not come to court until he had avenged himself on Cai. He overcame sixteen knights and sent them to Arthur to submit to his justice. (7) He came to a lake where a richly dressed old man sat with youths fishing from a boat. Peredur stayed at his court and was instructed in arms. The old man revealed himself as Peredur's maternal uncle and gave his nephew new advice on manners. He was instructed not to ask about strange sights unless he was told about them. (8) Peredur then left his uncle and went on to another court where an old man ruled. Here he was challenged to break an iron column with a sword – each time the sword and column broke in two and reunited, but his third attempt was unsuccessful. The man revealed himself as Peredur's second

maternal uncle; he said that his nephew had reached only two-thirds of his strength, but when he was fully grown he would be invincible.

(9) As they talked at dinner, a spear was borne into the hall, which dripped three drops of blood, followed by a platter on which was a man's head floating in blood. Peredur did not ask about either event, true to his first uncle's advice. (10) The next morning he rode off and heard a woman cry. It was a maiden lamenting a dead knight. She addressed Peredur as accursed because he had been the cause of his mother's death. She explained that the two dwarfs were once servants of his parents, and that she herself was his foster-sister. The knight which slew her husband appeared and Peredur overcame him and bade him marry his foster-sister and submit to Arthur. He sent a message to Cai that he would yet avenge the dwarfs. Arthur was impressed by Peredur's deeds and vowed to set out in search of him since Peredur would not come to court nor would Cai leave it in search of him otherwise. Peredur meanwhile came to a castle where he was welcomed by (11) a poorly dressed but beautiful maiden. Her household was being kept alive by the nearby convent of nuns, since its goods had been seized by a young earl who had courted her, to her displeasure. Her foster-brothers bade her sleep with Peredur that he might champion their cause. Peredur sent her from his chamber to sleep and fought the young earl, overcoming him and restoring the tattered maiden's lands. He also overcame the Proud Knight of the Clearing and bade him forgive his lady, who was innocent.

(12) He came to a mountain castle where a tall woman ruled. She bade him sleep elsewhere if he valued his life, since nine hags lived near with their parents and were laying waste the country. Peredur stayed and at dawn heard screams. A hag was attacking the watchman, but Peredur struck her: she acknowledged him by name and spoke of a prophecy in which she would train him in arms. He stayed with the hag for three weeks, learning battle skills and then he chose a horse and arms and set out.

While staying with a hermit he saw (13) a sight which transfixed him: the blood of a wild duck upon the snow as a raven fed on it. The redness of the blood, the whiteness of the snow and the blackness of the raven put him in mind of the woman he loved best. While rapt in his vision, Arthur's men approached. Cai tried to rouse him but Peredur absently struck him down. (14) Then Gwalchmai, with more tact, approached him and led him to Arthur. Peredur realized that he had avenged the dwarfs on Cai, albeit absent-mindedly, and he returned to Caerleon with Arthur. (15) While there Angharad

Golden-Hair rejected his suit, but he was insistent that he loved her so much he would speak to no Christian until she confessed she also loved him. For this he was afterwards called the Dumb Knight.

He resumed his wandering and slew a lion which was guarding a giant's castle. A maiden bade him beware the Round Valley, the name of their land, since all the giants would kill him. Peredur fought and killed many but overcame the chief giant and granted him mercy on condition that he be baptized and submit to Arthur. The giant admitted that no Christian had previously ever remained alive in the Round Valley, and Peredur was glad he had not broken his oath of silence. (16) He slew a serpent which had been wasting the land and won the golden ring it guarded. Growing weary of solitude, Peredur turned back to Arthur's court and on the way met Cai who, not recognizing him, asked him who he was three times. He then struck Peredur in the thigh with his spear, but Peredur did not respond. He defeated an unknown knight who challenged Arthur's men and returned to court on foot. Angharad professed her love for Peredur, who was then enabled to speak, and everyone who had not recognized him until then did so now.

(17) While out hunting the stag with Arthur, Peredur came to a hall in the wilderness where lived the Black Oppressor and his daughters. The eldest begged Peredur to leave, and made her father refrain from killing him. The man told Peredur, who asked a taboo question warranting death, that he had lost his eye while fighting the Black Serpent of the Dolorous Mound. This serpent guarded a stone which, when it is clasped in one hand, gives as much gold as the possessor wishes in the other. In the ensuing combat, Peredur over-came the Black Oppressor.

(18) The Black Oppressor gave Peredur directions to find this serpent. He would come first to the court of the sons of the King of Suffering, so called because an *addanc* (underwater monster) killed one of them each day. After this he would come to the court of the Countess of the Feats who had a retinue of 300 men; every stranger who came there heard the tales of her war-band. After that he would find the Dolorous Mound. He would then kill the Black Oppressor (19) At the court of the sons of the King of Suffering, Peredur witnessed the revival of the dead sons in a bath of water, after which they were anointed. (20) The next day he followed the men to their assignation with the *addanc* and he encountered a beautiful woman seated on top of a mound. She advised him that the *addanc* hid behind a pillar in its cave from where it killed its foes. If he promised to love her beyond

all women, she would grant him the stone of plenty. She gave him a
ring, bestowing invisibility. When asked by Peredur where he would
find her again, she bade him look towards India.

(21) He then came to a valley divided by a river. On one bank a
flock of black sheep grazed, on the other a flock of white sheep. As
they crossed over to the other sides they would exchange colours. On
the bank was a divided tree: one half burning and the other half
green. (22) Beyond it on a mound sat a royal youth with a brace of
greyhounds. He heard hounds flushing out a stag across the valley.
The royal youth told Peredur that the three roads ahead led to his
own court, where Peredur was welcome to stay, to a fortress where he
could pay lodging, or to the *addanc*'s cave. Peredur found the cave
and slew the *addanc*. The three sons of the King of Suffering begged
him to choose one of their sisters as a wife, but Peredur refused. (23)
He took Etlym Red-Sword, a young earl, as his companion and
together they came to the court of the Countess of the Feats. Peredur
overthrew the 300 knights of her war-band in order to sit next to her
and offered her Etlym as her lover which she accepted. The 300 men
surrounding the Mournful Mound refused to do homage to Peredur,
who killed 200 of them; the remainder submitted to him. He then
killed the serpent and gave its stone to Etlym.

He lodged at a miller's house, in a valley full of mills. Because the
Empress of Constantinople was there, there was great need for grain
to be milled. (24) Peredur went to gaze on her daily and was
overcome for love of her. The miller lent Peredur money in order to
purchase arms for the coming tournament, which angered the miller's
wife. On the third day the miller roused Peredur from his reverie of
love by striking him with his axe-handle. He bade him attend the
tournament. Peredur was known as the Knight of the Mill and
overcame all comers, sending all the knights to the Empress and the
horses and arms to the miller's wife. He eventually got to see the
Empress with whom he was talking when a black man entered,
asking the Empress not to give the cup except to the knight who
would fight for her. (25) Peredur asked for the cup and was given it;
he sent it on to the miller's wife. Another black man came, bearing a
cup in the shape of a monster's claw, which Peredur likewise had and
sent on. Thirdly a red-haired man brought a crystal cup which was
likewise given to him. He then killed the three cup-bearers. The
Empress bade him remember the promise he made her when she
advised him about the *addanc*. He remained with her for fourteen
years.

(26) When Arthur was at Caerleon, with Peredur and others, a hideous damsel rode into court who greeted the whole assembly but berated Peredur for not having asked about the spear and the dish at his uncle's court. He had been the cause of great suffering. She told of a besieged castle, near Castle Syberw (the Proud Castle) her home, where whoever lifted the siege would gain the greatest honour in the world. Inside was a maiden to be rescued. Gwalchmai resolved to rescue her, while Peredur swore he would not rest until he discovered the meaning of the spear and dish. Each man went his separate way. Gwalchmai first slew a knight. (27) Then he proceeded to a castle where he was met by a maiden. An old man taxed the girl with welcoming her father's murderer. When her brother returned, Gwalchmai did not either admit or deny the deed but asked for a year's respite during which time he was on Arthur's business.

(28) Peredur set out to find the hideous damsel and met with a priest who told him it was Good Friday, on which he should not bear arms. Peredur spent Easter there and asked the priest to tell him of the Castle of Wonders, and then set out. He met a king out hunting and was imprisoned because of the familiarity he showed to the king's daughter. (29) While in prison Peredur learnt that the king was threatened by a neighbouring earl. The king's daughter provided Peredur with arms and let him out to help her father. Peredur overcame the earl and returned to prison, from whence he was released and offered the king's daughter as wife. He refused, asking the way to the Castle of Wonders. (30) He found it and, inside the castle, a *gwyddbwyll* board playing against itself. The side he supported lost and he threw the pieces and board into the lake, whereupon the hideous damsel appeared, telling him it was the Empress's board. If he wanted to retrieve it, he had to go to the Castle of Ysbidinongyl where a black man ravaged the Empress's lands. He granted the black man mercy on condition he gave back the board. The hideous damsel appeared and berated him for not killing the black man. He was forbidden to see the Empress until he had killed a further oppressor. (31) A stag with a single sharp horn on its forehead had laid waste the forest and had drunk up the fish-pools, leaving the fish exposed. Peredur took the Empress's lapdog to help flush out the stag, which he beheaded. A horsewoman appeared and berated him for killing the best jewel of her realm. She bade him seek a stone slab beneath a bush and there fight three times with a man.

A black man rose up from under the slab and fought him, but he disappeared before Peredur could slay him. At last he came to a hall

where a lame old man sat next to Gwalchmai. (32) A golden-haired
youth came in, saluted Peredur, and told him that he, the youth, had
been the hideous damsel, the horsewoman and the black man. He
had also carried the dish and the spear. The head belonged to
Peredur's first cousin, beheaded by the hags of Gloucester who had
lamed his uncle. The youth was Peredur's first cousin and it was
destined that Peredur should avenge him. Peredur and Gwalchmai
sent for Arthur and his men and then they fought the hags. Peredur
struck one who proclaimed that Peredur was come, the one they had
taught battle skills, who was destined to destroy them. Arthur and his
men then killed the hags of Gloucester. So runs the story of the Castle
of Wonders.

Commentary

1. Two triads speak of Peredur; number 86 calls him one of three
knights who won the Grail, and number 91 calls him one of three
fearless men. The name of his father, Efrawg, is derived from
Eboracum (York). There was a historical Peredur, possibly he
who is mentioned in the *Gododdin*, that epic by the sixth-century
poet Aneurin, which tells of the battle of Catraeth fought between
the Britons of the north and the men of Bernecia and Deira.[14,74]
In the long arguments that have raged about the pre-existence of
this story before Chrétien it must be remembered that while
Peredur was a common British name, Perceval was not – prior to
the written evidence of the Grail romances. It would seem, then,
that Perceval was derived from Peredur, not the other way
about.

2. The upbringing of Peredur is archetypal: he is raised in
seclusion, brought up in ignorance of arms and, according to
Chrétien, has no name. It is tempting to compare his youth with
that of Llew, who similarly has no name and is fated never to be
given the arms of manhood nor a wife of human stock. This
seems all part of the hard destiny that the hero has to overcome,
but whereas Llew's relationships with Sovereignty via Arianrhod
and Blodeuwedd are abrasive, Peredur is considerably assisted by
the many women whom he encounters. His exploits with the deer
are paralleled exactly in the *macgnimartha* of Fionn, where the two

women warriors who are fostering the boy find themselves unable to catch two deer; Fionn drives them back with only his hands.[8]

3. The three knights whom Peredur mistakes for angels are three of the most prominent of Arthur's court: Gwalchmai (Gawain), Gwair and Owain. They are searching for 'the knight who had distributed apples in Arthur's court'; a curious detail this, which is not explained further. Peredur claims to have seen the man. It is not stated whether the knights are seeking to harm him or detain him, and no other details of this lost story appear elsewhere. We may only speculate, drawing upon traditional lore for the answer. It is usual, before the appearance of a great wonder or before the institution of a quest, for an Otherworld personage to make an appearance, bearing some token of the wonder or quest. Often the bearer carries a branch from the Otherworldly tree, which boasts fruit, blossom and buds all on one bough. The fruits of the Otherworld sustain life and enhance awareness, as Maelduine finds on his voyages.[146] It is possible, then, considering the importance of these knights, that the man who distributed apples at Arthur's court was the messenger of the coming adventures and that Gwalchmai, Gwair and Owain (all seasoned Otherworldly visitors) have set out on the quest already. Gawain's part of the Grail quest figures largely in Chrétien, and while in later romances Gawain proves to be an unworthy Grail-winner, in a lost original he may have played a larger part than he does in *Peredur*.

4. His mother's advice to Peredur is a sweeping précis of courtly behaviour. The story-teller makes him implement this advice in the very next incident. Up until the point when he reaches his uncles' castles, Peredur behaves totally as the *Amadan Mor*, the Great Fool, in his headlong career to become trained as a knight.[61]

5. A careful analysis of this incident shows us that the Maiden of the Tent is not synonymous with the frightened girl in Chrétien's version. This maiden shows no fear and is described in much the same way as the Orchard Woman of *Gereint and Enid*, for she wears a golden diadem and sits in a golden chair. She offers food

to Peredur, which is one of Sovereignty's first actions, and allows him to take her ring. The text indicates that she does not rise in alarm; she remains seated because Peredur kneels to kiss her. We may take this to be Peredur's first encounter with Sovereignty, but because he is immature, no empowering exchange takes place between them yet (see note 20). The Proud Knight of the Clearing is, like the Black Knight in *Owain* and Mabonograin in *Gereint and Enid*, Sovereignty's champion. It is possible that the story-teller did not fully comprehend the implications of this incident: to accuse Sovereignty of adultery is really implausible, since she is not bound by the laws of earthly marriage and selects her own champions at will. Her encouragement of Peredur shows that she recognizes in him a future champion. All the tests and encounters that he subsequently has only go to develop him as a man and as a knight.

6. The insult to Gwenhwyfar is the most grave instance appearing in the three romances, for it is a gross insult to Sovereignty herself. As Arthur's queen, Gwenhwyfar represents the land and the Goddess. Triad 53 intriguingly speaks of three harmful blows which were struck in Britain. The first is that which Branwen received at the hands of Matholwch and the second is the blow which 'Gwenhwyfach struck upon Gwenhwyfar, and for that cause there took place afterwards the Action of the Battle of Camlann'.[38] This is further borne out in Triad 84, where Camlann is described as one of three futile battles brought about because of a quarrel between these two protagonists. Gwenhwyfach was Gwenhwyfar's sister, according to *Culhwch and Olwen*.[23] Triad 54 further confuses matters by telling us that Medrawt (Mordred, who is seen not as Arthur's son in early tradition but as an independent and worthy young man) *left neither food nor drink* in Arthur's court and, moreover, dragged the queen from her royal chair and struck her.[38] This gives notice of a tradition much concerned with this very incident of the queen's insult. The theft of the queen's cup is a loss of sovereignty to Arthur, since the Goddess bestows kingship by means of her cup. On p. 250 a whole text is devoted to telling this archetypal story.

The curious incident of the dumb dwarf couple is paralleled in

Chrétien by a maiden who has not laughed for six years, and whom the fool says will laugh to acclaim the best knight.[7] Kay strikes them both, as here. Goetinck is of the opinion that Chrétien's version was drawn from the original or proto-story, and I am inclined to agree. Dwarfs appear frequently in Breton stories but seldom in British ones. The prophetic laugh is also a feature of Celtic tradition, especially where Merlin exhibits this very feature in the *Vita Merlini*.[11,149] The function of both maiden and dwarfs is to name the hero and prophesy his future merit. This is the first time anyone speaks Peredur's name, which may not, in the proto-story, have been known to him.

Peredur defends Arthur's sovereignty by vanquishing the insulting knight and avenging Gwenhwyfar's affront by returning her cup. His refusal to come to court until avenged on Cai shows one part of the unfolding vengeance motif of this story. Cai is reproached by the arrival of the sixteen knights overthrown by Peredur, each of whom bears the same message. Cai's renown is somewhat dinted since Peredur is not a knight, nor does he have any training in arms but relies on his strength alone.

7. Much ink has been spilt concerning the number, function and designation of Peredur's uncles. The first uncle does not fish himself: his squires do so and he watches. Is he the Fisher King? He is also said to be lame. So is he also the Wounded King? It is revealed (see note 32) at the conclusion that the Witches of Gloucester lamed him, though Peredur is not told this until the end. But what of the second uncle? Within the context of *Peredur* we can find no clear answer to these questions, nor, perhaps, should we attempt to squeeze this story into the mould of the later Grail romances, which give us either clear or even more confused archetypal roles to draw on. It is sufficient to remark that the roles of these figures of Wounded or Lame or Fisher Kings became hopelessly confused during the transcription and reweaving of these stories.

The first uncle tests Peredur and prophesies that he will be the best swordsman of Britain. He gives the advice that obviates the asking of the Grail question, as later texts call it. He also makes Peredur a knight.

8. While Peredur fought with a stick at the court of the first uncle, his second bids him fight with a sword in a test of strength which is Otherworldly in its magical property of reuniting pillar and sword. The implication of Peredur's entire career to this point is that if he can perform tasks which outdo other men when he is not yet an experienced knight, what will he not be able to do when he is fully experienced and possessed of his whole strength? The broken sword became an emblem of the Grail quest in later texts.

9. This second uncle is neither lame nor wounded, according to the text, nor do we know the name of the castle where Peredur is at this point. These details are inconsistent within the text. The Grail procession, if it can be truly called such, consists of very different hallows from those of later sources. The spear appears to be that very weapon which causes the Dolorous Blow: this is the weapon that wounds the Wounded King and causes the devastation of the land, hence the blood that flows continually from it indicating the unhealing nature of the Dolorous Blow on both flesh and earth. The head in the dish is later revealed to have been Peredur's first cousin – doubtless the son of the second uncle at whose table he sits. A fuller discussion of this incident follows.

10. For the first time Peredur obeys his mother's dictum about answering a woman's cry. This incident seems strangely astray and in other texts is usually the signal for the Black Maiden to appear to reproach Peredur for not asking the Grail question. The sum of Peredur's thoughtless deeds is increased at this point by the accusation of his killing his mother by leaving her. It is possible that the foster-sister, of whom no previous mention has been made, was originally the same as the Black Maiden.

As in both *Owain* and *Gereint and Enid*, Arthur is eventually forced to go and seek his new knight, since Peredur will not visit him. The removal of Arthur from court enables the three heroes of the romances to acquire some of Arthur's authority, as they become his champions in the retention of sovereignty.

11. The Tattered Maiden goes unnamed here, though Chrétien names her Blanchflor. Her description fits the later Blood in the

Snow episode (see note 13), but what is puzzling is that Peredur does not take up her offer to sleep with her. Like Pwyll with Arawn's wife (*Mabon*, p. 24),[111] Peredur is chaste both from honour and because he has a combat to face. After he has restored her lands, she thanks him by name and offers her help if he should ever stand in need. It has been suggested that this episode owes something to *The Tragic Death of Cu Roi mac Daire* (*Mabon*, p. 49),[111] and the Tattered Maiden's original name may indeed have been a British variant of the Flower Bride's, if Chrétien's Blanchflor is any proof. The acquittal of the Tent Maiden seems extraneous and is but one instance of the doubling and sometimes tripling of incidents in the text.

12. The mountain castle seems analogous to the ubiquitous Castle of Maidens or Island of Women. Its gatekeeper is a prodigious child who bears arms, and its lady a seated countess. She is yet another appearance of Sovereignty who suffers under the affliction of a *gormes* (plague) of witches. This is the first mention of a prevailing theme throughout *Peredur*: the ridding of the land by the hero of a host of plagues – a thorough clean-up of the land. Dressed only in his shirt and trousers Peredur pursues and captures one of the witches, who acquiesces to a prophecy which says she shall train him in arms. She and her sisters are in the Celtic tradition of women warriors who train unskilled youths in battle.[120] The most famous instance of this is, of course, Cu Chulainn's training at the Rath of Scathach. There are faint traces of this story within *Peredur*. It is also possible that Peredur has had transferred to him a story once told of Cai, since the poem 'Pa Gur'[44] speaks of Cai's destruction of the Nine Witches of Gloucester. Possibly the similar incident of the Pitch-Black Witch in *Culhwch and Olwen* may be part of this fragmentary tale: that *anoeth* (impossible task) is fulfilled by Arthur himself, we will recall (see *Mabon*, p. 93).[111]

13. The hermit does not, as in other texts, explain the events of the quest to Peredur; that is left to others. The Blood in the Snow episode forms one of the central tableaux of the story. The white, red and black colours in proximity are an archetypal kaleidoscope into which the hero or heroine of a folk-tale looks to see their

lover revealed. The simplicity of this motif should not be dismissed, since these very colours signify the symbolic processes of alchemy also. Here a kind of soul-alchemy is effected in Peredur, who at last responds fully to the dream-image within his heart. He has met Sovereignty in many guises and has been propositioned by one earthly woman, Blanchflor, whose colouring this image represents. The Blanchflor of Chrétien's story is blond, since romantic convention made all beautiful women fair not dark. But in British and Irish tradition the desired one is dark not fair. This episode is very like that in *Culhwch and Olwen* when King Doged's wife swears the destiny of marrying only Olwen upon Culhwch. Peredur, like Culhwch, has never lain with a woman. This episode, therefore, represents his sexual maturity, when the dream-image of his heart matches the one woman who has offered him her love (see section III).

14. For the last time Cai insults and is bested by the hero in these romances. Again Gwalchmai is the intermediary. In this case he is the most suitable of Arthur's knights for this task. His own experience in matters of love and Otherworldly quests makes him a sensitive choice. The Triads speak of Gwalchmai as one who is most courteous to strangers and guests, and this makes him, with Peredur, one of the most fearless men in Britain.[38]

15. Peredur exhibits his new-found facility of courting women, as advised by his mother. Peredur lays a *geas* on himself not to speak to a Christian soul, in an excess of courtly love. This is but one of many tasks which, as a newly recognized knight, Peredur undertakes as a test of his increasing powers. He then enters an Otherworldly place, the Round Valley. His encounter and that of note 17 are very similar in kind. They remind the reader of Culhwch's meeting with Custennin at Yspaddaden's court (see *Mabon*, p. 97).[111] The old giant is a shapeshifter who is close-lipped in his agreements, like Yspaddaden, and, also like him, has an obliging daughter who helps Peredur.

16. The serpent lying on the gold ring is the first of three such monsters which Peredur slays. Cai's wounding of Peredur, in the terminology of the Grail corpus, makes our hero a wounded

knight, but the wound is healed by Gwenhwyfar: a fair exchange for the healing that he brought to her. Peredur is here under one of his many aliases as the Dumb Knight. When Angharad proclaims her love for Peredur, thus releasing him from his self-imposed *geas*, he does nothing about it according to the text. In other texts the hero who has reached sexual maturity thinks little of sleeping with many court ladies before he marries. This is especially true of Lanzelet and Guigamor, Gawain's son.[42]

17. The Black Oppressor with his one eye is very like Balor, the grandfather of Lugh (see *Mabon*, p. 84).[111] Like Balor, the Black Oppressor is a *gormes* or plague who lays waste the surrounding countryside. The encounter of Peredur and the giant is very like that between Culhwch and Yspaddaden, for Culhwch asks a question which breaks the custom of the giant, namely, to marry his daughter. Here Peredur asks about the loss of the Black Oppressor's eye. He receives information only after he has bested him.

18. Like both Yspaddaden, who lays *anoethu* upon Culhwch, and the Wild Herdsman, who acts as a guide to Owain, the Black Oppressor gives directions to the Mournful Mound. The triplication of serpents is very confusing for the reader, who feels that he or she is reading in circles. Before Peredur finds the Black Serpent, he kills an *addanc*, a water-monster, sometimes described as a giant beaver. The episode of the court of the sons of the King of Suffering that follows is a familiar theme in Celtic literature, associated with the *Ridere gan Gaire*, the Laughless Knight story. In this the hero's task is to find the cause of the knight's sorrow and to make him laugh once again. This always involves the restoration of his dead sons, slain by giants who are then made to share their victims' fate; this causes the knight to laugh. In some measure Custennin's role is as the Laughless Knight in *Culhwch and Olwen* (see *Mabon*, p. 97).[111] This episode is also a parallel of the sorrow at the Castle of Wonders, where Peredur saw the Grail procession. The King of Suffering is wounded by grief, not by the Dolorous Blow; but it is as though Peredur, having failed the earlier test, fulfils his role as liberator on the human level by restoring the sons.

19. This episode of reviving the sons is, of course, analogous to the Cauldron of Rebirth in *Branwen, Daughter of Llyr*, into which dead man are put, to be pulled out alive but dumb. The properties of the Grail include the gift of immortality or regeneration, but here the vessel of rebirth is a bath of warm water. In Celtic folk-tradition such a vessel is often employed by an old woman, or *Cailleach*, who aids the hero. She is not only able to revive the dead, but also, sometimes, has two vessels: a cauldron of poison and a cauldron of cure[69], into both of which she plunges the hero to harden him in his combats and to heal his wounds. The *Cailleach* is, like Ceridwen or the goddess depicted on the Gundestrup cauldron, plunging warriors into a vat of immortality, a prime figure in the regenerative mythos of the cauldron. In later tradition, which inherits all the earlier analogues, the Grail is represented by two figures: the Grail Maiden and the Loathly Lady. These representatives of Sovereignty have this joint role of healing and hardening the hero.

20. Peredur finally meets Sovereignty in her undisguised form, seated on top of a mound, symbolic of the land she guards. Whereas before he took a ring from the Maiden of the Tent, now he is given one in return for his undisputed love. This is one of the clearest sovereignty-bestowing episodes in the whole *Mabinogion*, for Peredur receives a ring from Sovereignty's hand. The juxtaposition of this incident with his slaying or overcoming of so many serpents may lead us to conclude that in the proto-story Peredur may have disenchanted the Black Maiden from her dark aspect into the beautiful maiden. In all other key Sovereignty stories the hero has to perform the *fier baiser*, kissing the hag or lying with her for her to change into her beautiful queenly aspect. The fact that Sovereignty disappears at this point, to re-emerge as the supreme royal woman, the Empress of the Eastern World, is significant.

In Celtic folk-story the woman destined to become the hero's wife is invariably the daughter of the King of Spain or Greece, or is simply called the daughter of the King of the Eastern World: in these stories the Otherworldly location is subsumed in an exotic Eastern province, though the East is described in exactly the same terms as one of the Blessed Isles. In *Parzival*,[40] where von Eschenbach attempted to replace the proto-story's Otherworld location with a more contemporary Middle Eastern origin, Parzival's half-brother, Feirfitz (who is piebald, being the son of a white father and a black mother), marries the Grail Maiden, Repanse de Schoy, with whom he returns to India, where their son Prester John is born.

21. From here on it is impossible to doubt that Peredur does indeed enter the Otherworld on his quest. The sheep that change colour also appear in the *imram* of Maelduine, where his ship comes upon an island bounded and divided by a brass fence with black sheep on one side and white on the other. They are guarded by a giant shepherd who transfers white sheep into the black sheep's pen, where they become black instantaneously.[146] We have, of course, already come upon the Otherworldly shepherd in *Owain*, where the Wild Herdsman guards the animals. Custennin in *Culhwch and Olwen* occupies the same role. It is possible that the noble youth whom Peredur meets was intended in the proto-story to occupy the same place in this story.

The Green and Burning Tree with both flames and leaves is the tree guarding the perimeters of the Otherworld. It reminds the traveller that the Otherworld is a mirror image of the earthly realms, that here things become or meet their opposites.

22. The meeting of Peredur with the noble youth is very like that of Pwyll with Arawn, even down to the invitation to visit the youth's wife (see *Mabon*, p. 23).[111] As in *Pwyll, Prince of Dyfed* there is more than a suggestion that Peredur and the youth change places, for, as the text states, this border of the Otherworld is where opposites meet and change places. The youth acts as guardian and way-shower for Peredur, offering him a choice of paths.

23. The sudden appearance of Etlym may lead us to suppose that he and the noble youth are one and the same, for Peredur is instrumental in obtaining his bride for him. We will recall that Pwyll and Arawn changed places in order that Arawn's enemy, Hafgan, might be overthrown. Pwyll, though he has the opportunity to sleep with Arawn's wife, abstains. Moreover, he

occupies the place of the King of Annwn while Arawn becomes merely a prince of Dyfed, just as Etlym agrees to be Peredur's man. Although the noble youth already has a wife, it is possible that he is unable to come to her save through Peredur's offices, since the Countess of the Feats already knows and loves him. The Countess herself is an aspect of Sovereignty in her guise as Mistress of the Games. We also note that Peredur gives up his right to the Countess, just as Cu Chulainn forgoes sleeping with Aoife during his weapon training, but gives her up to his brother-in-arms, Laegaire.[8]

24. The Valley of the Mills is rationalized by the story-teller, who remarks that the reason there are so many is that the Empress's army requires much grain to make bread. The Otherworld's components are consistent between texts of great variance, and it is clear that this valley is analogous to the island encountered by Maelduine and Ua Corra, where the miller of hell grinds to dust all possessions hoarded in the world. This valley, together with the Green and Burning Tree and the sheep, all indicate that we are indeed in the Otherworld (see Chapter Eight).

The Empress of the Eastern World is *Amherodres* of Constantinople, the great Byzantine empire which, by the time this tale was transcribed had become a place of fabulous reputation. She and the Woman of the Mound are identical, for when she gave Peredur the ring in order to slay the *addanc*, she told him to look to India to find her again. Her beauty corresponds so closely with his mystic Blood in the Snow vision that Peredur falls into a trance of contemplation again until roused by a blow from the miller, who acts here in the role of the Beheading Knight. The blow makes him come to his senses.

25. The three cups that Peredur drinks from are crucial to the Sovereignty theme, for, in Irish tradition, she offers three cups to the hero: the milk of fostering, the red wine of lordship and the dark drink of oblivion – the white, red and black of Peredur's vision. Here all the cups contain wine, but he drains them all (see Chapter Nine). There is also a suggestion, since one of the cups is a monster-foot, that the three men and cups are symbolic of the three serpents that Peredur has overcome.

Peredur reaches the conclusion of one of his quests, to find a wife, for he lives with the Empress for fourteen years. As in *Owain* and *Gereint and Enid*, whose pattern *Peredur* is almost bent to fit, the hero lives content with his wife for a time but re-emerges to continue his adventures and conclude his other task, which is invariably to fulfil his knightly duty.

26. The appearance of the Black Maiden here seems misplaced if, indeed, she has come to complain about Peredur's failure to ask the Grail question. There is an inconsistency in the text also, because she accuses him of failing to ask about the spear and the dish at the court of the Lame King, but it was at the court of his second uncle that Peredur saw the spear drip blood. Other Grail texts place this incident directly after the Grail Procession. The Black Maiden's appearance here seems more in keeping with the parallel incident in *Owain* where Lunet rides into Arthur's court to accuse Owain of failing to return to his wife, the Countess, since Peredur has indeed just left his wife. Either the incident is misplaced or the story-teller has changed the Black Maiden's speech.

The Black Maiden is the Goddess in her guise as the Dark Woman of Knowledge. Since Peredur is no longer united with his Empress, she takes on the form of the hag to reproach him. Her appearance is very like that of Eriu (Ireland): 'One time she was a broadfaced, beautiful queen and another time a horrible, fierce-faced sorceress, a sharp-nosed, whitey-grey, bloated, thicklipped, pale-eyed battlefiend.'[70] Besides reproaching Peredur, she brings news of a quest which Gwalchmai immediately sets out upon.

The adventures of Gawain occupy a great part of Chrétien's *Perceval*, where he is seen to be on a parallel quest to that of Perceval. The one who lifts the siege of the maiden will earn the greatest honour, says the Black Maiden. In Chrétien the prize is the Sword of the Strange Baldric. The knight that Gwalchmai kills in the *Mabinogion* in Chrétien accuses Gawain of killing his Lord.

27. The story-teller has little time to relate Gwalchmai's exploits in his enthusiasm for Peredur's adventures and so they are much reduced here. Although Chrétien left *Perceval* unfinished, it rather

looks as though he intended to tell the story of the finding and wielding of all the Hallows, for Gawain's concern is with the sword and the chessboard, and Perceval's with the Grail and spear. In Chrétien, Gawain defends himself in this incident with the chessboard while the maiden of the tower throws the pieces as weapons against their assailants. The incident as it remains in *Peredur* makes very little sense, and one needs to supplement the story with reading Chrétien from line 4,684 to 6,216 and from 6,519 to the end, where it will be seen that Gawain's quest takes him into some deep, Otherworldly adventures.

28. Peredur's quest has taken him a year and he arrives at a priest's house on Good Friday. We will remember that part of his quest is to discover the story and meaning of the Spear Which Drips Blood, but there follows no disquisition on the Christian analogues with the spear which a priest might well have given; the Spear of the Dolorous Blow of Celtic tradition, that which lamed Bran and which is the rightful weapon of the young hero (as typified by Lugh/Llew), was later associated with the Lance of Longinus, the centurion who pierced Christ's side on the cross, causing blood and water to flow therefrom. This biblical story (John 19:34) flowed into apocryphal Grail tradition as the origin of the two cruets borne by Joseph of Arimathea to Europe (see p. 247).

There is another inconsistency in the text where Peredur asks for instructions on how to find the Castle of Wonders, as this is the first mention of the place. The story-teller clearly intends us to understand this to be the court of the second uncle, where the Grail procession appeared.

The king's daughter seems to be yet another aspect of Sovereignty, since she upholds Peredur's cause and arms him herself. This incident, where the hero is unjustly imprisoned and let out to help fight a tournament, is almost obligatory in medieval literature.

29. She clothes him in traditional fool's colours, but Peredur triumphs, refusing yet another bride and winning yet another combat against an encroaching earl.

30. The following two incidents are part of Sovereignty's games. The *gwyddbwyll* board is one of the Hallows of Sovereignty and appears in the list of the Thirteen Treasures of Britain (see *Mabon*, pp. 51–2),[111] where the board is of gold and the pieces of silver, and the pieces play by themselves. The board represents the land and is a prime symbol of Sovereignty, so Peredur's action of casting it into the lake is doubly unfortunate, since the board belongs to the Empress, his wife. The games that Sovereignty imposes like tests upon him entail the ridding of the land of yet another plague, Ysbidinongyl, whom Peredur kills, but only after unwisely sparing him. It has been suggested that Ysbidinongyl may derive from Yspaddaden Pen Cawr in *Culhwch and Olwen* or from the knight called Espinogre who appears in Malory.[74]

31. The stag with one horn appears as a malefic unicorn. With only the Empress's dog for a guide, Peredur overcomes it. The unicorn seems to fulfil much the same role as the two dragons of *Lludd and Llefelys*, and is no mere Otherworldly messenger intended to lure the hero, as in *Pwyll, Prince of Dyfed* and *Gereint and Enid*, but the emblem of an Otherworldly power loosed chaotically upon the earth. All green things are dead and the waters are dried up, creating the wasteland so familiar from the other Grail texts. Like the two dragons the unicorn is Sovereignty's beast, and it is Peredur's task to overcome it or bring it under control. The fact that the huntswoman takes up the dog suggests that she is none other than the Empress, and that she and the Black Maiden aspect of herself are playing off one against the other in order to guide Peredur to the heart of his quest, rather like a pair of sheepdogs with a sheep. It is this killing of the unicorn that causes Peredur's later guise to be called 'the Freer of the Waters', which becomes the honoured title of the Grail-winner.

The combat with the black man under the stone who disappears before Peredur can strike him dead is the last of the tests that keep him from reaching his destination.

32. The golden-haired youth who admits to having been the many characters within Peredur's adventures is somewhat of a

puzzle, since these guises have all been the Otherworldly masks of Sovereignty and her representatives male and female. The shape of the story almost demands that the Empress appear here as the Black Maiden and drop her last disguise to be once again restored to Peredur as his rightful wife and royal Sovereignty. Goetinck suggests that the story-teller has misheard or misread *damoisel* (youth or page) for *damoiselle* (maiden).

It is at last revealed that the Spear Which Drips Blood is the weapon with which the Witches of Gloucester lamed Peredur's uncle, and that the head in the dish is none other than that of his cousin. Gwalchmai and Peredur join forces once more to do battle with the Witches. Peredur is responsible for killing their leader while Arthur and his men destroy the rest. Thus the Witches are no longer a *gormes*, free to waste the land.

II GRAIL FAMILY AND HALLOW QUEST

Throughout the *Mabinogion* we have noted the way certain heroes succeed to Otherworldly roles, becoming Sovereignty's champions or partaking in the Succession of the Pendragons (see *Mabon*, p. 18).[111] There is also, as we find in *Peredur*, a hereditary guardianship with which Peredur's family is deeply concerned. In this pattern the Grail and other Hallows are virtually heirlooms which successive members of the Grail family both guard and wield.

Within Peredur's family the guardianship is still upheld, but the active wielding of the Hallows awaits the Freer of the Waters, as the Grail-winner is traditionally known. How the Hallows come to be within the guardianship of a particular family is often the missing part of the story.

We have seen in *Branwen, Daughter of Llyr* how the cauldron – that earliest analogue of the Grail – comes from a lake in Ireland and is brought by Llassar and Cymeidei, titanic underworld figures (see *Mabon*, p. 42).[111] Matholwch of Ireland proves unworthy of it, and Llassar and his wife bring it to Britain where it is given into Bran's keeping. Its unworthy use and Efnissien's subsequent destruction of it render it inoperative in the earthly realms. Bran becomes its Otherworldly guardian, for he is wounded by a spear in his heel: a wound which causes him to become the Lame or Wounded King, struck by the Dolorous Blow, which afflicts both land and king. His hall at Gwales and Harlech is caught in time, both an Otherworldly overlay where heroes rejoice and sing in unending bliss, and a place where the laws of life and death are suspended for, though beheaded, Bran still speaks with his faithful companions.

The suspension of time in Bran's hall is a direct ancestor of the Otherworldly time-scale in the hall of the Grail Castle where the Wounded King, smitten by the Dolorous Blow, does not die but holds court in expectation of the Freer of the Waters. Bran himself has long been understood as the prototype of the Wounded Kings of later Grail romances.[124] But Bran's guardianship is not a hereditary one, for his sister, Branwen, dies childless and his own son is slain by Caswallawn. The guardianship both of the Hallows and of Sovereignty is, therefore, a mystical one in which later characters appear to fulfil the roles of Bran and Branwen. As we have seen in *Mabon* (pp. 47–8)[111] it is Arthur who succeeds to the guardianship of the cauldron in the Succession of the Pendragons. The female role in this cycle is that of a Daughter of Branwen, a long succession of women who exemplify Sovereignty but who seldom wield her power themselves: Peredur's mother is one such and Rhiannon is another.

When a hereditary guardianship is established, the Hallow (or Hallows) is normally bestowed upon a worthy ancestor, or is won by him or her from a god. As not all descendants of the ancestor are worthy, one may lose the Hallow, or it may be stolen from him by an enemy. The empowering sovereignty is thus robbed from that family and it falls to a young champion to win it back. Such is the pattern within *Peredur*. For further verification of this we need to consult the parallel career of Fionn mac Cumhail whose youthful exploits closely follow those of Peredur.

The Fionn cycle is amorphous and almost as sprawling an epic as the Matter of Britain itself. It is not generally thought of in terms of a Hallow quest, though that is indeed the theme of the *Macgnimartha Fionn*, for it is about the recovery of the Crane-Bag, the receptacle for the Treasures of Ireland.

The Crane-Bag belonged to Manannan, Otherworldly King of the Blessed Isles, and was made from the skin of a woman, Aoife, who for love of Manannan's son had incurred the jealousy of Iuchra, an enchantress. Iuchra bespelled Aoife into crane-shape and so she lived for 200 years. When Aoife died, Manannan placed all the Treasures of Ireland into the bag made of her skin: the shirt and knife of Manannan, Goibhne's belt and smith's hook, the King of Scotland's shears, the King of Lochlann's helmet and the bones of Asail's swine.

> When the sea was full, its treasures were visible in its middle; when the fierce sea was in ebb, the crane-bag in turn was empty.[76]

The Crane-Bag was then given to Lugh, the many-gifted champion of the Tuatha de Danaan, and, after his withdrawal from the affairs of men, it descended to many kings and heroes, among whom was Cumhail, brother-in-law of Lugh.

Cumhail was the chief of Ireland's *fianna* [war-band] and the primacy of his clan was due to his possession of the Crane-Bag. During the battle of Cnucha, the man who guarded Cumhail's treasure-bag treacherously struck a blow at his master and thereafter ran away with the bag, leaving Cumhail to be slain by the sons of Morna, his enemies. Cumhail had left his wife, Muirne, the half-sister of Lugh, pregnant and she bore a boy called Demne. She was so fearful of Cumhail's enemies that she gave her son into the fostering of a druidess, Bodmall, and a woman-warrior, Liath Luachra. Demne's youthful exploits were prodigious during his secret upbringing. He beat all the youths at hurling and when they complained to the king, the king asked for a description of the boy. 'He is fair,' they said. 'Then let him be called Fionn,' said the king.

Fionn was on his way to seek the remnant of his father's troop of *fianna* when he came upon a wailing woman, weeping tears of blood, with a bloody mouth, lamenting for her dead son, slain by a mighty champion. Fionn pursued the warrior and slew him. In the man's possession was the Crane-Bag, for it was he who had struck Fionn's father. Taking the bag with him, he found his father's old companions-in-arms and showed them the bag. One of them, Crimnall, opened the bag:

> and laid bare its priceless treasures one by one, and as his old comrades watched him, their eyes grew bright, their weapon-hands tightened on their spears and swords, and age seemed to drop from them instantly.[76]

Then Fionn left them and apprenticed himself to the poet, Finneces, who was awaiting the day when he might eat the salmon of knowledge. Fionn caught it and while preparing it to eat, licked the drops that had fallen upon his thumb. Forever afterwards he bore the thumb of knowledge which he only need put under his tongue in order to predict the future.[76] (See also *Mabon*, p. 122ff.)[111]

We note that Fionn's upbringing follows the classical pattern of the hero: raised in obscurity, given a boyhood name, he yet succeeds in besting his enemies and in winning back the Hallows of which his father was guardian. His subsequent career shows the empowerment that the Crane-Bag gives, for Fionn becomes chief of the *fianna* and a great hero, though his career comes to its close when he attempts to impede the representative of Sovereignty, whom he seeks to marry, from eloping with a younger man.

In a similar manner Peredur, though raised in ignorance of arms and without knowledge of his family's heritage, finds his feet led along the path to vengeance and the restitution of the Hallows, which are not lost in this story but inoperative. The family tree of Peredur may be tentatively reconstructed as shown in Figure 7.1.

The responsibility of wielding the Hallows is, at any time, an awesome burden and, looking at the characters in the family tree in Figure 7.1, one that has taken its toll. Efrawg and his six sons do not seem to have ever entered into the guardianship, since their main occupation is war and tournaments, in which they have all died. Peredur's mother, the Widow, seems to have guarded him from the knowledge of both his father's heritage and his matrilineal family's guardianship. Her brother, whom we will call the Fisher King, though he does not actually fish in the text, may be the father of the shapechanging cousin who has attempted to wield the Hallows and been enchanted by the Witches of Gloucester for his pains, and who appears at the end to explain matters. The Lame King, at whose court the Hallows appear, may be the father of the cousin whose head is paraded in the dish, causing such lamentation. It is possible that the head-in-the-dish cousin was also a failed Grail-winner. Certainly his father, the Lame King, bears the unhealing wound of the Dolorous Blow.

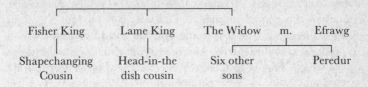

Figure 7.1: *The Descent of Peredur*

The attempt to match *Peredur* with later Grail symbolism becomes a struggle. The title of Fisher King is a case in point, since it is an amalgam of two ideas from the French romances, wrought of *pécheur* (sinner) and *pêcheur* (fisher); the one who has lost the empowerment of the Hallows loses them through sin, according to this scenario, which, as we have seen, is but a Christianized way of interpreting the king's failure to ratify his bond with Sovereignty. But behind the title Fisher King we may discern a faint trace of the proto-story in which Peredur's uncle was the King Under the Wave, Ri faoi Thonn. We may establish such a connection via a body of Celtic folk-stories which, though collected in the nineteenth century were found in oral tradition, that most persistent preserver of stories lost from literary sources.

The stories upon which I draw here are *Coldfeet and the Queen of the Lonesome Isle*, *Wishing Gold and the Queen of the Moving Wheel*, *Baranoir and the Daughter of the King Under the Wave*, *Gold Apple*,[68, 69] and *The Well at World's End*.[83] I shall not attempt to tell them here in full but merely to establish an archetypal pattern from their contents, which are remarkably similar and corroborative. All five are from Irish traditional story-tellers, and it is indeed doubtful whether any folklorist could prove cross-fertilization with later literary sources; the stories magnificently represent the innerworld archetypes of a shared Celtic culture and show a marked resemblance to those images and characters appearing in *Peredur*.

Coldfeet is so named because of his extraordinary growth, which is titanic, as are his prodigious exploits in running down cattle and bringing them home in one hand for dinner. His mother, unable to feed him or clothe him adequately, sends him away to make good. He meets three giants whom he overcomes, and then the giants' mother, a *Cailleach*, lays on him a *geas* to bring to her from the Lonesome Isle the Sword of Light which never fails, a loaf of bread which is never eaten and a bottle of water which is never drained. Coldfeet is the *Amadan Mor*, but he sets off on his quest. He encounters three old men, one 700 years old, one 1,400 years and the other 2,100 years old, who direct him on his quest. The Lonesome Isle is ruled by a queen who sleeps, her castle revolves and round her bed the Hallows are to be found. Coldfeet takes them all, with the old men's advice, but also lies with the queen while she sleeps. He takes them to the *Cailleach*, but refuses to yield them to her, that not being part of the bargain. He beheads her with the Sword of Light.

On his return to his mother's house Coldfeet is tricked into parting with each of his treasures, which the cunning householder of his lodgings replaces with mundane and similar-looking objects. Coldfeet and his mother are poor as before. Nine months later the Queen of the Lonesome Isle awakes and finds a child at her side, which grows unusually fast. She vows to seek out the one who took the Hallows and made her pregnant. She stops at each of the three lodgings and observes the inexhaustible loaf and bottle of water and the supernatural light of the sword, which she appropriates until she finds Coldfeet's house, where he admits to taking them and fathering the child. Together they return to the Lonesome Isle with the Hallows.

This humorous folktale might stand beside *Peredur* only as a faint parallel if it were not for the wealth of corroborative material to be found in the other stories. *The Well at World's End* is a near variant of *Coldfeet*. In this the King of Connacht has a wounded foot and sends out his three sons to fetch the curative bottle of water from the Well of World's End. The two eldest brothers are cunning and the youngest simple, but he is the destined finder of the Well. He is hosted by a *Cailleach* who sends him on to her sister hag. On his way Ceart, the youngest brother, meets a queenly figure dressed in red silk who encourages him on his quest. The second *Cailleach* sends him on to her brother, an old man, who bears Ceart on his shoulders across the waters that guard the island of the Well. The castle where the queen of the island sleeps, as in *Coldfeet*, is guarded by beasts and monsters, which Ceart overcomes. A wheel throws up the water of the well. Ceart fills two bottles – one for his father and the other for the old man. He is told to touch nothing else, but takes a bottle marked 'Water for the World' and the loaf marked 'Bread for the World' together with the Sword of Light. He also lies with the queen and her eleven waiting women, who are asleep. The old man pours the water on himself and becomes young, as do his sisters. Ceart is tricked into giving up his Hallows, though he retains the bottle intended for his father. His brothers steal it and cure their father. The Queen of World's End and her ladies all bear children, and she goes in search of Ceart, rejecting the false brothers and bringing with her the three Hallows. Ceart and the queen marry.

In *Wishing Gold* the hero is already the offspring of the Queen of the Lonesome Isle and the King of Erin: Wishing Gold's father marries a false queen who wishes the boy dead. She causes the King to send Wishing Gold to fetch the curative water from the well of the Queen of the Moving Wheel. On his way Wishing Gold is hosted by three women, each of whom tends one of three senile, sick old men who turn out to be his uncles, brothers to his mother. They give him advice on entering the Castle of the Moving Wheel where the queen is asleep. The castle is in the sky and it can be brought to earth only by Wishing Gold picking three apples from the tree and throwing them up in the air. He gains his prize, sleeps with the queen, and the castle is again withdrawn to the sky by his casting up the three apples. Wishing Gold makes all his uncles young again by application of the water. Wishing Gold's stepbrothers, sons of the false queen, waylay him, steal the water and pretend he is dead.

Meanwhile Wishing Gold returns to the Lonesome Isle. His mother commands him to return to Erin and defend his father's kingdom, which is threatened by the Queen of the Moving Wheel, who is demanding the head of the man who visited her while she slept. Wishing Gold and the Queen of the Moving Wheel fight and are reconciled. The false queen is punished.

In *Baranoir*, the quest is for the destined wife and the curing of the Seven Kings of Gleann Glas (the Grey Glen). Baranoir is aided by *Fear Gansaol* (the Lifeless Man) and by *Bromach Caol*

Donn (the Slender Dun Filly), which bears him through the great Wheel of the World to the Well of Fortune, where the curative waters are. Baranoir also gains the Sword of Light from three battle hags and engages in a riddle game with the King Under the Wave's daughter, who turns out to be his destined wife, though Baranoir has to overcome many tests to gain her. The Dun Filly is revealed to be a woman under enchantment, the sister of the Seven Kings, whom Baranoir disenchants. The *Fear Gansaol* is revealed as a dead man whose debts Baranoir has lifted, thus enabling him to rest in peace.

In *Gold Apple* the King of Erin marries a hag who turns into a beautiful queen; however, she plots to destroy Gold Apple, the king's son by a former wife. She lays a *geas* on him to bring her the eight-legged dog's head. Gold Apple stays with each of three giant uncles, who each give him an apple with which to find the next uncle's house. Lastly Gold Apple comes to his grandfather's house. Following his family's directions he finds the place where the eight-legged dog is kept: the realm of the King Under the Wave, whose daughter he promptly falls in love with. He refuses his stepmother the head of the eight-legged dog, since the agreement was only that he should bring it home. She subsequently falls dead at his touch. He returns to his grandfather's house, where he learns that the Queen of the Lonesome Glen stole away his grandfather's ring of youth, pot of health and rod of enchantment, the lack of which renders him old and ill. Gold Apple regains these Hallows and marries the Queen of the Lonesome Glen,[69] having disenchanted his uncle, who was bespelled into the eight-legged dog.

It will become clear to the reader that a cohesive pattern is emerging from which we may perhaps deduce the outline of Peredur's proto-story (see Figure 7.2).

The many common elements that can be derived from these stories lead to a startling discovery: the Hallow quest is usually prompted by the hag's *geas*, and the Hallows themselves are in the keeping of an Otherworldly queen. While the Hallows vary in kind, there is a consistent emphasis on their restorative properties, paramount among which is the healing quality of Otherworldly waters. The hero is aided and directed by three siblings

Text	Origin of Quest	Object of Quest	Hero Aided By	Keeper of Hallows	Hallows Guarded By	Nature of Enchantments Lifted
Coldfeet and the Queen of the Lonesome Isle	hag's *geas*	to fetch the Hallows to the hag	three ancient men	Queen of the Lonesome Isle	revolving castle	not specified, though hero overcomes giants
The Well at World's End	King's wound	to fetch curative water	two *cailleachs* and their elderly brother	Queen of the Well at World's End	water-wheel and monsters	helpers regain youth, father healed
Wishing Gold	false queen's *geas*	to fetch curative water	three sick uncles	Queen of the Moving Wheel	Castle of the Moving Wheel	uncles healed and made young, false queen punished
Baranoir	Fear Gansaol's *geas*	to fetch curative water	Fear Gansaol and woman enchanted into a filly	three battle hags and daughter of the King Under the Wave	Wheel of the World	Fear Gansaol able to rest, enchanted filly becomes a woman
Gold Apple	false queen's *geas*	to fetch eight-legged dog and Hallows	three giant uncles and grandfather	Queen of the Lonesome Glen and grandfather	not specified	implied healing of grandfather
Peredur	Black Maiden's *geas*	to discover meaning of dish and Spear Which Drips Blood	two uncles	Empress of Constantinople	Valley of the Mills	implied healing of lame uncle, implied disenchantment of cousin ridding land of plagues (witches, giants, serpents, etc.)

Figure 7.2: *The Proto-Hallow Quest in Celtic Folk-Story*

whose sex, though it varies, is usually male; they are, moreover, related to the hero. In *Coldfeet* these uncles are increasingly elderly, representing a tradition which we perceived in the 'oldest animals' story in *Mabon* (p. 134).[111] It is possible that this was a feature of the proto-story of *Peredur*, since this tradition of Hallow guardians of increasing ages is found in the German Grail cycles of *Parzival* and *Diu Cröne*, where three generations of Grail guardians are represented by Parzival, Anfortas and Titurel in a Chinese-box-like gradation.[39,40] These helpers aid the hero by training him in certain magical skills or in feats of arms, as in *Peredur*, and act as staging-posts along the path of his quest.

In three of the stories the hero begets his successor upon the sleeping Hallow Queen, and here we may perceive the mythic foundation for Galahad's conception by Lancelot upon Elaine, who is disguised as Guinevere. The hero's act is not a rape but an Otherworldly engendering of his successor in the Hallows guardianship. The Hallow Queen is magical and deadly to any but the bravest champion, as we find in *Baranoir*, who has a magical riddle contest with his bride and in *Gold Apple*, who physically fights with his.

The restoration of the Hallows to the earth must be effected by the hero's penetration of the Otherworldly gates, represented by the revolving castle or wheel. This image is paramount in the initiation of the seer–poet, as we saw from Taliesin's experience: he physically enters the womb of Ceridwen and speaks figuratively of his initiation: 'I have been three periods in the prison of Arianrhod.'[23] (see also *Mabon*, p. 128.)[111] Arianrhod, the Silver Wheel, has for her castle Caer Sidi, the turning castle, which is a place of death or wonder, depending on the abilities of the one who approaches it. As we saw in *Math, Son of Mathonwy* (*Mabon*, p. 86),[111] Arianrhod's mythos is paralleled by that of Ethniu, Balor's daughter, who is similarly marooned upon a solitary island because her son will oust her father. Only the daring hero can impregnate her because of the dangers of the island. As Ethniu's son is the great god Lugh and Arianrhod's child is Llew, we do not have to stretch the parallel at all. Both gods wield the spear or the Sword of Light, wrenching it from their grandfather's evil use – under which it becomes the weapon of the Dolorous

Blow, enchanting the land – and restoring it to its regenerative function, to rid the land of plagues and invasion and to bring healing. Thus the Sword of Light in our stories is really an analogue of the Spear Which Heals and Wounds.

Consistent throughout the stories is the wheel or turning castle. It is both an Otherworldly barrier, as we have seen, but it is also the Wheel of Life and Death. In *Peredur* this symbolism is not totally lost but is rationalized providing us with a Valley of Mills. The juxtaposition of this episode with Peredur's final encounter with the Empress should leave us in no doubt that the mills are a relic of this powerful Celtic symbol.

Despite the variety of the heroes' adventures the outcome of the quest is the same: the land is put to rights; the false queen, who here takes the place of the Black Maiden, and perhaps of the false Sovereignty (see p. 49), is punished or killed; the helpers are disenchanted or healed; and the hero wins his queen, going with her to live in the Otherworld and start a new line of Hallow guardians.

This hereditary guardianship of the Hallows becomes a prime feature of later Grail stories and represents the passing over of one mythic pattern for another. In the Succession of the Pendragons successive heroes win and wield the Hallows in order to be king; in the hereditary guardianship of the Hallows, specifically the Grail, this royal role becomes a holy one. This process reveals a deeper association with the roots of kingship, which is holy as well as royal: a combination which is not lost even today in Britain's constitutional monarchy, which, while relegating its political right of government to Parliament, retains the sacral bond of monarch with land.

It is this linking of holy and royal roles that lies at the heart of *Peredur*, for it is his encounter with Sovereignty, the Hallow Queen herself, that establishes the shape of the Grail corpus for all time.

III THE ROYAL BLOOD IN THE HOLY SNOW

Much has been made of the etymological pun arising from the medieval *San Greal* (Holy Grail): by the rearrangement of one letter it readily becomes *Sang Real* (Royal Blood). It is a pleasing and mythically veracious pun appropriate for the story of *Peredur*, for there is a way in which the Grail is holy and the Blood royal, without recourse to Christian paradigms, though these are likewise appropriate and mythically bonded with both Christianity's own mystical tradition and the earlier, pagan glyphs discussed below.

Peredur is not a Grail-quest story in the later sense of that term, for at no point does the Grail appear in the story, either in a vision or to physical sight, as it does in other texts. The only direct quest that Peredur undertakes is voiced by the Black Maiden as follows:

> When you went in to the court of the lame king and saw the squire carrying a sharpened spear, with a drop of blood running from the point to the lad's fist like a waterfall, and other marvels as well, you asked neither their cause nor their meaning. Had you asked, the king would have been made well and the kingdom made peaceful, but now there will be battles and killing, knights lost and women widowed and children orphaned, all because of you.[22]

This admonition is made only in the last quarter of the story. It is possible that this episode is misplaced as I suggested on p. 180, but it still follows that part of Peredur's quest is to discover the meaning of the Dolorous Blow, for that is struck by the very spear which he sees paraded about the hall.

It will be seen then that Peredur's quest is to undo the damage wrought by the spear and by his own silence and thereby to lift the enchantments upon the land. This theme, as we have already seen, is pervasively present throughout the *Mabinogion*. It is the motivation of Manawyddan, Branwen, Culhwch (in the Twrch Trwyth hunt), Lludd and Peredur.

Let us briefly examine the theme of the Dolorous Blow in *Peredur*. The first dolorous stroke happens before the beginning of the story, in the laming of Peredur's second uncle, the Lame King. We are told by Peredur's shapeshifting cousin that this blow was struck by the Nine Witches of Gloucester; from this we must conclude that the witches had the Hallow of the Spear Which Heals and Wounds in their possession.

This brings us to a consideration of the witches themselves. What is their function in *Peredur*? We have already seen in *The Well at World's End* (p. 188), as well as in the *Balor on Tory Island* story (*Mabon*, p. 84),[111] that the Hallow Queen is accompanied by a number of waiting-women – usually eleven or twelve – whom the hero impregnates while they sleep. In the Balor story they are set to protect and guard Ethniu, by whom Sovereignty may be won, together with monsters and other barriers to the hero's success. The witches may be seen from this viewpoint or, alternatively, we can look to a feature of Celtic mythology in which nine sisters or priestesses guard an Otherworldly island.

We can instance Morgen and her eight sisters from the *Vita Merlini*, who guard the island of Avalon to which Arthur is ferried by Barinthus for the healing of his wounds.[11] These sisters are Otherworldly women, possessed of specific arts, each being the genius of a quality or Otherworldly gift. The Celtic and Greek mythologies overlap on this feature, as the Celtic ninefold sisterhood is analogous to the Greek muses, who are the Daughters of Memory, Mnemosyne. Their function is similar but not identical, for the Celtic sisterhood has two modes of manifestation: in the Otherworld they are beauteous women to whose island heroes sail in order to enjoy unending bliss; in the realm of the earth they frequently assume the guise of hags. They are aligned with the archetype of the Dark Woman of Knowledge.

We have already noted how aspects of the Goddess of Sovereignty are similarly polarized: she appears as a beautiful maiden bearing kingship or as a fearful hag bearing a loathly challenge. The transformative nature of Sovereignty is, like the land or the seasons that change the land, a major feature of the hero's quest. She is beautiful and may bestow kingship on the hero, but she is likewise deadly, dangerous to the unworthy.

The Witches of Gloucester are a ninefold sisterhood who represent the hag aspect of the Goddess of Sovereignty in her guise as Hallow Queen. They function as a group of female warriors who guard the Hallows and who are able to bestow battle skills upon Peredur, whom they train *so that he can overcome them*, as it is prophesied. The hero who goes to seek the Hallows and their empowerment is always met by a hag – in Peredur's case, the ninefold Hags of Gloucester. They are the three times three, the ninefold emanation of the Triple Goddesses of Celtic tradition and, more specifically, of the Goddess of Sovereignty herself.

In *Baranoir* and *Gold Apple* we saw how these two aspects are combined in the Hallow Queen, who actually engages in personal combat with the hero. In *Peredur*, this identification is obscured by the polarization of aspects into different characters. The extreme danger in approaching the Hallows unworthily is instanced in all Grail texts: Lancelot is unable to enter the Grail Chapel in Malory[25] because of his sin with Guinevere; attempting to help the priest who is raising the Grail, he rushes forward and is blinded for his temerity. This is the very action of the spear: it may heal or it may wound.

All the Hallows are Otherworldly tokens of high powers; their ability to regenerate does not impede their ability to devastate. This polarity of function is demonstrated in all the texts involving a Hallow quest, and it is the moral integrity of the bearer of the Hallows that determines whether their effect is destructive or regenerative. Unworthy bearers or heroes become protagonists of cosmic evil, while worthy ones become protagonists of cosmic good.

There is no such dichotomy in the Celtic proto-story. The Hallows are amoral in their application because they abide eternally in the Otherworld; it is the manner of their wielding by Otherworldly figures in the earthly realms that cause them to be regenerative or destructive.

Thus an unworthy hero seeking the empowerment of the Hallows (an action which symbolically entitles him to be a consort of Sovereignty and a ruler in his own land) suffers an encounter with a hag and receives the Dolorous Blow, which causes him to bear an unhealing wound and his land to become waste.

The implications of this understanding provide us with a conundrum: the hag aspect of Sovereignty is responsible for the wasteland and the Wounded King, administering a Dolorous Blow which causes the Hallow Queen to be without a consort and for the land to assume its dark or wasted appearance. *Yet*, simultaneously, the hag aspect of Sovereignty encourages the hero, even to the extent of providing him with the skills that will enable him to overcome both these ills.

Thus Peredur's Lame Uncle was doubtless once a Hallow-quester who failed. It is left to his nephew to succeed, with the misleading advice of his family and the battle skills that the Witches of Gloucester provide. The Dolorous Blow may also be seen as extending to the cousin whose head is in the dish.

Further 'dolorous blows' may be discerned in *Peredur*, notably the insult to Gwenhwyfar. The absence of a Grail proper has worried some commentators, who have discarded *Peredur* as a corrupt text, tangential to the mainstream tradition. If we focus once more upon this incident, however, it will become obvious that Gwenhwyfar's cup is the prototype of the Grail, since it is Sovereignty's own cup, which she offers to kings. Its possession by Gwenhwyfar is totally apposite, since she is Arthur's manifest Sovereignty.

At the opening of Peredur's active career the imbalances wrought by the unwielded Hallows are already at work. The warrior who insults Gwenhwyfar by casting wine upon her, snatching her cup and boxing her ears is an agent of the Hallow's Otherworldly guardian. The power of the Grail, which is properly the empowering Hallow wielded by a queen, is almost withdrawn. Only the action of Peredur prevents this happening, although he is powerless to prevent the cup's regenerative powers being reversed prior to his arrival. His immediate handling of the situation and his championship of Arthur's queen show his immature ability to champion Sovereignty in a like manner.

Another 'dolorous blow' is effected by the unicorn, which dries up the fish-pools, devastates green and growing things and kills other beasts. The description of the unicorn reveals that its function is like that of the spear:

> '[the] single horn on its forehead [is] as long as a spear shaft and as sharp as the sharpest thing.'[22]

As the spear wounds the Lame King, so the unicorn devastates the land. The horsewoman who appears to remonstrate with Peredur for killing this beast is shown to be none other than the Empress, whose lands the unicorn devastates (p. 168). Peredur is himself wounded by Cai, though he is healed by Gwenhwyfar, which is a parallel of the wounding and healing of the Lame King.

It would perhaps be valuable to scan the list of objects that might be possible Hallows in this text, which Peredur either wins or is given. They are as follows:

Ring – taken from the Tent Maiden

Cup – restored to Gwenhwyfar, stolen by Otherworldly knight

Sword – given by the second uncle, the Lame King, to test Peredur's strength

Ring of Invisibility – given to Peredur by the Woman of the Mound, alias the Empress

Three cups – won in combat with three Otherworldly champions, given to Miller's Wife

Chessboard – cast away by Peredur and won from Ysbidinongyl

Unicorn's head – taken by Empress

To which list we must add the Spear Which Drips Blood and the head in the dish, which Peredur sees but does not win. The archetypal list of Hallows in later Grail literature is normally whittled down from the Thirteen Treasures of Britain to four items:

SWORD   SPEAR   GRAIL   DISH

As we noted in *Mabon* (p. 51),[111] the Thirteen Treasures list is repetitive, and so is the above list from Peredur. The ring, which appears in the Thirteen Treasures list as Luned's Ring of Invisibility, appears twice; the Tent Maiden and the Woman of the Mound are one and the same character and can be identified with the Empress. Gwenhwyfar's cup and the Three Cups of Sovereignty overlap, since Peredur restores the first cup to the queen, and the three cups are sent, by him, to the Miller's Wife, who is analogous to the Witches of Gloucester and to the Black Maiden in her admonitory role. The sword is minimal in *Peredur*, although greatly developed in later texts[119]; it is analogous to the Sword of Light, which the hero requires to enact his role as Sovereignty's champion. The Spear of the Dolorous Blow remains a mystery, responsible for the Lame King's wound; but the unicorn's head, which, as we have seen, serves the same function, is won by Peredur.

It is the spear that opens the Hallow quest; it is the winning of the unicorn's head that ends it. The spear was wielded by the Witches of Gloucester; the unicorn's head is given into the hands of the Empress, who is Hallow Queen in *Peredur*. A complex polarity thereby brackets the quest.

There remains the chessboard, which belongs to the Empress. This was always one of the Thirteen Treasures. It represents the land itself and its interrelationship with the Otherworld; its black and white squares are a formalization of the mystic image of the sheep. The chess-pieces represent the earthly and Otherworldly characters that appear in Sovereignty's games, for such is the Hallow quest.

A further discussion of the Hallows that relate to Sovereignty will follow in Chapter Nine, where I will attempt to give a restored list of each Hallow and its Otherworldly properties.

A The Ring of Invisibility, which is also the token of his union with Sovereignty
B The Sword of Light
C The cup of Sovereignty, from which he drinks three times
D The horn of the unicorn, analogous to the spear
E The chessboard, representing the lands in which Sovereignty will empower him

As well as winning these Hallows he achieves many great feats, overcoming many *gormesiad*. The triple nature of these *gormesiad* is perhaps not irrelevant to Peredur's devotion to the Triple Goddess. He defeats:

three serpents (the ring-bearing serpent, the Addanc and the Black serpent)
three 'Black' men (Black Oppressor, Ysbidinongyl and the Black Champion)
nine Witches (three times three)

The time has come to encapsulate these wondrous feats and

apply them to a study of the figures of Sovereignty in *Peredur*, as promised. How is the blood royal and the snow holy? We shall see.

In our discussion of the Hallows of Sovereignty we have noted her polar aspects of hag and beautiful maiden; we must not exempt the aspect that unites both, for Sovereignty is also the queen, Mother of the Hallows.

Each of these three aspects is symbolically denoted in Celtic tradition by the colours black, white and red. This is why the Blood in the Snow episode is so crucial to an understanding of *Peredur*, for these colours are not just the physical appearance of his fantasy mistress but the mystic emblems of Sovereignty in her three aspects. This is borne out in Irish tradition, where the hero is offered the white milk of fostering, the red wine of lordship or the dark drink of forgetfulness at various points in his career (see Chapter Nine).

In order to understand the complex relationship that Peredur has with Sovereignty, it will be useful to enumerate the female characters in the story in the order in which they appear.

A   Peredur's mother
B   The Tent Maiden
C   Gwenhwyfar
D   Female Dwarf
E   Dish-bearing maiden
F   Peredur's foster-sister
G   Tattered Maiden (called Blanchflor in Chrétien)
H   Countess of the mountain castle
I   Nine Witches of Gloucester
J   Angharad Golden-Hair
K   Maiden of the Round Valley, Black Oppressor's daughter
L   Woman of the Mound
M   Countess of the Feats
N   Miller's wife
O   The Empress of Constantinople
P   Black Maiden
(Q Chess-playing maiden [Gwalchmai's adventures])

R   King's daughter
S   Horsewoman of the forest

To find so many female characters in a text is by no means
remarkable, but their effect upon Peredur's life is more than
usually important. Peredur's mother (A), although determined to
shield him from danger, actually endangers him more seriously,
since he is unprepared for his quest. We have already remarked
upon the misfortune wrought in Peredur's family by its failure to
wield the Hallows; this misfortune also falls upon members of their
household, since both the Female Dwarf (D) and her husband
suffer under a ban of enchanted silence at Arthur's court, while
the foster-sister (F) loses her husband to the Otherworldly forces
that cause chaotic violence. Peredur is himself the cause of his
mother's death.

Peredur's encounters with the other women may be seen as a
cumulative set of meetings with Sovereignty's three aspects.
Blanchflor (G), Angharad (J) and the king's daughter (R) may
be seen as types of the beautiful maiden, whom he desires but
does not marry. The Tent Maiden (B), Gwenhwyfar (C), the
mountain castle countess (H), the Woman of the Mound (L), the
Countess of the Feats (M), the Empress (O) and the Horsewoman
(S) are all types of the royal or queenly aspect of Sovereignty.
The hag aspect is represented in this text by the Nine
Witches (I), the Maiden of the Round Valley, whom the text
implies is less than lovely (K), the Miller's Wife (N) and the
Black Maiden (P). The two exceptions to this scenario are the
Dish-bearing Maiden (E), who partakes of all three aspects, being
the potential maiden, bearing a proto-Hallow of Sovereignty's
queenship, but bound to carry the lamented cousin's head as a
sorrowful woman; and the chess-playing maiden (Q), who only
appears in Gwalchmai's part of the quest and whom Peredur
never meets, though her chessboard makes her a Hallow-bearing
guardian of queenly stature.

Peredur is offered in marriage G, K, M and R. He professes
love to J and L, who is the same as the Empress. He defends or
avenges B,C,D, F,G,H, and R. He compensates C, F, N, O and
S. He marries the Empress (O). There is little space here to

consider each of these relationships, though the reader is invited to contemplate their interaction with our hero, for this is usually illuminating. I am aware that Sovereignty may be said to operate under four as well as three aspects, and have assigned the Black Maiden to the *Cailleach* here.

Although the Grail as a manifest Hallow seems absent from *Peredur*, it is nevertheless still present within the text. The clue to this resides in Peredur's Blood in the Snow vision, where the combination of the white, black and red puts him in mind of the woman he loves best. His unfocused yearning after Sovereignty takes on the shape and colouring of the Tattered Damsel, whom we shall call Blanchflor, after Chrétien. The unattainable longing in Peredur is wrought not of spiritual desire but of physical attraction. He is virgin, unmated, incomplete. He does not seek union with the divine, which is the gift of the Grail in later texts, but seeks physical union with the object of his desire.

Peredur's Grail is a woman, whether the earthly representative or the Otherworldly Hallow Queen herself; the Empress in this text.

Such an understanding can be verified by reference to *Parzival*. At the end of the Grail quest, when the chaos of wasteland, war and wounded king have been resolved, Parzival's half-brother, Feirfitz, sits at the table as the Grail-bearer, Repanse de Schoy, (Fullness of Joy) enters and serves the company from the holy vessel. He is entranced by her beauty and charmed by the mysterious way all the cups seem to be filled:

> Then [said] the fair Anfortas, who sat by the heathen's side,
> 'Seest thou not the Grail before thee?' But Feirefiz replied,
> 'Naught I see but a green Achmardi [emerald] that my Lady
> but now did bear.'[40]

Feirfitz is stricken with love for the Grail Maiden, but he is totally unable to see the Grail itself. He asks what he has to do to win her love. The old Grail guardian, Titurel, judges that Feirfitz's inability to see the holy vessel is due to his being a pagan, and that baptism will rectify matters. The font, when it is turned towards the Grail, miraculously fills with water and Feirfitz is baptized; shortly afterwards he marries Repanse de Schoy and returns to India where they have a son, Prester John, who becomes the great Christian king of the East.

It would be simplistic to overstate von Eschenbach's case that pagans perceive the Grail-bearer and Christians the Grail itself, but there is a manner in which this is valid. Although Peredur is nominally Christian, his motivation is Otherworldly; his Christianity is shown to be minimal, since he mistakes a pavilion for a church and is uncertain about the rites of Holy Week. His helpers are mainly Otherworldly, not angelic beings. His inspiration are the representatives of Sovereignty who lead him to marry the Hallow Queen herself, the Empress of the East. (Constantinople was the Christian centre of Eastern Europe, though the Empress's retainers seem strangely Otherworldly.)

In *Peredur* there is no dual vision: he perceives the spiritual benefits of the Hallows through the mediation of Sovereignty: her gifts and her love are one and the same.

It is this very vision that is obscured in later Grail texts, for, though she is still present, Sovereignty becomes fragmented into more and more distressed damsels, disinherited maidens and lamenting widows. The pattern of Sovereignty within the Grail texts can still be perceived by the presence of the Loathly Lady, the Black Maiden or Cundrie in *Parzival*: for where the hag aspect of Sovereignty is present, Sovereignty herself as the gift-bearing Hallow Queen cannot be far away. (See Chapters Nine and Ten for a further discussion of Sovereignty as Grail Queen.)

Peredur's quest for a wife has been amply explained in this chapter. He seeks none other than Sovereignty, whose final appearance is in the person of the Empress herself. But in the mythic pattern of the Transformative Goddess (p. 77) we would normally expect Peredur to have to face and embrace the Loathly Lady before being allowed to possess the Empress. This episode does indeed occur, though it is obscured by the story-teller, in the episode at the mountain castle where Peredur first confronts the witches.

Clad only in shirt and trousers he brains one of the witches with his sword – a feat which no one else has been able to perform, for, as the Countess says, 'they have overrun and laid waste the entire realm except for this one house'.[22] This is no embrace, save one of combat perhaps, which reminds the reader of the grappling of Scathach, Cu Chulainn's female battle teacher.[8] The story-teller shows the witch totally at Peredur's mercy, and though he does not say so, she is firmly gripped by her prophesied doom-bringer. One of the disenchanting skills in folk-song is this very ability:

'to hold me fast and fear me not'[64]

which Tamlin's mistress employs in that ballad, as the Faery Queen changes Tamlin into fearsome shapes. Likewise Peredur may, in the earlier proto-story, have transformed Sovereignty.

In Peredur's Blood in the Snow vision he is aware of these same three aspects of Sovereignty which rearrange themselves into the configuration of his inner woman – the woman he loves best. Its alchemy works upon his senses until he passes from boyhood to manhood during his contemplation. Even the three birds that bring about the vision correspond to the three aspects of the Goddess: the wild hawk representing the dangerous Hallow Queen, the duck representing the innocent maiden, and the raven the hag aspect. Peredur's career is encompassed by this vision, for he defies the challenges of the Hallow Queen, liberates the innocent from danger and enchantment, and is admonished by both the witches and the Black Maiden who serve as his teachers and guides.

Implicit within the vision also is the wounding of both land and people: from the king down to the youngest child orphaned by the *gormesiad*, which devastate the country. The enchantments upon the land can be overcome only if Peredur succeeds in his quest and becomes the consort of Sovereignty, for only then can the royal blood of the Grail family become one with the holy earth of the land. The order in which *Peredur* is written makes it very difficult to perceive the shape of the Hallow quest and the Sovereignty challenge, for in our story Peredur lives with the Empress for fourteen years before he is challenged to find the meaning of the spear. However, his severance from the Empress brings him greater maturity, in which he completes his quest and passes further tests: those of the chessboard, the unicorn and the man under the stone.

The meeting and mingling of two levels of existence – the earthly and Otherworldly – brings honour and an awesome responsibility upon the worthy hero, for he is representative of his race. He does not, like Gereint, marry an earthly woman who is Sovereignty's representative, but marries Sovereignty herself. He may no longer live a personal life but must live a redemptive one, standing between the worlds as the burning-glass of the Otherworld and a channel between mortal and immortal realms. Empowered by the Hallows he is responsible for wielding them and holding the land in balance until the next cycle, when he will no longer be able to maintain his role and it will pass to another.

Once more the land will become waste; Sovereignty will assume her guise of hag and wander the land in search of a new champion; the Hallows will be lost to the earthly realms and a new Grail quest will begin. This cycle of barrenness and fertility, success and failure is repeatedly found within the Grail legends. The empowerment of the Hallows is never permanent. Even great kings like Arthur fail, diminish and pass back into the Otherworldly realms, like the Hallows they once wielded. Sovereignty, like the face of nature itself, changes from hag to maiden to queen, returning to hag as her consort's power wanes.

How such a vision and such a quest may be relevant to ourselves in our own time is the Grail question we have yet to answer. The very existence of humanity and the earth may yet depend upon it, for we all share the holy blood of Grail-winners and we all succeed to the Grail family's responsibility of finding and wielding the Hallows to balance our holy land.

CHAPTER EIGHT

THE GREEN AND BURNING TREE

Even at the confines
  Where this is that, that, perhaps was this,
even there, where is the moving wall of mist where
was the pillared hall . . .
Yet, even here,
  Where the mixed-men most mix their magic, where the
exchanges are . . .

DAVID JONES
The Roman Quarry

I IN THE LANDS OF THE LIVING

The *Mabinogion* presents the reader with a unique vision of the Otherworld. While the Otherworld narratives of Irish tradition are perhaps better known, through the stories of *immrama*, the voyages to the Blessed Isles, the British tradition reveals its own view of the paradisaical realms inhabited by gods and other beings.[146]

While the texts comprising the *Mabinogion* were transcribed very late in terms of pre-Christian traditional survival, in the twelfth and thirteenth centuries, the stories nevertheless stem from early oral tradition, where the gateways and methods of entry to the Otherworld were yet remembered, where the old gods were to be found shimmering on the borderlands between the worlds.

The stories betray certain characteristic patterns from which a map of the Otherworld may be drawn; they show how, time and again, certain characters constellate in mythic configurations which are recognizable as a distinct tradition. In *Mabon* I explored the earlier stories, those that stemmed from the mythical past in which the protagonists were recognizably god-forms conforming to the unrecorded Mysteries of Britain; in this book we have seen how the mantles of these earlier mythic personae fall upon Arthur and his court. The protagonists are now analogous to earthly heroes and heroines, but they still meet Otherworldly personages who challenge, help and grant gifts.

Certain features that appear consistently in the *Mabinogion* combine to give us a fairly developed view of the British Other-world tradition. The presence of the Otherworld and its operators is usually discerned by characters and events which originate in the Otherworld but which affect the earthly realms. The way in which the two worlds interlock is quite subtle. Rarely do characters visit a distinct Otherworld location as Pwyll does in his visit to Annwn. Even Arthur, who as we know from the 'Preiddeu Annwn' poem (*Mabon*, pp. 107–8)[111] does voyage to the Underworld, is said to sail to Ireland in his ship *Prydwen*. The Otherworld borders the earthly world so subtly, almost as a supra-reality superimposed upon the landscape, that the reader is often unaware when a story becomes operational on another level.

In Figure 8.1 we see a table of brief clues to Otherworldly activity within the stories. One of the most obvious ways to travel into the Otherworld is to follow an unearthly or totemic beast. Such animals are harmonics of both the Otherworld and the earthly character's destiny, as I have already discussed in *Mabon* (Chapter 8).[111] The hunting of such beasts draws the character from one world into another without his knowledge. As Pwyll is drawn into an encounter with Arawn, so his son, Pryderi, falls prey to the Otherworldly trap set by Llwyd. In *Culhwch and Olwen* the chase is somewhat different: the search for Mabon is in the nature of a conscious quest, but the totemic oldest animals draw the seekers into deeper time-scales to the roots of time itself in order to find the Divine Youth. The hunting of the White Hart

Protagonist	Pwyll	Branwen	Manawyddan	Math	Culhwch	Lludd	Rhonabwy	Macsen	Owain	Geraint	Peredur	Taliesin
Animal leading to Otherworld	stag		white boar		the oldest animals					White Hart	hawk, duck, raven and unicorn	salmon
Threshold Guardians	Arawn				Custennin, Glewlwyd	Iddawg			Wild Herdsman		the noble huntsman	
Otherworldly Hallow Guardian	Rhiannon's bag	Llassar and Cymeidei's cauldron Caswallawn's mantle			Twrch Trwyth's treasures	Gwyddno's hamper	Arthur's sword, ring, mantle, chessboard	Eudaf's chessboard	Luned's ring	Orchard Woman's horn	hag's spear, Empress's cup, ring and chessboard	Ceridwen's cauldron
Characters who shape-shift	Rhiannon (mare) Pryderi (foal)		Rhiannon (mare) Pryderi (foal) Llwyd's wife (mouse)	Gilfaethwy and Gwydion (deer, pigs and wolves) Llew (eagle) Blodeuwedd (owl)	King Tared (boar) Gwrhyr (bird)	dragons become pigs	Owain's family (ravens)					Taliesin (hare, fish, bird and wheat-grain) Ceridwen (greyhound, otter, hawk and hen)
Otherworldly plagues (gormesiad)		cauldron-folk and magic mist	magic mist and mice		Twrch Trwyth, Yspaddaden	Corannyeid, dragon's shout and theft of provisions			Black Oppressor	Enchanted Games	witches, serpents, Black Oppressor, unicorn	
Otherworldly combatants	Hafgan	revived cauldron warriors	Llwyd	Pryderi and Gwydion	Twrch Trwyth, Yspaddaden	Gwyddno	Owain and Arthur		Black Knight, Black Oppressor	Edern, Mabonagrain	witches, insulting knight, Black Oppressor, Ysbidinongyl, Black Man under stone, two black men and a churl	

Figure 8.11: *Otherworldly Features of the Mabinogion*

likewise draws the hunters into participation in an Otherworldly game in *Gereint and Enid*. It is Peredur's Blood in the Snow vision, involving the hawk, duck and raven, that initiates him into manhood and into the realm of the Empress, who represents Sovereignty. The one-horned stag or unicorn of *Peredur* has a malefic effect upon the land and is more in the nature of a *gormes* than an Otherworldly messenger, except in so far as it denotes the imbalance that exists between the worlds.

The borderlands of the Otherworld are always guarded by an awesome figure who challenges all comers. There are distinct archetypes apparent here. In *Pwyll, Prince of Dyfed* Arawn acts as both King of Annwn and Otherworldly guardian; his majesty and nobility are reflected in *Peredur* by the noble huntsman whom Peredur meets near the Green and Burning Tree. Both characters invite the hero into their world and offer a choice of roads or possibilities. Neither Pwyll nor Peredur choose to sleep with the guardian's wife. Related to this tradition is Lord Bertilak of *Gawain and the Green Knight*, who similarly acts as the Hospitable Host and Way-shower to the Green Chapel for Gawain. Just as Bertilak appears both as a genial and obliging mortal man and as the Green Knight, an awesome Otherworldly figure, so too does the Threshold Guardian assume a more fearsome guise in the figures of Custennin and the Wild Herdsman. The semi-giant, semi-bestial figures who appear in both *Culhwch and Olwen* and *Owain* represent challenge at the gateway between the worlds. Those who pass muster may travel onwards into the Otherworld; those who fail or fear too much are already barred by their own inadequacies.

The ability to command speech, set riddles and ask questions is also a feature of the Threshold Guardians, both male and female, as we discern from the figure of Iddawg in *The Dream of Rhonabwy*. It was by his misleading words that the Battle of Camlann was caused, and it was he who first conducted Rhonabwy into the interior of his dream to confront the historical Arthur. Prime among such guardians is, of course, Glewlwyd Mighty-Grasp himself, Arthur's porter, whose importance in *Culhwch and Olwen* and in the romances has been mentioned in some detail. Instead of guarding some lonesome ford in the forest, he stands forthrightly at the doors of Arthur's court, forbidding entry to the unworthy. As we have noted, Arthur's court, especially in *Culhwch and Olwen*, takes on an Otherworldly dimension as the feasting and assembly hall of all the mighty dead of Britain. Culhwch's ride thither is really an Otherworldly journey.

The presence of the Otherworld within earthly realms is usually signified by the appearance of the Hallows and their guardians. Such Otherworldly treasures are usually wielded by people of power who, if not immortal themselves, derive their empowerment from close association with the Otherworld. Both Rhiannon's bag and Ceridwen's cauldron are treasures wielded only in the Otherworld. But Gwyddno's hamper is brought from the Otherworld in order to take the provisions from Lludd's court. The reviving cauldron of Llassar is used to terrible effect in *Branwen, Daughter of Llyr*, where the dead Irish warriors fight on, to Britain's loss. This incident is closely related to Arthur's voyage to Annwn for the Hallows and to the quest for the treasures of Twrch Trwyth. These sets of regalia or Otherworldly treasures are primarily the objects of sovereignty quests. As the Cauldron of Rebirth is responsible for the devastation of Britain's troops in Ireland, so the hag's spear wreaks havoc in *Peredur*, where both king and land are laid waste. The land itself is represented by the chessboard or *gwyddbwyll* board. Peredur goes on a quest to recover the Empress's chessboard, which he so carelessly threw away, while in *The Dream of Macsen Wledig* Elen's father, Eudaf, is shown creating the pieces for the board: in a symbolic manner he empowers Britain's war-bands who accompany Macsen to Rome, for chessmen and warriors are identical in the mythic schema of the Otherworld.

The Ring of Invisibility is closely related to the Mantle of Invisibility, which both Caswallawn and Arthur assume. In the case of Luned's ring, it denotes an Otherworldly talisman which Owain wears while in the earthly realm. Arthur has both ring and mantle in *The Dream of Rhonabwy*, as well as his Sword of Light and chessboard, for Rhonabwy travels to the Otherworld in his dream and sees Arthur in his full regalia as King of Avalon. The horn of the Orchard Woman in *Gereint and Enid* is the horn of disenchantment by which Otherworldly afflictions are lifted. It is paralleled in folk-tradition by the horn that awakens the sleeping Arthur in the Sewingshields legend (*Mabon*, p. 160).[111]

The ability to shapeshift denotes an Otherworldly affinity in certain characters in the *Mabinogion*. These are noticeably present mostly in the earlier stories of the Four Branches and in *Taliesin* and *Culhwch and Olwen*, though, as we have seen, Owain's ravens are likely to be of the same shapeshifting Otherworldly kin as his mother, Modron/Morgan.

The most telling evidence for Otherworldly interference in human affairs is the *gormesiad* or enchantments or plagues that afflict the land of Britain. As we have noted on p. 196, the Otherworld, its archetypal characters and its empowering Hallows are not in themselves either good or bad, but when the balance between the worlds is shifted – by an unworthy king's greed or weakness – then this imbalance results in a series of plagues and enchantments which affect the whole kingdom.

The magic mist that shrouds Arberth in *Manawyddan, Son of Llyr* and *Branwen, Daughter of Llyr* and the garden in *Gereint and Enid* shows a localized infringement of the borderlands that separate the worlds. The *gormes* of invading peoples afflicts the land in both *Branwen, Daughter of Llyr* and *Lludd and Llefelys* with the cauldron-folk and the Corannyeid respectively being totally out of control. Similarly in *Peredur* it is the witches who afflict the country. Serpents and dragons emerge from the earth in *Peredur* and *Lludd and Llefelys* as a result of unbalanced forces loose in the land; these are related to the tradition of Merlin Emrys and the dragons who sleep under Vortigern's tower.[10] When the unworthy Vortigern attempts to erect his tower, his masons disturb the slumbering dragons, which causes the edifice to fall down, just as Vortigern's kingship is also without foundation.

Sometimes the afflictions and enchantments are caused by a giant like Yspaddaden who, Balor-like, attempts to sustain his kingdom by forbidding his daughter to marry a husband who will replace him. The Black Oppressor of both *Owain* and *Peredur* is akin to him. Yspaddaden is also responsible for setting the *anoethu* (impossible tasks) that Culhwch has to fulfil. These are likewise akin to the Enchanted Games of Owain's Otherworldly court. In both incidents the heroes, Culhwch and Gereint, accept the challenge and win the prize: sovereignty over lands and control over their destinies.

Sometimes the affliction is in the shape of an Otherworldly beast, like Twrch Trwyth or the unicorn of *Peredur*, which, like other serpents and dragons, exhibits a devastating ability to sear the land, drying up waters and rendering the fields infertile. The Otherworldly folk of Llwyd, in the shape of mice, actually help to devastate Manawyddan's crops.

These *gormesiad* are invariably overcome by the combat of the hero, who represents the afflicted land and its peoples, with an Otherworldly champion. Many of these combats take place at a ford (see Figure 8.2), the borderland between the worlds which is neither water nor dry land. Alone among these combats only Manawyddan does not engage in a hand-to-hand fight with Llwyd; being a great Otherworldly archetype himself, Manawyddan needs only to outwit his opponent through the use of superior skill. But this is not the case between Pryderi and Gwydion, who are both semi-mortal. Gwydion's magic overcomes Pryderi's human fairness in a single combat. The overcoming of Twrch Trwyth and of Yspaddaden is strangely familiar: Twrch Trwyth vanishes after the scissors, comb and razor have been filched from behind his ears; and it is with these items that Yspaddaden is ignominiously overcome by the shaving of his hair and beard. The combat between Owain and Arthur in *The Dream of Rhonabwy* is a sportsmanlike contest over the *gwyddbwyll* board. But Owain, Gereint and Peredur overcome their opponents in a more warrior-like fashion.

British tradition as represented in the *Mabinogion* lacks the sumptuous description of the Otherworld that abounds in Irish tradition, yet we are still able to discern its general configuration from the consistent images that arise in the stories (see Figure 8.2).

Certain natural features of the landscape have always acted as Otherworldly doorways. These places are normally considered sacred, are surrounded by traditional lore and are numinous and well avoided by ordinary mortals, such as the Mound of Arberth, which can inflict blows or wonders depending upon the nature of

	Pwyll	Branwen	Manawyddan	Math	Culhwch	Lludd	Rhonabwy	Macsen	Owain	Gereint	Peredur	Taliesin
Otherworldly gateway	Arberth		Arberth				dream	dream	forest	magic mist	water	dream
Otherworldly castles	Arawn's fortress	Harlech, Gwales	Fort of the Golden Bowl	Caer Arianrhod	Forts of Ysypaddaden Wrnach, Caer Loyw, Seven caers of Annwn, Oeth and Anoeth			Caer Seint	Shining Fortress, Countess of Fountain's castle	Court of Joy (orchard), Limwris's castle (of death)	Castle of Wonders, chessboard castle	Caer Arianrhod
Otherworldly tree				Tree of Nantllew					fir-tree	apple-tree	Green and Burning tree	
Otherworldly birds		Birds of Rhiannon							Birds in fir-tree			
Water-crossing as Otherworld entry		voyage to Ireland			voyage to Ireland	Voyage to France		voyage to Britain	river		lake-crossing, river valleys of the Tree and the Castle of Wonders	
Ford-combats	Hafgan and Pwyll at ford in Annwn			Pryderi and Gwydion at Yellow Ford			chess-game of Owain and Arthur at ford		Black Knight and Owain at Fountain			
Mounds and their guardians	Arberth (Lords of Dyfed)		Arberth		Custennin				Wild Herdsman		Woman of Mound	

Figure 8.2: *The Configuration of the Otherworld in the Mabinogion*

the Lord of Dyfed who stands upon it. Pwyll sights Rhiannon from its top, but Pryderi, his son, finds himself and his family under Otherworldly enchantment. The tradition among the Lords of Dyfed was to sit upon the mound after or during a feast, which may give us another important clue to the way to gain Otherworldly entry. Otherworldly gateways open more easily at the sacred overlays of linear time with Otherworldly timelessness; that is, during the major Celtic agricultural feasts of *Samhain* (the New Year and the time when the dead are abroad, marking the beginning also of winter), *Oimelc* (the coming of Brighid, spring-lambing and the combat between the *Cailleach* of Winter and her rival the Spring Maiden), *Beltane* (May-Eve, time of enchantments, the beginning of summer); and *Lughnasad* (harvest-time, marked by the Autumn Games of Sovereignty, when the Summer and Winter Kings often fight).

The custom of the Lords of Dyfed is remarkably like the custom of Arthur, who, in later texts, refuses to eat the feast set before him until a marvel happens. The *geas*, for such it appears to be, prevents the king from eating before an adventure has begun. The most famous example of this is in *Sir Gawain and the Green Knight*, which occurs on the solar festival of the Winter Solstice. In many of the later versions of the romances, Arthur's court meets at Whitsun (Pentecost) to compare adventures, and it is at one such gathering that the Grail appears.[29] Time plays an important part also in the stories of both *Lludd and Llefelys* and *Taliesin*, for the dragon's shout goes up at Beltane, and Taliesin manifests in the waters of the weir on May Eve.

Water is also a means of crossing into the Otherworld, as both Bran's and Arthur's voyages to Ireland testify. The dreams of Macsen and Rhonabwy gain them access to the Otherworld, but Macsen's dream journey is soon followed by an actual voyage to Britain, whose Otherworldly loveliness is much extolled in the text. Interestingly the 'lands to the west' act as the Otherworld in relation to earthly realms in these stories: Ireland is Britain's Otherworld, Britain is Rome's. Rhonabwy, though he comes to the ford and meets Arthur, does not cross over the river but remains an observer rather than becoming a participant.

The earthly paradise of British tradition is a rugged place of hills, valleys, forests and running rivers: as much like British topography as it could be. Here is no pretty paradise garden, no *hortus conclusus* for the meeting of medieval lovers, but an awesome landscape in which mighty archetypes are met.

Central to the landscape of the Otherworld is the tree of tradition, the axial World Tree around which the symbols and archetypes constellate. This is nowhere more apparent than in *Owain*, which affords us one of the most detailed accounts of the Otherworld in the *Mabinogion*, with a complete itinerary for us to follow. The tree in *Owain* is a fir- or pine-tree and under it is the very fountain of Otherworldly life, akin to the Irish well of nine hazels, the well of knowledge, sometimes called the Well of Segais. In *Gereint and Enid* the magic garden, surrounded by its hedge of stakes with very typically Celtic severed heads, encloses an apple-tree, the emblematic token of the Orchard Woman or Sovereignty herself. Her fruits, like those of the Avalonian apple-trees, or like those fruits which Thomas the Rhymer offers to pick for the Queen of Faeryland, bring Otherworldly knowledge but death to mortal-kind. In *Peredur* we meet the Green and Burning Tree wrought of leaf and flame, emblematic of the mortal and immortal lives of human-kind and faery-kind respectively. The Tree of Nantllew in *Math, Son of Mathonwy* partakes of this tradition: in its branches the wounded Llew, bereft of human shape, sits as an eagle, awaiting the restorative magic of Math and Gwydion to transform him again.

The Birds of Rhiannon are virtually alone in representing the British tradition of Otherworldly birds, so prevalent in Irish tradition. Their singing brings the suspension of linear time, as in *Branwen, Daughter of Llyr*, where Bran's company sits feasting in an Otherworldly time-scale. The birds of the fir-tree in *Owain* descend only when the tree is defoliated by the force of the storm; they seem related both to the Birds of Rhiannon, because of their sweet singing, and to the birds in the combat-at-the-ford episode in the *Didot Perceval* (see p. 93), where Perceval fights Urban of the Black Pine; the birds are really Otherworldly women who fight on Urban's side.[32]

Ford combats, fought at the borders between the worlds, occur in *Pwyll, Prince of Dyfed, Manawyddan, Son of Llyr, The Dream of Rhonabwy* and *Owain*, although Owain's combat with Arthur is fought on the *gwyddbwyll* board and not with arms and warriors.

Lastly we note that the Otherworldly gateways are frequently depicted as mounds and that these mounds have guardians. The monstrous totemic shepherds like Custennin and the Wild Herdsman are typical Threshold Guardians, but in *Peredur* we meet the Woman of the Mound, herself a type of Sovereignty and an aspect of the Empress whom Peredur vows to marry. The Green Chapel of *Sir Gawain and the Green Knight* (see p. 123) is obviously intended to be a hollow mound like the examples above. It is fortress, stronghold and gateway all in one. The superstitious dread in which such mounds were held was due to the correct belief that they were burial mounds wherein lay the ancient dead.

Later Celtic and early medieval tradition invested the Otherworld with castles or *caers* from which the Otherworldly archetypes operated.

Caer Arianrhod appears twice: once as the abode of Gwydion's sister, and again as the initiatory *caer* of Taliesin's poetic vision. Even earthly castles take on supernatural roles in *Branwen, Daughter of Llyr* and *The Dream of Macsen Wledig*, where real places come under Otherworldly rules. Even Gloucester, Caer Loyw, has its place in legend as the site of Mabon's imprisonment, and a similar Shining Fortress reappears in *Owain*, where, in place of Peredur's nine witch tutors, an array of beautiful maidens and youths wait on the hero. These Otherworldly castles are treasure-houses also, like the Fort of the Golden Bowl, whose powerful magic lures Rhiannon and Pryderi into enchanted servitude, or like the Castle of Wonders, where Peredur sees the undying splendours of the Hallows exhibited. But the treasures are often housed within the dark *caers* of Annwn, to which both Pwyll and Arthur descend. Pwyll's experience of Annwn is of a magnificent palace of entertainment and joy, while Arthur's face is said to be scarred with anxiety after the experience of the raid upon Annwn for the cauldron and other empowering Hallows.

Sometimes the castles are places of testing, as in the forts of Yspaddaden and Wrnach, or in the Court of Joy where the

Enchanted Games are played out. Even the Castle of Wonders partakes of this traditon, since it is a place where Peredur ought to have asked the Grail question. In the Countess of the Fountain's castle Owain is able to gain entry only with Luned's help; in Earl Limwris's castle Gereint is saved from oblivion and death by the force of Enid's impassioned shrieks.

In the Lands of the Living that are the Celtic Otherworld, the ways are clearly marked so that no chance traveller might stray in unaware. For those who know the customs of the country the path is clear to see; but there are many challenges and dangers to be faced before he or she emerges into the earthly realm once again. Like Arthur, Rhiannon or Pryderi they may return haggard though vindicated from their sojourn in those lands. Like Culhwch and Gereint they may return victorious to their lands and loved ones. Or like Bran, Arthur and Owain they may never truly return to affairs of earthly estate, remaining in the Otherworld to resume guardianship over the inner sovereignty until they in turn succeed to the role of Mabon once more in the long Succession of the Pendragons – guardians of the inner lands which lie under and around us even today.

II THE BRIGHT AND THE DARK

It will be apparent from reading these stories that Otherworldly characters often bear 'bright'-meaning names and appear to be fair when they are in the Otherworld. When they appear in earthly realms their names and appearances reflect blackness and ugliness. Like the sheep that change colour from black to white or white to black in *Peredur*, so do Otherworldly characters when they cross the way between the worlds. Others have bright names and dark natures.

It is not possible to give definitive etymological meanings to the names of all such characters in the *Mabinogion*. But we may note the following:

PWYLL, Prince of Dyfed: Hafgan (summer song); Gwawl ap Clud (radiance). Hafgan bears a marked resemblance to

Gromer Somer Joure of *Gawain and Ragnell*[78], for that Otherworldly challenger is Lord of Summer's Day.

BRANWEN, Daughter of Llyr: Llassar Llaesgyfnewid gives his name to the blue enamel that Manawyddan uses in the next branch. The root of the name is *glas* or bluey-green, indicating the transparent colour of sea and sky. The same root is incorporated into the name of the 'Glass Caer' of Glastonbury, under whose tor another bright/dark figure, Gwyn ap Nudd, was said to have made his abode.[80]

MANAWYDDAN, Son of Llyr: Llwyd ap Cil Coed is 'the Grey One'. We have already noted his similarity to both Caswallawn, in his ability to spread the magic mist, and to Cu Roi mac Daire of Irish tradition (*Mabon*, Chapters 3 and 4),[111] who might well be called 'the Man in the Grey Mantle'.

CULHWCH and Olwen: provides us with many such characters. Apart from the Shining Fortress (Caer Loyw), there are Goleuddydd (Bright Day), Gwyn ap Nudd (White Son of Night), the Bright-White Witch, Pitch-Black Witch and Gwenhwyfar (White Phantom) among many more.

OWAIN: the Yellow Man, host of the Shining Fortress, is mirrored in reverse by the Black Oppressor. The Wild Herdsman is black, one-eyed and one-legged.

GEREINT and Enid: Edern ap Nudd (Eternal Son of Night)

PEREDUR: innumerable black men, including the Black Oppressor, become opponents to Peredur in this story. It has been suggested that Ysbidinongyl is Lord of the Black Pine[92], which may associate him with Urban of the Black Pine whom Perceval fights in the *Didot Perceval*.[32]

TALIESIN: Ceridwen's son is Afagddu (utter darkness) and is also called Morfran (great crow) in accordance with his appearance. He is contrasted with Taliesin himself, 'the Radiant Brow'.

These are but a few of such characters appearing in the stories of the *Mabinogion*. However, these polarities show not only the transformative nature of the borderlands between the worlds where the Green and Burning Tree represents mortality and immortality, but also the nature of the combatants who fight for the hand of Sovereignty. The patterns that arise from the stories are telling evidence of a mythic pattern subsumed in British tradition, that of the combat for the Flower Bride, in which the maiden aspect of the Goddess of Sovereignty is fought over by a mortal and an immortal being, a hero and an Otherworld king, or the Bright and Dark Kings of Summer and Winter.

This fascinating discovery shows how it is that Gwenhwyfar succeeds to all the panoply of the Flower Bride of proto-Celtic tradition (see Figure 8.3). However, before we look at the final development of this tradition, let us attend to the mythic pattern of this combat in the *Mabinogion* and related Celtic texts.

Seven of the twelve stories comprising the *Mabinogion* reveal distinct combats for the possession of a woman. The woman in question is always possessed of some gift, either sovereignty or one of the Hallows, and is always beautiful. The prime template for this pattern is established in *Culhwch and Olwen*, where we read of Creiddylad, daughter of Lludd Llaw Eraint (Geoffrey of Monmouth's Cordelia and Lear), who, before she can sleep with Gwythyr ap Greidawl, is abducted by Gwyn ap Nudd. The judgement upon them is given by Arthur, who orders that:

> 'Creiddylad was left in the house of her father undisturbed by either side, and every May Day the two men would fight, and the one who conquered on the Judgement Day would keep the girl.' [22]

Such is the mythic pattern, preserved in the capacious bag of the story-teller, where it huddles with other torn fragments of great mysteries. But this is no lone scrap of tradition, for this mythic pattern is found again in related British tradition in the early Welsh text of *Drustan ac Essyllt* (Tristan and Isolt). The lovers, pursued by March (King Mark), submit their case to Arthur, who rules that Essyllt shall be with Drustan while leaves are on the trees, and with March when the trees are bare. Essyllt acclaims this Solomonic pronouncement with glee:

A   In the *Mabinogion*

Text	Flower Bride	Bright Combatant	Abductor/Otherworldly Dark Combatant
Pwyll, Prince of Dyfed	Arawn's wife (possibly Rhiannon)	Arawn (championed by Pwyll)	Hafgan
	Rhiannon	Pwyll	Gwawl
Branwen, Daughter of Llyr	Branwen	Bran (championed by Efnissien)	Matholwch
Math, Son of Mathonwy	Goewin	Math	Gilfaethwy
	Arianrhod	Gwydion	Math
	Blodeuwedd	Llew	Gronw
Culhwch and Olwen	Olwen	Culhwch	Yspaddaden
	Creiddylad	Gwythyr ap Greidawl	Gwyn ap Nudd
Owain	Countess of the Fountain	Owain	Black Knight
Gereint and Enid	Enid	Gereint	Brown Earl and Earl Limwris
	Gwenhwyfar	Gereint	Edern
	Orchard Woman	Gereint	Mabonograin
Peredur	Blanchflor	Peredur	the Earl

B   In Related Celtic Texts

Text	Flower Bride	Bright Combatant	Abductor/Otherworldly Dark Combatant
Tochmarc Etain	Etain	Eochaid Airem	Midir
Toruigheacht Dhiarmada Agus Ghrainne	Grainne	Diarmuid	Fionn
Aided Cu Roi Mac Daire	Blathnait	Cu Chulainn	Cu Roi mac Daire
Triad 67 and Poem Cynddelw	Fflur	Caswallawn	Julius Caesar
Drustan Ac Essyllt	Essyllt	Drustan	March

It should be remembered that the Bright and Dark Combatants above are to some extent interchangeable, since in most instances. the Flower Bride determines with whom she shall live.

Figure 8.3: *The Combat for the Flower Bride in Celtic Tradition*

'Blessed be the judgement and he who gave it! There are three trees that are good of their kind, holly and ivy and yew, which keep their leaves as long as they live!'[81]

Both Creiddylad and Essyllt are in the role of Flower Bride: the Otherworldly woman of unearthly beauty who will succeed to the Goddess of Sovereignty, and for whose hand many men fight. The prime example of the Flower Bride in the *Mabinogion* is, of course, Blodeuwedd, wrought of flowers by Math and Gwydion to be given to Llew. The text of *Math, Son of Mathonwy* reveals a succession of Flower Brides, for the reason for Blodeuwedd's creation is the *geas* that Arianrhod lays upon her son: that he shall never have a wife of earthly kind. Arianrhod is herself in the role of Flower Bride at the beginning of the story: a role which she strongly wishes to occupy and remain in. But Math's wand reveals the true state of his disposition, and she gives birth to twin sons. Gilfaethwy, meanwhile, has raped Goewin, the foot-holder of Math. Goewin's virginity is symbolic of the inviolability of the land; while Math's feet are in her lap, there is no war. The war magically provoked by Gwydion gives Gilfaethwy the opportunity to rape Goewin and steal the sovereignty.

A similar succession of women to the role of Flower Bride appears in *Gereint and Enid*; Gereint champions them all in the manner we have discussed (see Chapter Six). Owain's Flower Bride, the Countess of the Fountain, is really a fully developed representative of Sovereignty; her maiden aspect is exemplified by Luned, who loves Owain and helps him to achieve her mistress's hand. The role is split between Luned and the Countess in much the same way as it is between Enid and Gwenhwyfar in *Gereint and Enid*.

Rhiannon represents the most Otherworldly of Flower Brides, since she is stolen from Annwn itself. The prior combat that Pwyll fights on behalf of Arawn with Hafgan may well be fought over her also, for, as we have discussed (see *Mabon*, p. 25)[111] Rhiannon and Arawn's wife may be one and the same. In the later combat Pwyll wins her from Gwawl, in the manner of King Orpheo.[64]

Branwen's undoubted claim to the role of Britain's Sovereignty is championed by Efnissien, her brother, in another kind of combat, which involves the dishonouring of the Irish king, Matholwch.

The Flower Bride is usually easily identified by her flowery name. Olwen means 'white-track'. Peredur's first love is unnamed in the story, but Chrétien calls her Blanchflor, and it is she whose image kindles Peredur's devotion to Sovereignty.

This mythic pattern is discernible among many other stories within Celtic tradition, a few of which are noted here. The *Tochmarc Etain* (Wooing of Etain) tells of the abduction of Etain, a woman of the sidi (faery-hills), by Eochaid Airem. But Etain has forgotten, since she has been through a number of reincarnations, that she was once the wife of Midir, a lord of the sidi. He comes to take her back and fights Eochaid in a series of chess-matches to win one kiss from her mouth. He embraces her and they fly through the roof-opening back to the sidi where they are besieged by Eochaid.[5] The prior relationship between the Flower Bride and her dark combatant is a feature of *Pwyll, Prince of Dyfed* and, as we shall see, is perhaps part of the submerged cycle attached to Gwenhwyfar.

Related to *Drustan ac Essylt* is the proto-story of the *Toruigheacht* [Pursuit] *of Diarmuid and Grainne* by Fionn mac Cumhail. This triangular relationship is the basis for the later Tristan and Isolt stories. It tells how the beautiful Grainne was to be given in marriage to the elderly Fionn; she remarked on her intended husband's grey hair and cast her eyes upon Diarmuid, his handsome young follower. By laying a *geas* upon Diarmuid and causing the company to be drugged into sleep, she escaped her fate and fled with Diarmuid. Their long flight from Fionn, during which time they were forbidden to lie more than one night in the same bed, is attested in Irish topography where numerous prehistoric monuments and standing stones are still termed 'the beds of Diarmuid and Grainne' to this day.[142]

We have already noted the lost story, alluded to in the triads and in Welsh poetic tradition (see *Mabon*, p. 80),[111] of Fflur and Caswallawn. Fflur was carried off to Rome by Julius Caesar in this lost Sovereignty story, but Caswallawn followed her to Rome, dressed as a shoemaker, in order to win her back again.[38] Fflur (flower) may well have represented the sovereignty of Britain over whom the invading Julius Caesar and the native king, Caswallawn, fought.

The *Aided Cu Roi mac Daire* (tragic death of Cu Roi) is a story concerning the proto-Irish Flower Bride, Blathnait (see *Mabon*, p. 49). Like Blodeuwedd, Blathnait overcomes her husband by guile in order to escape with her lover.

The combatants who fight over the Flower Bride may be earthly or Otherworldly ones; they may bear bright names, like Gwawl or Gwyn, but they are none the less dark combatants. The earthly combatants usually appear in the role of Summer King; the Otherworldly combatants, who are often versed in magic, like Math, usually take the role of Winter King. This schema may appear arbitrary, but there is much evidence to support it, notably from the Creiddylad and Essyllt stories, where the Flower Bride is fought over by a young lover and elderly or Otherworldly husband or abductor. Matholwch, King of Ireland, appears as an Otherworldly king, because Ireland is the opposite pole to Britain as the Otherworld to the earthly realm; whereas Yspaddaden is a Winter King, almost paralysed in his Cronos-like grip upon his kingly powers and his daughter, Olwen. It was once the fashion of scholars, following in the footsteps of Fraser's *Golden Bough*, to sort all deities into two heaps, the Solar and Lunar, in a simplification which I would wish to avoid here. However, the combatants for the Flower Bride do fall into the pattern of Summer/Winter antagonists, after the mythic schema established above.

These combatants and the role of the Flower Bride appear endlessly within the progressive unfolding of the Arthurian legends, but, though the combatants or abductors vary, the Flower Bride is always present in one woman – Gwenhwyfar, the Guinevere of early tradition, as we shall see in Chapter Ten.

III THE MYTHIC COMPANY

Certain characters within the *Mabinogion* betray traces of ancient mythic archetypes which have been almost forgotten. The gentle erosion of powerful gods into the status of heroes, queens and mighty adversaries was greatly aided by the Arthurian legends, which have acted as a kind of clearing-house for this transformation. Usually, the later the text, the less we can perceive the resemblance of a character to a mythic archetype, but nevertheless there are some surprises and exciting confirmations of older patterns to be found.

It would be simplistic merely to associate each character with a mainstream god-form, after the fashion of certain classical mythographers: such a process would be totally inappropriate for archetypes of a proto-Celtic provenance. The problem of the pigeon-holing of Celtic gods is perhaps associated with the dearth of native statuary depicting them. The custom of depicting deities representationally was not a British or Irish obsession, though it was a Roman habit which spilled over into local custom.

Celtic tradition reveals that deities and spirits, as well as mythic heroes, were associated with places. Land features, natural outcrops of rock, springs, wells and trees are the loci of these deities, not temples built by men. The Irish *dindschencas* (place-name stories) relate the topography of Ireland by association with deities and mythic peoples whose great deeds are remembered at particular spots and who gave their names to those loci. The British chroniclers, such as Nennius, reveal a very similar tradition. History is the land beneath our feet. The earth is sacred because it is deeply infused with mythic activity, invisible to mortal sight but perceptible to seers and story-tellers, who, in Celtic tradition, are the priests of the gods.

Imperceptibly the mantles of gods fall on to the shoulders of earthly men and women who, due to the Celtic story-teller's total disregard for proper definitions, merge with the mythic arche-types, becoming their exemplars. This process is very clearly visible in, for instance, Hindu tradition, where men and women are seen to embody characteristics of the gods, becoming their avatars, through whom the gods are active in human affairs. The Other-world tradition of the Celtic countries is at once similar and very different from this, for it replaces a formal religious tradition. Although there are constants among the characters who appear and the locations that are described as existing within the Other-world, the variations of detail within the Otherworld boundaries are immense. The borders between the worlds are but a thought away within the Celtic imagination.

The sacred points of the Celtic year mark the overlapping of the earth and the Otherworld. Temples existed only after Roman occupation and before that *nemetons* (sacred groves) and springs were visited by those seeking communication with the Other-worldly entities whom we call gods.

When gods of the wild places were subsumed into Christian saints, a further interesting variation crept into the mythic con-sciousness of Britain. But if we look for permanent shrines for the ancient god-forms, we need look no further than the *Mabinogion*, whose stories enshrine these old archetypes, mixing history, myth and tribal belief in one rich draught. Like the Cauldron of Rebirth, which made the dead alive again, these stories ensure the immortality of the mythic archetypes; the roll-call of Arthur's court in *Culhwch and Olwen* shows us the feasting-hall of the Otherworld, where heroes, gods and kings assemble in one throng under the aegis of Arthur as Pen Annwn, Lord of the Underworld.

Figure 8.4 shows some of the many mythic archetypes that can be found in the *Mabinogion*; this diagram shows only the main ones that have emerged from this special study of king with Sovereignty. It will be noted that some characters appear in more than one role: this is consistent with the mythic progressions that occur in the stories, wherein a woman who is the Flower Bride in one part of the story may become Sovereignty or even the Dark Woman of Knowledge in another.

The Sovereignty figures are those women who represent the full-blown qualities of the Goddess: they are queens, like Gwenhwyfar or Rhiannon, or Otherworldly women who appear wearing the diadem of royal rule, seated in the golden chair that represents the earth, like Elen.

The Dark Woman of Knowledge shows the dark aspect of Sovereignty, which may be admonitory hag, like the Black Maiden in *Peredur*, or she may retain her maiden beauty, as does Luned. As Lady of the Wheel she shares, with the Guardian of the Totems, the role of adjuster, a restorer of balance. As we saw on p. 192, she guards the portals of the Otherworld from her revolving castle. Arianrhod's Caer Sidi is a prime example of this gateway (see below).

The Daughters of Branwen are those women who are rightful heiresses of Britain's sovereignty, but those who seldom, if ever, embody this for long. They are those from whom the land is repossessed. Custennin's wife is important in this role, for she is one of the daughters of Amlawdd Wledig, the 'Cornwall sisters' of later Arthurian tradition (see *Mabon*, p. 96).[111] If we look at her sisters' role, we will find that Igerna (Igraine) becomes Uther's queen and that Goleuddydd becomes the Queen of

Title	Function	Typified by
Flower Bride	sovereignty-bestowing maiden	Blodeuwedd, Goleuddydd, Olwen, Creiddylad, Enid, Gwenhwyfar, Blanchflor, [Fflur]
Sovereignty	the Goddess of the Land	Rhiannon, Gwenhwyfar, Elen, Countess of Fountain, Orchard Woman, Woman of the Mound, Empress, [Morgan, Brigantia]
Dark Woman of Knowledge/ Lady of the Wheel	initiator and guide; Lady of Death/Rebirth	Ceridwen, Arianrhod, Nine Witches, Black Maiden, Custennin's wife, Luned, Countess of Fountain, Modron as Raven Queen, Miller's Wife, [Morrighan]
Daughter of Branwen	heiress of Britain's sovereignty	Branwen, Goewin, Custennin's wife, Luned, Peredur's mother, [Eigr/Igraine, Morgause, Elaine]
Black Maiden	messenger of Sovereignty; admonisher and guide, of the Voice of the Land	Luned, Black Maiden, Peredur's sister, [Scathach, Morrighan, Elene]
Mabon	Sovereignty's son; restorer of innocence	Pryderi, Gwern, Llew, Goreu, Peredur, Gwion, [Segda]
Pendragon Pen Annwn	Sovereign lord of land sacrificial king; guardian of the land	Pwyll, Manawyddan, Pryderi, Math, Macsen, Lludd, Arthur Bran, Math, Arthur, Yspaddaden, Lame King, [Vortimer]
Thief of Sovereignty	dispossesser and despoiler of land	Gwawl, Caswallawn, Llwyd, Gwydion, Black Oppressor, Edern, Knight of the Apples, Gwyddno, Earl who dispossesses Blanchflor, [Medrawt]
Guardian of the Totems/ Lord of the Wheel	Lord of Wild Things; instructor and guide; Lord of Death/ Rebirth	Custennin, Wild Herdsman, Noble Huntsman (Peredur), Black Oppressor (Peredur), Miller, [Green Knight], Curoi, Mog Ruith]
Provoker of Strife Seer–poet	guardians of Sovereignty inspired prophet of Sovereignty	Iddawg, Efnissien, Cai, [Bricriu, Medrawt] Llefelys, Taliesin, [Merlin, Segda]

(The characters in square brackets are from parallel Celtic tradition.)

Figure 8.4: *Mythic archetypes in the Mabinogion*

Cilydd. Custennin's wife is nameless but it is possible that her rightful name should be Anna.

The Daughters of Branwen – those women who stand for the manifest Sovereignty of Britain – often suffer an obscure fate or else are the bearers of great burdens. The archetype is difficult to establish in many cases, but the prevailing guidelines seem to be that the woman in question is rarely queen in her own right but is married, and her blood confers the sovereignty of the land upon her children. One of the old medieval names for Britain was 'the Nest of the Pelican' and this seems a very apposite title when applied to the Daughter of Branwen archetype. The pelican was, according to medieval bestiaries, supposed to peck open its own breast in order to feed its young upon its own blood; this erroneous belief became attached to the symbolism of Christ's sacrifice upon the cross, since his blood redeemed the world. Britain as the Nest of the Pelican, then, symbolizes the fostering-place of Christ and, more especially, of his mother, for whom England was called Mary's Dowry. The Daughter of Branwen is accustomed to sacrifice, suffering and sorrow, but she is also tenacious of her children's rights.

The role of king, corresponding to Sovereignty, falls to many characters in the earlier stories of the *Mabinogion*, but is exemplified primarily by Arthur, whose mythical influence extends beyond the Heroic Ages into medieval times. Kings may come and kings may go, but Arthur is king for ever, it seems.

When the king is withdrawn to the Otherworld, he sometimes becomes a special guardian of the land, as Bran, whose head is buried under White Mount, and as Arthur, who, though undying, is said to sleep beneath the land of Britain in very many places, awaiting a time of need when he will come again. To this list we might add Vortimer, Vortigern's worthy son, who is buried as a palladium against invaders on the shores of Britain. The Lame King of *Peredur* extends his role as guardian of the Hallows, like Bran with the cauldron. Yspaddaden is no longer operative within his archetype: like Cronos, who devours his children, he keeps a vice-like grip on Olwen's life, never allowing things to progress. Likewise Math passes from his kingly role into that of withdrawn king as Llew grows up.

One of the characters that emerges from our study in a startling way is the Thief of Sovereignty, who is often one and the same as the Flower Bride's abductor, like Caswallawn or Edern. He may be an Otherworldly warrior who comes to steal away the goods and possessions of the kingdom, like Llwyd in *Manawyddan, Son of Llyr*, or Gwyddno, the mysterious figure in *Lludd and Llefelys*. Medrawt appears to follow this role in Triad 54. Gwydion empties Pryderi's kingdom of pigs. Gwawl, in *Pwyll, Prince of Dyfed* is closely associated with Rhiannon's bag of plenty, and, considering he attempts to abduct her also, he consistently exemplifies this role of thief.

The Guardian of the Totems is also Lord of the Wheel; he is an adjuster, like the Dark Woman of Knowledge, the Lady of the Wheel. Together they exemplify the ancient parents of all the gods. The guardian is often also the Threshold Guardian of the Otherworld, and he presents tests and challenges to the hero. He directs the way forward into the Otherworld and may appear as a lordly man, like the Noble Huntsman whom Peredur meets near the Green and Burning Tree, or else as a forest man, uncouth and of giant stature, like the Black Oppressor or Wild Herdsman. Celtic tradition supplies further characters in this role: Lord Bertilak as the Green Knight[78] and Cu Roi mac Daire, who both play the beheading game and challenge the heroes Gawain and Cu Chulainn to become the best warriors. Mog Ruith, whose name means literally 'Servant of the Wheel', appears in Irish mythology as one who flew through the air by means of his rowing-wheel – a kind of air-boat. He is said to have been a disciple of Simon Magus (who, we will remember, also tried to fly). Mog Ruith's dwelling-place in the south-west of Ireland is very near Cu Roi mac Daire's revolving castle, and it is possible that there are mythological parallels between the two men. The Lord of the Wheel is concerned with the progress and initiatory testing of the hero, and it is not surprising that he makes an unusual appearance in *Peredur* as the Miller who patronizes Peredur.

A subtle role which might be overlooked is that of the Provoker of Strife, who acts as a contradictory guardian of his land's sovereignty. It is possible that, originally, this role was an extension of the Lord of the Wheel's. Iddawg, Churn of Britain, provokes the Battle of Camlann by his rash words. Similarly

Efnissien provokes war between Ireland and Britain after Branwen's marriage to Matholwch. And though Cai does not start
wars in any of our stories, he certainly follows in these footsteps
by provoking arguments and dissension among Arthur's knights
in each of the romances. Furthermore, in *Perlesvaus*, it is Cai who
kills Arthur's son, Loholt (Llacheu).[29] It is interesting to recall
that in *Culhwch and Olwen* he reminds Arthur that he is breaking
custom by allowing Culhwch into the hall after the feasting has
begun. It is possible that Cai's original role was as a preserver of
the traditions or the Mysteries of Britain. The satirist Bricriu, in
the Ulster Cycle, is a parallel of this role.

The opposite character to the Provoker of Strife is the Black
Maiden, whom I have identified as a fourth aspect of Sovereignty.
Her role has been considerably obscured in the texts, but is
clearly very important to our study. She often appears as the
sister/helper of the hero and as such appears to play no great
part, but the Black Maiden archetype acts as the representative
of Sovereignty in a very definite way. The Black Maiden of
Peredur is shown to be the admonitory voice of the land, urging
Peredur to rectify his mistakes and face up to his responsibilities,
while Luned, in *Owain*, gently encourages Owain to win Sovereignty's games with skill and flair. This role is related to that of
foster-mother or woman warrior in Celtic tradition, for it is the
responsibility of each of these characters to arm, name and give a
destiny to her fosterling or student. Cu Chulainn's boyhood was
spent on the Isle of Skye, being taught his battle skills by
Scathach.[8] Later on in his career, Cu Chulainn encounters the
goddess Morrighan, who is disguised as a female satirist, with
whom he conducts a heated debate.[88] We have already seen how
the role of Provoker of Strife is often portrayed by a satirist whose
stinging rejoinders and wicked wit cause cracks to appear in the
king's realm.

The Black Maiden aspect of Sovereignty may also be seen as
the Voice of the Land, for she voices the messages of Sovereignty.
Her voice, like the nagging of conscience, sometimes swells to
indignation and fury. The shriek of the dragon of Britain in *Lludd
and Llefelys* denotes the suffering of the land and causes devastation, acting like a vocal 'dolorous blow'. The shriek of the Lady

of the Fountain at the death of her champion heralds a possible interregnum during which her lands are laid waste: but it is Owain who hears her cries and answers them by marrying her and thus becomes the land's champion. The cries of Enid, struggling in the embrace of Earl Limwris, cause Gereint to come to his senses and to return almost from the dead to save her, his representative of Sovereignty. And, as we shall read on p. 250, the land is served by the damsels of the wells, whose unworthy treatment causes a terrible silence to fall on the land, since no one is able 'to hear the voices of the wells', the indwelling voice of the land, of Sovereignty herself. Arthur hears the voice of the Goddess and is restored to his former glory and courage (p. 301).

The Black Maiden became the *Damoiselle Maldisante* in medieval romances – the maiden whose nagging tongue spurs the hero on to magnificent deeds by dint of her encouragement. We have seen her in the person of Elene in *Libeaus Desconus*; she appears also in Malory as Linnet, the sister of Lionors.

The heroic role of the Black Maiden, so clearly defined in Celtic tradition, did not again surface until its revival in Shakespeare, whose heroines, such as Imogen and Viola, combined the roles of Black Maiden and of Daughters of Branwen in their guise as young men. This combination of roles is also present in two medieval romances: *The Story of Grisandole*, in which a young woman dressed as a man is enabled by Merlin to wed the Emperor of Rome; and in *Le Roman du Silence*, in which Silence dresses as a young man in order to obtain her inheritance.

Lastly there is the seer–poet, of whom we have only two examples: Taliesin, the prophet of the race of Troy, and Llefelys, Lludd's brother. Both uphold the role of the king and prophesy or advise the ruler about the nature of his reign. Sometimes, as does Merlin Emrys and Segda, he stands in for the king when the reign is an unworthy one, acting as a judge or standard of justice for the realm in the absence of true judgement. Here the seer–poet acts as a harmonic of Mabon, Sovereignty's son.

It will be seen that some of these archetypes fall into polarized pairs between whom energy is exchanged or power represented. The male and female roles of each archetype are similar in function:

Female Roles	*Male Roles*
Flower Bride	Mabon
Sovereignty	Pendragon
Dark Woman of Knowledge	Pen Annwn
Daughter of Branwen	Thief of Sovereignty
Black Maiden	Provoker of Strife
Lady of the Wheel	Lord of the Wheel/Guardian of the Totems

RECONCILER:
Seer–poet

Figure 8.5: *Corresponding Male and Female Archetypal Roles*

The interrelations of these mythic archetypes are as various as the many turnings of a story. Some of the main points of relationship have been dealt with in *Mabon*, pp. 127–8 and pp. 164–5,[111] where the male and female archetypes are exemplified by the roles on the Poet's Wheel and in the Succession of the Pendragons. Each of the female and male roles above represents a level or pitch of Otherworldly energy. They are reconciled by the seer–poet, a neutral role which can be wielded by either a male or female character, who embodies the archetype of Mabon, skilfully tuning and playing upon the strings of the Otherworldly archetypes. The purity of the seer–poet's role is the result of a perfect balancing of earthly and Otherworldly modes of operation. He/she reconciles each primal pair of archetypes to a state of perfect neutrality, as we see in the examples of Merlin Emrys and Segda. In both cases the king is in an unbalanced relationship with the land's Sovereignty, and the wise men of the land require the sacrifice of an innocent child. This does not, in fact, happen, although in the case of Gwern, who in *Branwen, Daughter of Llyr* is thrown upon the fire by Efnissien, the sacrifice is enacted. Likewise the casting of Taliesin upon the waters by Ceridwen is part of this theme. The ancient punishment among Celtic peoples for certain offences, including incest, was to put the offender in a boat without rudder or oars so that he or she drowned or survived at the mercy of the waters.

It is possible that Dylan's plunging into the waves at birth may be a remembrance of this theme, for, as we have noted (see *Mabon*, p. 87),[111] his death is remembered in the Triads as an unfortunate accident, or possibly a sacrifice. There is also a submerged tradition concerning Arthur's slaughter of the innocents. This comes about because Mordred, the child conceived by Arthur upon his half-sister, is born on May Day, and Arthur commands that all children born on that day must be set adrift in an open boat, in order to purge his own child of his incestuous origin.[87] It is interesting to remember that Taliesin also suffers the ordeal of the waters about May Eve.

We shall return to this tradition again on p. 286, when we look at the many possible candidates for the Sovereignty of Britain. But it is clear that the earliest harmonic of the seer–poet may well be tied to a primitive cult of child sacrifice in which chieftains established their sovereignty by 'giving' a child to the Otherworld. Although this tradition clearly does not obtain later in the Arthurian cycle, there is still the mystery of the deaths of Arthur's various children, Llacheu, Amr and Gwydre, who are not the sons of Gwenhwyfar in early Welsh tradition. They are said to have died in Arthur's lifetime: Gwydre is slain by Twrch Trwyth in *Culhwch and Olwen*; Llacheu dies in battle in the early sources, but is killed by Kay in *Perlesvaus*;[29] and Amr is said to have been killed by Arthur himself.[28] Of course, in early tradition Mordred was not considered to be a son of Arthur, only a nephew.

If we look at Figure 8.4, where the Pendragons are listed, we will see that there are few kings in whose reign a child is not killed or abducted to the Otherworld. Pryderi suffers a dual abduction in *Pwyll, Prince of Dyfed* and *Manawyddan, Son of Llyr*, Dylan is lost in *Math, Son of Mathonwy*, and Arthur's reign, laid alongside the evidence of the *Mabinogion* stories, shows a similar pattern.

The later harmonic of the seer-poet show it to be firmly lodged in its mode of prophet, giver of justice and revealer of inner wisdom. This is the role of Merlin in later Arthurian tradition, who establishes Arthur in his sovereignty and afterwards retires from the world's affairs to his observatory of seventy doors and windows, from whence he can view the heavens and earthly realms. It is due to this myth that Welsh tradition, perceiving the overlay of our world with the Otherworld, called Britain Clas Merddin, or Merlin's Enclosure; to anyone aware of the depths of Britain's mythological heritage, this guardianship is still active, perceptible in meditation and ritual insight.

We can see how the seer–poet is a figure who steps in and out of the Otherworld at will, since he is a son of Sovereignty who never aspires to the kingship yet who functions as its guardian on a mystical level. Within Clas Merddin lies Llys Arthur, the mystical centre of the land – the Hollow Hills, the subterranean chamber of Arthur's return. It is perhaps of this concept that William Blake, one of Britain's great mythographers, wrote when he caused Enitharmon, the Great Mother of his poem *Jerusalem*, to say:

> I will Create secret places,
> And the masculine names of the places, Merlin & Arthur.
> A triple Female Tabernacle for Moral Law I weave . . . [53]

Whether we see Sovereignty in her three or four aspects, she is the land itself, surrounded by the palladium of Merlin's Enclosure, and at her heart is Llys Arthur, the Court of Arthur, where the mythic company still throng her hills, valleys and secret places.

CHAPTER NINE
THE JOY OF THE COURT

Now tell me the name of that wondrous queen,
With her couch of crystal and robe of green.
Bruighean Caerthainn
(trans. P. W. Joyce)

And Peredur stood, and compared the blackness of the raven
and the whiteness of the snow, and the redness of the blood, to
the hair of the lady that best he loved, which was blacker than
jet, and to her skin, which was whiter than the snow, and to
the two red spots upon her cheeks, which were redder than the
blood upon the snow.

Peredur
[my trans.]

I THE SYMBOLS OF SOVEREIGNTY

Every British sovereign at his or her coronation receives numerous
objects called regalia, with which he or she is invested at the
solemn moment of saining or consecration. This hallowing of an
earthly being with what are, in effect, Otherworldly empowerments is an awesome enactment, causing frissons of atavistic
remembrance among many of its witnesses. The importance of the
sovereign's regalia is not based upon the extrinsic value of each
object, though many are indeed beyond price, nor on each

piece's association with the former sovereign who caused it to be made, though, again, such association invests the object with commemorative value. We have to look beyond these considerations to the function of the regalia, for each piece, whether it be worn, carried or used, is symbolic of the qualities of Sovereignty herself.

There is a mysterious symbolism attached to the present British coronation regalia, with its swords, sceptres, bracelets, spurs, crown, ring and mantle, all of which derive from earlier models,[50] and some of which we can see plainly from the traditions embodied in the *Mabinogion*. Celtic kings were not crowned and so had no coronation; they were, however, inaugurated upon the sacred earth of their kingdom. The present Queen of England was crowned while seated over an ancient inauguration stone, the Stone of Scone, which once belonged to the kings of Scotland, but now resides within St Edward's Chair in Westminster Abbey. So an ancient tradition continues.

Within the *Mabinogion*, the land is symbolized by the *gwyddbwyll* board: its possession denotes sovereignty. The list of the Thirteen Treasures of Britain (see also *Mabon*, p. 51)[111] awards the board to Gwenddolau ap Ceidio, who was the patron and protector of Myrddin, and one of the leaders of the factions who died at the Battle of Arderydd (see p. 97). But in our stories we see the board in operation in three different ways. Eudaf, Elen's father, seems to be its possessor, for he also makes the chess-pieces for the board. The appearance of the *gwyddbwyll* board in *The Dream of Macsen Wledig* denotes his future sovereignty over Britain. It is Arthur who owns the board in *The Dream of Rhonabwy*, where he fights Owain in a game, perhaps for the sovereignty of the Otherworld, while in *Peredur* the board is owned by a Sovereignty figure, the Empress. Peredur is unable to achieve his quest until he retrieves the board he has so rashly thrown away.

The royal chair, or throne of the king, may once have been a sovereignty-investing seat in Celtic tradition. It is paralleled by the golden chair in the *Mabinogion* and in it is found sitting a representative of Sovereignty: Elen, the Orchard Woman or the Maiden of the Tent. It is Gereint who seats himself on the vacant golden chair in the Orchard, though later tradition goes on to

The Symbols	King or Sovereignty Figure and Representative, Objects
golden chair	Elen (MW), Orchard Woman (G), Maiden of the Tent (PR)
ring	Arthur (R), Luned (O), Woman of Mound (PR)
mantle	Caswallawn (B), Llwyd (M), the dragon's covering (L), Arthur (R)
gwyddbwyll board (chessboard)	Eudaf (MW), Arthur (R), Empress (PR)
Sword of Light	Lluch Llenlleawg (C), Arthur (R), Goreu (C), Peredur (PR)
spear	Irish spear (B), Gronw (MM), Yspaddaden (C), Peredur and Nine Witches (PR)
Cauldron of Rebirth	Llassar (B), The King of Suffering (PR), Diwrnach (C)
Cauldron of Knowledge	Ceridwen (T)
vessel of plenty	Rhiannon's bag (P), hamper of Gwyddno (C, L), Diwrnach (C)
Sovereignty's cup	golden bowl (M), Empress (PR), Gwenhwyfar (PR)
horn	Orchard Woman (G) Gwlgawd Gododin (C) Peredur (PR)

Abbreviations to stories in the Mabinogion:

P = Pwyll
B = Branwen
M = Manawyddan

MW = Macsen Wledig
L = Lludd
C = Culhwch

R = Rhonabwy
O = Owain

PR = Peredur
G = Gereint
T = Taliesin

Figure 9.1: *The Hallows Associated with Sovereignty in the Mabinogion*

speak of the rash way in which Perceval sits in the 'Siege Perilous' – the place at the Round Table at which only the destined or worthy champion can sit. This role later passes to Galahad.[32,106]

The ring with which the British sovereign is invested is called the Wedding Ring of England. When she was urged by her councillors to marry and beget heirs, Elizabeth I held up the hand on which her coronation ring was and said, 'England is my husband and all Englishmen my children.'[50] The ring that most often appears in the *Mabinogion* is also sovereignty-bestowing or has some other Otherworldly property. Arthur's ring in *The Dream of Rhonabwy* confers the power of remembrance upon all who see it, which is how Rhonabwy is able to relate his dream afterwards. The Woman of the Mound gives Peredur a ring, which is a token of devotion and also empowers him to become invisible to the dreadful *addanc* he goes to slay. Similarly, Luned's ring has two properties: it confers invisibility, but there is also the suggestion that this ring betokens Owain's union with the land and with the Countess of the Fountain.

The mantle of invisibility is mentioned in the Thirteen Treasures as the possession of Arthur, as indeed we find it in *The Dream of Rhonabwy*, although Caswallawn and Llwyd both use its power to create a magic mist: the mist becomes the mantle in their stories. Later in Arthurian tradition, the mantle becomes a chastity-proving garment, which will cover chaste women and shorten upon unfaithful ones. The Mantle of Tegau Gold-Breast is one such garment, mentioned in an appendix to the Thirteen Treasures.[38] This represents the diminution of the Sovereignty tradition where the Goddess of the Land and her relationship with the king was portrayed in a more mundane way by the 'what women most desire' quest, which is found in the stories of both *Gawain and Ragnell*[78] and the *Wife of Bath's Tale*.[6]

But the mantle also represents the land, if we follow a hint from Nennius, where he is describing the incident of Vortigern's tower. Emrys interprets the dragons but says of the cloth that covers them: 'The cloth represents your kingdom.'[28] We have seen how the story of Merlin Emrys and the dragons is associated with the story of Lludd (cf. Chapter Two). I have therefore included the dragon's covering cloth as a type of the mantle.

The Sword of Light, borne by the hero, is represented in *Culhwch and Olwen* by the flashing sword of Lluch Llenlleawg, which, says the 'Preiddeu Annwn', flashed and possibly distracted the cauldron-watchers. Goreu accomplishes singular feats at Wrnach's castle, where the sword is the object of one of Culhwch's *anoethu*: it is also Goreu who beheads Yspaddaden at the conclusion of the story. Traditionally only a weapon of light can defeat the giant of darkness. Arthur's sword depicts the twin dragons of Vortigern's tower upon its blade, for when it is unsheathed, they breathe fire. Although Peredur's sword that breaks in two is an unlikely candidate for the Sword of Light, we have seen how his prototypes always find and wield the sword (Chapter Seven).

The cauldrons and vessels of the *Mabinogion* represent the inner wisdom and the bounty of the land. The Cauldron of Rebirth is amply demonstrated in *Branwen, Daughter of Llyr*, where the Sovereignties of Britain and Ireland eventually contend. The sons of the King of Suffering are likewise revived in two baths in *Peredur*. Diwrnach's cauldron will not boil a coward's food, according to the list of the Thirteen Treasures and to *Culhwch and Olwen*; however, it is analogous to the cauldron of Annwn in the 'Preiddeu Annwn' and to the fragmentary traces in *Culhwch and Olwen*, which make the voyage to Annwn a journey to Ireland. The prime cauldron of knowledge is Ceridwen's, prepared over a year and a day, whose outpouring wisdom is imbibed by Taliesin not Afagddu. Rhiannon's bag, which is never full, and Gwyddno's bottomless hamper seem part of the same tradition of bounty.

The Spear Which Heals and Wounds represents the way in which sovereignty can be promptly removed from a ruler or restored if he proves worthy. Bran is wounded mortally by such a spear but he does not die; neither does the Lame King, Peredur's uncle, wounded by the Nine Witches of Gloucester. Peredur is able to bring the spear under his control when he slays the unicorn and takes its spear-like horn. Gronw's spear, magically forged, like Ceridwen's own careful alchemical preparations for her cauldron, defeats Llew's by making him break the *geasa* that surround his death. But Llew does not die either; his career is checked temporarily and he is forced to consider his relationship with the Flower Bride, Blodeuwedd. Yspaddaden's rule has been an onerous one by the time Culhwch and his company come to the giant's castle: the spears that the giant sends after the men of Arthur are all returned with devastating effect upon Yspaddaden, wounded in knee, breast and eye.

Sovereignty's cup is perhaps the earliest prototype of the Grail. While the cauldron shares its properties, we note three appearances of the cup in our stories. The golden bowl to which Rhiannon and Pryderi become stuck is an Otherworldly Hallow used by Llwyd to snare them and avenge the insult to Gwawl. The bowl on chains appears also in *Owain*, and in *Perlesvaus*, where it reveals the sufferings of those trapped in the Underworld.[29] It cannot be achieved by the unworthy, and the reason why Rhiannon and Pryderi suffer is possibly because Pryderi has relinquished his father's sovereignty into the hands of Manawyddan instead of taking it up himself. The Empress's cups are harmonics of the cup that is stolen from Gwenhwyfar in *Peredur*. Like the cup that Sovereignty pours for Irish heroes, it is offered only to the worthy candidate.

The horn appears in the Thirteen Treasures list as the Horn of Bran the Niggard, which supplies whatever drink one desires. There is a tradition that Myrddin was trying to gather the Thirteen Treasures together, and all their possessors swore to relinquish them if Myrddin was able to gain the Horn of Bran. He did get it and afterwards took all Thirteen Treasures with him into his Glass House on Bardsey Island, where he is still supposed to reside.[85] The horn of Gwlgawd Gododin is specified as one of Culhwch's *anoethu* by Yspaddaden and seems to be a similar vessel. But we note two further horns: that won by Peredur when he cuts off the unicorn's head, and the horn in the Orchard when Gereint has successfully achieved the Enchanted Games test. This horn is for blowing, not drinking out of, and it signifies the end of the hero's testing and his worthy joining with Sovereignty. We will have more to say about this object in section IV.

These are Sovereignty's regalia, the Hallows of the Goddess, which she gives into the keeping of her worthy champion. While he remains faithful to her, he is empowered by these gifts; when he fails to uphold the rights of the land, he is bereft of their empowering help. It is in such a way that the Grail is withdrawn from the earth in later tradition, as we shall see in section III of this chapter.

It remains only to consider how later story-tellers portrayed Arthur's sovereignty with the symbol that is known by every child: the sword in the stone. The sword, set in an anvil by Merlin, may not be drawn by any save the rightful king. Symbolically the sword cannot be drawn by any save Arthur because it is stuck into the stone, which represents the land. This is a very pure myth of the Goddess of the Land. When Arthur receives his manhood's sword, Excalibur, (as opposed to his inauguration or coronation sword) from the Lady of the Lake, he receives a clearer empowerment. At the conclusion of his reign he commands Sir Bedevere to cast Excalibur back into the lake because the sword must return to Sovereignty; it may not be kept as an heirloom or bequeathed to some future king. Each monarch makes his own agreement with Sovereignty, who will not give her gifts to the unworthy.

II QUEEN DRAGON

The gaining of the Hallows of Sovereignty depends upon the hero's successful encounter with the Loathly Lady or *Cailleach* aspect of the Goddess. The transformation of the hag into a beautiful maiden is effected by the hero's kiss, or by his willingness to sleep with her. A Scots Gaelic version of *The Daughter of the King Under the Wave* retains this feature.[61] The *fianna* are encamped on a wild rainy night when an ugly woman with hair down to her heels approaches them. She asks at the tent of Fionn and Oisian to be let in, but it is only Diarmuid who receives her. After drying herself at the fire, she begs to be allowed to come under Diarmuid's blanket. The story-teller says, with a phrase which might have been drawn straight from *Peredur*:

> She was not long thus, when he gave a start, and he gazed at her, and he saw the finest drop of blood that ever was, from the beginning of the universe till the end of the world, at his side.

It is this willingness to accept the most unpromising appearance of Sovereignty that lies at the heart of the hero's success. Like a man promising to marry a woman 'for richer, for poorer, in sickness and in health', the kingly candidate takes on the government of the land and all that it entails *out of love for the land*. The land that is loved and respected gives of its best, as do its people, and the reign of that king is bountiful and wise, strong and loving. It is all too easy, under the rule of a worthless king, for the land to turn sour; its crops wither, its people turn to violent crime and the whole body politic is racked with strife.

It is at such times that the sovereignty-bestowing maiden and queen of the Hallows transforms into her *Cailleach* aspect. As we have seen in folk-stories, this transformation is often effected by an evil stepmother or magician who enchants the maiden into a monstrous shape, into a worm or dragon (see Chapters Three and Five). But we note also that Sovereignty has the ability to shapeshift at will, as we have seen from *Peredur*, and that this voluntary transformation is, in fact, the earlier of the two models.

Each of the three romances reveals the transforming Goddess of Sovereignty in the persons of her representatives. In *Owain*, the Countess of the Fountain appears first as a mourning woman, ugly with grief, yet Owain still perceives her inner beauty; in *Gereint and Enid* Enid is both the most beautiful maiden and also the most poorly dressed; she receives the highest honours and then the lowest degradation; in *Peredur*, Sovereignty shows all her aspects, from the Empress right down to the Black Maiden and the Nine Witches of Gloucester. Underlying both *Owain* and *Peredur* are the substrata that connect the figure of Sovereignty as a transforming hag with the enchanted damsel who is doomed to take the shape of a monster. While most Irish Sovereignty figures appear as hags, British folklore variants show how the enchanted damsel can be released by means of the *fier baiser* (the daring kiss of medieval romance), given her by the worthy knight. In the case of *Owain*, we have seen how the overlay of the *Libeaus Desconus* story (p. 71) and the folk ballad *Kemp Owyne* (p. 121) can be perceived; in *Peredur*, the disenchantment scene is missing, but it may be vestigially present in the incident when Peredur slays the *addanc*, but only after having been given a ring of invisibility by the Woman of the Mound.

Each aspect of Sovereignty helps or interrelates with the others. As we have observed on p. 195, the action of the *Cailleach* aspect of

Sovereignty is not evil. Hers is a scouring, catabolic function by which the disintegration of order and fertility within the land is hastened. The *Cailleach* clears the way with the harsh broom of purgation, bringing a spiritual winter whereby the land can be renewed and hearts made ready to receive the spring.

The action of the *Cailleach* and her transformation into the sovereignty-bestowing maiden is clearly seen in the following story, which relates the joint functions of the transformative aspects to the seasons. This story appears in both the *Leabhar Breac* and the *Book of Lismore* and is remarkable in that it shows how enduring was the seeming combat between the hag and maiden aspects of Sovereignty, even into the Christian era.

The story is called *Don T-Samain Beos* and it relates the meaning of the pagan feast of Samhain (31 October) and how it is connected to the Christian feast of All Saints (1 November). It is probably the work of a clerical commentator who wished to explain, in Irish terms, how such a pagan festival could stand side by side with one of the greatest Christian holy days; certainly customs pertaining to ancient pagan seasonal rites were practised on the occasion of the Christian feasts, and are still so practised today.

This is the reason why the feast of Samhain is called the Feast of All Saints. It came about as Boniface, the successor of St Peter, was contemplating the Pantheon, the pagan house of the gods in Rome. He remarked to the Emperor that the Pantheon, despite the coming of Christianity, had grown in influence. At this, the Emperor caused the Pantheon to be consecrated to Mary and all the saints of the world, those who stand in the first nine ranks of the blessed. This is why Samhain is called All Saints, because the pagan house of the gods has now been consecrated to all saints. There is another reason also, namely a game which was played by the boys of Rome every year on the same day: it was a board game with the figure of a hag at one end and the figure of a virgin at the other. The hag set a dragon on the virgin, calling all the demons, while at the other end the virgin let loose a lamb so that the lamb overpowered the dragon. At that the hag set a lion upon the virgin, but the virgin let loose a rain, and the rain was victorious over the lion. Boniface who watched this told the boys that this farcical game was unseemly and asked them how they came to know it. The boys replied: 'Sibyl, the brilliant prophetess, has taught us this game, through the grace of a prophecy in which she prophesied Christ's combat with the devil.' 'Thank God,' answered the pope, 'He who was prophesied has come and the devil is defeated.' He added, 'Give thanks to God and do not play this game any more.' At that this game was not played any more upon Samhain eve.[35]

The game, supposedly Roman in this story, is exactly the kind of game that the Irish played themselves: the story-teller gives the game away by telling us that they played it on 31 October, Hallowe'en or Samhain: the night when the Celtic New Year began, when winter truly started, when the *Cailleach* reigned. Both Irish and Scottish Gaels (Scottish Celts) personified winter as the Cailleach Bheare or Bheur. She held sway until Oimelc (spring) when, on St Brigit's day, 1 February, the maiden Goddess challenged the hag and began battling for the rule of spring. The hag and maiden of this game are clearly identifiable with the *Cailleach* and the goddess Brighid. The *Cailleach* held folk in the grip of winter with her icy winds and clouds of snow, whereas the goddess Brighid was the fosterer of lambs born at this time of year. She was honoured with great celebrations on both sides of the Irish sea up until recently. On Bride's morn, in Scots Gaelic tradition, the serpent is supposed to come forth from the ground, signifying the attack of the *Cailleach*, who normally chooses to increase her winter chill at this time:

> Thig na nathair as an toll
> La donn Bride,
> Ged robh tri traighean dh'an t'sneachd
> Air leacd an lair.

> La Bride nam brig ban
> Thig an rigen ran a tom
> Cha bhoin mise ris an rigen ran,
> 'S cha bhoin an rigen ran rium

> The serpent will come from the hole
> On the brown day of Bride,
> Though there should be three feet of snow
> On the flat surface of the ground.

> On the day of Bride of the white hills
> The noble queen will come from the knoll
> I will not molest the noble queen,
> Nor will the noble queen molest me.[63]

We note that, even here, the serpent is referred to respectfully as queen. Thus the beasts that hag and maiden set against each other in the 'Roman' game, the dragon and the lamb, are clearly drawn from Celtic association. It is conceivable that we have here a lost game in which Sovereignty's transformations were played as a form of *fidhchell* during the long winter months when stories and indoor games were the only entertainment. Certainly we know that some *fidhchell* boards were decorated or formed in the shape of a human body, with arms and legs protruding from their corners.[104]

The second move in the game, when the lion is overcome by a shower of rain, is similar to the behaviour of the characters of Owain and the Lady of the Fountain; but this similarity must be considered coincidental.

Certainly the story above is derived from a genuine mythical understanding of the seasonal rituals concerning the transformation of winter into spring, although the change that is brought about here is that from paganism to Christianity. The models that the story-teller has chosen to express his views are from existent Irish pagan customs, carefully selected to have the most profound effect upon his hearers, who would have known very well about the struggle between the *Cailleach* and the maiden. We note that the beast that the hag first sends against the maiden is the dragon, and that this tradition is reflected in the Scots Gaelic customs concerning the serpent that comes out of the ground to signify the ending of winter, the 'noble queen' herself, the *Cailleach*. If we set this identification of the *Cailleach* as dragon side by side with the tradition of the maiden enchanted into a serpent shape, we discover an interesting thing: that Sovereignty may choose to take the shape of the dragon.

Dragons have a curiously contradictory symbolism: they appear in some stories as ravagers of lands and devourers of maidens and youths, and are fit only to be destroyed by great knights like St

George. In other stories, while they are awesomely powerful and to be approached respectfully, they are also guardians of treasure, some of which they may give up to the one who is brave enough to engage in a contest of wits with them. Both sets of symbols may seem familiar to the reader, and this is not surprising since both are analogues of the symbolism surrounding Sovereignty herself, who, depending upon the aspect she is manifesting, guards great treasures, devastates the land, gives advice and indulges in games by which she may be overcome or for which she is the victor's reward.

The most striking thing about the Samhain Eve story is that the game describes the chessboard of the land over which hag and maiden battle for sovereignty. The sacred games of Sovereignty appear throughout Celtic tradition, and in the *Mabinogion* we have seen some prime examples, notably in *Gereint and Enid* where the games concern the hunting of the White Hart, the winning of the Sparrowhawk contest and the Enchanted Games. The chess-games of *The Dream of Macsen Wledig*, *Peredur* and *The Dream of Rhonabwy* are also rooted in the whole question of who shall gain the sovereignty of the land. Even the horse race that Elphin stakes against King Maelgwn in *The Story of Taliesin* may be seen as part of this tradition, for Taliesin ensures that Elphin, his patron, gains the sovereignty of honour and even compensates for Elphin's persistent misfortune by enabling his master's winning horse to stumble over the place where lies hidden a great golden treasure.

It is not incidental that the sovereignty of the land is guarded by a *Cailleach* or a woman in dragon's shape who has to be overcome in a game or else disenchanted. It is not incidental that the treasures that the dragon guards are those very Hallows that empower the rightful king. Such considerations may lead us into deeper waters.

The mysteries of Sovereignty are expressed by means of many symbols besides the emblems of the Hallows. The union of the land with the king and the two Christian symbols of the Grail are intimately related: the red and white dragons that appear in both Nennius and Geoffrey of Monmouth as well as in *Lludd and Llefelys* have their symbolic analogues with the two cruets brought by Joseph of Arimathea to Europe, for these contain blood and sweat from the world's Redeemer. As Bob Stewart has already remarked in his essay 'The Grail as Bodily Vessel':[115] 'the interaction of male and female characteristics ... [has] long been expressed as The Seed and The Blood.'

The basis of the Grail's existence in British tradition is, as we see, founded on the union of the king with Sovereignty: the emblems of this union are the Hallows, which include the Grail in its earliest form – the empowering cup or cauldron. Beneath this understanding is the ancient, tribal concept of the mingling of the royal seed with the holy blood of the land: the magical image is of king and Sovereignty's representative or priestess joined in sexual union. This union is that same disenchanting kiss or ritual bedding with the *Cailleach* that results in the transformation of the hag into the sovereignty-bestowing maiden and of the wasteland into a fruitful garden. The archetypal symbols representing this union are the two dragons, the red and the white.

All texts speak of the dragons in a political not a mystical light, but the deeper symbolism emerges. The sleeping dragons, locked safely away, represent the dormant state of Britain's sovereignty. They are chained during Lludd's reign because their uncontrolled manifestation renders the kingdom chaotic. It is during the reign of Vortigern that they are uncovered at the prophetic behest of Merlin Emrys, who comes to rid Britain of a worthless ruler and re-establish the true union of the land with a new dynasty – the Pendragons.

The later reign of Arthur, according to all traditions, ends because the union of the king with his land is ruptured; the cause may be the incestuous begetting of Mordred upon Arthur's half-sister, or it may be the loss of Guinevere to Lancelot, but the energies of the dragons run uncontrolled towards the conclusion of Arthur's reign, bringing in the Saxon invaders, devastating the land and bringing the Round Table Fellowship to an end (see p. 158). It is also possible to see the end of Arthur's reign from the point of view of the Queen Dragon herself – the transforming Goddess, who, having been Flower Bride and representative of Sovereignty, chooses a new consort to rule her land; such is the career of Gwenhwyfar in the earliest traditions, as we shall see in

246

the next chapter. It is significant that the Battle of Camlann is provoked by an adder, whose appearance causes one of Arthur's men to strike out, thus breaking the truce between Arthur and Mordred in Malory.[25] The serpent comes out of the ground just as the *Cailleach* of winter does.

The maintenance and wielding of the Hallows is the duty of the king, and if he once wavers, the kingdom soon tilts out of balance. The popular belief in the Sleeping Lord, who lies buried at certain sacred sites throughout Britain and who guards a golden cup or other treasure, is a deeply rooted remembrance of an ancestral mystery. There is a sense in which the Hallows are hidden within the land itself at the four quarters of the realm of Logres, the 'inner' Britain. These do not constitute 'buried treasure', which can be found with a metal-detector and dug up, but the guardianship by Sovereignty's champion of the elemental, power-bestowing energies that hold the realm in balance.

It is this tradition that underlies the importance of the Grail in British consciousness. An apocryphal gnostic tradition speaks of the two cruets of Joseph of Arimathea, which constitute a Christianizing of the native Hallows; they are thought to be buried in France and Britain. These emblems are guarded by Joseph and by Mary Magdalene; in British tradition these figures can be viewed as the Guardian of the Hallows and the Dark Woman of Knowledge, or the Lord and Lady of the Wheel, for they are jointly responsible for the relics of the Dead Redeemer and the dissemination of his tradition. The cruets, containing the Blood and the Sweat, are the Christian analogues for the Blood and Seed.

Such is the power of this mystery that its symbolism has accordingly been made dense and obscure to human understanding, lest it be reduced to atavistic levels involving ritual sacrifice or into modern perversions of genetic manipulation. The mysteries of Sovereignty are those of life itself, of the exchange of energies between man and woman, king and Sovereignty, god and goddess.

Within the framework of the Celto-Arthurian world the Blood and the Seed and the red and white dragons are symbols which may be applied to the Goddess and the king, or to the Queen

Dragon and her consort, the Pendragon. They are the maintainers of Logres, the inner Britain; they are the dragons who are loose once more, scouring the land with their strong breath, rekindling the dreaming fires of creation in each heart.

III THE MAIDENS OF THE WELLS

As we are beginning to appreciate, the Grail legends lie at the heart of the Sovereignty story. There is little space here in which to track the course of the Grail's progress from Sovereignty's cup to Vessel of Redemption, but we can see how the figure of Sovereignty persists throughout the legend's unfolding.

The purest example of Sovereignty is drawn from *Baile in Scail*, where Conn is abducted into the Otherworld in order to have a vision of his kingly destiny. In it we see the earliest pagan analogues of the Grail tradition, but here the vessel confers kingship not spiritual redemption.

> They went into the house and saw a girl seated in a chair of crystal, wearing a golden crown. In front of her was a silver vat with corners of gold. A vessel of gold stood beside her and before her was a golden cup. They saw the Phantom himself on his throne . . . 'My name is Lug . . . and I have come to tell you the span of your sovranty' . . . The girl was the Sovranty of Ireland and she gave food to Conn . . . When she went to serve the ale, she asked to whom the cup of red ale [Dergflaith or red lordship] should be given, and the Phantom answered her 'For Conn.'[70]

When Sovereignty appears as herself and not in any changed form, she invariably offers food or drink. We have already seen how this happens in *Peredur* with the Maiden of the Tent (p. 170). The giving of nourishment was of course a prime requisite of Celtic hospitality.

The function of giving cups to the worthiest hero occurs in *Bricriu's Feast*, where the great queen Medbh (Maeve) gives cups to all the heroes whom Conchobar sends to her for judgement (see p. 126). Her own name means 'intoxication', referring to her reputation as a sovereignty-bestowing woman; this is further borne out by her many lovers and husbands to whom she grants, briefly, the right of kingship beside her.[142]

Different kinds of sovereignty deserve different kinds of drink, which is shown in an Irish genealogical tract concerning the succession of the Munster kings, the Eoghanacht. The founder of that line was Corc; his wife, Aimend, had a dream in which she gave birth to wolf-cubs. She bathed one in wine (the royal drink), one in ale (the noble drink), one in new milk (the drink of the fosterling) and one in water (the drink of slaves). A fifth cub came to bed and she bathed him in blood (the drink of the warrior) and he gnawed at her breasts.[60] This dream is prophetic of the sons she bears and who settle in various parts of Munster with better or worse success. The fifth wolf-cub refers to her stepson, who proves treacherous. Here the candidates for kingship are bathed rather than given something to drink, but the classic pattern is shown quite clearly.

Sovereignty offers three cups in all to her candidates; these correspond to the three symbolic colours of her transformations:

the milk of fostering	white	maiden
the wine of lordship	red	Hallow Queen
the drink of forgetfulness	black	Dark Woman of Knowledge/ Cailleach

It is possible that the three cups that are offered to the Empress in *Peredur* are based upon this understanding, representing Peredur's complex relationship with Sovereignty in that text (cf. p. 179).

The cup of Sovereignty, which later becomes the Grail, cannot be robbed of its original symbolism, to which the Grail texts attest in showing the Grail-bearer as a beautiful maiden, and the Grail messenger – she who summons and prompts the seeker – as an ugly hag.[119] This polarization of two of Sovereignty's aspects within one story appears in each of the romances, as we have noted. The later Grail texts show a further diminution of the tradition by bringing into the Grail quest numerous dispossessed or raped maidens, widowed wives and enticing enchantresses; the Grail-seekers go to great lengths to rescue the former and escape the latter, even though their quest is thereby lengthened. We perceive a glimpse of the hero's championship of Sovereignty in such episodes.

A. C. L. Brown in his book *The Origins of the Grail Legend*[58] has shown how the quest for the Grail sprang out of a long Celtic tradition of Otherworld journeys in which kings and heroes achieve wonders and bring back types of the Hallows. The women who guard these treasures are clearly Otherworldly or faery women, and it is not until the mainstream Arthurian romances that we find Sovereignty being represented by earthly women, although she is often present as a faery mistress in the Breton *lais* and related stories.[134]

From this fusion of traditions arises a prime story, which shows how the usurpation of Sovereignty's function by an unworthy king brings about the wasteland and the ensuing Grail quest. *The Elucidation*, as it is hopefully called, is of unknown authorship, though possibly written about 1230. It serves as an introduction to Chrétien's *Perceval* or *Conte du Graal* and is supposed to elucidate the hidden meanings of that story. Since Chrétien left his story unfinished, numerous writers attempted to continue and conclude it; these episodes are called 'the continuations', and serve to explain Chrétien's intentions for his heroes, Gawain and Perceval. *The Elucidation* was probably written during this period and is doubtless an attempt at a 'prequel' to the Grail quest. However, it is a peculiar kind of introduction, since it refers to stories which happen nowhere in either Chrétien or the continuations, and moreover seems bent on mystifying the reader rather than enlightening him, as the title might suggest.

For our purposes it is a key story, since it shows an understanding of Sovereignty's association with the Hallow of the Grail more clearly than any other text.

In ancient times Logres was a rich country but it was turned into a Wasteland so that it was worth scarcely a couple of hazelnuts. For the kingdom lost the voices of the wells and the damsels that were in them. These damsels would offer food and drink to wayfarers. A traveller had only to wish for food and seek out one of the wells and a damsel would appear from out of the well with the food he liked best, a cup of gold in her hand. No wayfarers were excluded from this service.

But King Amangons broke this custom. Although it was his duty to guard the damsels and keep them within his peace, he raped one of them and took away her golden cup for his own service. After that time no damsel was seen issuing from the well and the only service which wayfarers received was done invisibly. The king's vassals followed their king's actions and raped the other damsels also, carrying off the golden cups. And so the service of the wells ceased. The land was laid waste: trees lost their leaves, meadows and plants withered and the waters were dried up so that no man might find the Court of the Rich Fisherman, he that once made the land bright with his treasures.

After this time, King Arthur instituted the Knights of the Round Table, who, when they heard this story, were determined to recover the wells and protect the damsels. They swore they would totally destroy the kindred of Amangons and his men. But though they made vows to God, they could never hear a voice from the well nor could they find any damsel, for these had been pierced by the swords of Amangons's followers or else hanged.

The Round Table knights found damsels in the forest accompanied by well-armed knights. One of these was captured and brought back to Arthur's court where he told the following tale. 'All of us are the children born of the damsels whom Amangons and his men raped. These great wrongs shall never be redeemed in worldly time. We are bound to travel in common, knights and damsels, through this land until God wills that the Court of Joy be found, for that will make the land bright again. Whoever seeks that Court shall find greater adventures than were ever in this land before.'

The Round Table knights decided to seek for the Court of the Rich Fisherman, who was a shapeshifter. Although many knights sought it and a few found it, none asked the right questions when the Hallows were processed about the hall of the Rich Fisherman who appeared in such splendour that none recognized the fisherman they had seen earlier that day. At that table the Grail appeared by itself and served all who sat there, providing food in great variety.

[At this point the writer tells us about the stories we will hear and says that each branch of the story has a guardian appointed to it.]

On the day that the Court of the Rich Fisherman was found, and the correct answers received by the seeker, the waters flowed again, fountains which had been dried up ran into the meadows. Fields were green and fruitful and the forests clothed in green leaf on the day that the Court of Joy was found.

Then there came up out of the wells a pitiable kind of people who made for themselves castles, cities and strongholds. They made for the damsels the rich Castle of the Maidens, but they knew not the service of the wells. They made the Perilous Bridge and the Orguellous Castle. They founded an order called The Knights of the Rich Company, in opposition to the Round Table knights. They made war on Arthur and such were their numbers that it was hard to overcome them. For four years they fought against him, and they were at last overcome on the day when the Court of Joy was found.[36]

This mysterious story has many surprising elements, considering it was written as a 'prequel' to the Christian Grail-quest cycle. The reign of Amangons obviously predates Arthur's reign by more than one generation and in some measure represents an earlier, pagan tradition. Amangons is a mythical, not a historical king, and indeed the whole story reads very like a gnostic parable of the fall of humanity from innocence. Just how much the author or transcriber of this tale was drawing upon imagination or oral tradition is hard to say. Certainly there is something about the damsels of the wells which ranks them with Sovereignty's representatives.

The rape of the damsels and the stealing of their cups is, of course, a parallel to the theft of Gwenhwyfar's cup and her abduction in Arthurian tradition, which, as we shall see, is crucial to an understanding of the mythic patterns within the *Mabinogion*. The fertility of the land is bound up with the fate of the damsels of the wells, and when they are raped and their golden cups taken from them, the harmony that should exist between king and land is ruptured. We note that these prototypes of the Grail are symbolic of the damsels' service in Logres; it is not until the more developed Grail legends that we see Sovereignty's role devolve to that of Grail-bearer. Interestingly the Grail question that so many knights fail to ask when the Hallows are paraded about the Grail castle is 'Whom does the Grail serve?' strikingly reminiscent of Sovereignty's question to Lugh in the *Baile in Scail* story (see p. 67), 'For whom should the cup be poured?'

The relationship of the damsels of the wells with the court of the Rich Fisherman is not explicitly dealt with by the author, but we can hazard that the damsels are Otherworldly women who offer food and drink to travellers along a network of holy sites and springs, which are the meeting-places between the worlds. The court of the Rich Fisherman, which is also called the Court of Joy in the text, is analogous to the Otherworld paradise, wherein the treasures or Hallows are guarded by the Rich Fisherman himself, who is possibly a type of Manannan or Manawyddan. (Manannan traditionally represents the King of the Otherworld and is, like the Rich Fisherman, a shapechanger who can take on humble personae as well as appear in his guise as King of the Blessed Isles.)

It would appear that access to Otherworldly communion was effected at the wells by means of travellers drinking from the damsels' cups. By the time that Arthur and his knights appear and swear to destroy Amangons's kind, they have a substantial problem: they cannot destroy the descendants of Amangons without also destroying the descendants of the damsels. Earthly and Otherworldly stocks are now totally mingled and, like the parable of the tares and the wheat in the Gospel, these people must be left alone to effect their own destiny. But among them there are story-tellers, like Master Bleheris, who tells Arthur about the Court of Joy, the blessed Otherworld, access to which, for mankind, has been withdrawn, but which may yet be found.

The one who finds the Court is, of course, the Grail-winner, who is Perceval in the earliest legends and Galahad in the later versions. In the fully developed Arthurian stories we may see that while Arthur himself encounters Sovereignty and becomes king after the early Celtic pattern, it is his knights, Perceval, Galahad and Bors, who achieve the Grail quest. Thus a twofold association is effected: Arthur establishes his championship of Logres, his communion with the land, and becomes its king, while the

Grail-winner establishes a communion with the Otherworldly/ heavenly realms by crossing the barrier between the worlds.

The Grail-winner is always a scion of a royal line, having in him a share of the mixed parentage that we all inherit; but in him the blood of Sovereignty's representative is paramount. His opponents upon the Grail quest are drawn from a similar mixture of earthly and Otherworldly races; they are the Order of the Rich Company in whom the blood of Amangons is paramount. What they do not have, they steal; whoever obstructs them, they destroy. And so the powers of light and darkness oppose each other in a conflict; Sovereignty's cup becomes not only a power-bestowing vessel but also a chalice of spiritual redemption in the late Grail romances.

The text tells us that the land of Logres 'lost the voices of the wells', which descriptively evokes not only the loss of the Otherworldly communion but also the withdrawal of the Grail from earthly realms. In order to obtain this wonder-working Hallow by which the land will be restored to its former fertility, the Grail-seeker has to find the gate and enter the Otherworld, where he will be subjected to tests and challenges which will establish whether he is the rightful champion, 'he who frees the waters', the destined Grail-winner. He must be attuned to the needs of the land so that he may hear the voice of Sovereignty in his heart and answer her urgent questioning.

IV THE COURT OF JOY

The Elucidation, then, may be considered to be a parable of the loss of the Otherworld by the earthly realm of Logres. It is also, though we should be cautious about utilizing traditional Celtic texts in other cultural contexts, about the loss of communion with the Divine Feminine, with the Goddess of the Land. The later incorporation of Christian motifs of redemption is in no way at variance with the native model of Sovereignty, since both are about the loss of the creative, Otherworldly realm that we all stand in need of, whether we see this as a loss of innocence, a loss of paradise or a loss of creative imagination. For both models the symbol is the same, the redemptive vessel or Hallow that may be Grail, cauldron or cup.

We immediately notice a strong connection between *The Elucidation*'s inherent prophecy that the Court of Joy will be found by the most worthy knight and the story of *Gereint and Enid* or Chrétien's *Erec and Enid*, where it is foretold that someone will achieve the Joy of the Court. How these two texts correspond is vital to an understanding of the nature of the Grail quest and the restoration of the land's fertility. As we have already seen, there is some confusion arising from the meaning of the word *cor*, which may be interpreted in one of many ways. The two meanings that most concern us here are:

$$li \ cors \ = \ \text{horn or body}$$
$$la \ cors \ = \ \text{court}$$

We will remember from *Gereint and Enid* that the horn was to be blown by the victor of the Enchanted Games; it is also the horn by which the Joy of the Court is announced in *Erec and Enid*, *Gereint*'s French variant. This feat is called the Joy of the Court in that text and signifies the court's happiness at the release of Mabonograin from bondage and the cessation of his enforced combat with challenging knights. In *Erec and Enid* the court at which this joy is announced is the castle of Brandigan, where Evrain (Owain) presides. The horn (*li cors*) announces a great joy to the court (*la cors*) according to this tradition, but there is yet another meaning which underlies this shapeshifting word – that of 'body'.

We are already familiar with the archetype who is a key to the mystery, for he likewise possesses a horn, which gives one whatever drink one desires – Bran the Blessed himself.

It is impossible to stray far from the Grail legends without encountering Bran in some form or other. We have already seen that his sister, Branwen, is intimately associated with the archetype of Sovereignty. Bran himself is a prototype for the Fisher King, as many commentators have pointed out.[93,125] We saw how, in *Branwen, Daughter of Llyr*, he was wounded in the foot with a poisoned spear, yet he threatened the Irishman thus: 'Dogs of Gwern, beware of Pierced Thighs.'[22] Of course, the

Wounded King of Chrétien's *Perceval*, who is called the Fisher King, is likewise wounded in the thigh by a spear.[7] The *Didot Perceval* names the Fisher King 'Bron', while de Boron's *Joseph* calls Bron 'the Rich Fisher'.[92] The numerous parallels between the pagan demi-god of the *Mabinogion* and the Christian semi-mortal of the later Grail romances has already been admirably dealt with by Helaine Newstead in her *Bran the Blessed in Arthurian Romance*,[124] so I will not reproduce her arguments here.

We have noted that the castle at which the Joy of the Court takes place is called Brandigan, which, although Evrain (Owain) lives there, is closely associated with Bran. Chrétien describes the castle as a strong castle, secure from attack, with rich orchards and meadows all about; its hospitality is famed, but it is also known as a place of great danger, since all are awaiting the Joy of the Court. Evrain's castle is obviously in another, Otherworldly dimension. It is like the hall at Harlech and Gwales where the surviving warriors feast with Bran in perpetual, unallayed joy. It is also like the court of the Rich Fisherman in *The Elucidation* at which great hospitality can be had but in which great sorrow is experienced, rather as the Assembly of the Noble Head in *Branwen, Daughter of Llyr* discover when they open the forbidden door that brings them to reality again.

The manner in which Bran represents the Rich Fisherman is overlaid with symbolism. It is possible that Robert de Boron, the first to call the Fisher King 'the Rich Fisher', was calling upon classical antecedents. One of the titles of the Lord of the Underworld, Hades, was Plutus, which means wealth, and it was one of Heracles' labours to take the Amaltheian horn filled with Hesperidian fruit to Tartarus for Plutus, after which it became known as the Cornucopia. We have already seen in *Mabon* (p. 53)[111] how Bran is associated with Cronos, who is likewise seen in classical tradition to sleep on rocks of gold. Bran is also described in the list of the Thirteen Treasures as the owner of a horn. The richness of the Fisherman's court is due to its being an abode of the Otherworld – not a gloomy place of the dead but an earthly paradise in which the mighty ancestors live on, feasting and fighting as they do in *The Dream of Rhonabwy*. It is worth noting that Bran has a connection with Owain, who, in *Gereint and Enid* and *Erec and Enid*, is the guardian of Brandigan castle. Owain's guardianship of the castle is quite natural, since he is likewise a guardian of the inner realms to which his mother's blood entitles him. Both Owain and Bran share the raven as their totem bird.

One of the chief features of Owain's castle is the hedge of stakes with heads upon them that surrounds the enchanted orchard where the Joy is to take place. This is echoed in *Branwen, Daughter of Llyr*, when Bran's head is cut off and brought to Harlech, where it continues to entertain and converse with his followers. Bran's head is nowise horrific to them but conveys the comforting presence of their lord. His sacrificial decapitation is in order to keep the land of Britain safe from invasion, although the immediate result of his foray to Ireland is devastation and the usurpation of his throne by Caswallawn. He remains alive, though beheaded. This is also a feature of the wounded Fisher King in the Grail legends: he is wounded but cannot die until a successor comes to guard the Hallows in his place; the land lies wasted but will be restored by a suitable successor.

The means by which the horn of Bran derives from the Cauldron of Rebirth to become the Christian Grail is one of the great mysteries of folklore. As we have seen above, the story-tellers shift their ground by the same process that one word may, by the removal of one letter and its replacement by another, be transformed into a totally different word which yet remains a harmonic of the original meaning. We are reminded of the medieval word-game played with San Greal (Holy Grail), which becomes Sang Real (Holy Blood). Such a game has been played with that innocent word *cors* with similar effect.

One of the later Grail romances in the Vulgate Cycle,[33] calls the castle of the Fisher King 'Corbenic'. The text tells us that the castle was called this 'after the holy vessel'. Now at no point in the Grail legends has the Grail ever been called anything like Corbenic. This would make sense only if the vessel had ever been referred to as the *cor beneit*, or blessed horn. In the later Grail romances the horn of Bran, which gives one the liquid one most desires to drink, becomes the chalice of the mass by which the wine of earthly realms is transubstantiated into the blood of the

Lord Christ, who is of heavenly kind. Bran's cauldron had the property of restoring the dead to life; Christ's covenant with humanity likewise brought new life, to both the soul and to the body, which would be raised up on the Day of Judgement. It is very doubtful that any Grail story-teller was consciously aware of these harmonics, but the line of tradition is remarkably consistent.

Of course the word Corbenic has another interpretation, which is equally valid; as *cors beneiz* or blessed body. The blessed body was, of course, Corpus Christi; the bread of earthly food became the transubstantiated body of the Saviour by which the faithful were nourished. The resonances between the mystical Christian symbolism and the legends of both Grail and the Blessed Bran are overwhelming. The Grail gives people the food they most crave or need in many texts, noticeably *The Elucidation*, and in the de Boron text it is the vessel that the Rich Fisher uses in his role of provider to the remnant of Joseph of Arimathea's family. The Grail, like the transformed bread and wine, sustains the life of the Grail guardian so that, though wounded, he does not die. In the *First Continuation*[93] the Grail procession includes a bier upon which is a sword. The King of the Grail Castle leads Gawain to it and says:

> Ah, noble body, lying here, for whose sake this kingdom is desolate, may God grant that you may be avenged so that the people may be glad thereof, and that the land which has long been desolate may be restored.

Such words might well have been spoken by Branwen over her brother Bran's body, for he sacrifices himself to become the Pen Annwn, the Sleeping Lord, whose physical presence in the land will safeguard it from invasion and keep it harmonized with Sovereignty.

It has been suggested by Francis Rolt-Wheeler that Corbenic is derived from the Welsh *cor-arbennig*, or Sovereign Chair;[141] though this is persuasive, it must be rejected as unlikely, for the *Cor y Fendigeid Fran*, the Horn of Bran the Blessed, must take prominence in this argument. The suggestion is hard to square with accepted Welsh etymology, which would make *cor-arbennig* mean 'the privileged (choir) stall', rather than kingly throne. (Although there are places in the locality of Llangollen that might well endorse this speculation: Cadair Fronwen (Branwen's Seat) and Gorsedd Fran (Bran's Throne).)

There is no purpose in advancing one meaning of *cors* to the detriment of all other definitions, for they are all valid in this knot of related symbols. The body (*cors*) of the imprisoned guardian is liberated by the sound of the horn (*cors*) to the joy of the whole court (*cors*). The finding of the Court of Joy is a task best handled by the worthiest champion, who, in the person of Gereint, wins Sovereignty, or who, as Grail-winner, like Perceval or Galahad, wins the Grail. Both sets of heroes achieve a breakthrough in the barriers that separate the earthly from the paradisaical realms, making their riches and wisdom available to common humanity. They are uniters of kingdoms rent apart. The hero thus wins his appointed portion and the king his empowering Hallows.

Sovereignty as Grail Maiden, Hallow Queen and Loathly Lady comes to invest the world in fresh garments, for the stain of devastation and the marks of wasting are cleansed as the new guardian takes up his appointed task. Bran is succeeded as Sleeping Lord (Pen Annwn) by Arthur just as Mabonograin and the Fisher King are succeeded by heroes like Gereint, Perceval and Galahad. The Hallows are brought out as the king is solemnly invested with their symbolic power: with his dragon-sword of light upon his thigh, symbolic of the dynamic dragons whose union is of blood and seed; with the mantle of the land about his shoulders by which he may pass in many shapes to all regions; with his ring upon his finger, seated in his golden chair; with the vessels of healing, plenty and rebirth before him, his spear of justice in his hands and, at his feet, the chessboard charged ready with pieces to fight for the rights of the land, the king is invested by Sovereignty with all the powers of earth and of the Otherworld.

CHAPTER TEN

THE SOVEREIGNTY OF BRITAIN

It is believed that when her time has come, this lady will declare herself: she will choose for herself a man, and he will be the Secret King of the Island of the Mighty, he will be Bran, reincarnate!

JOHN ARDEN AND MARGARETTA D'ARCY
The Island of the Mighty

Consider how to honour her and to perform so well that she will remain with you and may God aid me, but I wish in faith that all the women of the realm of Logres might be of her beauty.

Didot Perceval

I THE FOSTER-MOTHER

Throughout this book we have examined many aspects of Sovereignty as she appears in Celtic tradition. The time has come to see if we can discover the Sovereignty or Goddess of Britain. There are many contenders for this title, and, in order to narrow the field, I shall confine this last chapter to a consideration of Sovereignty in Arthurian tradition.

We have seen throughout the *Mabinogion* countless examples of Sovereignty's representatives, but here I shall discuss four distinct archetypes in relationship to Arthur himself: the Foster-mother, the Queen of the North, the Flower Bride and the Otherworldly Consort. These aspects of Sovereignty arise from a study of the Celto-Arthurian tradition and its fusion with the later romantic tradition: in order to encompass this study it is necessary to throw our net wide and catch the mythological drift of our elusive quarry.

It will be argued that nowhere does Arthur have a direct encounter with Sovereignty, but this proves not to be the case. He encounters her representatives in the persons of his mother, his sister and his wife as well as in more indirect relationships, which, when analysed, are very revealing.

We have seen how Arthur's knights champion their sovereign lord and by virtue of their quests and adventures actively maintain his passive relationship with Sovereignty. When we look again for Arthur's own encounters with the Goddess, we find the evidence is scanty. It is necessary to collate snippets from the various strata of Arthur's development from oral to literary tradition in order to amass sufficient evidence to create an overview.

This partially lost mythos of Arthur contains tantalizing clues and fragments, which can give us only a suggested reconstruction. Early tradition hints at his premier role as the first Grail-winner, in the 'Preiddeu Annwn': an event which probably figured largely in his *macgnimartha*.[105] It instances his retention in prison by Gwen Pendragon: a possible Sovereignty reference, which is almost impossible to reconstruct (see *Mabon*, p. 154).[111] All levels of tradition speak of his efforts to restore Britain to a state of order and harmony. He is supposed to be ubiquitously available to his country in time of need. Yet there is no extant story that tells of his marriage with the land. At no point does he meet a figure who bears the name of the land. He does not embrace an ugly hag by a well. However . . .

Almost the whole of Arthur's story, in whatever tradition we approach, bears such weighty testimony to the underlying presence of Sovereignty, her support and help within his reign, and such Otherworldly intervention in his affairs and those of the kingdom, that it is hard not to construe her influence in his career. From birth to death, the mythic witness sets its seal upon the life of Arthur, as well as upon his family, his court and his kingdom.

Let us see first what the evidence of genealogy, which has a mythic structure all of its own, has to offer.

The birth, conception and childhood deeds of Arthur are derived straight from the proto-Celtic story-telling tradition, in terms of archetypal stories of the young hero. As we noted from the story of Mabon (see *Mabon*, p. 167),[111] the young hero is conceived by the union of a worldly and Otherworldly parent; he is then fostered secretly because his very existence endangers the order of things. During his fosterage he is taught many deep wisdoms and is prepared for the task to come. His youth and strength, combined with his other advantages of birth into the royal house and his foster-mother's empowerment, bring him quickly to prominence and he is soon recognized as a prime candidate for kingship.[112]

This pattern is not confined solely to Arthur's story but is clearly discerned in the stories of such heroes as Peredur, Pryderi, Galahad, etc. Since Arthur's legend has been assembled cumulatively over generations of story-tellers, embroidered and reworked, we might well expect to find something rather different. Unexpectedly we find that the later story-tellers have inherited and enhanced the patterns of earlier British story-tellers, even though the former are working from a medieval Continental tradition. We have no means of telling what is their invention and what is traditional.

If we look to the earliest traditions, evidence for Arthur's parentage is sparse apart from the Welsh genealogical tracts, which can hardly be relied upon. The bardic skill of imparting and memorizing a patron's lineage was one slow to fade, but the early medieval period back to the sixth century was a time in which genealogical emendation and enhancement was quite an industry. It is normal to find the eponymous ancestor linked with Roman emperors, Celtic saints and Arthurian battle-lords with great impartiality. The resultant effect is similar to reading the list of Arthur's court in *Culhwch and Olwen*. If we look to the patrilinear and matrilinear descents of Arthur (see Figures 10.1 and 10.2) we note divergent traditions that predate the accepted family of Arthur that was derived from later sources in the

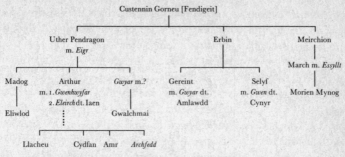

Figure 10.1: *Patrilinear Descent of Arthur*

French romances. Both of these simplified family trees derive from Welsh genealogical tracts.[12]

We see that Arthur's paternal grandfather is Custennin of Cornwall, a figure later confused by Geoffrey and others with Constantine III, the man proclaimed emperor by the British troops in 407. Uther's brothers sire families which figure largely in Arthurian legend: Gereint, whom we know from the *Mabinogion* story (see Chapter Six), and March – the King Mark who marries Isolt or Essyllt. Uther himself marries Eigr, or Igraine. This tradition gives them three children: Madog, of whom we hear nothing, Arthur and a daughter, Gwyar, whose identity will prove to be of some interest (see Figures 10.4 and 10.5).

Arthur marries Gwenhwyfar, according to all traditions, but in Figure 10.1 he also marries Eleirch, by whom he has three sons and a daughter. Tradition speaks only of Llacheu who is killed by Kay, and Amr whom Arthur is responsible for killing, according to the earliest sources.[28,87]

Figure 10.2 shows the six daughters of Amlawdd Wledig – a legendary character whose name, Amloth, seems to derive from the same root as that of Hamlet. Whoever he may have been, his daughters certainly seem to have been key figures in the sovereignty of Britain. This genealogy, largely derived from a twelfth-century life of St Illutud – here a cousin of Arthur – shows Eigr (Igraine) marrying Rhica, the chief elder or counsellor of Cornwall, rather than the more usual Gwrleis (Gorlois). We have

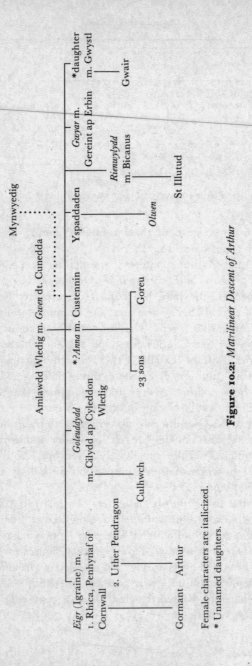

Figure 10.2: *Matrilinear Descent of Arthur*

Female characters are italicized.
* Unnamed daughters.

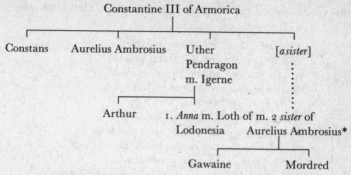

Figure 10.3. *Arthur's Family Tree according to Geoffrey of Monmouth*

already met Goleuddydd in Chapter 6 of *Mabon*,[111] and her mysterious unnamed sister who marries Custennin ap Mynwyedig, who is ousted by Yspaddaden. Rienwylydd is the mother of St Illutud. Gwyar – a different woman from the Gwyar, daughter of Uther and Eigr – marries Gereint. A second unnamed sister marries Gwystl, the hostage; their son, confusingly called Gwair, is one of the knights whom Peredur encounters in the forest and whom he believes to be angels.

A glance at Figure 10.3 will show that Geoffrey had linked his Arthur with the imperial line of Constantine III. Arthur's sister is called not Gwyar but Anna and she is married to Loth or Lot, of whom more in section II of this Chapter.

There is doubtless much in these family trees which is fantastic and unhistorical but, despite the many interpolations created by well-meaning genealogists, they show certain traditional consistencies. Uther and Eigr are always Arthur's parents. Arthur has a sister. He always marries Gwenhwyfar. He is always uncle to Gwalchmai or Gawain.

Yet what can be gained from this accumulation of traditions? We are able to see Arthur's relationship with his cousins and nephews: those knights who will play so great a part in the stories associated with him and who will often stand in the place of the king, as his champions. For Arthur's relationship with Sovereignty we

* This is an error on Geoffrey's part. It should be Arthur's sister not Ambrosius'.

must look beyond genealogy into the complex webs of the sisters:

> He is a King crouned in Fairie,
>> With sceptre and with his regally
> Shall resort as Lord and Soveraigne
>> Out of Fairie and reigne in Britaine;
> And repaire again the Round Table.
>> By prophesy Merlin set the date,
> Among Princes King incomparable,
>> His seate againe to Caerlion to translate,
> The Parchas sustren sponne so his fate,
>> His Epitaph recordeth so certaine
> Here lieth King Arthur that shall raigne againe.[23]

This verse by Lydgate emphasizes the manner in which Arthur is seen mythologically: he is a king aided by the Otherworld and his fate is administered by the mystic sisterhood of women who represent Sovereignty and the land.

This tradition, which neatly ties together the beginning and ending of Arthur's career, is founded mostly in Breton-influenced *enfances* (childhood stories) now lost to us but still perceptible in the childhood of Lancelot, whereby the hero becomes the foster-son of a powerful Otherworldly woman who endows him with supernatural gifts, powers and objects. We find traces of this in the English Layamon, in which the elves are attendants at Arthur's birth and his body is finally received by Argante, Queen of Faery.[43] Three fays are said to attend Arthur's birth and give him gifts in the Second Continuation of *Perceval*.[134] We see, too, traces of this tradition in Malory, where Arthur is endowed by the Lady of the Lake with Excalibur and its magical scabbard of invulnerability.[25]

Within British tradition there is no such fostering story, though Igraine seems to revert to the Otherworldly queen archetype in Chrétien's *Perceval*, where she appears as the Queen of the Castle of Maidens, visited by Gawain. Within this Otherworldly castle, in which are many women awaiting the coming of a great champion to restore their rights, we see a vast, collective Sovereignty assembled. Three royal women administer the place: Ygerne (Igraine/Eigr), Arthur's mother; Morcades, who appears in later tradition as Ygerne's daughter and Gawain's mother; and Clarrisant, Gawain's sister. Although Gawain liberates the castle and thus becomes its lord by right, he does not recognize these women at all and is astonished when told who they really are:

> 'The white-haired queen (is) . . . King Arthur's mother.' – 'By the faith I owe God and His power, as far as I'm aware, King Arthur has had no mother for a long time, not for a good sixty years, to my knowledge, and even for much longer than that.' – 'Yet it's true, sir; she is his mother. When his father Utherpendragon was laid to rest, it came about that Queen Ygerne came to this country bringing with her all her treasure . . . And I'm sure you saw the other queen, that tall, handsome lady who was King Lot's wife and . . . the mother of Gawain.'[7]

It would seem that Ygerne has established herself in the Island of Women or the Land of Youth, in the manner of the Celtic *immrama* stories on which this incident is clearly based, since one of the conditions of the champion who overcomes all obstacles to become its master is that he has no leave to depart from the castle again. The same thing happens to Maelduine and Bran when they reach the Land of Women.

Arthur's ancestry aligns with this tradition in *Parzival*, where von Eschenbach describes Arthur's great-grandmother as being called Ter de la Schoy (the Joy of the Land), a faery from the land of Feimurgan, (Morgan le Fay).[40] So Arthur's ancestry is shown to be Otherworldly and perhaps intimately related to Sovereignty.

As for Igraine – Eigr herself – like Modron, she represents a Daughter of Branwen, one of the great matriarchs of the Island of the Mighty. In Malory it is Igraine's daughters by Gorlois – 'the famous Cornwall sisters' as T. H. White calls them – whose dynastic marriages secure the sovereignty of their mother's line in Britain: a role we will examine in the next section. But earlier tradition clearly identifies Igraine as an Otherworldly woman, or a representative of Sovereignty able to retreat to her unearthly 'fastness'. The attempt to give Arthur a faery godmother or foster-mother is a persistent tradition.

The custom of fosterage was strong among the Celts. A child of good birth would be fostered within a noble household and raised with that family, thus enforcing ties of tribal obligation and reducing the likelihood of feud between those families. The foster-mother would suckle her fosterling with her own children, thus making them brother and sister. Malory makes Kay Arthur's foster-brother, after Uther's death when Merlin ensures Arthur is fostered with Sir Ector of the Forest Sauvage.[25] But in Arthur's case we need to see if there is any likelihood of his fosterage by a representative of Sovereignty, for the mythological tradition is very potent.

Within Celtic tradition the archetypal foster-mother is the goddess Brighid, whose cult became subsumed in that of Saint Brigit. This powerful figure was a territorial goddess particularly worshipped in Britain by the Brigantes – hence her other name of Brigantia – a tribe living in the north Midlands. Irish apocryphal tradition credits St Brigit with fostering none other than Christ himself, and many commentaries give her goddessly titles: *mathair mo rurech*, 'mother of my lord' and *oen mathair Maicc Rig mair*, 'the unique mother of the Great King's Son'.[58] In some senses these titles are true, for such was the ancient goddess's power that her mythos and attributes passed entire into the cult of the Christian saint. Brighid was the mother of the gods and patron of the queenly arts of smithcraft and poetry as well as of women. It was logical that St Brigit reflected these abilities.

In Brighid we see traces of the Goddess of Sovereignty, sponsoring her chosen candidate from his very birth, giving him to drink of her bountiful wisdom by laying him at her own breast. The apocryphal story of St Brigit's fosterage of Christ must be seen in this light. As the Goddess of the old dispensation she fosters the god of the new faith, giving him a stake in the Otherworldly consciousness of all British and Irish believers by a process quite natural and harmonious, for he is her Mabon, quite as much as any other of her foster-sons.

If there was ever any story relating Arthur's fosterage by Sovereignty, under the aspect of Brighid Brigantia, we do not know of it. The fact that the Dark Age Arthur, presumed to have lived between 470 and 527, was contemporaneous with the historical St Brigit of Kildare (470–523) does not necessarily count for anything. However, the identity of the true Sovereignty of Britain may lie within her jurisdiction (see p. 304).

We have seen how Sovereignty sets tests for her champions. Arthur is not exempt from her scrutiny. In order to be secure in his kingship he needs to perform two important deeds: to openly welcome the *Cailleach* aspect of Sovereignty in order to transform his kingdom, and to successfully obtain the Hallows, which confirm his kingship. If we look to assorted legends and levels of tradition, we do indeed find both factors present.

Arthur is the primary Grail-winner: a fact which is not at all clear from later tradition. His descent into Annwn may be classed with the other great redemptive acts usually associated with gods and heroes. He enters Annwn in order to secure the cauldron of Pen Annwn, according to the ninth-century poem of 'Preiddeu Annwn' (*Mabon*, p. 107).[111] This cauldron combines all the primal aspects that surface later in the Grail stories: it is a life-giving vessel, it gives prodigious amounts of food to the courageous possessor and it bestows wisdom. Like the rest of the Hallows it is a withdrawn part of the mythological regalia of Sovereignty, who appoints her guardians and puts many obstacles in the way of the Hallows being reived by the unworthy.

The poem tells us of the cauldron being warmed by the breath of nine maidens or muses. These are the archetypal guardians of the cauldron/Grail. The three-times-three sisterhood, the chorus of sibyls who keep the vessel, are Underworld harmonics of the Goddess of Sovereignty herself; that much can be deduced from the evidence of the later Grail legends. We have only to look at *Peredur* to find that the Nine Witches of Gloucester are responsible for wielding yet another of the Hallows – the spear – and that they enable Peredur to gain his manly training in weapon skills after the old Celtic fashion of women warriors who teach heroes. We have already noted the dichotomy in this story: that the witches hinder the Grail quest but actively help its eventual champion (see p. 195). This ninefold sisterhood represents the same harmonic as the ninefold muses of the cauldron.

I have already suggested (see *Mabon*, p. 108)[111] that Arthur's right to the cauldron is, to some extent, a royal and mystical one, that he succeeds to Bran's ancient guardianship of this Hallow; but there is another possibility raised by Welsh genealogical tracts – that Arthur's right is also an ancestral one. Independent genealogies trace both Arthur's maternal and paternal lines back to Bran ap Llyr Llediath – Bran the Blessed himself.[2]

The ninefold sisters never allow any of the Hallows to fall into the hands of unworthy heroes, however well descended, and it is only by great toil and loss of men that Arthur is able to obtain the cauldron at all. Finding and maintaining the Hallows is no sinecure, for any champion soon finds out that there are strings attached: any king who falls out of harmony with his land and its people is likewise out of harmony with Sovereignty, who hides her fair face and assumes the garment of wasteland – a major theme of Grail literature.

It is interesting that the repositioning of the Grail legends tells us much about Arthur's unfolding role within tradition. The earliest story, told in 'Preiddeu Annwn', undoubtedly happened quite early in Arthur's reign. By the time of the later Grail romances we find that the stories occur towards the end of it. Arthur's kingdom, in these romances, is in disarray; part if not all of it has fallen into wasteland. His early prowess and reputation are obliterated by the ever-present menace of disorder, ruin and mismanagement. This is especially so in *Perlesvaus*, where Guinevere begs Arthur to re-establish his early glory by attending to the state of his soul. It is on her advice that he resorts to the Chapel of St Augustine in the forest and there, during many adventures both supernatural and mundane, he experiences a vision.

He has a vision of the Virgin, in which she presents her own child as the offering at mass. But as Arthur gazes on this scene, he sees the child turn into the crucified Christ, bleeding from his hands and feet. After admitting his own lack of responsibility towards his kingdom, Arthur hears a voice:

Arthur of Britain, you may truly rejoice in your heart that God has sent me to you. He commends you to hold court as soon as possible, for the world, which has suffered much harm because of you and your neglect of great deeds, will now profit most greatly from your action.[29]

At the sound of this Arthur's heart is filled with joy – perhaps that very Joy of the Court that results from the successful endeavours of Sovereignty's champion.

This episode is crucial to an understanding of Arthur's role and shows his active involvement in maintaining his sovereignty, which is at risk through his own inaction. At the bidding of Guinevere, who, as we shall see, is the representative of Sovereignty, he rides into a perilous place, putting his person at risk. There he is granted the vision of the Blessed Virgin and her Son; and though the text tells us that the wasteland and the wounding of the Fisher King are caused by the unworthy knight (Perlesvaus or Perceval), it is Arthur himself who has caused much suffering.

The mysterious voice is unidentified, though clearly intended to be angelic at the very least, if not the voice of the Virgin herself, to whom, during the Middle Ages, was ascribed the special patronage of England, called the Dowry of Mary. The reproof of Arthur is very similar to the reproof that Perceval receives from the Black Maiden in other texts. Clearly the story-teller responsible for *Perlesvaus* understood the harmonic under-lying the earlier traditions of Arthur's Grail questing. This concept was lost sight of almost entirely in the later stories, where the Grail is sought by Arthur's champions, not the king himself.

However, although Arthur has, in *Perlesvaus*, temporarily fallen out of harmony with Sovereignty, he is reconciled to her and is able to hear her voice once more. This is very significant if we return briefly to the Amangons story (p. 250) where, because of Amangons's rape of the damsels of the wells, no one is able to hear 'the voices of the wells'. This telling phrase indicates the articulation of the land itself in the heart of the rightful king. We will recall that, in that story, Arthur and his knights were also unable to hear the voices of the wells, although they were well intentioned towards the damsels. This silence is broken, in *Perlesvaus*, where Arthur hears the voice of the Virgin herself. Interest-ingly Arthur likewise hears the voice of Ragnell singing to the lute in the story told on p. 273.

It was said earlier that there is no parallel tradition concerning Arthur's marriage to Sovereignty, but this is not strictly true. Elements remain within the Arthurian corpus which are in-triguing and indicative of earlier traditions. If we look to Uther's kingship, we find interesting traces of something called 'the custom of the Pendragon'. This appears first in Chrétien's *Erec and Enid*, where it is called 'the custom (or the honour) of the

White Hart'. Anyone who is able to win the head of the White Hart is permitted to kiss the fairest of the maidens at court. Arthur judges Enid to be the most beautiful damsel there and says:

> It's the business of a true king to uphold the law, truth, good faith and justice ... I do not wish the traditional custom to lapse which my family habitually observes ... Whatever may become of me, I must safeguard and uphold the practice of my father Pendragon.[7]

Arthur then asks the opinion of the court, who unanimously accord the 'kiss of the White Hart' to Enid, whom Arthur kisses, saying:

> My sweet friend, I give you my love in all honesty. I shall love you with all my heart without baseness or impropriety. (ibid.)

And thus we hear from Arthur's own lips the vows that a king makes to Sovereignty, whose representative Enid is at this point. We have dealt in Chapter Six at some length with the implications of the *Gereint and Enid* story, where we saw on how many complex levels the Sovereignty motif is repeated. This same theme is taken up in the *Lanzelet* text, where we hear again of the chase for the White Hart and the kiss, but it is slightly different:

> And then the king was to take by right, and as it became him, a kiss from the most beautiful woman; that was his reward. His father Uther Pendragon instituted this custom; and his son has maintained it ever since.[42]

It is the king, not his champion, who awards this honour, we note.

Perhaps here we have some relic of the king's marriage with the land. Certainly this is a Celtic custom, which may have been present once within the earliest Arthurian oral traditions but which Chrétien and von Zatzikhovan have chosen to ennoble in their courtly language. We have only to look at Irish tradition for confirmation of 'the custom of the Pendragon'. In *The Birth of Conchobar* we read, 'Every Ulsterman rendered Conchobar a great honour [sending] his daughter to lie with Conchobar on the first night that he was her first husband.'[105] We further discover that Conchobar Mac Nessa, Cu Chulainn's king, was under a *geas* to sleep with every bride on her first night of marriage. This causes considerable problems for the hero, and Cu Chulainn is sent on an errand to hunt some game for his king, while Conchobar sleeps in the same room as the hero's wife, Emer. A druid also sleeps in the same room to restrain the king's sexual activity, and honour is satisfied without Conchobar's breaking his *geas*.[135]

Submerged somewhere in this is the tradition of Arthur's marriage with the land. Enid is but one representative of Sovereignty. But there is yet one more telling example which we may call up to add to our knowledge. The long-neglected story of Gawain's marriage with Ragnell has recently been rediscovered by a wider readership, both feminist and folkloric, but it is still seldom noted that though Gawain weds Ragnell, it is Arthur who first encounters her.

Arthur encounters a fearsome knight called Gromer Somer Joure, who lays a *geas* on Arthur to find what it is that women most desire, within a twelvemonth. It is perhaps not insignificant that Arthur is hunting for a wild stag when he meets his adversary. Confiding his task to Gawain, the two of them try to amass suitable answers to this riddle. It is Gawain, his nephew and *tanaiste*, to whom Arthur turns and whom, eventually, he implicates in the events that will fall out.

Just like the kings of Celtic tradition, Arthur meets a hideous hag while on his quest. She knows his thoughts and offers him the answer in return for Gawain as her husband. Arthur promises to do his best and Gawain obliges him by agreeing to marry the woman. The answer is given by Ragnell and supplied by Arthur to Gromer as the riddle's solution:

'Our desire is to have sovereignty over the most manly of men.' And so Arthur overcomes Gromer, who appears to represent the Provoker of Strife archetype in this story. Amid great lamentation, Gawain is married to Ragnell, though the king's life is no longer at risk. Alone in their chamber, Ragnell demands a kiss, at least.

'I will do more than kiss you,' Gawain says, 'and before God.'

She turns into a beautiful maiden, but there is a catch. Gawain may have her fair by day, for his honour at court, and foul by night; or foul by day, to his dishonour, and fair at night for his delight. He bids her choose and by so doing answers the riddle again, for she exclaims:

'I would have been transformed until the best man in England married me and gave me sovereignty over his body and his goods.'[78]

The original Sovereignty story is here shared between Gawain and Arthur: Arthur's life and kingdom are preserved by Gawain's sacrifice of his will to Ragnell in a medieval denouement to the primal Sovereignty theme.

And so we discover that Arthur indeed stands in intimate relationship with Sovereignty on many levels. He is successful in finding the Hallows and in some measure encounters the Dark Woman of Knowledge, Sovereignty in her *Cailleach* aspect. He knows and accepts his fated part in the marriage of king with land.

But for the main part Arthur's chief enounters with Sovereignty are with the women in his own family, particularly his sisters, and, of course, his wife. It is to these women that we turn next.

II QUEEN OF THE NORTH

During the lifetime of Uther, Arthur's father, a supernatural event took place in the skies over Britain on the evening of Ambrosius' death:

At that time appeared a star, which was seen of many. [It] shone marvellously clear, and cast a beam that was brighter than the sun. At the end of this beam was a dragon's head, and from the dragon's mighty jaws issued two rays. One of these rays stretched over France, and went from France even to the Mount of St Bernard. The other ray went towards Ireland, and divided into seven beams. Each of these beams shone bright and clear, alike on water and on land.[43]

Calling Merlin to him, Uther demanded of him some explanation of this wonder. Merlin announced the death of Ambrosius, Uther's brother, and interpreted the comet thus:

The dragon at the end of the beam betokens thee thyself, who art a stout and hardy knight. One of the two rays signifies a

> son born of thy body, who shall become a puissant prince, conquering France and beyond the borders of France. The other ray which parted from its fellow betokens a daughter who shall be Queen of Scotland. Many a fair heir shall she give to her lord, and mighty champions shall they prove both on land and sea. (ibid.)

According to Geoffrey and Wace, this daughter is called Anna. She is the prototype for the half-sister that tradition will later give Arthur in the shape of Morgause.

In the accretions of Arthurian tradition we see an interesting development in Arthur's sisters or half-sisters. This development may be summarized as shown in Figure 10.4.

It will be seen how one full sister gradually becomes several half-sisters. Consistently, however, the sister or half-sister of Arthur is always the mother of Gawain. We also note that it is Chrétien who is responsible for Arthur's relationship with Morgain.[52]

The importance of Arthur's sister or sisters may not be immediately apparent. We must return to our first concepts of Sovereignty in order to see the connection. We recall that the primeval concept of Sovereignty involved the matriarch of a tribe; she was the priestess or royal woman whose blood conferred sovereignty. From her descendants might be drawn the rulers of the tribe. In this regard we can see Eigr, or Igraine, and her many sisters as the manifestation of this concept. All the descendants of Eigr hold prime positions in the Arthurian cycle, so that while Arthur leaps into prominence as the main focus of the stories, Eigr's daughter likewise follows a royal destiny.

Whether this daughter is called Anna, Gwyar, Morcades or Morgause is not a matter of great import. In all instances this woman marries Loth of Lothian (Lleu ap Cynfarch), a character to whom Geoffrey of Monmouth imputes great strength and loyalty to the throne of the Pendragons. It is into Loth's care that Uther places his kingdom before Arthur is acknowledged as king.[10] In this we can see the working out of the old Celtic kingship and the explanation of the strong tradition of distrust between Arthur and his Orkney nephews in later legends. For Arthur is not the only possible heir of his line: his sister bears the

Source	Name of Sister(s)
Welsh genealogical tracts	**Gwyar**, d. of Uther and Eigr
Geoffrey of Monmouth	**Anna**, d. of Uther and Igerne
Birth of Arthur (14th-cent. MS)	**Gwyar** and **Dioneta**, ds. of Gwrleis and Eigyr
Chrétien (*Erec and Enid*)	**Morgain and an unnamed woman**, mother of Gawain
First Continuation of *Perceval*	**Morcades**, wife of Loth, mother of Agravain, Guerrehes, Gaheriet, Mordred and Clarissans
Robert de Boron (*Merlin*)	**Two unnamed girls**, wed by Loth and Urien, and **Morgain**, all ds. of Igerne and Gorlois
Vulgate Cycle	**Blaisine, Brimesent, Morgain** and **one unnamed d.**
Malory	**Morgause, Elayne** and **Morgan**, ds. of Igraine and Gorlois

Figure 10.4. *Arthur's Sister(s) in Arthurian Tradition*

same blood and her descendants have as much of a right to the throne. The sevenfold rays of light emanating from the prophetic comet do indeed become Arthur's champions, but do not, as in Geoffrey's version of the episode, become the heirs to the throne of Britain.

If any woman stands to inherit the title Daughter of Branwen, then it is Arthur's sister. This archetype, discussed in Chapter Eight, is the basis for all those women who are the great matriarchs of the Island of the Mighty; they are the Sovereignty-bestowing mothers of the royal line, whose queenship is mystical rather than actual. If one glances at the texts in which the variously named sisters of Arthur appear, it will be seen that they are anything but passive, yea-saying women; rather they exemplify the energies of Sovereignty in being initiators, arch-conspirators and sometimes actual enemies in the order of things.

It is, of course, the nephews of Arthur, Gwalchmai and Medrawt (or Gawain and Mordred), who spectacularly effect the outcome of Arthur's reign. In the earliest texts both men have very different roles: Gwalchmai is Arthur's champion and faithful

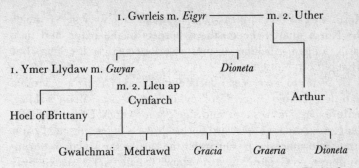

Figure 10.5. *Relationship of Arthur and Gawain According to* Birth of Arthur *MS*

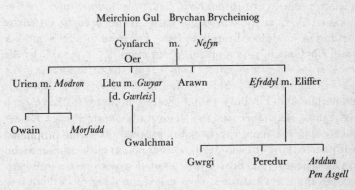

Urien and *Efrddyl*, Owain and *Morfudd* are twins, while the children of Efrddyl are triplets.

Figure 10.6. *Descent of Lleu (Loth) ap Cynfarch according to Triad 70*

warrior in the service of Sovereignty rather than the blundering, obstinate Gawain of Malory's story; Medrawt is the abductor of Gwenhwyfar and the Thief of Sovereignty rather than the incestuously begotten child, whose death by exposure in an open boat is decreed by Arthur in the later stories.[87] The original men are more like Nissien and Efnissien of the second branch story, *Branwen, Daughter of Llyr*, in their natures: one fair and compassionate, the other embittered and unforgiving. But there are other *Mabinogion* parallels lying within this tradition which we have yet to lay bare.

Arthur's sister becomes, by her marriage to Loth, Queen of the

North – a position of great power strategically, for whoever holds the North guards the northern borders of the realm and may easily foment rebellion or muster troops against the king. But what of Loth himself?

He seems to have been a formidable figure, having a venerable tradition behind him. Geoffrey calls him: 'a valiant soldier, mature both in wisdom and age',[10] to whom Uther gave his daughter, Anna, as a reward for his prowess in leading the British army, and to whom he entrusted the care of the kingdom during his illness. As Geoffrey tends to ignore female characters, we hear little of Anna herself, but she would seem to be much younger than her husband.

Loth's name runs throughout Celtic tradition in one form or another. A. C. L. Brown suggests that it has been inherited by Arthurian tradition from the Irish Fomorian leader's mother Loth Luamnach, which means 'destruction of the active'. In the *Book of Invasions* the name Loth occurs twice, appearing the second time as Loth, the grandfather of the Fir Bolg. Both the Fomorian and Fir Bolg peoples were considered to have been ugly, dark, misshapen and evil. This tradition, in which a former race comes to represent negative aspects, the country aligned with barbarians or even devils, is common in both historical and mythological terms. Brown points out that Loth seems to inherit certain mythological titles: he is called the King of Lothian and Norway in Geoffrey, while in the *Perceval* of Chrétien he is called King of Orkney – an appellation which continues into later tradition. Lothian is the area above Hadrian's Wall between Galloway and Gorre, in Arthurian legend. Mythically Norway is known as Lochlann, in Celtic tradition – literally the 'land overseas' – and it is associated with the Land of the Dead. Orkney itself has accumulated much of the same reputation, both from its association with the classical name for Hades, Orcus, as well as an aboriginal tradition concerning the burial of the dead upon Orkney.[58]

To summarize this, we may posit Loth as a latter-day King of the Dead who marries a young, sovereignty-bearing woman, whose children will have as much right to the throne as do Arthur's. If we look to parallel British tradition, which drew upon oral records as well as interpolating much of Geoffrey's work, we find, in Triad 70, that Loth becomes Lleu ap Cynfarch. Moreover his brothers are none other than Urien, husband of Modron (herself a daughter of a King of the Underworld), and Arawn, whom we met in *Pwyll, Prince of Dyfed* (see *Mabon*, p. 21)[111] as King of Annwn, the British Underworld. A glance at Figure 10.5 will show that Lleu marries not Anna daughter of Uther, but Gwyar, daughter of Eigr and Gwrleis, which may represent an earlier tradition than that of Geoffrey's *History*.[10]

Loomis further suggests that Loth's Underworldly antecedents may not end there. He posits that Loth is derived from or analogous to Llwch Lleminawc, the man who appears twice in British tradition: once in *Culhwch and Olwen*, where he is described as the great-uncle of Arthur who comes from overseas, and once in the 'Preiddeu Annwn' and the later part of *Culhwch and Olwen* relating to the Theft of the Cauldron.[22] In this episode Llwch seizes Caledfwlch (Excalibur) and wields it with great skill: the implication being that this deed helped Arthur get the cauldron of Pen Annwn.

The implications of this identification are immense. The 'Preiddeu Annwn' poem represents one of the earliest recorded traditions about Arthur which we may take to be authentic and uncontaminated by French romanticization. It represents Arthur as entering Annwn for the purpose of reiving the cauldron of Pen Annwn, the King of the Underworld, and it is Llwch Lleminawc who helps him achieve this. In later traditions, from Geoffrey onwards, Arthur is acclaimed king on the death of Uther, but it is Loth who has held the kingdom during Uther's declining years and who enables him to gain his rights within the kingdom. Loth is therefore an enabling hero, in earlier tradition; one who helps Arthur to maintain his sovereignty within Britain. And it is to this man that Arthur's sister, or half-sister, is married.

Loomis further suggests that the wars between Arthur and the Roman general Lucius Hiberius, described by Geoffrey, can be correlated with the later *Huth Merlin* text, in which Arthur wars with Loth.[92] Such divergences show the meandering of the tradition until it reaches Malory's full-blown account of the enmity between Loth and Morgause's family, and Arthur.[25]

Which brings us back once more to the Queen of the North and the fate of her children, so lyrically and prophetically announced by the comet. There have been many examples of women being used as political cement in history, but Arthur's sisters or half-sisters, along with the other women appearing in the Celto-Arthurian cycles, occupy a different kind of role. Whether we wish to call this lady Anna, Gwyar, Morcades or Morgause does not matter, for she retains her inalienable power of sovereignty inherited from either Eigr (or Igraine), as the representative of Sovereignty, or from Uther, as the Pendragon's daughter. Once ensconced in the North she plays her own game – a royal and often crafty one – against her brother. Traditions vary on this point, but she is seen to take two forms of opening play: she either accepts supporters or champions who will advance her own cause as royal woman, or else she jockeys her children into positions of power, urging on their efforts to displace their uncle, Arthur.

If we look closely at this activity of hers, we perceive that perhaps we are indeed looking at a single archetype who has three aspects: a seemingly passive princess who accepts the husband chosen for her; a queen determined to set herself on the throne of Britain to be the prime Sovereignty of that land; and a queen mother, who ceaselessly, tirelessly supports her children, particularly her sons' claim to sovereignty. If we return to Figure 10.4 where one sister became three half-sisters of Arthur, we are dimly aware of how the threefold Sovereignty has become embedded into Arthurian tradition as the three 'Cornwall sisters', Elayne, Morgan and Morgause, who correspond exactly to the threefold royal woman outlined above.

Elayne married Nentres of Garlot: an insignificant husband for an almost invisible woman in Malory. So thick on the ground are the Elaines of Arthurian tradition that even the writers of the romances themselves became confused. Yet we may recall the laudable figure of Elen, royal Helen of the Ways, as our prime archetype of the royal, sovereignty-bearing princess, as well as the daughter of King Pelles, another Elaine, whose fate is to become Guinevere for a night in order that she might compel the reluctant Lancelot to help her conceive the future Grail-finder,

Galahad (see p. 74). Both women submit to their fate, yet both gain a mystical triumph on behalf of the land. These are the true Daughters of Branwen, whose hearts are set on the well-being of the land and its people. Theirs is not a personal life but a redemptive one: a sacrifice which is often repellant to feminist politics, but which is nevertheless demanded at an Inner, Other-worldly level by the Goddess of Sovereignty.

The second sister, Morgan, is, in Malory, married to Urien, though as we have seen in Chapter Four, her antecedents are often quite other. She becomes, in later tradition, the chief enemy of Arthur, her half-brother, whom she tricks with her magic wiles. This deterioration of the archetype is a feature of later tradition, where the romancers were at their furthest remove from the primal images of their craft. Morgan – who may also be Morgain, Morgen or Modron –behaves like the Queen of the Hallows; she represents the Sovereignty of the Land, and the Hallows are rightfully wielded at her behest and by her champions. But the later writers have aligned her more nearly with the *cailleach*, the Dark Woman of Knowledge, in keeping with Morgan's earlier role as Queen of Avalon, and have assigned her a more mundane role as Arthur's half-sister. Chrétien perhaps achieves the nearest amalgam of these two roles in his *Perceval*, where a thinly disguised Morgan appears as the Proud Damsel. This character is not quite a Black Maiden, though she shares certain attributes with women such as Luned of *Owain* (see Chrétien, lines 8286–8648).[7]

This character's name, 'L'Orguelleuse de Logres' is interesting in that there is some scholarly debate as to whether the original name for Britain's Sovereignty translated into a more rational French title. We know from Irish tradition that Ireland's Sove-reignty calls herself 'Eriu' or Ireland. It has been argued that Britain's Goddess might well have been named 'Logres' and that the French writers made this into *L'Orguelleuse*, the Proud Damsel. Whether this can be proved or not, it is intriguing, since the Goddess of Sovereignty should indeed be the 'pride of the land', jealous of its welfare.

The third sister, Morgause – also called Morcades, a name derived from both Morgan and the Orkneys (Orcades), which she rules with Loth – represents the Queen Mother aspect of the threefold Sovereignty. She fights for the cause of her children in later tradition, though Malory causes her to sleep with Arthur in order to conceive Mordred incestuously. Although this theme of incest seems, at first sight, to be a later tradition there remains the ancient concept of re-enforcing the royal bloodline by inter-marriage of brother and sister, which existed in Egypt and among other peoples in early times. The incestuous union of Arthur and his sister is a persistent subtextual tradition, even in the earlier cycles where the sister, however named, is the mother of both Gawain and Mordred, though not of any other children.

What is the meaning of this in the light of Sovereignty? In order to answer this we must go deeper into this very tradition. We may well find some startling resonances between Arthurian and Celtic tradition; in the following text the most significant one being that Arthur's sister desires, above all things, to be seen and known as a virgin. It is worth bearing in mind that an unmarried woman, in medieval times, preserved her property rights on her own behalf; if she married, then those rights were transferred to her husband or sons. Beneath this understanding is the original foundation of Sovereignty herself – proud, single, independent and determined to keep her realm intact. In the interweaving of the triple Sovereignty archetype which Arthur's sisters betray we may well find ourselves back at the roots of one of the *Mabinogion*'s prime stories.

The following fragmentary story, *Les Enfances Gauvain*,[27] is from a French poem, written in the early thirteenth century; it relates the birth and conception of Gawain, and its contents are substantially the same as the twelfth-century Latin romance, *De Ortu Waluuanii* (*The Rise of Gawain*), ably translated by Mildred Leake Day.[9] The seeds for both versions lie in Geoffrey, but in the case of *Les Enfances Gauvain*, there may be tangled references to *Math, Son of Mathonwy*.

We may use the clues from *The Rise of Gawain* to fill in the lacunae of *Les Enfances Gauvain* (indicated in square brackets) to give the following summary:

[Uther took hostages for the good behaviour of his subjects. One of these was Lot, nephew of the King of Norway. Lot and Uther's daughter grew enamoured of each other so she became pregnant.] Morcades then went to her brother Arthur, requesting that she retire to the Castle of Bel Repaire, accompanied only by her handmaid, her squire – who was in fact Lot – and a small household, the porter to admit only such persons of known respect or Arthur himself. Arthur assented and seven months later, Morcades was delivered of a son, Lot assisting at the birth. Had circumstances been otherwise, she would have been glad to raise the boy herself, but she decided that she could not lose the reputation of being a virgin.

Nearby lived a wise knight called Gauvain the Brown who often sent game from his hunting to Morcades and whose handmaid he longed to marry. The latter refused him. Lot and Morcades decided that they would have to be rid of the child and requested the handmaid to take the boy away secretly. However, Gauvain accosted her as she was stealing away with the child and, knowing it could not be hers, he asked to be allowed to take care of it, for he was without wife, child or heir. The handmaid promised to wed Gauvain as soon as the child was baptised and Morcades had prepared his sending away. [She had arranged for merchants to take away the boy and raise him with care.] Gauvain baptised the boy by his own name and took especial care of the richly embroidered shawl and other precious things, betokening his birth. Gauvain also put a letter in a chest and wrapped it in the shawl before putting it and the little Gauvain into a barrel. This was to be thrown into the sea.

[Little Gauvain is found/stolen by a fisherman who brings him up.] The fisherman takes Gauvain to Rome on pilgrimage, during which the chest is opened and the truth is known. Up until this time, the fisherman has called Gauvain nothing but 'beau fils' (good son). Gauvain is subsequently adopted by the pope as his nephew, and he keeps the boy's possessions against the day he will be made a knight.

Meanwhile, Morcades preserved her secret from all, especially the King. She consented to attend Arthur's wedding to Guinemar (Guinevere) at Dinasdaron. Guinemar spent all her time with Morcades, delighted with her company. Gauvain the Brown marries the handmaid.

Little Gauvain was now twelve years old and was made a knight on St John's Day – a day sacred to both Christians and pagans. He was successful in all passages of arms and was never taken prisoner. The Emperor of the Roman Empire died without heirs [and Gauvain was proposed as his successor].

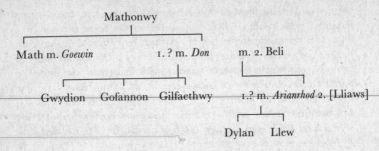

Figure 10.7 *Arianrhod's Family*

It is here that the fragment breaks off. *The Rise of Gawain*[9] goes on to relate the adventures of the young Gawain and how he came to Arthur's court and was at last named and recognized. The fragmentary *Enfances Gauvain* is the work of a French romance writer, but it nevertheless reveals some interesting features native to British tradition.

Arthur's sister is Morcades, a single, independent woman who demands her own household and gives birth to her lover's child in secrecy in order to preserve her reputation as a virgin. Although the text makes it unclear whether or not Lot eventually marries Morcades, he remains a shadowy figure, disguised as her squire. She relinquishes her own child, endowing him with objects that will enable him to be named, armed and supported in later life, but consigns him, via her handmaiden, to the sea. So far the tale is likely enough, but the interpolation concerning the fisherman and the pope is clearly derived from the famous medieval legend of Pope Gregory, who was similarly conceived – in incestuous circumstances – and thrown into the sea.[8] This interpolation rendered successive tradition more receptive to the idea of Arthur and his (half)sister incestuously conceiving a son, which indeed happens in Malory, though the child is Mordred, not Gawain. Yet this is in itself significant.

There seems to be an underlying story struggling to break out here, but it is one which can be only tentatively traced in. If we compare Figures 10.7 and 10.8, we will see a very rough similitude between two key stories: those of Arianrhod and of Gwyar/ Morcades/Anna, Arthur's sister. Both women are born of great

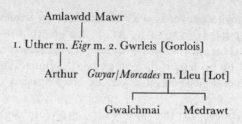

Figure 10.8. *Morcades' Family*

matriarchs who have important dynastic marriages. Both have half-brother(s). Both have two sons, usually twins. The isolation of both women – Arianrhod at Caer Arianrhod and Morcades at Bel Repaire – the fact that one of their children is thrown into the sea and that the fatherhood of that child is questionable all betray a subtextual pattern that is more than coincidental. What we see here is the fertility of mythological tradition, as one set of characters inherits the archetypal characteristics of another set.

It would be wrong to try and make more of this than merely to point out the parallels, but it does help us locate Arthur's sister in the directory of British archetypes, and it suggests also her role within the framework of Sovereignty. Arianrhod's role in *Math, Son of Mathonwy* (see *Mabon*, p. 73)[111] is notably equivocal, and the resulting story in which she appears leaves us with a correspondingly confused picture of her: sulky, independent, two-faced, unloving, passionate, vindictive and unforgiving is how the story-teller makes her appear. The confusion has been wrought by trying to force a goddessly archetype into the framework of a human woman.

Arianrhod is primarily a Queen of the Hallows: one whose empowerment will make kings famous, one who holds the balance of the land. But she is set against her half-brother, Gwydion, with whom, possibly, she has an incestuous relationship. Arianrhod is the royal woman whose blood makes her children royal in turn. The possibly mythological/dynastic conflict between her and Gwydion should not, therefore, exist, but it does. Like the Queen of the Turning Wheel (see p. 189), Arianrhod is outraged at being pregnant: her intrinsic sovereignty is at risk, and she denies both her children. Dylan is fostered by Math, his great-uncle (who corresponds to Gauvain the Brown in *Les Enfances Gauvain*), and Llew is fostered by his father/uncle, Gwydion (in much the same way Arthur always promotes Gawain in every version of the legend.)

Dylan is, of course, lost at sea, but Llew grows up to oppose and be opposed by his mother. Arianrhod's anger arises from not being chosen to be Royal Footholder – a post for which the candidate must be virgin. Similarly Morcades seeks to preserve her virginity by retiring to Bel Repaire, but her secret eventually comes to light with the return of Gauvain, although the story-teller has lost the impetus for this tale, not understanding the underlying subtext that makes Morcades a royal woman like Arianrhod. Both women refuse to name or arm their sons or choose wives for them. This alone shows us where the mythological trail has led us. These are the conditions or *geasa* placed upon the candidate for kingship by Sovereignty; if he is successful in overcoming them and winning himself a name, arms and a wife, he is found worthy and welcomed by Sovereignty in one of her many forms.

Morcades/Morgause's two children conform to very similar archetypal patterns to those of Arianrhod's. Mordred is the child whom Arthur causes to have cast into the sea, according to Malory.[25] Arthur realizes too late that he has begotten a child on his sister, Morgause, and orders that all children born on May Day should be cast adrift in an open boat. Only Mordred survives, as fate dictates in many mythologies, leaving Arthur with the reputation of Herod and the Innocents on his conscience. Gawain's career is quite different. His upbringing is rarely disputed; he is Lot's son, loyal to Arthur, often headstrong, but always sensitive to the vocation of Sovereignty, whom he defends and champions. Mordred is thus the Thief of Sovereignty and Gawain her champion, rather in the same way that Efnissien and Nissien are in *Branwen, Daughter of Llyr* (see *Mabon*, p. 41).[111] The two men are the Dark and Light Twins of mythological archetype. And indeed there may be a tradition, now lost, which made them twins. If we refer to Figure 10.6 we will see that twins ran in Lleu's family. Since tradition is adamant in making Gwalchmai and Medrawt the sons of Arthur's sister, it is possible that they are indeed the children of one birth.

As we will see in the next section, Mordred and not Gawain is responsible for the final ruination of Arthur's kingdom. Within the mythological pattern it seems that both men are necessary: one to build up Logres, the other to tear away the old administration. Following our parallels with Dylan and Llew it is interesting to note that Gawain, like Llew, marries an Otherworldly woman (or rather a series of them), although there is no trace of the old *geas* against marrying a woman of earthly stock. He espouses Ragnell, a type of the Loathly Lady or Black Maiden; in other stories he encounters faery women and has children by them. The ubiquitous title 'solar hero' has been attached to Gawain quite as often as it has to Llew, since he is knighted at St John's Day, midsummer, and his strength is correspondingly more effective at midday. Mordred, as we shall see, involved himself in the abduction of the Sovereignty-bearing woman of Arthur's reign – another royal woman, Gwenhwyfar herself.

Thus we see that Arianrhod's and Morcades' seeming heartlessness in abandoning their sons is part of a larger pattern. We see that the king's sister occupies, even within medieval Welsh retelling and French Arthurian romance, the place of Sovereignty. It is also appropriate that the symbolism of both women should be so consonant: Caer Arianrhod is the Welsh name for the Corona Borealis, the Crown of the North; while Arthur's sister, in all her appellations, remains Queen of the North, proclaimed by a comet as a mother of champions.

But sisters, even of kings, find the severest rivalry when the king marries. Yet in the case of Gwenhwyfar, even the most ardent supporter of Sovereignty must acknowledge the right to her queenship, for she is possessed of all the attributes of the Flower Bride. Layamon's *Brut* richly describes Arthur's assembly at Caerleon and shows how Arthur's sovereignty is upheld by the four kings of the Island: Cador of Cornwall, the King of Scotland and the Kings of North and South Wales. Guinevere is likewise attended by:

> ... four chosen queens; each bare [sic] in the left hand a jewel
> of red gold, and three snow-white doves sate on their shoulders;
> (these) were the four queens, wives of the kings who bare in
> their hands the four swords of gold before Arthur, noblest of
> kings.[43]

In this most Saxon version of a British legend, we see the fourfold
Sovereignty attendant upon Gwenhwyfar – those same four
queens who will later bear to Avalon the most famous of Sovereignty's consorts.

III THE FLOWER BRIDE'S FAREWELL

Gwenhwyfar, or Guinevere, is probably established in all minds
for all time by now as the one who caused the Round Table to
fall, particularly since Malory's and Tennyson's versions of the
Arthurian legend were printed. She inherits the beauty and
sovereignty-bestowing power of the Flower Bride, not to mention
the reputation that attends this role – that of the fickle, unfaithful
and deceiving woman. In Triad 80, she speaks of the three
unfaithful wives of the Island of Britain, she appears appended to
the triad thus:

> And one was more faithless than those three: Gwenhywfar,
> Arthur's wife, since she shamed a better man than any of the
> others.[38]

When earthly women inherit the role of Flower Bride, story-
tellers assume the worst and portray a veritable Delilah.
Gwenhwyfar's later appearances within the Arthurian legend
certainly attest to this treatment. But in the mythic schema the
Flower Bride is portrayed as being totally amoral, for she alone
bestows sovereignty upon her chosen champion, selecting and
discarding her candidates with impunity. This is what makes the
marriage of Blodeuwedd to Llew so terrible, for Blodeuwedd the
Flower Bride, is captured by the magic arts of Math and Gwydion
to serve their purposes, brought from the Otherworld and fixed
in a form wrought of flowers. The Flower Bride is not a mortal
woman but an appearance of Sovereignty, and we should not be

surprised to find that Gwenhwyfar was originally of Otherworldly origin.

We have noted that Sovereignty has her three aspects, appearing as Flower Bride or sovereignty-bestowing maiden, Sovereign Queen and admonitory hag or Loathly Lady. The division of a deity into such a triplicity was a common Celtic understanding: an indivisible unity to the Celtic mind, just as the Three Persons of the Trinity were to the Greek mind. In Triad 56 we find a triple Gwenhwyfar:

> Three Great Queens of Arthur's Court:
> Gwenhwyfar daughter of Cywryd Gwent,
> and Gwenhwyfar daughter of Gwythr ap Greidawl,
> and Gwenhwyfar daughter of Gogfran the Giant.'[38]

The meaning of this obscure triad has puzzled scholars. Are three separate women intended? Was there an extant tradition of Arthur marrying three women so identically named? Have traditional stories become so inextricably mixed that the collator of the Triads has juxtaposed what he saw as a single tradition?

We are not helped much by the dearth of material relating to any of these putative fathers for Gwenhwyfar. Rachel Bromwich suggests that Gwent should perhaps be emended to Kent – not necessarily the county but the title.[38] Of Gwythyr we have already heard, since he fights with Gwyn ap Nudd for the possession of Creiddylad, another Flower Bride and, according to this triad, perhaps also Gwenhwyfar's mother. Of Gogfran the Giant, we have only the popular rhyme recorded by Sir John Rhys, which tells us about: 'Gwenhwyfar, daughter of Ogfran the Giant, bad when little, worse when big'.[139]

Hidden beneath the detritus of tradition is a tempting but perhaps implausible pattern of a succession of Flower Brides, all representatives of British sovereignty, who are the mystical mothers or predecessors of Gwenhwyfar. If the reader will permit a Gravesian digression, I will explain.

The three fathers of Gwenhwyfar mentioned above may each represent one of three sets of a single pattern. Gogfran is a form of cogfran or jackdaw, in which *fran* is a mutated form of *bran* or raven. Whether the giant Gogmagog of Geoffrey of Monmouth[10] bears any relationship to this tradition is impossible to say, but we do have a tradition concerning a sovereignty-bestowing woman related to a giant in the form of Branwen. In that story Branwen is called one of three great ancestresses of the Island of Britain.

Gwynn Jones's translation gives us 'one of the Three Matriarchs'.[24] In some measure Branwen is indeed the very first of a long line of women who become 'daughters of Branwen' in a mystical sense, for they bear the sovereignty-bestowing blood of Britain.

Gwythyr ap Greidawl is, of course, the suitor of Creiddylad, the other great Flower Bride of British historical tradition. Creiddylad is none other than Cordelia, the daughter of Lear, one of three sisters. It is interesting that Cordelia and Branwen are confused with each other: a confusion which might perhaps be significant? In Gough's additions to Camden (in 1789 edition), as discussed in the Triads, the following gloss is given to the grave of Branwen on the banks of the Alaw in Anglesey: 'We have a tradition that the largest cromlech in this country is the monument of Bronwen, daughter of King Leir, who is said to have begun his reign about the year anno mundi 3105.'[38] This is an interesting confusion because it was Cordelia who buried her father in an underground chamber near the river Soar in Leicestershire. The grave was dedicated to the two-faced god Janus, and it was the meeting place of craftsmen, who would commence a new piece of work at that site at the turning of the old and new years. In Geoffrey, Cordelia succumbs to grief and kills herself.[10] In *Branwen, Daughter of Llyr*, Branwen dies of grief at Bran's wounding, which is also Britain's devastation. Cordelia is also briefly queen in her own right. Branwen is a daughter of Llyr; Cordelia, a daughter of Leir. Both Llyr and Leir are variants of the ancestral god of the sea.

The last father of Gwenhwyfar, Cywryd Gwent or Kent, is the most puzzling character. But we may make an inspired guess and relate him to the tradition concerning Fflur. It is known only that Fflur's father was called Ugnach Gorr or Dwarf. She is loved by Caswallawn and stolen away by Julius Caesar. If we turn to Geoffrey's historical tradition once more, we find an interesting piece of information that Cassivelaunus' nephew, Androgeus, is created Duke of Kent. (Cassivelaunus is Geoffrey's version of Caswallawn.) Androgeus betrays his uncle to Julius Caesar after Cassivelaunus has ravaged Kent. Perhaps we have here a part of the lost Fflur cycle? Interestingly Cassivelaunus lays waste Androgeus' lands in much the same way as Gwyn ap Nudd does to the captives of Gwythyr's army. We also note that in *Branwen, Daughter of Llyr*, it is Caswallawn who devastates Britain while Bran is in Ireland rescuing Branwen.

It is therefore possible that Triad 56 represents a hidden tradition concerning the Flower Bride. Although three men's names are given as 'fathers of Gwenhwyfar', the traditional lore hidden in each of these lines is about the Daughters of Branwen, the women who represent the sovereignty of Britain in mythical/historical tradition: Branwen, Creiddylad/Cordelia and Fflur. Gwenhwyfar's role as Arthur's queen has always been rather mysterious, but this triad perhaps enhances her status as a person in her own right.

Turning back to Gwenhwyfar herself we discover that her name is related to the Irish *siabair*, meaning phantom, spirit or faery. In the Ulster cycle we see that the daughter of another prime representative of Sovereignty, Queen Medbh, has a similar name – Finnabair, meaning White Phantom.[38]

The earliest Welsh poets do not mention Gwenhwyfar at all. Indeed, the first mention of her being Arthur's wife appears only in the *Vita Gildae*[21] by Caradoc of Llancarfan, and in Geoffrey's *History*.[10] This is not to say that Gwenhwyfar did not exist in a prior tradition in her own right; we have only the evidence that has come down to us. What becomes clear is that she was originally an Otherworldly queen, like Rhiannon or Etain of Welsh and Irish tradition, whom Arthur steals for his bride. The many attempted abductions of Gwenhwyfar/Guinevere as outlined in Figure 10.9 attest to this lost tradition of Arthur's queen as the Flower Bride. Even when, in the later stories, Guinevere loses her Otherworldly status, story-tellers substitute a false Guinevere, as in the Vulgate text.[33]

I shall not attempt to tell the stories of each abduction, for these are so complex and so various that another book would be

Text	Date	Abductor
Vita Gildae	1130	Melwas of the Summer Country
History of the Kings of Britain	1136	Mordred, Arthur's nephew
Chevalier de la Charette (Chrétien)	1160s	Meleagant
Lanzelet	1190s	Valerin
Roman de Brut (Wace)	1155	Mordred, Guinevere's brother
Yder	1220s	Yder
Gereint	13th cent.	[Edern]
Diu Cröne	1230s	Gasozein
Vulgate Cycle	1220s	False Guinevere's men and Lancelot
Livre D'Artus	13th cent.	Urian, Lot and Galehot
Perlesvaus	13th cent.	[Madeglans of Oriande]
De Ortu Waluuanii	12th cent.	[Gawain]
Durmart	13th cent.	Brun de Morois
Morte d'Arthur	1470	Meliagrance and Lancelot

(Square brackets indicate potential abductors.)

Figure 10.9: *The Abduction of Gwenhwyfar/Guinevere as Flower Bride in Arthurian Legend*

required. The reader is directed to read K. T. G. Webster's study entitled *Guinevere, a story of her abductions*,[156] or to refer to other texts in the bibliography.

The proto-story of Gwenhwyfar's abduction is found in the *Vita Gildae*, where Melwas of the Summer Country abducts her to his kingdom in the region of Glastonbury, where she lies hidden among the marshes. Arthur, described as a tyrant, besieges the place and prepares terrible war until the conciliatory services of Gildas the Wise cause Melwas to render Gwenhwyfar to Arthur once more.[21, 80] We have already noted that in early tradition Arthur is called 'a red ravager' of Britain (see p. 36).

This story, with a few variations, is substantially followed in

Chrétien's *Chevalier de la Charette*[7] and Malory's *Morte d'Arthur*,[25] where Lancelot rescues Guinevere from Meleagant and Meliagrance respectively. In Malory we note that Guinevere is abducted while out maying with her unarmed knights.

Wace's *Roman de Brut*[43] and Geoffrey's *History*,[10] follow another tradition, which, as we have already noted (see p. 171), is referred to in the Triads, concerning Gwenhwyfar's connection with Mordred. Arthur gives Britain into the joint regency of Mordred, his nephew, and Guanhumara (Guinevere), while he goes off on campaign against the Romans. However, Guanhumara lives adulterously with her nephew-in-law, who seizes the crown in Arthur's absence. There follows the last battle of Camlann and the consequent deaths of Arthur and Mordred, and Guanhumara enters a convent in Caerleon.

More shockingly Wace makes Mordred Guinevere's brother and tells us that Mordred loved her secretly before becoming regent. Interestingly Wace and Geoffrey interpolate the hoary tradition about Rome demanding tribute from Britain, so that Arthur is forced to go and fight the Romans, thus leaving Britain and Guinevere alone, though in Mordred's keeping. This seems to hark back to the Fflur/Caswallawn/Julius Caesar story once more. Mordred, as Arthur's nephew and (in Celtic terms) his *tanaiste*, seizes Guinevere, who, as Flower Bride, represents Britain's sovereignty.

We will recall our discussion of Triad 54, which tells how Medrawt (Mordred) took the food and drink from Arthur's court, dragged Gwenhwyfar from her throne and struck her. This tradition seems related to the theme of his theft of the sovereignty of Britain. Related to this is Triad 53, which tells of the Three Harmful Blows of the Island of Britain, the first of which is the striking of Branwen by Maṭholwch. The second blow is that which 'Gwenhwyfach struck upon Gwenhwyfar: and for that cause there took place afterwards the Action of the Battle of Camlan'.[38]

Gwenhwyfach appears only once within British tradition, in *Culhwch and Olwen* as the sister of Gwenhwyfar. Triad 84 further tells that the Battle of Camlan was caused by a quarrel between the two. Since there is no tradition extant of Gwenhwyfar having a sister at all, we are faced by two possibilities. Either we have here a tradition concerning Arthur's queen and the False Guinevere, who appears in much later sources, or Gwenhwyfach is not a sister but a *brother* of Gwenhwyfar.

Triad 54 tells us quite firmly that Mordred struck the queen. But if there is any way that Wace's tradition of Mordred and Guinevere being brother and sister can be brought to bear on this tangle, a solution may appear. Following Mordred's theft of Arthur's kingdom and wife, the Battle of Camlann ensues: this makes sense of Triad 53 above.

Further explanation can be wrought from the little popular rhyme:

> 'Gwenhwyfar, daughter of Gogfran the Giant: bad when *little*, worse when *big*.'[139]

In Gwenhwy*fach* the last syllable is a mutated form of *bach*, or 'little'. In Gwenhwy*far* the last syllable might have once been *fawr*, a mutated form of *mawr*, or 'big'. What does this leave us with? We are back to the three Gwenhwyfars again, or rather, a tradition which speaks about two of them.

Out of this tangle I would draw the following conclusion: that Gwenhwyfar is a woman firmly in the role of Flower Bride, who, as we have seen, is both warm and loving as well as cunning and faithless when she chooses. This dual nature has been polarized into two characters, as we have seen happen to both the Countess and Luned in *Owain* and to the Witches of Gloucester and the Empress in *Peredur*. The Flower Bride can indeed be a beautiful, gift-bestowing maiden, as is Guinevere at the beginning of Arthur's reign; but she partakes also of the nature of the Loathly Lady, the Hag, the Dark Woman of Knowledge, the form adopted by Sovereignty time and again in her testing of the king, a role which Guinevere adopts at the conclusion of Arthur's reign when she discards her former husband and seeks a new champion.

Side by side with the Mordred tradition we find numerous other abductors or potential abductors of Gwenhwyfar/Guinevere. Most of them are not significantly attached to the British tradition at all, but are the invention of French or German story-tellers; they all, however, derive from the general tradition relating to the Flower Bride's Otherworldly abduction.

We have already noted in *Gereint and Enid* the residual traces of this tradition, in that Edern may once have been an actual abductor in a proto-version of the story. There exists a corroborative text in the shape of *Yder*.[92] It tells of how Yder (Edern) left his mother and grandmother in order to discover the whereabouts of his father Nuc (Nudd). At Caruain he fell in love with a Queen Guenloie and immediately set out to prove his manly prowess in a series of adventures. These included the overcoming of Arthur in knightly combat, the rescue of Arthur's queen,' Guenievere, from a bear's attack and the finding of his father. Guenievere provokes Arthur's jealousy by proclaiming that, if she were to marry again, she would choose Yder. Yder succeeds in defeating two giants and bringing back their knife according to Guenievere's command as a condition of their marriage. Yder and Arthur's queen marry.

This strange story gives us two Guineveres and provides the Flower Bride with a lover whose father is the King of the Underworld. Gwyn ap Nudd, as we have seen, is one of the prime combatants for the Creiddylad's hand; his son, Yder or Ider, as he is called in William of Malmesbury's *De Antiquitate Glastoniensis Ecclesiae*, is further credited with the defeat of three giants near Glastonbury in that chronicle. Glastonbury Tor, according to the Life of St Collen, was the entrance to Gwyn ap Nudd's realm. It is also the place where Gwenhwyfar is abducted by Melwas.[21, 87]

Our dogged pursuit of the tradition of Guinevere as Flower Bride is proving fruitful. But what do we make of the similarly named women Guenloie and Guenievere in Yder's story? Like the wife of Arawn and Rhiannon, who share an identity, it is possible that these two ladies also do. Both are called queens, and the story-teller describes Queen Guenloie in a manner which suggests that it was really Arthur's queen who is intended, since the queen harps on Arthur's prowess.

We note that the later Arthurian texts rarely show Arthur in action. He remains a figurehead, seated at the Round Table: a crowned sovereign whose knights fight on his behalf and champion the king's justice. But when Guinevere is threatened, things change. It is only in the last flowering of the Arthurian legends, in Malory, that Arthur is merely content to sit and let justice take its course with his faithless wife by having her burned. Many of the earlier texts show him to be concerned enough to fight for her himself.

We also note that Guenievere sets Yder on a Hallow quest for the giant's knife; the Sword of Light, such as Cai and company steal from Wrnach the Giant in *Culhwch and Olwen*. It is also apparent that Guinevere shows a marked preference for her would-be abductor; this emerges in many texts.

Durmart, a thirteenth-century French romance, features Ider (Yder) again; in a similar way to Gereint he champions Guinevere, who has been seized by Brun de Morois, who is possibly a figure related to both the Brown Earl and Earl Limwris in *Gereint and Enid*. We get some insight into the nature of the light and dark combatants once more because Brun swears that he will not force the queen while the sun shines, indicating that Brun is of Otherworldly stock.

In Figure 10.9 potential abductors – that is, knights who show a marked interest in Guinevere but who do not actually abduct her in the story – are indicated by square brackets round their names. In each of these texts we see traces of a prior liaison, as in *Yder*, between Guinevere and her would-be abductor. In *De Ortu Waluuanii* (*The Rise of Gawain*), we find Guinevere remarking to Arthur that a better knight than he is on his way to court, one who will send her tokens. This is none other than Gawain, who overcomes Arthur, significantly, at a ford.[9]

In *Perlesvaus*, a *Percival* variant, Guinevere, like Enid in *Gereint and Enid*, criticizes Arthur for his inability to keep a strong court, and provokes him to seek adventures by which he might win glory. He is further admonished by a maiden similar to both Luned and the Black Maiden of *Peredur*. Guinevere's role is strangely altered in this text, but in such a way that her role as Sovereignty of Britain is enhanced. While on a pilgrimage to Avalon, Arthur wins in combat a crown and war-horse. It is awarded with the following words:

'Sire, you have won . . . this golden crown and this war-horse, for which you should rejoice indeed, so long as you are valiant enough to defend the land of the finest lady on earth, who is now dead . . .

'*To whom did the land belong?*' asked the king. '*And what was the name of the queen whose crown I see?*'

'Sire, the king's name was Arthur, and he was the finest in the world, but many people say that he is dead; *and the crown belonged to Queen Guinevere, who is now dead and buried.*'[29]

Guinevere is indeed dead, from grief at her son's death and from worry over Lancelot's safety, for this text makes her the mother of Loholt or Llacheu, slain by Kay. Here the sovereignty of Britain is in Guinevere's gift.

Later on in the story, Madeglans of Oriande comes to court, demanding that Arthur yield up the Round Table and the sovereignty to him, since he was Guinevere's nearest kinsman, and now that she is dead, Arthur is no longer entitled to it. Madeglans likewise bids Arthur renounce Christianity and marry Madeglans's sister, Jandree, for which he may be permitted to remain king.

There is no text which presents Guinevere's sovereignty-bestowing role more clearly. The land and the crown are all derived from her. Her death, which is substituted for an abduction in *Perlesvaus*, is the occasion of the Otherworldly kin coming to claim their rights on her behalf.

Diu Cröne, a German text by Heinrich von dem Turlin establishes Guinevere's Otherworldly provenance beyond doubt. Guinevere provokes Arthur, as in *De Ortu Waluuanii*, when she finds him huddling over a fire on a cold winter's day, saying that he was never so enduring as the knight who rode at the ford of Noirespine dressed only in a silk shirt. She describes this knight with some warm appreciation, and Arthur sets out to find him. Arthur learns that the stranger knight is the Otherworldly Gasozein, who claims Guinevere as his own, for she was destined to be his mistress by nocturnal spirits when she was born. He accuses Arthur of having stolen her and they go to fight a duel, but it is decided to leave the matter to Guinevere's judgement.

Her indecision is ended by Gasozein's abduction of her. Gawain eventually rescues her.[39] This story is related to Marie de France's *Lai d'Espine*.[26]

We have already noted the abduction by Valerin in *Lanzelet* on p. 143. The *Livre d'Artus* is a mangled tale in which duplications of incidents tirelessly occur, including several abductions of Guinevere by Urian, Lot and Galehot. Guinevere's lover in this text is Gosengos, and he implies that she has had many lovers whom she has treated badly. (A similar complaint is made by the Sumerian Gilgamesh, when the goddess Inanna demands his love!)

This leaves only the *Vulgate Cycle* and the false Guinevere. This curious duplication of characters probably arises as a result of the dual nature of the Flower Bride. Story-tellers probably reasoned that Arthur's queen could not bear the burden of such a reputation, and transferred the queen's apparent wickedness on to another character. Much the same happens in the Tristan legend where, having been banished from Isolt, Mark's queen, Tristan takes up with another Isolt when he arrived in Brittany, who is eventually responsible for his death.[81]

In the *Vulgate Cycle*, Guinevere's father, Leodegran, begets the real Guinevere on his queen and the false Guinevere upon his seneschal's wife. The false Guinevere arranges for her half-sister's abduction after her wedding to Arthur, substituting herself as his new bride, but she is discovered and banished. In the *Prose Lancelot*, it is Lancelot who is at first deceived by the false Guinevere, and then Arthur.[33] A distant version of this tradition is present in Lancelot's bedding of Elaine, Pelles' daughter, under the impression she is Guinevere.[25] This might indeed have been the solution to Triad 53 (see p. 171) had these texts not been at such a remove from each other in terms of the date of their transmission; Lancelot's sleeping with Elaine under the mistaken impression she is Guinevere results in the conception of Galahad. In the later texts it is the quest for the Grail that empties the Round Table of its worthy knights, and the guilty love of Guinevere and Lancelot that brings the action to the Battle of Camlann. In one sense Elaine, as 'the little Guinevere', does indeed strike 'the big Guinevere' a terrible blow, for it is the dream or false Guinevere who conceives the Grail-winner, a role which is denied the real Guinevere.

It will be seen that Guinevere's most famous 'abductor', Lancelot, appears as such only in the later texts, as in Malory, where he rescues the queen from burning at the stake. He is not the sole abductor of this tradition, though he certainly succeeds to the role of Otherworldly lord, as he is fostered by the Lady of the Lake.[42]

There is one tradition in which Guinevere's role as Flower Bride passes to her daughter and that is in a fragmentary folk ballad, *King Arthur and King Cornwall*. In this song, Guinevere provokes Arthur to search for the Round Table, whose provenance is known to the queen. Arthur rides out disguised as a pilgrim with some of his knights and comes to the castle of King Cornwall, where he hears a story about himself which gives him cause for dismay. King Cornwall relates:

> Seven yeere I was clad and fed,
> In Litle Brittaine, in a bower;
> I had a daughter by King Arthur's wife,
> That now is called my flower.
> For King Arthur, that kindly cockward,
> Hath none such in his bower.[64]

The apparent lack of issue from the marriage of Arthur and Guinevere (his sons are all by other women – see Figure 10.1) testifies to the rupture of the king and his Sovereignty, though not to an ending of the influence of their roles, which are inherited by other characters in other time-scales.

The career of Guinevere is the Flower Bride's farewell in British tradition, for she represents the final manifestation of Sovereignty's distinct maiden aspect within our mythic history; she is remembered still in May revels and seasonal rites where, with her crown of flowers and virginal smock, she smiles down from every May Day float in the person of every little May Queen. There are few who remember as they watch the combat of the May King with his opponent, that the prize was once more than the honour of being king for a day; that the Flower Bride brought as her dowry the Sovereignty of Britain.

IV THE ANASTASIS OF ARTHUR

Arthur's interaction with Sovereignty is nowhere more apparent than in the days leading up to his departure from Logres. Few story-tellers have been willing to speak of the death of Arthur; a tradition which is extended to all of royal blood in many parts of the world today. We may instance modern Ghana where the people assert:

> Ordinary people die and are dead. But the king is never dead. He is still alive. We do not talk of the death of the king.[62]

Just so does *Stanzas of the Graves* state: '*Anoeth bid bet y Arthur*',[44] or 'difficult to conceive a grave for Arthur'. For this reason I have adopted a Greek liturgical form *anastasis*, and titled this section 'the Deathlessness of Arthur'.

The encounters of Arthur with Sovereignty in stories of the early tradition are mainly lost to us. All that is possible here is to trace the mythological path leading from the obscure sign-posts of fragmentary stories into the well-documented later Arthurian tradition. We have seen how Arthur drinks from the white drink of fostering, as well as from the red drink of lordship; now is the time for him to drink of the dark drink of forgetfulness, after which his earthly kingdom of Logres is laid aside in exchange for the realm of the Goddess of the Otherworld, the Royal Virgin of Avalon herself.

Arthur encounters many aspects of Sovereignty throughout his life in the shape of his mother, foster-mother, sisters, wife and in the many unspecified damsels who come to seek his help in guarding the land; at the point of his departure he encounters them all at once, in a single dream which is a recapitulation of his life and relationship with the land.

This episode occurs in a single source: the *Alliterative Morte Arthure*, a fifteenth-century Middle English prose romance, which stands in the tradition of Geoffrey of Monmouth rather than of the French romances. It predates Malory and, though it represents a rather late tradition, it does present us with one of the fullest encounters of Arthur with Sovereignty.

It opens with Arthur dreaming he is in a wood, in a lovely valley. He sees descending from the sky a richly dressed woman, bedecked with jewels and with a crown upon her head. She whirls a wheel with her hands. In the centre of this wheel is a kingly throne, and clinging to the outer hub are six kings, each of whom bewails that ever he was enthroned. She welcomes Arthur, saying that she alone has been responsible for the honour he has won in battle. She sits him on the throne, combs his hair and then gifts him with three gifts: a diadem; an orb, symbolizing Arthur's sovereignty over the land; and a sword, which is Arthur's own. Entering an orchard she bids the boughs bend low and present Arthur with apples, and tells him to eat as many as he chooses.

> Then she went to the well, by the woodside,
> That welled up with wine and wonderously flowed.
> She caught up a cupful and covered it fairly,
> And bade me drink deeply a draught to herself. (My trans.)[3]

But at midday her soft mood changed and she whirled the wheel, violently crushing Arthur.

A philosopher duly interprets Arthur's dream as being one of Fortuna; the six other men are six of the Nine Worthies (Alexander, Hector, Julius, Judas Maccabeus, Joshua and David), to whom will be added Charlemagne, Godfrey de Bouíllon and Arthur himself.[3]

The figure of Fortuna enjoyed a new lease of life during the Middle Ages. She had previously been a popular goddess among the Romans, particularly among soldiers, who frequently set up shrines to both her and to Victory. The question here is whether *Alliterative Morte Arthure*'s depiction of Fortuna has any relationship with our Sovereignty. Certainly she behaves like a Celtic Goddess: she empowers Arthur's kingship by victory in battle; she gives him royal regalia and arms him; she commands apples to fall into his lap and is clearly mistress of the orchard; and, most significantly, she gives him to drink of the red cup of lordship. And, while the concept of the Nine Worthies is a medieval one, the Succession of the Pendragons is not.

As we saw in *Mabon*, p. 114,[111] the wheel turns inexorably, so that there is always a king, his *tanaiste* and his predecessor – in Arthur's case, Mabon and Uther. Yet the symbol of the wheel is not usually a goddessly emblem among the Celts, but one wielded by Taranis, the god of thunder. Our story depicts not a mere *genius* of the spring, but a queenly character whose influence empowers kings, just like Sovereignty; nor is this the only appearance of Fortuna in the Arthurian legends.

We saw in Chapter Nine how the Grail derives, in part, from the vessel that Sovereignty guards, whether it be well, spring or cauldron. In *Perlesvaus*, a thirteenth-century Grail text, we read how Gawain encounters many adventures on his quest to recover the Grail to the kingdom of Logres. He is the first to seek it, at the behest of the Bald Maiden of the Cart and her two maidens, who have come to Arthur's court to request his help in healing the Wounded King and the wasteland. While following these maidens, Gawain comes upon a fountain with a golden vessel hanging from it. As he goes to touch it, a voice tells him: 'You are not the good knight who is served from the vessel and cured by it.'[29] He then sees a priest approach, bearing a four-square golden cup, which he rinses and then fills with the contents of the fountain cup. Then three maidens appeared:

> all draped in white robes with white drapes to cover their heads; one of them carried bread in a vessel of gold, another brought wine in a vessel of ivory, and a third bore meat in a vessel of silver. They came up to the golden vessel . . . and in it they placed their offerings. And after waiting awhile at the foot of the pillar, they began to walk back, but as they went, *it seemed to Sir Gawain that there was but one of them*. [ibid., my itals.]

Later Gawain comes to the Castle of Enquiry, where a hermit explains the wonders he has seen. The Bald Maiden is Fortuna, who has lost her hair because a knight has not yet asked the Grail question that will heal the land and the Wounded King, and her cart is Fortuna's Wheel. Her two maiden companions are dressed, one better, one poorly so, to signify the changing patterns of fortune. But when Gawain asks for an explanation of the three maidens at the fountain, the hermit gnostically replies:

Of that . . . I will tell you no more than you have heard . . . for no one should reveal the secrets of the Saviour; they should be kept secret by him to whom they are entrusted. (ibid.)

This passage helps us clearly to associate Fortuna with Sovereignty in the person of the Bald Maiden, who is the *genius* of the land, her beautiful hair never to be restored until the Grail question is asked by a knight who will become not only the Grail-winner but also the champion of Logres. The three mysterious and very Celtic maidens who appear at the fountain bearing food and drink in rich vessels seem to have strayed in from one of the *immrama*, the Otherworldly voyages of Maelduine or Bran mac Febal. The hermit implies that these maidens are at the centre of the Grail cult; his silence is as strange as his comment about the 'secrets of the Saviour'. However, we may conclude that here, perhaps, is the meeting place of the Christian mysteries of the Grail and the original damsels of the wells whom we met in the Amangons story from *The Elucidation* (see p. 250).

These three maidens appear to be one woman in Gawain's sight: a highly significant factor, if we consider both Gawain's noted association with Otherworldly women and the configuration of the archetypes of the Divine Feminine in Celtic culture. It is known that the native threefold goddesses depicted as the *Matres*, or the Mothers, in Celtic Europe were intimately associated with the Roman cult of the *Parcae*, or Fates – also a threefold sisterhood.[75] While fusion of Roman and British deities tended to produce sets of divine couples such as Rosmerta, a native goddess of plenty, with Mercury, the Roman god of skill, certain goddessly archetypes remain obstinately unmatched.

At Corstopitum (Corbridge, Northumberland), two reliefs have been found of such goddesses. One shows a figure standing beside a vat, with a dish or cup in her hand. The other shows two goddesses; the right-hand figure is standing and has been identified as Fortuna, with cornucopia and rudder. The left-hand one is seated and much larger. She holds an orb-like object in her lap, while in her left hand is a sceptre. Beside her is an altar with a bird upon it. At this site the goddess is invoked as *Caelestis Brigantia*, the Heavenly Brigantia.[142] Is it possible that the

Sovereignty of Britain, as depicted in these selections from the Arthurian legends, can be this once-mighty goddess of the native Britons? Brigantia, whose name means 'High One', or 'Queen'?

We will recall that early tradition credits Arthur with bearing an image of the Virgin upon his shoulder at the Battle of Badon, and to this his victory is attributed (see p. 29). Perhaps this is indeed so, but in the shifting association of mythological archetypes, perhaps Arthur's spiritual allegiance was given to Sovereignty herself? Brigantia's name was invoked to bring victory among both native tribes and Roman auxiliaries stationed in the British north. A relief found at Birrens depicts Brigantia with a mural crown, depicting the crenellations of a fortress, showing her to be a territorial goddess; she is standing on a globe, symbolic of victory and sovereignty, she is carrying a spear and wearing the gorgoneion of Minerva on her breast – the gorgon mask which should unman the enemy with its fearful glance. In this single depiction we have all the symbolism of Sovereignty, even down to the *Cailleach* or fearful aspect assumed by the Black Maiden. It is not inconceivable that the fifth-century Arthur might have worn a Roman cuirass, on which the gorgoneion of Minerva was embossed, at the Battle of Badon.

Sir John Rhys has shown that the Welsh 'brenhin', or king, derives from the Celtic root word 'bríg', meaning power, authority or high esteem: all terms signifying sovereignty. The legendary judge of Ireland, Sencha, had a daughter called Bríg; it was her duty to criticize and correct her father's judgements. This is a role we recognize from Sovereignty's aspect as Black Maiden, where she harangues her protégés. The goddess Brighid was frequently called Bríg also.[140]

It is possible to further associate Brighid with the later appearance of Fortuna as Sovereignty. Brighid is primarily a goddess of nurture, whether it be the growth and well-being of children or beasts, or the development of wisdom. On the feast day of St Brigit, to this day in Celtic countries (Oimelc, 1 February), people still make Bride's Cross – a three- or four-spoked cross of rushes resembling a wheel. In times past it is possible that such an emblem was set alight and thrown into the winter skies to herald the return of the light and the turning of the year's wheel of seasons. Certainly there is much weather-lore relating to this day. We have already seen how Brighid mitigates the influence of the *Cailleach* at this time of year (see p. 242). Her mythos, whether of goddess or saint, speaks of power, wisdom, nurture and new beginnings. And so we may conceive the Celtic Goddess of Sovereignty.

But we should not forget that the Irish triple, Brighid, is associated with smithcraft and that her wisdom-in-battle aspect is the bestower of victory upon her successful clients: which leads us to the last contender for the title of the Sovereignty of Britain.

Within the last days of his life, Arthur encounters the Lady of the Wheel: the aspect of the Goddess that governs the cutting of the thread, she who gathers to herself all those champions who have lived in her service, for she is the Otherworldly mistress and she demands her tithe. As we might expect, Arthur puts Gwenhwyfar, the Flower Bride, behind him when the end is near. The Orkney clan, the sons of Morcades/Morgause, Gwalchmai and Medrawt, briefly take up opposite roles in the conflict that stands between king and land – one championing the king, the other ready to wreak havoc. We note that Medrawt, in the early texts, attempts to steal the Flower Bride, thus becoming the Thief of Sovereignty (see p. 158). It is Arthur's lot to encounter the Battle Goddess, the Taker, the Washer at the Ford: Queen Dragon herself.

The earlier texts tell of Gwenhwyfar's abduction – whether willingly or not – by Medrawt: Arthur is thus without his representative of Sovereignty. But they also tell of how the Battle of Camlann is provoked by various incidents. One of these is in *The Dream of Rhonabwy* where Iddawg, the Churn of Britain – so called because of his habit of stirring up trouble – took a message of truce from Arthur to Medrawt and delivered it in such a way as to provoke the battle. In this instance Iddawg appears to act as the Provoker of Strife – one of Sovereignty's henchmen, whom she utilizes only when she is in her catabolic phase, breaking the kingship down in order to start again. The *Stanzaic Morte Arthur* also tells us that the Battle of Camlann was provoked by the appearance of an adder, which bit the foot of one of Mordred's company when both sides were drawn up in truce. He drew his sword to slash at it and so the conflict began.[3] Here is the *Cailleach*, Queen Dragon herself, in the form of the adder, which comes out of the ground to bring the reign of winter upon earth, only returning once more at the festival of Brighid (see p. 243).

And so the two champions fight: Arthur against Medrawt/Mordred, who is, according to different viewpoints, Arthur's son or nephew, or the young champion of Sovereignty herself:

> When Medrawd heard that Arthur's host was dispersed, he turned against Arthur, and the Saxons and the Picts and the Scots united with him to hold this Island against Arthur. And when Arthur heard that, he turned back with all that had survived of his army, and succeeded by violence in landing on this Island in opposition to Medrawd. And then there took place the Battle of Camlan between Arthur and Medrawd, and Arthur slew Medrawd, and was himself wounded to death.[38]

And so the story told in Chapter Two of Vortigern and Merlin Emrys, in which the dragons were released from the foundations of Vortigern's tower, is to some extent recapitulated: Medrawt is Vortigern come again – a man who allies himself with the enemies of Britain. But Merlin's prophetic insight is no longer available to Arthur. Standing in the wings is Morgan, the Battle Goddess, the Otherworld Mistress, ready to claim her lord from the field of the slain. The adder as well as the raven is her totemic beast and, like the dragons' release by Merlin, betokens the end and beginning of a phase of Britain's sovereignty.

We have to some extent anticipated this discussion in Chapter Four where we dealt with Morgan in her aspect as Battle Goddess. Perhaps here we truly understand how the *gwyddbwyll* combat of the Pendragons with Sovereignty reaches its end-game.

Morgan's oldest and perhaps least understood role in Arthurian legend is that of Otherworldly Mistress and Healer. When she first appears in Arthurian tradition in Geoffrey of Monmouth's *Vita Merlini*[11] as Morgen, Queen of the Otherworldly realm of Avalon, she bears little trace of the curious, changeable creature later tradition will make of her. She appears as the mistress of her eight companion sisters; she is able to fly, to shapechange and to heal, as well as being a mistress of wisdom. All these attributes seem at odds with the malevolent Morgan of Malory, for instance.

We note, however, that she is one of nine sisters, a feature we have met previously:

Nine Muses who warm Pen Annwn's cauldron
Nine Witches of Gloucester who help/hinder Peredur
Nine Avalonian sisters

All three examples are from British tradition, but are consonant with European traditions of the Nine Korrigans of Brittany, a cell of priestesses, whom Pomponius Mela described as being called the 'Gallenciae'.[134] This ninefold sisterhood is the three-times-three multiplication of the three-fold Goddess herself, which classical tradition represented in the *Parcae* or Fates, but which in Celtic tradition remained firmly associated with the *Matres*, the Mothers.

Morgan has been through so many transformations and shifts of emphasis that the welter of material surviving shows clearly the synthesis of the Otherworldly Goddess into a series of Otherworldly women. It is when these supramortal qualities are bestowed on the very mortal figure of Morgan as Arthur's sister in later tradition that story-tellers are reduced to explaining away such power by making Morgan an enchantress. There is no space to recapitulate this complex development here; readers are directed to the excellent studies by Paton[134] and Harf-Lancner[79] where this will be made apparent.

Morgan retains many Celtic characteristics. She has been mostly replaced by the figure of the Lady of the Lake as a foster-mother of heroes, but that element is still there, submerged in Arthur's career, that of the Otherworldly woman who endows him with his sword: the Hallow by which he defends the kingdom of Logres. It is this very sword which is returned to the Lady of the Lake at the conclusion of his earthly life, since it belongs to Sovereignty and must be won again by every candidate for the kingship. The Lady of the Lake, although developed in the French romances, is clearly derived from Celtic models of the insular Goddess who rules over a land of women, the famous Tir na mBan of Irish traditional *immrama*. The Lady of the Lake also is seen to arm her young fosterling, as we find in Lancelot's story:[107] this is resonant of the Celtic woman warrior who trained her fosterling in arms and combat and finally sent him out into the world with a worthy blade to assist him, having taught him all her skills.

In her opposition to Arthur, Morgan displays characteristcs of the Black Maiden. She acts as an irritant, becoming the nagging reminder of Arthur's oath to the land, to Sovereignty herself. She reminds him of his *geasa*. She is also jealous of her affianced champion, and when, as we have seen, Arthur weds Gwenhwyfar, who is the manifest Sovereignty of Britain, Morgan extends her opposition to the queen herself. (This is rationalized in the romances by Morgan having loved a cousin of Guinevere's: a relationship which the queen brought to a close.)[134] Morgan also takes lovers and rival champions, whom she sets in active opposition to Arthur, notably Accalon of Gaul, who briefly holds the sword of Sovereignty, Excalibur, before being overcome by Arthur.[25]

But it is perhaps as Battle Goddess, Queen of Ravens, that Morgan's chief Celtic characteristic is manifested. The Morrighan of Irish tradition – herself a triple-aspected Goddess – plays a key part in the changing of dynasties and the succession of the land to a new champion. This earlier resonance of Morgan declares who is victorious at the Second Battle of Mag Tuired, the great battle fought between Lugh and the Tuatha de Danaan and the occupying Fomorians, thus:

> (She) proceeded to proclaim that battle and the mighty victory which had taken place, to the royal heights of Ireland and to its faery hosts and its chief waters and its river-mouths.[8]

In other words, she proclaims the land itself to be victorious, though Lugh and the Tuatha have fought successfully for the sovereignty. She goes on to prophesy the end of the world in an apocalyptic manner:

> I shall not see a world that will be dear to me.
> Summer without flowers,

> Kine will be without milk,
> Women without modesty,
> Men without valor,
> Captures without a king . . . (ibid.)

Her role is analogous to that of the figure who appears at the end of Merlin's prophecies to end the world:

> The Moon's chariot shall run amok in the Zodiac and the Pleiades will burst into tears. None of these will return to the duty expected of it. Ariadne will shut its door and be hidden within its enclosing cloudbanks.[10]

Likewise Morgan appears to end the reign of the Pendragons, to make an end because she is the Lady of the Wheel, Fortuna herself, who turns the Wheel of the Pendragons. In her many aspects she has been everything except the Flower Bride – a role reserved for Gwenhwyfar. But now her time has come to take her consort home; time to checkmate the king-piece on the *gwyddbwyll* board of the land.

Her last transformation is perhaps the most amazing to modern readers. She changes from being the chooser of the slain, the Raven Queen – an archetype predominantly found in many cultures in north-west Europe, from Ireland to Scandinavia – to being the healer-goddess who will mend Arthur's wounds. She takes him away on a barge accompanied by two other queens in the version most familiar from Malory: the threefold Sovereignty incarnate. But the barge is only an ill-disguised version of the Otherworldly crystal *curragh* that bears ardent travellers to the Land of Women or the Blessed Isles, where time is not.

Among the mysteries of Sovereignty the passing of the king into the land is the most profound. After his earthly career, worn out by toil in the defence of the land, the land restores him by means of its Otherworldly fruit; its everlasting fountains restore his youth and strength until the time comes for the wheel to turn again, when he, too, will change from being Lord of the Underworld, Pen Annwn, and become the Goddess's fosterling, her Mabon once more.

The *Vita Merlini* describes Arthur's passage to Avalon in the barque of the mysterious Barinthus, accompanied by Taliesin and Merlin, to the place where Morgen heals his wounds.[11] Another text, *Le Dragon Normand* by Etienne de Rouen, slightly post-dates this tradition and gives us a fresh insight into the nature of Arthur's passing:

The grievously wounded Arthur requested healing herbs from his sister:
These were kept in the sacred isle of Avalon.
Here the eternal nymph, Morgan, helped her brother.
Healing, nourishing and reviving him, making him immortal.
The Antipodes were put under his rule. As one of Faery,
He stands without armour, but fearing no fray.
So he rules from the underworld, bright in battle,
Where the other half of the world is his. (My trans.)[134]

This text gives details not found in Geoffrey, notably the references above. Interestingly the whole poem is about sovereignty, the sovereignty of Brittany, and includes a correspondence between Arthur and Henry II in which Henry becomes a vassal of Arthur's! We note that Arthur is king of the southern hemisphere, though this is clearly intended to mean the Underworld, that subterranean kingdom whose unearthly influence governs the sovereignty of the land. It is so that Arthur becomes Pen Annwn, in truth the Sleeping Lord.

The *Gesta Regnum Britanniae* of c. 1235 confirms Arthur's relationship with Morgan, the royal virgin of Avalon:

At that same time when Arthur bequeathed the diadem of royalty and set another king in his place, it was she who brought him over there in the five hundred and forty-second year after the Word became incarnate without the seed of human father. Wounded beyond measure, Arthur took the way to the court of the King of Avalon, where the royal virgin, tending his wound, keeps his healed body for her very own and they live together. (*Mabon*, p. 163)[111]

And so Arthur is established in tradition as an Otherworldly king with Morgan at his side, with whom he administers the important business of Britain's sovereignty. As the king who does not die, he is thus always potentially available to his land and its people.

Thus Arthur had himself borne to Avalon and he told his people that they should await him and he would return. And the Britons came back to Carduel and waited for him more than forty years before they would take a king, for they believed always that he would return. But this you may know in truth that some have since then seen him hunting in the forest, and they have heard his dogs with him; and some have hoped for a long time that he would return.[32]

And so we come full circle in our study of the *Mabinogion*, for here is where we began, in the first branch story of Pwyll, where the King of Dyfed met Arawn, Pen Annwn, out hunting and the Otherworldly adventures began. This extract from the *Didot Perceval* above proclaims the ongoing, mythological existence of a king for whose return, indeed, many have hoped.

The hunting by Arthur in the forests of Brocéliande,* that great forest, which once covered the land of Logres, still pursues its quarry: the White Hart, which is Sovereignty's own beast and one which only the best of champions can win for the most sovereign of ladies.

The names of the land are as various as the aspects of Sovereignty that we have met in this book; the calling of the Pendragon is a serious undertaking. These two riddles have underlain this study. However we call her – whether Elen of the Dream-Paths, Brighid, Morgan, Gwenhwyfar, Rhiannon, Modron, Arianrhod – Sovereignty will never cease to call her own champion.

And what of those who stumble into the subterranean chamber where Arthur, the Sleeping Lord, lies awaiting the call? Will they find that the horn of awakening is, after all, the horn that restores the Court of Joy? By what empowerments will they find the sword within their hands, the cup raised to their lips? Only those who are attuned to the voices of the wells, the voice of Sovereignty herself, can ever truly know the land. But that is an adventure that awaits us all . . .

* See John Matthews's *Broceliande: a novel of the Forest* (in preparation).

THE WHEEL OF THE YEAR: KING AND GODDESS

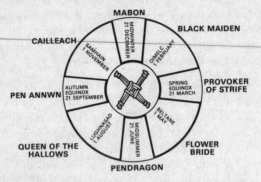

Figure 11.1. *The Wheel of the Year: King and Goddess*

Amid the welter of evidence for Sovereignty in Celto-Arthurian tradition presented in this book, it is perhaps best to try and achieve a degree of clarity. Figure 11.1 shows the Wheel of the Year upon which the major harmonics of Sovereignty and king have been placed.

The centre of the diagram shows a cross plaited out of reeds, which is traditionally made on St Brigit's day on 1 February in Ireland today. Each arm of the cross indicates one of the four major aspects of Sovereignty. This is superimposed upon an equilateral Celtic cross, each arm of which indicates one of the four major aspects of the king. The Goddess corresponds to the Celtic festivals; the king corresponds to the quarter days, or sun festivals.

The Celtic year begins at Samhain with the rule of the *Cailleach*. In the depths of winter, when the sun is at its lowest in the sky, Mabon is born, remaining hidden until his epiphany or finding. It is during this time that the king is fostered secretly by the Dark Woman of Knowledge or *Cailleach* and is taught battle skills by the Black Maiden, who appears at Oimelc, when the rule of the *Cailleach* is challenged by her in the manner spoken of on p. 243. The young king, in order to be acceptable to Sovereignty, must become aware of the needs of the land he seeks to govern.

In so doing, he becomes a Provoker of Strife, by stirring up trouble for the reigning king and spearheading resistance to a reign that has grown stale or corrupt. It is in this manner that he becomes the Champion of Sovereignty and proves worthy of the Flower Bride, Sovereignty's manifest representative, whom he marries. He may even be responsible for carrying her off, as her abductor.

The Flower Bride is properly seen as the Queen of May, and her time of manifestation is at Beltane. It will be seen from the diagram that this position is diametrically opposite that of the *Cailleach*. On the Wheel of the Year, the young king has used the *Cailleach*' knowledge to understand the needs of the land and has experienced the Goddess's transformatory nature as she appears as Flower Bride: the land puts off its wasted appearance, which it affected during the previous reign of an unworthy king, and becomes fair once more. This is the land that the king marries.

As Pendragon, recognized King of Britain, the king is at his strongest at the time of midsummer, but in order to maintain his kingdom he must seek the gifts and empowerments of Sovereignty and ratify his union on a deeper level. The Hallows are held by the Queen of the Hallows in her Otherworldly castle. She appears at Lughnasad, the festival that in ancient tradition saw the *banais rigi* – the wedding of the kingship to the land. Throughout the long summer he seeks her gifts, eventually journeying into the regions of the dead, to the Underworld itself, to bring back the Hallows. It is in this way that the king succeeds to his new role as Pen Annwn, Lord of the Underworld, the Sleeping Lord, who enters the realms of the *Cailleach* to be reborn and remade. This transformation may take many turns of the wheel to effect, but the king is mythically tied to this wheel until his own deeds release him into the Otherworld, from whence he will come again.

This schema shows the barest bones of a deeper pattern, which the reader is invited to uncover by means of reading, meditation and personal revelation. The yearly cycle it represents may be enacted ritually, or made the focus of a reverent *anamnesis*. It may be combined with the many fragmented and partially restored texts exemplified in this book for the reconstruction of a more coherent cycle. For a visual summary of the major themes in this book, readers are directed to *The Arthurian Tarot*.[113]

LIST OF REFERENCES
AND FURTHER READING

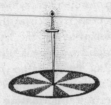

TEXTUAL SOURCES

1. Bartrum, P. C., *Early Welsh Genealogical Tracts*, Cardiff, Univ. of Wales Press, 1966

2. Bartrum, P. C., *Welsh Genealogies AD 300–1400*, Cardiff, Univ. of Wales Press, 1974

3. Benson, L. D. (ed.), *King Arthur's Death: The Middle English Stanzaic 'Morte Arthure' and Alliterative 'Morte Arthure'*, Exeter, Univ. of Exeter Press, 1986

4. Best, R. L. (ed.), 'The Adventures of Art, Son of Conn', in *Eriú*, vol. 3 (1906), pp. 146 *et seq.*

5. Bruce, J. D. (ed.), *Historia Meriadoci and De Ortu Waluuanii*, Baltimore, Johns Hopkins Press, 1913

6. Chaucer, G., *Canterbury Tales*, Oxford, OUP, 1912

7. Chrétien de Troyes, *Arthurian Romances*, trans. D. D. R. Owen, London, Dent, 1987

8. Cross, T. P. & Slover, C. H., *Ancient Irish Tales*, Dublin, Figgis, 1936

9. Day, M. L., *The Rise of Gawain, Nephew of Arthur*, New York, Garland Pub. Inc., 1984

10. Geoffrey of Monmouth, *History of the Kings of Britain*, Harmondsworth, Penguin, 1966

11. Geoffrey of Monmouth, *Vita Merlini*, ed. & trans. J. J. Parry, Illinois, Univ. of Illinois Press, 1925

12. Gerald of Wales, *Journey Through Wales*, ed. & trans. L. Thorpe, Harmondsworth, Penguin, 1978

13. Gildas, *The Ruin of Britain*, ed. & trans. M. Winterbottom, London & Chichester, Phillimore, 1978

14. *The Gododdin*, ed. & trans. K. H. Jackson, Edinburgh, Edinburgh Univ. Press, 1969

15. Hartman von Aue, *Erec*, trans. J. W. Thomas, Lincoln & London, Univ. of Nebraska Press, 1979

16. Hartman von Aue, *Iwein*, trans. J. W. Thomas, Lincoln & London, Univ. of Nebraska Press, 1979

17. Joynt, M. (ed. & trans.), 'Echtra Mac Echach Muígmedoín', in *Eriú*, vol. 4 (1910), pp. 91–111

18. Kitteridge, G. L., 'Arthur and Gorlagon', *Studies and Notes in Philology and Literature*, vol. 8 (1903), Boston, pp. 149–275

19. *The Laws of Hywel Dda*, trans. M. Richards, Liverpool, Liverpool Univ. Press, 1954

20. *Life of St Brigit* in *Lives of the Saints*, ed. W. Stokes, Oxford & Clarendon Press, Anecdota Oxoniensis, Medieval and Modern Series 5

21. 'Life of St Gildas' (*Vita Gildae*), *Lives of the Saints*, ed. S. Baring-Gould, Edinburgh, Grant, 1877

22. *The Mabinogion*, ed. & trans. J. Gantz, London, Penguin, 1988

23. *The Mabinogion*, ed. & trans. Lady C. Guest, London, Ballantyne Press, 1910

24. *The Mabinogion*, ed. & trans. G. Jones & T. Jones, London, Dent, 1976

25. Malory, Sir T., *Le Morte d'Arthur*, New York, University Books, 1961

26. Marie de France, *French Medieval Romances*, ed. & trans. E. Mason, London, Dent, n.d.

27. Meyer, P., 'Les Enfances Gauvain', *Romania*, vol. 39 (1910), pp. 1–31

28. Nennius, *British History and Welsh Annals*, ed. & trans. J. Morris, Chichester, Phillimore, 1980

29. *Perlesvaus* (*High Book of the Grail*), trans. N. Bryant, Cambridge, D. S. Brewer, 1978

30. *Sir Clèges and Sir Libeaus Desconus: Two Old English Metrical*

Romances rendered into prose, Frans J. L. Weston, London, David & Nutt, 1902 31. *Sir Gawain and the Green Knight*, trans. Rev. E. J. B. Kirtlan, London, Charles Kelly, 1912

32. Skeels, D. (ed. & trans.), *The Romance of Perceval in Prose* (*Didot Perceval*), Seattle, Univ. of Washington, 1966

33. Sommer, H. O. (ed.), *The Vulgate Version of the Arthurian Romances*, 7 vols., Washington, The Carnegie Institute, 1909–1916

34. Stokes, W. 'The Death of Muirchertach MacErca', in *Revue Celtique*, vol. 23 (1892), Paris, pp. 396–437

35. Stokes, W. H. & Windisch, E., *Irische Texte*, Leipzig, Verlag con S. Hurzel, 1884

36. Thompson, A. (ed)., *The Elucidation: a Prologue to the Conte del Graal*, New York, Publications of the Institute of French Studies, 1931

37. Thorpe, L. (ed.), *Le Roman de Silence*, Cambridge, Heffer, 1972

38. *Trioedd Ynys Prydein,* ed. R. Bromwich, Cardiff, Univ. of Wales Press, 1961

39. Von dem Türlin, *Diu Cröne,* ed. G. Scholl, Stuttgart, Bibliothek des Litterarischen Vereins, 1852

40. Von Eschenbach, W., *Parzival, a Knightly epic*, trans. J. L. Weston, London, 1894

41. Von Eschenbach, W., *Titurel*, ed. C. E. Passage, New York, Frederick Ungar Pub. Co., 1984

42. Von Zatzikhovan, U., *Lanzelet*, ed. & trans. K. T. G. Webster, with revisons by R. S. Loomis, New York, Columbia Univ. Press, 1951

43. Wace & Layamon, *Arthurian Chronicles*, ed. & trans. E. Mason, London, Dent, 1962

44. Wilhelm, J. J. & Gross, L. Z.., *The Romance of Arthur*, (2 vols.), New York, Garland Pub. Inc., 1984 & 1986

GENERAL

45. Adler, A., 'Sovereignty as the Principle of Unity in Chrétien's *Erec*', Publications of the Modern Language Association of America (PMLA), vol. 60 (Dec. 1945), no. 4, pp. 917–36

46. Adler, A., 'Sovereignty in Chrétien's *Yvain*', PMLA, vol. 62 (June 1947), no. 2, pp. 281–305

47. Anderson, A. O., 'Gildas and Arthur,' *Celtic Review*, vol. 8 (1912–13), pp. 149–65

48. Arden, J. & D'Arcy, M., *The Island of the Mighty*, London, Eyre Methuen, 1974

49. Ashe, G., *Kings and Queens of Early Britain*, London, Methuen, 1982

50. Barker, B., *Symbols of Sovereignty*, Newton Abbot, Westbridge Books, 1979

51. Bartrum, P. C., 'Was There a British "Book of Conquests"?', in *Bulletin of the Board of Celtic Studies*, vol. 23, part 1 (1968), pp. 1–5

52. Blaess, M., 'Arthur's Sisters', *Bibliographical Bulletin of Institute of Arthurian Society*, vol. 8 (1956), pp. 69–77

53. Blake, W., *Poetry and Prose*, London, Nonesuch Library, 1975

54. Breatnach, R. A., 'The Lady and the King: a theme in Irish Literature', *Celtic Studies*, vol. 42 (1953), pp. 321–36

55. Brewer, E., *From Cuchullin to Gawain*, Cambridge, D. S. Brewer, 1973

56. Bromwich, R., 'Celtic Dynastic Themes and Breton Lays', in *Etudes Celtiques*, vol. 9 (1960/1), pp. 439–74

57. Brown, A. C. L., 'The Individual Character of the Welsh Owain', *Romanic Review*, vol. 3 (Apr–Sept. 1912), pp. 143–72

58. Brown, A. C. L., *The Origins of the Grail Legend*, Cambridge, Mass., Harvard Univ. Press, 1943

59. Bullock-Davies, C. 'Lanval and Avalon', *Bulletin of the Board of Celtic Studies* (n.d.), pp. 128–42

60. Byrne, F. J., *Irish Kings and High Kings*, London, Batsford, 1973

61. Campbell, J. F., *Popular Tales of the West Highlands*, 4 vols, London, Wildwood Press, 1983–4

62. Cannadine, D. & Price, S., *Rituals of Royalty*, Cambridge, Cambridge Univ. Press, 1987

63. Carmichael, A., *Carmina Gadelica*, vol. 1, Edinburgh, Scottish Academic Press, 1972

64. Child, F. J., *The English and Scottish Popular Ballads*, 5 vols, New York, Dover Books, 1965

65. Chotzen, T. D., 'Le Lion d'Owein et ses Prototypes

Celtiques', *Néophilologus*, vol. 18 (1932–3), Groningen, pp. 51–8.
66. Corkery, D., *The Hidden Ireland*, Dublin, Gill & Macmillan, 1967
67. Currer-Briggs, N., *The Shroud and the Grail*, London, Weidenfeld & Nicolson, 1987
68. Curtin, J., *Hero Tales of Ireland*, London, Macmillan, 1894
69. Curtin, J., *Irish Folk Tales*, Dublin, Talbot Press, 1944
70. Eisner, S., *A Tale of Wonder*, Wexford, John English, 1957
71. Ellis, T. P., 'Urien Rheged and his Son, Owain', *Welsh Outlook*, vol. 18 (1931), pp. 121–3, pp. 157–60, pp. 183–5
72. Evan, S., *In Quest of the Holy Grail*, London, Dent, 1898
73. Frazer, J. G., *The Illustrated Golden Bough*, London, Macmillan, 1978
74. Goetinck, G. W., *Perceval: a study of the Welsh Tradition in the Grail Legend*, Cardiff, Univ. of Wales Press, 1975
75. Green, M., *The Celts and their Gods*, Gloucester, Alan Sutton, 1986
76. Gregory, Lady, *Gods and Fighting Men*, Gerrards Cross, Colin Smythe, 1970
77. Grout, P. B., Lodge, R. A., Pickford, C. E. & Varty, E. K. C., *The Legend of Arthur in the Middle Ages*, Cambridge, D. S. Brewer, 1983
78. Hall, L. B., *Knightly Tales of Sir Gawaine*, Chicago, Nelson Hall, 1976
79. Harf-Lancner, L., *Les Fées au Moyen Age*, Paris, Librarie Honoré Champion, 1984
80. Henken, E. R., *Traditions of the Welsh Saints*, Cambridge, D. S. Brewer, 1987
81. Hill, J., *The Tristan Legend*, Leeds, Univ. of Leeds Press, 1977
82. Hull, E., 'Old Irish Tabus or Geasa', *Folklore*, vol. 12 (1901), pp. 41–56
83. Hyde, D., 'The Well of D'yerree in Dowan', *Great Fairy Tales of Ireland*, compiled M. McGany, London, Wolfe Pub. Ltd, 1973
84. Jones, D., *The Roman Quarry*, London, Agenda Editions, 1981
85. Jones, E., *The Bardic Museum*, London, A. Strahan, 1802
86. Knight, G., *The Secret Tradition in Arthurian Romance*, Wellingborough, Aquarian Press, 1983
87. Korrel, P., *An Arthurian Triangle*, Leiden, E. J. Brill, 1984

88. Le Roux, F. & Guyonvarc'h, C. J., *La Souverainente Guerrière de l'Irelande*, Rennes, Ogam Celticum, 1983

89. Lewis, C. S., *That Hideous Strength*, London, Bodley Head, 1945

90. Lewis, F. R., *Gwerin Ffristial a Thawl Bwrdd*, Transactions of the Hon. Society of Cymmyrodrians, 1941

91. Lloyd-Morgan, C., Perceval in Wales: Late Medieval Welsh Grail Traditions', *The Changing Face of Arthurian Romance*, ed. A. Adams, A. H. Diverres, K. Stein & K. Varty, Cambridge, Boydell and Brewer, 1986

92. Loomis, R. S., *Arthurian Tradition and Chrétien de Troyes*, New York, Columbia Univ. Press, 1949

93. Loomis, R. S., *The Grail: From Celtic Myth to Christian Symbol*, Cardiff, Univ. of Wales Press, 1963

94. Loomis, R. S., *Studies in Medieval Literature*, New York, Burt Franklin, 1970

95. Loomis, R. S., *Wales and the Arthurian Legend*, Cardiff, Univ. of Wales Press, 1956

96. Luria, M. S., 'The Storm-Making Spring and the Meaning of Chrétien's *Yvain*', *Studies in Philology*, no. 64 (1967), pp. 564–85

97. Luttrell, C., *The Creation of the First Arthurian Romance – a quest*, London, E. Arnold, 1974

98. Maccana, P., 'Aspects of the Theme of King and Goddess in Irish Literature', *Etudes Celtique*, vol. 7 (1956), Paris, pp. 76–114 & vol. 8 (1956), pp. 59–65

99. Maccana, P., *The Learned Tales of Medieval Ireland*, Dublin, Dublin Inst. of Advanced Studies, 1980

100. Maccana, P., *The Mabinogi*, Cardiff, Univ. of Wales Press, 1977

101. Mac Dougall, H. A., *Racial Myth in English History*, Montreal, Harvest House, 1982

102. McKenna, E. L. (ed. & trans.), 'Historical Poem VIII of Gofraigh Fionn O'Dálaigh', *Irish Monthly*, vol. 47 (1919), pp. 455–9

103. Macneill, M., *The Festival of Lughnasadh*, Oxford, OUP, 1962

104. Macwhite, E., 'Early Irish Board Games', in *Eigse*, vol. 5 (1945), pp. 25–35

105. Markale, J., *Le Graal*, Paris, Retz, 1982

106. Markale, J., *King Arthur: King of Kings*, London, Gordon Cremonesi, 1977

107. Markale, J., *Lancelot et la Chevalerie Arthurienne*, Paris, Editions Imago, 1985

108. Markale, J., *Merlin L'Enchanteur*, Paris, Editions Retz, 1981

109. Markale, J., *La Tradition Celtique en Bretagne Armoricaine*, Paris, Payot, 1978

110. Masefield, J., *Midsummer Night*, London, Heinemann, 1928

111. Matthews, C., *Mabon and the Mysteries of Britain*, London, Arkana, 1987

112. Matthews, C., 'Mabon, Divine Celtic Child', *The Second Book of Merlin*, ed. Bob Stewart, Blandford Press, 1988

113. Matthews, C. & J., *The Arthurian Tarot: a Hallowquest Pack*, Wellingborough, Aquarian Press, 1990 (forthcoming)

114. Matthews, J., *An Arthurian Reader*, Wellingborough, Aquarian Press, 1988

115. Matthews, J., (ed.), *At the Table of the Grail*, London, Arkana, 1987

116. Matthews, J., *Fionn Mac Cumhail*, Poole, Firebird Books, 1988

117. Matthews, J., 'The Grail Family', *Avalon to Camelot*, vol. 1., no. 3. (1983), pp. 9-10

118. Matthews, J., *The Grail: Quest for the Eternal*, London, Thames & Hudson, 1981

119. Matthews, J. & Green, M., *The Grail-Seeker's Companion*, Wellingborough, Aquarian Press, 1986

120. Matthews, J. & Stewart, B., *Warriors of Arthur*, Poole, Blandford Press, 1987

121. Moncrieffe of that Ilk, I. & Hicks, D., *The Highland Clans*, London, Barier and Rockliffe, 1967

122. Morduch, A., *The Sovereign Adventure*, Cambridge & London, James Clarke, 1970

123. Morris, J., *The Age of Arthur*, London, Weidenfeld & Nicolson, 1973

124. Newstead, H., *Bran the Blessed in Arthurian Romance*, New York, Columbia Univ. Press, 1939

125. Newstead, H., 'The *Joie de la Cort* Episode in *Erec and the Horn of Bran*', *P.M.L.A.*, vol. 51 (1936), pp. 13–25

126. Newstead, H., 'Perceval's Father and Welsh Traditions', *Romanic Review*, vol. 36 (1945), pp. 3–31

127. Nitze, W. A., 'Yvain and the Myth of the Fountain', *Speculum*, vol. 30 (1955), pp. 170–79

128. O'Corráin, D., 'Irish Origin Legends and Genealogy', *History of Heroic Tale: a symposium*, ed. T. Nyberg, Odense Univ. Press, 1985

129. O'Donovan, J., *Miscellany of the Celtic Society*, Dublin, 1849

130. O'Flaherty, W. D., *Women, Androgenes and Other Mythical Beasts*, Chicago, Univ. of Chicago Press, 1980

131. O'Rahilly, C., *Ireland and Wales*, London, Longmans, 1924

132. Ovazza, M., D'Apollon – Maponos a Mabonograin', *Actes du 14ème Congrès International Arthurian*, Rennes, Presses Universitaires, 1984

133. Parry. T., *History of Welsh Literature*, London, OUP, 1955

134. Paton, L. A., *Studies in the Fairy Mythology of Arthurian Romance*, New York, Burt Franklin, 1960

135. Power, P. C., *Sex and Marriage in Ancient Ireland*, Cork, Mercier Press, 1976

136. Proctor, C., *Ceannas nan Gáidheal*, Sleat, Clan Donald Lands Trust, 1985

137. Rees, A. & B., *Celtic Heritage*, London, Thames & Hudson, 1961

138. Reinhard, J. R., *The Survival of Geis in Medieval Romance*, Halle, Max Niemayer Verlag, 1933

139. Rhys, J., *Celtic Folklore*, vol. 2; 'Welsh and Manx', London, Wildwood House, 1980

140. Rhys, J., *The Hibbert Lectures: Lectures on the Origin and Growth of Religion as Illustrated by Celtic Heathendom*, London, Williams and Morgate, 1888

141. Rolt-Wheeler, F., *Mystic Gleams from the Holy Grail*, London, Rider, (n.d.)

142. Ross, A., *Pagan Celtic Britain*, London, Routledge & Kegan Paul, 1967

143. Scott, R. D., *The Thumb of Knowledge*, New York, Columbia Univ., 1930

144. Sheppard, O., *The Lore of the Unicorn*, London, Allen and Unwin, 1967.

145. Sims-Williams, P. P., 'Some Functions of Origin Stories in Early Medieval Wales', *History of Heroic Tale; a symposium*, ed. T. Nyberg, Odense Univ. Press, 1985

146. Spaan, D. B., 'The Otherworld in Early Irish Literature', Univ. of Michigan, 1969 (unpublished dissertation)

147. Stafford, G., *Pendragon*, Albany, Chaosium Inc., 1985

148. Stewart, R. J. (ed.), *The Book of Merlin*, Poole, Blandford, 1987

149. Stewart, R. J., *The Mystic Life of Merlin*, London, Arkana, 1986

150. Stewart, R. J., *The Prophetic Vision of Merlin*, London, Arkana, 1986

151. Sturm. S., 'Magic in the Bel Inconnu', in *Esprit Créateur*, vol. 12 (1972), Univ. of Kansas, pp. 19–25

152. Tolstoy, N., *The Quest for Merlin*, London, Hamish Hamilton, 1985

153. Van Duzec, M., *A Medieval Romance of Friendship: Eger and Grime*, New York, Burt Franklin, 1963

154. Van Hamel, A. G., 'The Game of the Gods', in *Archiv fur Nordisk Filogi*, vol. 6 (1934), pp. 218–242

155. Vansittart, P., *The Dark Tower*, London, Macdonald, 1965

156. Webster, K. G. T., *Guinevere: a story of her abductions*, Mass., Turtle Press, 1951

157. Weston, J., *From Ritual to Romance*, New York, Doubleday, 1957

158. Williams, R., The *Lord of the Isles*, London, Chatto & Windus/Hogarth, 1984

159. Wood, D., *Genisis*, Tunbridge Wells, Baton Press, 1985

160. Wyatt, I., 'Goddess into Saint: the Foster mother of Christ', in *The Golden Blade*, 1987, pp. 55–65

INDEX

Because many of the characters listed below exist in both Celtic and medieval Arthurian tradition, often with differing characteristics, some have entries under separate names (e.g. **Gawain** and **Gwalchmai**). Other entries are cross-referenced (e.g. **Kay**, *see* **Cai**) to indicate that the natures of these personae are substantially consistent throughout both traditions.

Dagda, 65
Daire Degamra, 46
Dark Woman of Knowledge, 20, 26,
    91, 93, 119–20, 124, 130, 145, 180,
    195, 225, 226, 228, 231, 247, 249,
    274, 281, 294, 312
Daughters of Branwen, 64, 76, 184,
    225–7, 230, 281
    as sacred queens, 53, 64, 276
Day, Mildred Leake, 282
Delbhchaem, 47, 49, 146
Désiré, 112, 155
Destruction of Da Derga's Hostel, 80,
    83
Diana, 103, 116, 117, 118
Diarmuid, 220, 222, 240
Didot Perceval, 35, 74, 78, 93, 95, 147,
    218, 260, 311
Dinas Emrys, 36
dinschencas, 224
Diu Cröne, 192, 292, 297
Diwrnach, 236, 238
Dolorous Blow, 38, 181, 184, 186, 192–
    3, 194, 196, 197
Don T-Samain Beos, 242–5
dragon(s), 32, 36, 38, 42, 44, 49, 100,
    182, 208, 211, 212, 229, 236, 237,
    242ff., 306
    as birds in Irish tradition, 47
    as symbols for seed and blood, 246–
    7
    transformed into pigs, 33, 39
Dragon Normand, 310
dream
    as gateway to Otherworld, 213
    -woman, 13, 27, 60, 65–9; 175; *see
    also aisling* and *speir-bhean*
Dream of Macsen Wledig, x, 7, 54–77,
    88, 107, 108, 208, 210, 213, 216,
    220, 235, 236
Dream of Oengus, 65–6
Dream of Rhonabwy, x, 27, 39, 60, 78–
    101, 102, 108, 113, 121, 141, 144,
    208, 209, 212, 213, 216, 235, 236,
    237, 256, 305
droit de seigneur, 143
Drustan ac Essylt, 219–20, 222
Dunadd, 15
Durmart, 292, 296
Dylan, 231–2, 284, 286, 287

Echtra Airt, 46–7, 48, 49
Echtra Mac Echach Muigmedoin, 1, 23

Ector, Sir, 5, 268
Edern ap Nudd, 89, 99, 135–7, 141,
    142, 143, 151, 156, 208, 218, 220,
    226, 228, 292, 295
Efnissien, 27, 39, 126, 183, 226, 229,
    231, 277, 286
Efrawg, 164, 169, 186, 187
Eigr, *see* Igraine
Elaine of Corbin, 64, 74ff., 226, 280
    as succuba, 75–6, 192, 298
Eleanor of Aquitaine, 16
Elements of the Goddess, xiii
Elen, 54ff., 110, 210, 225, 226, 235,
    236, 280
    as builder of roads, 57, 62
    as Goddess of dream-paths, 64ff., 76,
    311
Elene of Sinadoun, 71, 72, 76, 116,
    226, 230
Elizabeth I, 237
Elphin, 32, 42, 84, 85, 86, 99, 245
Elucidation, The, v, 161, 250–3, 254,
    255, 256, 258, 303
Emain Abhlach, 66, 154
Emer, 273
Empress of Constantinople, 167, 168,
    177, 179, 180, 182, 183, 191, 193,
    197, 198, 200, 201, 203, 204, 208,
    209, 210, 216, 226, 235, 236, 239,
    241, 249, 294
Enchanted Games, 118, 120, 128, 129,
    130, 133, 139, 141, 146–8, 154,
    156, 208, 211, 217, 239
Enfances Gauvain, Les, 282–3, 284, 286
engendering, mysteries of, 246–7, 262
Enid, xii, 38, 111, 133ff., 217, 220, 221,
    226, 230, 272
    as Sovereignty, 134, 143, 148, 151,
    158–9, 273
    as tattered maiden, 136, 137, 141,
    142, 145, 158, 159, 241
    dressed by Gwenhwyfar, 136–7, 142,
    160
    as Flower Bride, 151, 220, 221, 226
Eochaid Airem, 220, 222
Eochaid Muigmedon, 23–4
Eoghanacht dynasty, 249
Epona, 16
Erec and Enid, 7, 91, 96, 113, 119, 133ff.,
    255, 257, 271
Eriu, the Sovereignty of Ireland, 23,
    24, 67, 69, 70, 150, 180, 241, 248,
    281

Maiden, 25, 26, 59, 75, 76, 77, 177, 202
messenger, 26, 118, 145
pagan vision of, 75, 203
quest, xi, 73, 161, 162, 173, 202, 205, 252
question, 15, 77, 172, 180, 252–3
-winner, 4, 38, 43, 75, 76, 153, 170, 182, 183, 186, 205, 253–4, 261, 280, 303
Grainne, 220, 222
Gratian, 58, 59, 62
Greece, 82, 89, 177
Green and Burning Tree, 178, 206, 209, 213, 215, 219, 228
Green Chapel, 123, 127, 209, 216
green girdle, 123, 124, 129
Green Knight, 110, 209, 226, 228
Grisandole, 230
Gromer Somer Joure, 218, 273
Gronw, 220, 236, 238
gruagach, 145
Guardian of the Totems, 225, 226, 228, 231
Guest, Lady Charlotte, ix, x
Guigamor, Lay of, 144, 151–3, 155, 157, 159, 176
Guinevere (Guenievere), 74, 75–6, 124, 142, 158, 159, 160, 192, 196, 223, 246, 270, 271, 280, 287, 288–99; *see also* Gwenhwyfar
Guinglain, 71
Gundestrup Cauldron, 108, 177
Gwair, 76, 144, 170, 264
Gwalchmai, 17, 89, 106, 135, 137, 138, 168, 169, 170, 180, 183, 263, 265, 276, 277, 285, 305; *see also* Gawain
as peacemaker, 111–12, 146, 175
Gwawl ap Clud, 217, 220, 221, 222, 226, 239
Gwenddolau ap Ceidio, 97, 98, 235
birds of, 97, 98
Gwenhwyfach, 171, 293ff.
Gwenhwyfar, 5, 17, 104, 105, 111, 133ff., 142, 158, 176, 197, 200, 201, 222, 223, 232, 246, 263, 265, 287, 288–99
abduction of, 134, 141, 142, 151, 154, 157–8, 277, 291–9, 305
as Arthur's Sovereignty, 14, 28, 225, 226, 287, 297, 308, 311
as dream-woman, 75–6

as Flower Bride, 95, 96, 134, 159, 219, 220, 223, 288–99, 305, 309
as 'White Phantom', 218, 291
bad reputation of, 288
False, 292, 294, 295
insult to, 14, 108, 136, 141, 151, 171, 172, 197
theft of her cup, 171, 172, 198, 236, 239, 252
in Triads, 89–94
see also Guinevere
Gwern, 64, 231
Gwiffert Petit, 138, 145, 146
Gwion, 119, 226
Gwlgawd Gododin, 236, 239
Gwrthefyr, *see* Vortimer
Gwrtheyrn, *see* Vortigern
Gwyar, 263, 264, 265, 276, 277, 279, 280, 284
gwyddbwyll, 60, 79, 81, 87, 88, 97–101, 168, 182, 210, 212, 216, 235, 236, 306, 309
Gwyddno Garanhir, 42, 208, 210, 226, 228, 236, 238
Gwydion, 208, 212, 213, 215, 216, 220, 221, 226, 227, 284, 286, 288
Gwydre, 232
Gwyn ap Nudd, 218, 219, 220, 222, 289, 291, 295
Gwythyr ap Greidawl, 219, 220, 289, 291

Hafgan, 178, 208, 213, 217
hair, cutting of, 44, 51, 212
Hallows, xii, 4, 5, 15, 25, 30, 87, 149, 162, 181, 182, 183, 184, 186, 188, 190ff., 210, 216, 235ff., 269, 270, 274, 312, 313
coronation regalia as, 235–6
guardians of, 192, 193, 202, 247
Hanes Taliesin, x, 11, 31, 42, 84, 208, 211, 214, 218, 236, 245
head in dish, 162, 165, 173, 186, 187
Heilyn the Red, 81, 82–3
Helena, St, 56, 57, 62
Hengist, 36, 40, 43, 85
Henry II, 310
Henwen, 35
horn of joy, 147, 236, 239, 255ff., 311
Hospitable Host, 116, 122–30, 209
Hywel Dda, laws of, 61

Mabinogion, ix, x, xi, xii, xiii, 8, 13, 21, 48, 51, 64, 65, 69, 78, 97, 103, 111, 130, 134, 151, 161
  as repository of Celtic tradition, x, 22, 80, 128
  godly archetypes within the 206–33
  medieval romances of, x, 3, 7
Mabon, 4, 48, 50, 72, 85, 89, 91, 93, 95, 96, 119, 120, 121, 154, 155, 207, 217, 226, 230, 231, 262, 309, 312
Mabon the Enchanter, 71, 72, 96, 116, 147
Mabon and the Mysteries of Britain, x, 4, 48–50
Mabonograin, 96, 119, 135, 147, 154, 155, 156, 171, 208, 220, 255, 259
Macsen, 13, 53, 55ff., 90, 208, 210, 214, 226
Madawg ap Maredudd, 81, 82, 99
madness in Celtic tradition, 113–14
Maelduine, 162, 170, 178, 267, 303
Maelgwn, 32, 84, 245
Magnus Clemens Maximus, x, 55ff.
Malory, 3, 5, 72, 73, 74, 75, 110, 182, 196, 230, 247, 266, 267, 268, 276, 277, 282, 288, 292, 293, 300, 309
Manannan, 46, 68, 185, 253
Manawyddan, 17, 194, 208, 212, 218, 226, 239, 253
Manawyddan, Son of Llyr, x, 35, 211, 213, 216, 218, 232, 236
March, 219, 220, 263
Marie de France, 7, 151, 153, 298
Martin of Tours, St, 59
Mary, the Blessed Virgin, 20, 21, 29, 125, 270, 271, 304
Mary Magdalene, 247
Math, 37, 208, 215, 220, 221, 223, 226, 284, 286, 288
Math, Son of Mathonwy, x, 41, 192, 213, 215, 220, 232, 236, 282, 285
Matholwch, 183, 220, 223, 229, 293
Matres, 303, 307
matrilinear succession, 14, 96, 275ff.
Matter of Britain, xi, 1, 6–13, 22, 73, 184
Matthews, John, 125, 311
May Eve, *see* Beltane
Medbh (Maeve), 126, 127, 129, 248, 291
Medrawt, 83, 99, 171, 226, 276, 277, 285, 305, 306; *see also* Mordred
Melwas, 141, 142, 143, 292, 295
Mercury, 303

Merlin Emrys, 6, 40, 45, 48, 49, 65, 84, 109, 226, 237, 240, 268, 306, 310
  as Ambrosius, 44
  as dragon-priest, 11, 32, 211, 274
  as guardian of Britain, 232–3
  imprisonment by Nimue, 120
  prophecies of, 9, 172, 266
  retirement, 42, 98
  as Wise and Innocent Youth, 32, 43–6, 230, 231, 246
Wllyt (the Mad), 41, 97, 109, 113
Midir, 220, 222
Mill(s)
  Lord of, 167, 179
  Valley of, 179, 191
Minerva, 21, 304
mist, druidic, 98, 208, 211, 237
Mnemosyne, 195
Modena archivault, 142
Modron, xi, 80, 90, 91, 92–3, 94, 119, 124, 211, 277, 279
  as Sovereignty, 95, 226, 281, 311
Mog Ruith, 226, 228
Mongfind, 23–4
Morcades, 266, 275ff., 305
Mordred, 14, 39, 89, 171, 232, 246, 247, 265, 276, 282, 286–7, 306
  abducts Guinevere, 96, 158, 292ff.
  see also Medrawt
Morfran ap Tegid, 83, 89, 218
Morfudd, 90, 91, 277
Morgan (le Fay), xii, 14, 133, 211, 267, 276, 280, 281
  as Battle Goddess, 306, 309
  as Enchantress, 73, 74, 91
  enmity for Arthur and Guinevere, 28, 91, 95, 120, 125, 308
  as healer, 95, 114, 306, 309
  as male Welsh name, 91, 143
  as mother of Owain, 90–7, 121
  origins of, 92–3
  retains champions in Otherworld, 119
  as sister of Arthur, 91
  as Sovereignty, 96, 123, 124, 226, 306–11
  wife of Urien, 80
Morgan Tud, 137, 138, 143
Morgause, 14, 96, 275ff., 305
Morgen, 91, 195, 281, 306, 310; *see also* Morgan
Morrighan, 19, 27, 91, 92, 226, 229, 308
  prophecy of, 308–9